Praise for

BRENDA JOYCE's

bestselling de Warenne dynasty

An Impossible Attraction
"Best-selling Joyce matches up a strong-willed, proud…
heroine and a testosterone-rich, arrogant…hero…
[A] long, lushly sensual historical."
—*Booklist*

A Dangerous Love
"The latest de Warenne novel is pure Joyce with its
trademark blend of searing sensuality, wild escapades
and unforgettable characters. You'll find warmth and romance
alongside intense emotions and powerful relationships.
It's a story you won't easily forget."
—*RT Book Reviews*

The Perfect Bride
"Another first-rate Regency, featuring multidimensional
protagonists and sweeping drama… Entirely fluff-free,
Joyce's tight plot and vivid cast combine for a romance
that's just about perfect."
—*Publishers Weekly* (starred review)

"Truly a stirring story with wonderfully etched characters,
Joyce's latest is Regency romance at its best."
—*Booklist*

"Joyce's latest is a piece of perfection as she meticulously crafts a
tender and emotionally powerful love story. Passion and pain erupt
from the pages and flow straight into your heart. You won't forget
this beautifully rendered love story of lost souls and redemption."
—*RT Book Reviews*

A Lady at Last
"Romance veteran Joyce brings her keen sense of humor and
storytelling prowess to bear on her witty, fully formed characters."
—*Publishers Weekly*

"A classic Pygmalion tale with an extra soupçon of eroticism."
—*Booklist*

"A warm, wonderfully sensual feast about the joys and pains of falling in love. Joyce breathes life into extraordinary characters—from her sprightly Cinderella heroine and roguish hero to everyone in between—then sets them in the glittering Regency, where anything can happen."
—*RT Book Reviews*

The Stolen Bride
"Joyce's characters carry considerable emotional weight, which keeps this hefty entry absorbing, and her fast-paced story keeps the pages turning."
—*Publishers Weekly*

"A powerfully executed romance overflowing with the strength of prose, high degree of sensuality and emotional intensity we expect from Joyce. A 'keeper' for sure."
—*RT Book Reviews*

The Masquerade
"Jane Austen aficionados will delve happily into heroine Elizabeth 'Lizzie' Fitzgerald's family…Joyce's tale of the dangers and delights of passion fulfilled will enchant those who like their reads long and rich."
—*Publishers Weekly*

"A passionate tale of two lovers caught up in a web of secrets, deceptions and lies. Readers who love the bold historicals by Rosemary Rogers and Kathleen Woodiwiss will find much to savor here."
—*Booklist*

"An intensely emotional and engrossing romance where love overcomes deceit, scandal and pride…an intelligent love story with smart, appealing and strong characters. Readers will savor this latest from a grand mistress of the genre."
—*RT Book Reviews*

The Prize
"A powerhouse of emotion and sensuality, *The Prize* weaves a tapestry vibrantly colored with detail and balanced with strands of consuming passion."
—*RT Book Reviews*

BRENDA JOYCE

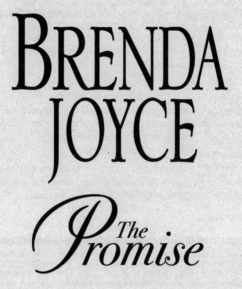

The
Promise

HQN™

Recycling programs
for this product may
not exist in your area.

ISBN-13: 978-0-373-77442-5

THE PROMISE

For Kathy Pichnarcik

Also by *New York Times* bestselling author
BRENDA JOYCE
and HQN Books

The Promise

PROLOGUE

Adare, Ireland

Summer 1824

THE ANIMATED SOUND OF adult conversation drifted from the mansion's formal dining room, where the Earl of Adare was having a supper party in celebration of his wife's birthday. The children had gathered in an intimate salon across the great, vaulted entry hall from the dining room, and Elysse O'Neill, who was eleven years old, sat on the gold brocade sofa in her most formal supper dress, wishing she had been allowed to join the adults. Her best friend, Ariella de Warenne, also dressed up for the party, was beside her, engrossed in a book. Elysse could not understand her friend—she hated reading. She would have been bored, if not for the boys.

They stood in a huddle on the other side of the salon, excitedly whispering to one another. Elysse stared at them, trying to eavesdrop, knowing they meant to cause trouble. Her eyes were riveted on Alexi de Warenne, Ariella's brother, as he was always the leader of the pack.

She had met him four years ago, when he had first arrived in London with his father and Ariella, from Jamaica Island where he had been raised. Upon being introduced, she had snubbed him instantly, although his dark, bronzed looks and swaggering air of confidence had instantly fascinated her. After all, he was a *bastard,* even if his mother was a Russian noblewoman, and she was a lady, so she meant to put him down. But he hadn't been affected by the rejection; instead, he had proceeded to regale her with his stories of his life. Elysse had expected him to be backward and gauche, but he was neither of those things. She quickly realized that she had never met any boy before who had lived through as much as he had. He had sailed across the world with his father, weathering hurricanes and monsoons, avoiding naval blockades and pirates, while carrying the world's most precious cargoes! He had swum with dolphins, climbed the Himalayan Mountains, trekked jungles in Brazil. He had even sailed a raft up a river in China without his father! In fact, he had bragged that he could sail anything, anywhere—and she had believed him. Within an hour, she had decided that he was the most interesting boy she had ever met—not that she would ever let him know!

She knew him well now. Alexi was an adventurer, like his seafaring father, and he could not stay on land for very long, or sit still, either. What were the boys up to? They hurried across the salon, and she realized that they were about to leave, their goal the terrace doors.

Pushing her golden hair behind her ears and smoothing down her blue satin dress, Elysse slid to her feet. "Wait," she cried. She rushed over to them. "Where are you going?"

Alexi grinned at her. "Errol Castle."

Her heart lurched. Everyone knew the castle ruins were haunted! "Are you mad?"

His blue eyes danced. "Don't you want to come, Elysse? Don't you want to see the old ghost who wanders the north tower in the light of the full moon?" Alexi leaned close. "They say he pines for his lady love. I know how you adore romance! She left him, you know, on a full moon—for another man. And so he killed himself, forever to walk the tower when the moon is full."

"Of course I know the story." Her heart beat with alarm and fear. She wasn't brave like Alexi or her younger brother, Jack, or Ned, the earl's heir, who stood with them. She had no desire to rush off into the night and meet the ghost.

"Coward," Alexi said softly. He touched her chin. "I'll protect you, you know."

She jerked away. "And how will you do that? You are only a boy—and a mad boy, at that!"

His smile faded. "If I say I will protect you, I will."

She believed he would do just that—even from a ghost. She hesitated, not wanting to go with them. "Ladies don't have to be brave, Alexi. They must only be graceful, politic, polite and beautiful."

"Of course they do! My stepmother has sailed the world with my father and even fought pirates at his side. She is brave *and* beautiful." His eyes gleamed.

Ned stepped forward. "Leave her be, Alexi. She doesn't want to come with us."

Her younger brother, Jack, snickered at her.

Ariella walked up to them, having actually put down her history book. "I'll go." Her blue eyes were wide and bright. "I would love to see the ghost!"

Alexi gave Elysse a daring look.

"Fine!" she cried, furious that he had taunted her into agreeing. "But how will we get there?"

"It won't take more than twenty minutes if we ride," Ned said. "The girls can ride double, behind us. Jack can ride by himself."

This was a horrible idea—Elysse simply knew it—but everyone else was wide-eyed with excitement. Within moments, she was following the boys and Ariella across the terrace to a paddock where they would steal their mounts.

The boys often rode bareback, with just a bridle or even a halter. Now, she wished they were horrid horsemen—but they were not. The night was so dark and so quiet! As she followed them across Adare's great gardens, she glanced up at the gleaming moon. It was full and bright. She prayed they would not encounter any ghost that night.

A few minutes later everyone was astride, and they were trotting away from the house. Elysse held on hard to Alexi, angrier with him by the minute. He was an excellent horseman, but she was a terrible rider, and she was afraid she would fall off.

"You are breaking my ribs," he said, with laughter in his tone.

"I hate you," she exclaimed.

"No, you don't."

They rode in silence the rest of the way. Ahead, in the moon's odd yellow light, she saw the dark shadows of Errol Castle. It was huge.

It was so quiet now. All she could hear was the rhythmic clip-clop of their horses' hooves and her own thundering heartbeat. Beneath her hands, she could feel Alexi's breath come more rapidly and thought she could feel his heart, racing more swiftly than it should. They passed through the piles of eerily white stones that had once been the outer walls of the barbican. She wanted to turn around and go home! Suddenly a wolf howled.

Alexi's slim body stiffened. Elysse whispered nervously, "There are never wolves this close to Adare."

"It isn't close." They halted their horses by the gaping entrance in the stone walls of the castle, which had once been the front door. Through the shadows of the maze of stone walls inside, she could see the lone standing tower at the other end of the ruins. She swallowed dryly. Her heart thundered.

Alexi whispered, "They say he carries a torch—the same torch he carried for his lost love." He gave her his hand, twisting a bit to do so. "Slide down."

Elysse did so, keeping her balance by holding his hand. Everyone dismounted. Ariella whispered, "We didn't bring candles."

"Yes, we did," Alexi said proudly. He produced a candle from a breeches pocket, and lit it with flint. "C'mon." He swiftly started inside, clearly intent on leading the way.

Everyone followed. Her stomach churning with dread, Elysse balked. She did not want to go inside.

The group of children vanished into the darkness inside the ruined castle. Elysse bit her lip, breathing hard. She became aware of being absolutely alone in the dark night, outside of the ruins. And perhaps that was even worse.

Something moved behind her. She cried out, leaping in fright, only to realize that one of the grazing horses had bumped into her. An owl hooted, the sound ominous. She *hated* adventure! She liked parties and pretty things! But being outside alone was worse than going inside with everyone else. Elysse rushed after the other children.

It was almost pitch-black inside and she could not see. She could hear their whispers, somewhere ahead, and she ran, trying to follow them. But the interior of the ruins was a stone maze. She hit a wall, panicked and turned, found a corner, and turned that, too. Her foot caught, and she tripped and fell.

She started to call out to Alexi, to tell him to wait, when she saw a flash of bright light in the darkness on the other side of the castle where the tower was. She froze, crouching by the wall, afraid to cry out. Had she just seen the light of the ghost's torch?

Afraid to move or make a sound, afraid the ghost would

find her, she became utterly still. She realized she couldn't hear her friends anymore. Where were they?

Panic overcame her. She saw the light again! Elysse rushed from the corner where she had been crouching, intent on fleeing the castle and the ghost. Instead, she found herself turning corner after corner, tripping and falling as she ran. She bumped her knees, skinned her hands. Why hadn't she left the ruins already? Where was the entrance? She realized she had reached a dead end. What might have been the huge wall of a fireplace blocked her. She fell against the rough stone, panting harshly, and that was when she heard the galloping horses.

They were leaving her?

She choked on a sob of fearful disbelief. She turned her back to the wall, and saw the ghost with his torch coming toward her. Fear paralyzed her.

"Elysse!" Alexi cried, hurrying forward.

She felt her knees buckle in absolute relief. It was Alexi, carrying the candle, not the ghost with his torch. She cried out, weeping. "Alexi! I thought you left me. I thought I'd be lost forever!"

He put the candle down and swept her into his arms. "It's all right. You're not lost. I'd never leave you. Didn't I say I would always protect you?"

She held on to him, hard. "I didn't think you'd find me—I heard the horses leaving!"

"Don't cry. I'm here now. You heard my father, the earl and your father pursuing us. They are outside—and they are furious." His gaze was searching. "How could you think that I wouldn't find you?"

"I don't know," she whispered, trembling, her face wet with tears. But she had stopped crying.

"If you are lost, I will find you. If you are in danger, I

will protect you," he said seriously. "It's what a gentleman does, Elysse."

She inhaled. "Promise?"

He slowly smiled and brushed a tear from her face. "I promise."

She finally smiled back at him. "I'm sorry I am not brave."

"You are very brave, Elysse. You just don't know it." Clearly, he believed his every word.

PART ONE

"Love Lost"

CHAPTER ONE

Askeaton, Ireland

March 23, 1833

ALEXI HADN'T BEEN HOME in more than two years, but it felt like an eternity. Elysse O'Neill smiled at herself in the gilded mirror hanging over the handsome rosewood bureau in her pink, mauve and white bedroom. She had just finished dressing for the occasion. She knew that her excitement was obvious—she was flushed, her eyes bright. She was thrilled that Alexi de Warenne had come home, at last. She couldn't wait to hear all about his adventures!

She couldn't help wondering if he would notice that she was a grown woman now; she'd had a dozen suitors in the past two years, not to mention five offers of marriage.

She smiled again, deciding that her pastel-green gown made her nearly violet eyes even more intriguing. She was accustomed to male admiration; boys had begun to look at her when she was barely more than a child. Alexi had, too. She wondered what he would think of her now. She wasn't certain why she wanted him to notice her this evening— they were only friends, after all. Impulsively, she tugged her neckline down, adjusting it to show off just a bit more of her cleavage.

He had never been gone for so long before. She wondered if *he* had changed. When he'd left on a run to Canada for fur, she hadn't known that it would be years before he would return, but she recalled their parting as if it had been yesterday.

He looked at her with that cocky grin he had. "And will you be wearing a ring when I get back?"

She'd known immediately what he meant. Startled, she had quickly recovered and her answer had been coy. "I always wear rings." But she had wondered if some dashing Englishman would sweep her off her feet before he returned. She certainly hoped so!

"Not diamonds." His thick black lashes lowered, shielding his brilliant blue eyes from her.

She shrugged. "I can't help it if I have so many suitors, Alexi. There will probably be many suits. Father will surely know which one to accept for me."

He shrugged in return. "Yes, I imagine Devlin will make certain you are properly married off."

Their eyes met and held. One day, her father would find her a great match. She had overheard her parents speaking about it and knew they wanted it to be a love match, as well. How perfect would that be?

"If I am not offered for, I will be vastly insulted," she said, meaning it.

"Isn't it enough that you are always surrounded by admirers?"

"I hope to be wed by the time I am eighteen!" she exclaimed. Her eighteenth birthday would be in the fall— only six months away—while Alexi was still in Canada. Hear heart lurched oddly. With confusion, she shook off the strange feeling of dread, smiling brightly at him. She took his hands. "What will you bring me this time?" He always brought her a gift when he returned from the sea.

After a pause, he spoke softly. "I will bring you back a Russian sable, Elysse."

She was surprised. "You are sailing for Lower Canada."

"I know where I am going," he replied, his gaze direct. "And I will bring you back a Russian sable."

She scoffed at him, certain he was teasing her. He had simply grinned. Then he had said goodbye to the rest of her family and swaggered out of the salon, while she rushed off to a tea, where her most recent suitors were eagerly awaiting her....

He had remained in Canada for several months, apparently having some problems acquiring a cargo for the run home. When he had finally raced back to Liverpool, he hadn't stayed. Instead, he had turned around directly for the islands for sugarcane. She had been surprised, even disappointed.

Of course, she had never doubted that he would follow in his father's footsteps. Cliff de Warenne had one of the world's most successful maritime transport companies, and Alexi had been at sea with his father for most of his life. It was a foregone conclusion that, when he came of age, Alexi would take on the most lucrative trade routes, carrying the most profitable cargoes, as his father had once done. At the age of seventeen he'd commanded his first ship. Elysse was the daughter of a retired naval captain, and she truly understood how much Alexi loved the sea—it was in his blood. Men like Cliff de Warenne and her father, Devlin O'Neill—men like Alexi—could never remain on land for very long.

Still, she had expected him to come home after his run to the West Indies. He always came home, sooner or later. But instead he had refitted his ship in Liverpool and set a course to China!

When Elysse had learned that he had leased his ship, the

Ariel, to the East India Company, which had a monopoly on the China trade, she had grown worried. Although retired, Devlin O'Neill frequently advised both the Admiralty and the Foreign Offices on matters of imperial and maritime policy, and Elysse was well versed in the subjects of trade, economics and foreign policy. She had heard all kinds of talk about the China trade in past few years. The China Sea was perilous—it remained mostly uncharted territory, with hidden reefs, submerged rocks and unknown shoals, not to mention monsoons and, far worse, typhoons. Beating up the China Sea was easy enough, if one didn't encounter one of those half-hidden rocks or reefs, with the south-westerly monsoons to aid you. But beating through the sea when homeward bound was difficult and dangerous. However, Alexi would think the danger the very best part of his voyage! Alexi de Warenne was fearless and loved a challenge—Elysse knew that very well.

But apparently Elysse had worried about him in vain. Last night, Ariella had sent her a note, telling her that Alexi had just arrived at Windhaven. It had been midnight when she'd gotten the hand-delivered message. She had been stunned to learn he had safely put into Liverpool a few days ago, with five hundred and five tons of silks and tea, having made the homeward run from Canton in one hundred and twelve days—a feat everyone was talking about. For a captain new to the route to make that kind of speed was terribly impressive, and Elysse knew it. He'd be able to command top dollar for his freight the next time he ran home from China. Knowing Alexi as well as she did, he would surely brag about *that.*

Elysse gave herself a final glance in the mirror and tugged at her bodice one last time, well aware that her mother would take her aside for being so daring. She was an acclaimed beauty—every suitor she'd ever had had raved about her striking blond looks. She had been told many times that she took after both of her parents—she was petite, with amethyst eyes, like her mother, and golden like her father. There had been many suits and five marriage proposals in the past two years. She'd turned every suitor and each proposal down, although she was now twenty, and her father had not minded. She hoped that Alexi wouldn't taunt her for still being single. Hopefully, he wouldn't recall her plan to be happily married by the age of eighteen.

"Elysse! We're here—Alexi is home and he is downstairs!" Ariella cried, knocking on her door from the corridor outside.

Elysse inhaled, suddenly so excited that she felt a bit faint. She ran for the door, opening it. Her best friend's eyes widened at Elysse's evening dress just before they embraced. "Are you going out tonight? Have I been excluded from an invitation to a dinner party?"

Elysse smiled. "Of course I'm not going out. I want to hear all about China and Alexi's adventures! How do I look?" She swiftly pirouetted.

Ariella was a year younger than Elysse, with exotic looks—light eyes, olive skin and dark golden hair. Unfashionably educated, she had a preference for libraries and museums, and an aversion to shopping and balls. "If I didn't know better, I'd think you were hoping to impress someone."

"Why would I bother to try to impress your brother?" She laughed. "But he had better notice that I am grown-up now—and the most desirable debutante in all of Ireland."

Ariella was wry. "Alexi has shortcomings, but a failure to notice attractive women isn't one of them."

Elysse closed the door. Alexi was a notorious ladies' man, but that was hardly a surprise—the de Warenne men were infamous for their rakish ways, which ended on their wedding day. It was an old family adage that when a de Warenne fell in love, it was once and forever, although it might take some time for that climactic event to happen. Elysse squeezed Ariella's hand as they started down the long corridor, lined with family portraits. "Did he say why he's been gone so long?"

"My brother is a seaman *and* an adventurer," Ariella said. "He is smitten with China—or the China trade, anyway. It was all he could talk about last night—he wants to build a clipper just for the trade!"

Elysse looked at her as they went downstairs. "Then he will continue to lease out to the East India Company? I was surprised when I had heard he'd leased the *Ariel* out. I can't imagine Alexi in someone else's employ." Alexi had never leased out his ship before.

"He was determined to get into the trade," Ariella said. "I do believe everyone within a league of Askeaton has called, to hear firsthand about China and his run!"

Elysse could hear the murmurs of conversation downstairs. Clearly, they had many callers. But of course, the neighbors would be interested in Alexi's return from China. News of his travels would have spread like wildfire. It was surely the most exciting event of the Season.

As they reached the bottom of the stairs, she could see across the great entry hall, where her neighbors and family had gathered. Askeaton was the ancestral home of the O'Neill family and the great hall was vast, with stone floors and walls, its ceilings timbered. Great, old tapestries were hanging on two of its walls. From one set of oversize windows, one could see out across the rolling green Irish countryside, and past the ruined tower behind the manor house. But Elysse did not look outside, or even at the crowd.

Alexi stood in front of the huge stone fireplace, his posture assured but indolent, clad in a riding coat, breeches and boots. The eighteen-year-old boy was gone. A grown man had taken his place. He was surrounded by their callers. Yet his gaze lifted immediately, moved across the crowd, and their eyes met.

For one moment, she simply stared. He had changed so much. He was a man of experience now. A man of confidence. She saw it in the way he stood, the way he shifted ever so slightly to face her directly. Then, finally, he smiled at her.

Her heart lurched oddly and the happiness was instantaneous. *Alexi was home.*

Her brother, Jack, slapped his shoulder. "Damn it, you can't leave it there, tell me about the Sundra Strait."

For one more moment, they stared at one another, that odd half smile on his face, while Elysse beamed. She couldn't help noticing that he was even more handsome than when he had left her. Then she saw that three of her girlfriends stood beside him, more closely than the rest of the crowd, their expressions rapt.

"It took us three full days to beat through, Jack." Alexi turned to her tall, golden brother. "I'll even admit I had a moment or two when I wondered if we'd be cast up on the shoals there—spending the next fortnight in Anjers making repairs."

Alexi turned and gestured, and a tall tawny-haired man in a frock coat, a stock and waistcoat, and pale trousers came over. Alexi seized his shoulder. "I don't think we'd have made our run in a hundred and twelve days without Montgomery. Best ship's pilot I ever had. Best thing I ever did was take him on board in Lower Canada."

Elysse finally looked at Alexi's pilot, who was probably a few years older than them both, and found him regarding her. Montgomery smiled at her as one of their neighbors, a gentleman squire, said eagerly, "Tell us about the China Sea! Did you weather a typhoon?"

"No, tell us about the tea," Father MacKenzie cried, smiling.

"Will China really stay closed to all foreigners?" Jack asked.

Alexi grinned at them all. "I got the first pick, black tea, the best you've ever had—I vow it. It's Pekoe. You won't find any other ship's captain bringing it home. Not this Season." Although he spoke to the crowded room, his gaze never wavered from her.

"How did you manage that feat?" Cliff asked, smiling proudly at his son.

Alexi turned to his father. "That is a long story, one that involves a few pretty pennies and a very astute and greedy comprador."

Elysse realized she had remained upon the last few steps like a statue. What on earth was wrong with her? She quickly started down them, still watching Alexi as he turned to one of her girlfriends, who asked him what Pekoe tea was like. Before he could answer, Elysse felt herself miss a step and stumble.

She seized the railing, mortified. She was usually very graceful. As she grasped the railing, someone caught her arm, preventing her from crashing to her knees and utterly humiliating herself.

Alexi slid his arm securely around her.

As he helped her straighten, Elysse looked up into his dazzling blue eyes.

For one moment, she was in his embrace. He began to smile, as if amused. "Hello, Elysse."

Her cheeks felt terribly hot, but that was from the embarrassment of being so foolishly clumsy, not from being in his arms—she was certain. Still, she was terribly confused and almost disoriented. She had never felt so small, so petite and feminine, and Alexi had never seemed so strong, so tall or so male. His body was hard and warm against hers. Her heart was thundering now.

What on earth was wrong with her?

Somehow, she stepped away, putting a proper distance between them. His smile seemed to widen. Her flush felt as if it had expanded—even her chest was hot. "Hello, Alexi. I have never heard of Pekoe tea." She lifted her chin.

"I am not surprised. No one gets first pickings—except, of course, for me," he boasted. His gaze seemed to be on her décolletage, then her eyes. She wasn't certain what had just happened. She wondered suddenly if he found her beautiful, as her many suitors did.

It took her a moment to recover. "Of course you got the best tea." Strangely unnerved, she said lightly, "I didn't know you were back. When did you get home?"

"I thought Ariella sent you a note last night," he drawled, and she realized that he had instantly seen through her deception. "I docked in Liverpool three days ago. I got home last night." He shoved his hands in the pockets of his riding coat, making no move to walk back into the salon.

"I'm surprised you even bothered to come home," she said, deciding to pout.

He gave her an odd look she could not decipher, and suddenly lifted her hand. "So you're not wearing a ring."

She pulled her hand free. His touch had made her heart slam. "I have had five offers, Alexi. And they were very good offers. But I turned each gentleman down."

His gaze narrowed. "If the offers were such good ones, why would you do that? I seem to recall that your intent was to be wed by the time you were eighteen."

He was laughing at her! Or was he? He was smiling, but he had glanced aside. "Perhaps I changed my mind."

His gaze flickered. "Hmm, why wouldn't that surprise me? Have you become a romantic, Elysse?" He laughed. "Are you waiting for true love?"

"Oh, I had forgotten how annoying you can be! Of course I am romantic—unlike you!" His teasing was familiar and it felt safe.

"I've known you since we were children. You are less a romantic than an insatiable flirt!"

Now she was truly annoyed. "All women flirt, Alexi—unless, of course, they are old, fat or ugly!"

"Ah, you remain rather uncharitable. I am thinking that your suitors must not have had the necessary qualifications to become your husband." His eyes danced now. "Have you set your sights on a duke, maybe? Or an Austrian prince? How suitable that would be! Can I play matchmaker? I know a duke or two!"

Surely he wasn't serious? "Clearly, you do not know me at all. I am *very* romantic. And no, you may not play matchmaker!"

"Really?" He was chuckling openly at her now. "We know each other very well, Elysse. So don't pretend we do not." He tilted up her chin. "Have I annoyed you, somehow? I am only teasing you, sweetheart."

She slapped his hand away. "You know you have! Nothing has changed! I had forgotten how you love to infuriate me. And who are you to talk? I have heard you have a woman in every port."

"Ah, a gentleman does not kiss and tell, Elysse."

"Your reputation is well-known." She scowled. Secretly, she wondered if he really had a mistress in every port. She wasn't certain why she should care, but she did.

He touched her chin again. "Why are you scowling?

Aren't you pleased to see me?" His tone softened. "Ariella said you were worried about me—that you expected me to vanish into the China Sea."

She inhaled, furious with her friend and uncertain what his murmur signified. "Ariella was wrong. Why would I worry about you? I am too occupied. I just got back from London and Paris, Alexi. In those salons, we are not talking about tea or typhoons!"

"Or me?" he asked, straight-faced but clearly trying not to laugh. "Everyone is talking about the China trade, Elysse. It's a new world. The East India Company can't possibly keep its grip on China, and China has to open up its ports to the world."

"I don't care about China, free trade or you," she huffed, aware of how completely she was lying. After all, he had been her friend since they were children—he would always be her friend.

"God, my heart is forever broken." He smiled slightly. "And we both know you do care about my travels—you're your father's daughter."

She folded her arms and his gaze slammed to her bosom. Taken aback, despite her earlier desire for him to notice how womanly she had become, she managed to speak. "Will you lease out to the East India Company again?"

"Oh, I am going back to China—I will get well over five pounds per ton, Elysse, after this last run. But there is gossip the Company will lose its charter soon."

So he would go make the run again. "And when will you leave this time?"

He grinned. "So you do care, after all! You will miss me!"

"I won't miss you—I will be too busy, fending off my suitors!"

"Now my heart truly is broken."

She trembled, dismayed. She *would* miss him this time, perhaps because he had been gone so long. She had forgotten how much she enjoyed his company—even his horrid teasing. And he had guessed.

"When will you go to sea again?" she heard herself ask. The best time to run to China was the summer. It was now the end of March. She couldn't imagine Alexi staying in the country, doing nothing, for another two months.

"So you did miss me," he said swiftly, his gaze piercing.

She wet her lips, refusing to answer. He leaned close and whispered, "I brought you a Russian sable, Elysse."

He had remembered his promise to her. Before she could answer, one of her neighbors approached. "I hope I am not interrupting," Louisa Cochrane murmured. "I should love an introduction to a China trader. I do love my Souchong tea."

For one more moment, Elysse stared at Alexi in disbelief that he would bring her such a luxurious and precious gift. He stared back, then finally turned to Louisa.

Gallantly, he bowed over her hand. "Alexi de Warenne at your service, madam," he said. He straightened. "And if you like Souchong, you will love Pekoe."

"I cannot wait to try it." Louisa smiled brightly at him.

Elysse had always liked Louisa. Now, hearing the sultry note in her voice, she couldn't abide her. Was Louisa intent on pursuing Alexi? She turned to stare at him.

"May I bring a sample to your door, say tomorrow? It would be my pleasure." Alexi grinned, *his* intentions suddenly clear.

"I hardly wish to put you out, Captain," Louisa murmured coyly.

"You can't put me out, Mrs. Cochrane, you are far too

beautiful to ever do so. I should enjoy delivering the tea, myself."

Louisa blushed, assuring him that he need not go to the trouble. Elysse's mind raced and she felt incoherent and confused. She had never really cared about his flirtations and seductions before. Why should she care about his next affair?

"You have so many admirers, Captain," Louisa said, ignoring Elysse. "Won't you escort me back into the salon so we can all hear your wonderful stories together?"

Alexi hesitated, glancing at Elysse. "Aren't you joining us?"

Elysse smiled. "Of course I am. I can't wait to hear about all of your adventures."

For one more moment, their eyes held, until Louisa tugged on his arm. Elysse followed them into the salon, noting every detail of Louisa Cochrane's dress and figure. Hadn't she heard that she was desperate to catch a wealthy husband? But Alexi was a determined bachelor. And she wasn't jealous, was she? Still, oddly, she wanted Alexi's attention. She had so many questions—she wanted to know what he'd been doing for the past two and a half years. And she wanted her Russian fur.

Inside, Alexi and Louisa were instantly surrounded, and Alexi was bombarded with more questions about his voyage. Elysse began to relax. Alexi was home, and she was fairly certain that he had noticed her charm, beauty and sophistication. She smiled as he responded to a question from Father MacKenzie.

Ariella came over. "I am so happy that my brother is back! Isn't it wonderful?"

"It is truly wonderful, but I hope Louisa won't take up all of his time. We both know he will not linger in the country for long."

Ariella raised her brows. "Hmm, he does seem very interested in Louisa. "

"You know, Louisa is a bit long in the tooth, don't you think?" Elysse heard herself say.

"She is a very nice lady!" Ariella exclaimed. "You aren't...*jealous* of her, are you?"

Elysse looked at her friend. "Of course not," she scoffed.

Ariella leaned close and lowered her voice. "Why don't you go speak with poor James Ogilvy? He is standing over there by himself, gawking at you with a moonstruck smile."

Oglivy had been courting her for about a month now, but Elysse realized she had lost all interest. Still, she smiled at him. He instantly came forward. As he bowed gallantly over her hand, she saw Alexi turn to glance at them. Pleased, Elysse turned her entire attention on James. "You promised me a picnic at Swan Lake."

His eyes widened. "I thought you were not interested, as you did not bring it up again."

She smiled and touched his arm. "I am *very* interested. In fact, I can't wait!"

"Then perhaps we can have our outing tomorrow afternoon?" he asked eagerly.

She glanced at Alexi, who was speaking to the squire now. She did not know how long Alexi would remain in the Irish countryside, and she wanted to be available until he left for London. She beamed at James. "Would next week do? I have an engagement tomorrow." That wasn't quite true, but it was only a tiny white lie.

They spoke for a few more moments. It was terribly hard to carry on a conversation with James while trying to hear every word Alexi uttered and keeping him in the corner of her eye. As she made her plans with Ogilvy, she became aware that she had another admirer. Montgomery, who was chatting with Ariella, kept glancing her way. Elysse hadn't paid much attention to him earlier. She did so now, deciding that he was very good-looking. Although he was a pilot, he comported himself like a gentleman. He glanced at her again and she knew he wished for an introduction. It crossed her mind that he had spent the past two years with Alexi. She excused herself from James.

He smiled at her as she approached. "I don't believe we have been properly introduced, Miss O'Neill. Of course, I have heard all about you from Captain de Warenne, but that is not why I am so eager to meet you."

Elysse comprehended the innuendo and was flattered. "Cliff has spoken about me?"

Montgomery smiled. "No, I meant my captain, Alexi." He shifted and stepped closer to her. "I am William Montgomery. It is a pleasure, ma'am."

He wasn't a gentleman, obviously—no well-bred man would ever pilot a ship, but Elysse was impressed by his charm. He had an unmistakable Southern accent, and she recalled that most American men from the Southern states were terribly gallant. "And it is my pleasure to receive you, sir." She laughed. "It isn't every day that I meet a fearless pilot who has sailed the high seas of China!"

He smiled warmly now, his glance quickly drifting down the bodice of her dress. "Our voyages are long, Miss O'Neill, and beautiful ladies are rare. I wasn't sure you would speak with me."

"You are our guest!" she exclaimed. She touched his arm lightly—flirtatiously. "Where are you from, Mr. Montgomery? My family has a tobacco plantation in Virginia."

"Baltimore, Miss O'Neill. Like the captain, I come from a long line of seafaring men. My father was a ship's master, and my grandfather was a pilot, as was my great-grandfather before him here in Britain. In fact, I grew up listening to my grandfather's sailing stories, mostly about the Ivory Coast and the African trade—in the last century, of course."

"My father was a naval captain, Mr. Montgomery, so I am fascinated." Elysse meant it. But more importantly, Alexi had just noticed their conversation. "Of course, we no longer trade in slaves here in the Empire, but in your grandfather's time, that was a very busy occupation, was it not?"

"It most certainly was," he agreed. "In America, we outlawed the slave trade in '08, well before I was born. In my grandfather's time it was a dangerous trade—I believe the African continent remains perilous, for those who dare to attempt to make their profits there still."

"I am against the slave trade," Elysse said firmly. The trade had been abolished in the British Empire in '07. "Even though my family has a tobacco plantation in Virginia, and we have slaves there, I also favor emancipation in the Empire and throughout the world."

"That is a bold position, Miss O'Neill. In my country, abolition is an issue that divides us. If I may be bold, I would love to visit Sweet Briar, if I was ever in Virginia again." He smiled, revealing strong white teeth. "I should especially enjoy such a visit if you were there to show me the plantation."

Elysse smiled archly at him. "I would *love* to give you a tour of Sweet Briar! But how could we possibly arrange that? The next time I am there, you will undoubtedly be running for China!"

"Yes, I could be crossing the Cape of Good Hope."

"Or beating up the China Sea." She laughed. "By the time you received my letter, I would have probably returned home."

"Probably—and it will be my loss."

They smiled at one another. "I heard Alexi say that you met in Lower Canada," Elysse said.

"We certainly did—in the midst of a blizzard. In fact, poachers were trying to steal the furs Alexi had just bought for his cargo home. I saved his life and we have been friends ever since."

Elysse was fascinated. "How did you save his life?"

From behind her, Alexi said softly, "The French had a few natives in their employ and I was seriously outnumbered."

She had been so engrossed that it took her a moment to realize that Alexi had come up to them. She turned, her heart exploding. He stood beside them, his arms folded across his chest, smiling. But she knew him well, and his smile did not reach his eyes.

She was taken aback. "What's wrong?" Could he be jealous?

"What letter will you send William?"

"An invitation to Sweet Briar," she said lightly, then turned her back on him and faced Montgomery.

"I so want to hear more about Lower Canada, the poachers and the natives," she said eagerly.

"That is a long story," the American began, glancing at Alexi.

"One unsuitable for a lady's ears," Alexi said flatly. "Would you excuse us, William?"

Montgomery hesitated. Then he bowed. "It has been my pleasure, Miss O'Neill. I hope we can continue this conversation another time."

"Of course we can," Elysse said, smiling at him. What was Alexi hiding? Did he really think her too frail to hear the truth about his travels? Had something terrible happened, which he didn't wish for her to know about?

William Montgomery walked off to join Devlin and Cliff. Elysse realized she was alone with Alexi. He was scowling at her. "What is wrong?" she asked. Surely he wasn't angry with her for speaking to Montgomery? "Your pilot is a very interesting man. And a handsome one, at that."

He took her arm, moving her into a corner by the drapery-clad windows. "Don't flirt with Montgomery, Elysse." His tone was filled with warning.

"Why not?" she cried, pulling free of his grasp.

"He is a *pilot,* Elysse, and a rogue."

She started. "*You* are a rogue, and I am allowed to speak with you!"

He glared. "He is not for you. I suggest you direct your flirtations at Ogilvy and his ilk."

She searched his eyes. He had never been jealous of her suitors before—and William Montgomery wasn't even a suitor. Alexi was right—as interesting as he was, he was a pilot, not a gentleman.

She began to smile. She touched his hand, which was large and hard, the knuckles cracked, the skin there suntanned. "You needn't be jealous, Alexi," she murmured.

"Don't even try to flirt with me! I am *not* jealous." He shrugged. "I am merely trying to protect you from a dangerous ladies' man, Elysse. Montgomery has a way with women, and I don't want you to fall under his spell."

"I am hardly under his spell." She glanced up at him from beneath her lashes, aware that she was flirting. "I'm glad you're not jealous, Alexi. Mr. Montgomery is very interesting—fascinating, actually—and very handsome. And he is a guest in this house."

For one moment he stared. Elysse knew him well, but she couldn't decide what he was truly thinking. Then he leaned closer, crowding her against the draperies. "Are you trying to play me?" he asked, very softly.

A little thrill swept her. She could barely breathe now. "I have no idea what you mean. But you can't object to my having a pleasant conversation with your pilot—or seeing him again." She batted her lashes at him while her heart raced frantically.

"Montgomery piloted the *Ariel* to Lower Canada and Jamaica and then to Canton and back. I trust him with my ship and the lives of my men, but I do not trust him with you." His stare darkened. He added, "You are impossible, Elysse. I am asking you to avoid him—for your sake, not mine."

His shoulder still pressed hers. It was becoming hard to think clearly. She whispered, "I will think about it."

Suddenly his gaze dropped from her eyes to her mouth. Elysse tensed. In that one moment, she thought he was going to kiss her. Instead, he straightened and slowly shook his head, appearing disgusted. "Fine. Think about it. But don't say I didn't tell you so."

CHAPTER TWO

HE WAS RESTLESS and he did not know why. After so much time away from his family, his mood should have been entirely different. Usually the time he spent in his family home in Ireland was somewhat aimless, his pursuits casual—long rides across the countryside, visits to his neighbors, tea with his sisters and raucous family suppers. He didn't feel casual now. Instead, he felt like rushing back to his ship and hoisting sail.

Last night, sleep had eluded him. All evening, he had thought about his run home from China, the price his tea had commanded from the London agents, and how fast his next run could be. He drew, in his mind's eye, the plans for the ship he intended to have built, just for the China trade. But in the night-darkened bedroom, his thoughts kept straying back to Elysse O'Neill. Even now, as he sat at breakfast with his family, his thoughts were on her.

She had always been beautiful. He'd thought so even as a small boy, when they'd first met. In fact, he would never forget walking into the drawing room at Harmon House for the very first time, having just arrived in London with his father after a long voyage from Jamaica, where he had been raised. He had read about London, of course, but he had never imagined such a large, bustling city, with so many palaces and mansions. As excited as he had been to finally visit his father's homeland, he had been taken aback—and very, very careful to hide it. On their way to

Harmon House, Cliff had pointed out many of London's sights to him and Ariella. Harmon House had seemed as majestic and imposing as Buckingham Palace.

To hide his nervous anxiety, he had increased the swagger in his stride and the set of his small shoulders. His father had been warmly greeted by his brothers, one of whom was the Earl of Adare. A number of other adults and children were present. He'd only seen the lovely golden girl dressed in pink silk and satin seated on the gold damask sofa.

He had mistakenly assumed her to be a real princess. He had never seen anyone as pretty, and when she had looked at him, he'd felt as if the wind had been knocked out of him. But she turned her nose up at him like a true snob. He'd instantly wanted to impress her. He had strutted over to her. Without even an introduction, he had boasted about his exploits on the high seas. Her purple eyes had become as huge as saucers….

The memory almost made Alexi smile. Within days, they had become friends. However, his smile failed him now. Last night, Elysse had been even more stunning than he recalled. Was it possible that he'd forgotten just how beautiful she was? He'd certainly forgotten how petite she was. When he'd rushed to her side as she'd tripped on the stairs, taking a firm hold of her, he'd been stunned at how tiny and feminine she had felt in his arms.

Of course, he wasn't the only man to have noticed her striking looks. Ogilvy was smitten—and if he didn't miss his guess, she had ensnared his pilot, too.

His heart turned over hard. She was damned beautiful—and she knew it. She'd known it since she was a little girl. She'd been a reckless flirt then and she was a reckless flirt now. He'd watched her casual flirtations for years. They'd always amused him. He hadn't ever really understood how her suitors allowed themselves to be so easily played, as if led around by her on a very short leash.

Had she really thought to flirt with *him?* Had she thought to put *him* on her leash? If she batted those lashes at him another time he might call her bluff and kiss her senselessly. She'd be shocked, wouldn't she?

Except he knew he was deluding himself. He would never treat her that way. He had been acutely aware of her from the moment they had met as children, and that had never changed. There had always been that special bond between them. Others might think her filled with airs, but he knew the truth—that a heart of gold beat within her chest. He also knew how kind she was—no one was as loyal— and she was exceptionally loyal to him. She couldn't help the fact that her parents spoiled her terribly, or that she had been blessed with so much privilege and such exceptional looks. None of that really mattered. What mattered was how well she understood him; sometimes, he felt that she knew his thoughts, when he wasn't even speaking. And how often had he known her thoughts—and secrets—without her having to verbalize them?

But that strong bond had been complicated for him from the start. There had always been a vague stirring of attraction for him, from that first moment when they had met as children. As a boy, he'd always assumed that one day, far in the future, when he was a grown man, she was the woman he would take as his wife. There had never been any ifs, ands or buts about it.

But at fifteen, he'd discovered women. Actually, he'd discovered sex. And any such beliefs or assumptions about Elysse had been buried deep.

Well, he had returned home now. He wasn't a naive eight-year-old boy or a randy sixteen-year-old. He was twenty-one and a very successful merchant sea captain.

He was also a bachelor—and he liked it that way. He was not interested in marriage, not any time soon. But that vague stirring of attraction wasn't vague any longer. It was a heated pounding in his loins. The desire was unmistakable, and no longer easy to ignore. It was powerful and disturbing.

The sooner he left Ireland, the better, he thought firmly. Then he could decide how to manage his feelings for her by the next time he came home.

"Your countryside is beautiful, Mrs. de Warenne."

Alexi came out of his brooding instantly.

"I am so glad you think so," Amanda, his stepmother, replied, smiling at William Montgomery from across the dining-room table.

"I thought I would only want to spend a day or two here in the countryside, but I was wrong," Montgomery said with his thick Southern accent, sipping from a cup of China tea. "I should enjoy riding across the Irish moors many times."

They were seated at the table with Amanda and Cliff. His sisters remained upstairs. His father was engrossed in the *London Times* and Alexi had been trying to read the Dublin newspapers, which were a treat, as they were impossible to come by outside of Britain. He especially liked the social columns—he missed the gossip about what everyone was up to—but this morning, he hadn't been able to concentrate on a single word. Now, he stared at his pilot. Montgomery had saved his life in Lower Canada. He'd risked his own life to do so. They were friends, but he happened to know that the pilot was ruthless when it came to his pursuit of beautiful women.

Montgomery would never try to seduce Elysse, surely. He was, after all, Alexi's pilot and a guest in his home. Their flirtation last night had been a casual, insignificant one. Yet why would he wish to linger in the countryside? "You'll be bored by this evening," Alexi said flatly, suddenly hoping he was right. "I am actually thinking of cutting my stay short."

Cliff laid down his newspaper, his blue gaze searching. "Why would you do that?"

"I want to get to London and start working on the plans for my new ship," he said. In London, he and Montgomery could carouse to their heart's desire.

Amanda smiled at the pilot. "I am so glad you are enjoying Ireland. I remember the first time I came here. I was so swept away by every single thing—the old homes, the green hills, the mist, the people! This is *your* first time here, is it not?"

"Yes, it is, and I can't thank you enough for your hospitality. Your home is so lovely, Mrs. de Warenne." Now, he looked at Alexi, smiling ever so slightly. "I enjoyed meeting the O'Neill family very much last night."

Alexi tossed the *Dublin Times* aside, sitting up straighter. He hadn't lied when he'd told Elysse that the American was a terrible ladies' man. They had spent ten days in Batavia, drinking, gaming and whoring, while waiting for a shift in the winds before running up the China Sea to Canton. Montgomery was a good-looking man with too much Southern charm and women flocked to him like ducks to water. His gallantry got him into the finer homes in the ports they put into, and he had seduced his share of married women—but he hadn't ever ruined an innocent daughter, not that Alexi knew of. Up until then, Alexi had considered him a true kindred spirit. Surely he did not wish to linger in Ireland in order to pursue Elysse. Or had she so thoroughly worked her wiles on him, already? When a man wanted a woman, it was often so hard to think clearly!

Cliff surprised them all by saying, "Elysse O'Neill is a very lovely woman."

"I don't believe I have ever met a woman as beautiful," Montgomery said shortly. "Or as charming."

He was stunned. Was Montgomery being polite—or was he smitten? He sounded very intense. "Be careful, my friend, or she will soon lead you about on her little leash as she does all of her *proper* suitors."

"Alexi!" Amanda gasped in disapproval. "That was terribly rude!"

Alexi fingered the saucer of his teacup. "Well, I am just worried about my friend. He hardly needs to have his heart broken. Elysse doesn't mean to hurt anyone," he added, knowing that was the truth. "But she is a skilled coquette. I have seen her gather admirers ever since she was twelve or thirteen. She is adept at it. And frankly, she is even more of an impossible flirt today than she was when I left."

Cliff shook his head. "This conversation is highly impolitic, Alexi."

"There is no harm in flirting," Amanda said to him, as reproof.

Montgomery added, "At home, a lady who doesn't flirt would be considered odd. Flirting is rather an art in Maryland."

Alexi folded his arms across his chest and refrained from scowling. He wasn't sure what had possessed him to speak so disparagingly of Elysse, whom he cared for, in front of his friend, who was still an outsider to the family. "I just think you should keep your distance, William. Her charms can be fatal."

Montgomery smiled slowly. "Are you speaking from experience?"

He tensed. "I have never had a broken heart—nor do I intend to ever have one."

"You know that ladies are few and far between on our runs. Last night was very enjoyable—I look forward to the company of all the ladies here again." The pilot picked up his cup and sipped.

But his intentions were clear. He meant to see Elysse again. Alexi stared thoughtfully at him. He truly didn't care if Montgomery and Elysse flirted once or twice, as long as Montgomery remained respectful. There was really no reason for him to believe that he would ever behave in any other manner—they weren't in Lisbon, Malta or Singapore now—but he continued to feel disturbed. He was sensing that Montgomery was simply too interested in Elysse for his own good—or her own good. When it came to Elysse, he simply didn't trust his pilot, as he had told her last night. "You know, Dublin is a very entertaining city. We should spend a few days there before we return to London."

Montgomery didn't respond.

"Please don't rush off so soon," Amanda said, rising from her chair. She came to stand beside him, placing her hand on his shoulder. "We have all missed you so."

Alexi knew he could not disappoint his family. He smiled at his stepmother. "I promise not to leave in any haste."

"Good." She kissed his cheek and excused herself.

"May I ask a question?" Montgomery said.

Alexi looked at him as his father returned to the *London Times*.

"Why isn't Elysse married?"

He almost choked. Before he could answer, Cliff rattled his paper and said, "Her father means to find her a love match. Devlin has said so often enough."

Montgomery sat up straighter. "Surely he means to find her a titled gentleman with deep pockets."

"I'm sure he wishes for Elysse to have every privilege,

but most importantly, he wishes for her to have genuine affection in her marriage," Cliff said. He laid his paper down. "I'm afraid I have some tenants to see today. Alexi, do you wish to join me?"

Montgomery was obviously surprised by Cliff's answer, and his mind was clearly racing. Alexi was disbelieving. Surely his pilot did not think to marry up? He couldn't help thinking about the boy he'd once been—the boy who had secretly assumed that one day he'd grow up and marry Elysse O'Neill. "I have other plans, Father."

Marriage was the last thing on his mind just then. All he wanted to do was escape his confusion and desire. He couldn't wait to run back to China, pick up another Pekoe cargo, and then race the clock—and his rivals—for Great Britain.

But he couldn't let this go.

Cliff left the dining room. Montgomery said soberly, "A great lady like Elysse O'Neill deserves all that life has to offer." He took up his teacup abruptly.

Alexi stared. Was the American suddenly considering the possibility that Elysse might truly like him? That he might seduce her into falling in love? Elysse admired Montgomery. He was masculine and attractive; *all* women liked him. Men like Montgomery married up all the time. And Montgomery was an opportunist. Devlin might even embrace the American as a fellow seafarer and set him up in his own shipping line. He was suddenly certain that, while Montgomery was intrigued with Elysse, he was now just as intrigued with the idea of marrying into the great O'Neill fortune.

The stakes had entirely changed.

He pushed his plate away. Elysse couldn't go to a dinner party, a dance or a ball without drawing every male in the room to her side and ensnaring them with her laughter, her looks and her charm. She had a way of hanging on to a man's every word, making him feel ten feet tall and impossibly masculine, impossibly virile. He'd seen her do it a hundred times—no, even more. She'd been mesmerizing the male gender since she was a child of seven! But attracting Montgomery was a terrible idea—he had said so to her. Now, it had even worse ramifications.

Alexi crossed his arms. "You seem deep in thought, William."

Montgomery glanced up. "I was trying to decide how to spend the morning."

"Let's ride."

"That's fine, as long as I am back by one."

Alexi sent him a questioning look. "And what happens at that bewitching hour?"

"I am driving in the countryside today with the loveliest lady I have ever met."

So they had made plans to meet again last night? Of course they had, because Elysse had ignored his warnings.

"Are you bothered with that?" Montgomery asked, his gaze riveted on Alexi.

"It's going to rain today." As a seaman, he could smell the impending rain. He damn well knew Montgomery could, too.

The American leaned across the table. "A bit of drizzle won't stop me from enjoying Miss O'Neill's company. Only a fool would postpone our afternoon. I asked you if you are bothered, Alexi."

Our afternoon. "Actually, I am."

Montgomery's eyes gleamed. "I thought so. So, you are interested in Miss O'Neill?"

He didn't move a muscle. "No. But I am very close to

her and her family, Montgomery. We are friends, so I will be direct. She is a lady. One I will always protect."

Montgomery wet his lips. "You don't have to protect her from me."

He laughed harshly. "What are you after, Montgomery? Since when do you play the gentleman and escort ladies about? I know what you want from a woman—we've caroused together far too many times. Elysse O'Neill is a lady—an innocent. She is *not* for you."

"I know very well that she is not some dockside whore. I enjoy her company. I mean no disrespect." His stare hardened. "And she enjoys my company."

He sat up straighter, certain Montgomery was calculating his chances of far more than seduction. What would he do if Elysse decided that she wished to marry the pilot? Could she be so foolish as to fall for him? "She flirts with everyone. You are taking her too seriously."

"I think you are jealous."

He was startled. "I have known her since we were children, Montgomery. I know her as well as I know my own sisters. Why would I be jealous of her shallow flirtations? I have watched her suitors come and go for years. I am merely concerned, as her friend and her protector."

"You would be jealous because she is too beautiful for words," he said, standing abruptly. "Any man with a drop of red blood in his veins would dream of receiving her smile and being allowed into her arms. I know you, too. You have dreamed of her just like all the rest of us."

Alexi stood, as well, his heart slamming. "I am trying to warn you that she is toying with your affections. I have seen her toy with men for most of my life."

"And I am trying to tell you that I don't mind. But if you must know, I believe she has a genuine interest in me." He added, "She likes me, Alexi. She is attracted to me. I have been around enough women to know when a woman is truly interested. Perhaps you will have to simply accept that."

He said harshly, "You are being played. And if you think she will consider a suit from you, you are *wrong*."

Montgomery smiled at him. "We are going for a carriage ride, Alexi. It is an afternoon's outing. I don't recall suggesting I might get down on bended knee."

Was he reading too much into what was merely an innocent flirtation? "Fine. Then enjoy your carriage ride." He added, perhaps unnecessarily, "But remember, she is a *lady* and my friend."

"How could I ever forget?"

"When she smiles at you as if you are the only man in the world, and you are alone, you might very well forget everything except what is pounding beneath your belt."

Their gazes remained locked. "I would never seduce her," he finally said. Alexi stared closely, but his expression was bland. "Do you realize that we are fighting?"

"We aren't fighting—we are friends," Alexi said tersely. But his words felt hollow and false. Montgomery felt like a dangerous adversary. The bottom line remained that he didn't trust the American with Elysse. And he was angry with her for ever flirting with his pilot in the first place. "In fact, we are more than friends—I owe you my life. If not for you, my scalp would be hanging outside some Huron's hut right now, in the Canadian territory." He tried to focus on that fact. It was impossible. He pictured Elysse in Montgomery's arms, their embrace passionate. God, he didn't even know if she had ever been kissed!

"And you saved my life in Jamaica, during the revolts," Montgomery returned.

"We might not have gotten up the China Sea in one piece without your mastery," Alexi said.

"So why are we arguing? Let's swear that we will not fight over a woman, even one as beautiful as Miss O'Neill." Montgomery held out his hand.

Alexi hesitated, his mind racing. An image of Elysse, impossibly beautiful in pale green, was engraved on his mind. He saw her laughing with the pilot—he saw her gazing deeply into his own eyes. He shook himself free of her spell and accepted Montgomery's handshake. "I wouldn't think of fighting with you."

"Good." Montgomery grinned. Alexi smiled back, but it was an effort to curl his mouth upward.

Montgomery left the breakfast room. They were at odds for the first time in two years. But worse, he no longer trusted the man who had saved his life. And it was entirely Elysse O'Neill's fault.

ELYSSE KNEW THAT STANDING by the window in the front hall, so she could have a view of the drive and who was coming up it, was childish. And she wasn't standing there because William Montgomery was calling on her this afternoon. Last night, she had overheard Alexi asking her father if they could have a private moment so he could ask him for advice. Devlin had suggested he come by at any time after lunch.

They hadn't spoken again last night after he had warned her to stay away from his pilot. There hadn't really been a chance, not with the house so filled with callers. Elysse had almost refused Montgomery when he had asked her if she'd drive with him the next day, but then, impulsively, she had decided that she was a grown woman. It hardly hurt to have another admirer on her arm, especially when that admirer seemed to annoy Alexi. While she trusted Alexi, he had no right to tell her who she could see. And a drive in the country was harmless, anyway.

Still, she was looking forward to having a moment or two with him now. She still had a hundred questions about his voyage, and she wished to know what had happened in Lower Canada. The more she thought about it, the more she was grateful that Montgomery had been there to save his life. If the adventure wasn't fit for a lady's ears, it must be ghastly, indeed. She couldn't imagine what she would do if anything had happened to him!

A movement behind her startled her. Elysse turned to find her tiny, dark-haired mother entering the hall. Virginia smiled at her. "Why don't you wait for him in the library? Those new shoes look terribly uncomfortable."

Elysse glanced down at her new, cream-colored patent-leather booties. The heel was fashionably high and her toes already hurt. But the shoes matched her ensemble perfectly. "It's really too early for Mr. Montgomery to arrive. Maybe I *will* wait for him in the library." As she spoke, she felt herself flush.

Virginia touched her arm, her purple gaze searching. "Elysse, I am your mother. We both know that the pilot is a nice enough man and that you couldn't care less about him."

"I hardly know him, Mother, but I am looking forward to getting to know him better. He has so many stories to tell!"

"Really? I noticed that *Alexi* has a great many tales of his adventures at sea, and that he has grown into a fine, capable man. Not only does he remind me of Cliff, he reminds me of your own father," Virginia said. "He is responsible and intelligent and industrious. I've been hoping that the two of you will have a chance to genuinely renew your friendship."

Elysse felt her heart race. "Only you, Mother, would speak openly about how hard he labors, even if at sea."

Most of the ladies and gentlemen she knew disdained any kind of labor for profit, never mind that they needed vast incomes to live well. But her mother was an American and she was very fond of pursuing profit. Elysse didn't mind. She just knew they should not speak openly of it. She smiled. "He has certainly had a successful voyage, hasn't he?"

"He is a very fine young man! And I know you think so, too. Has it ever occurred to you to tell him that you have missed him? I am sure he would be pleased to hear it."

She was aghast. What was her mother thinking? She would never tell Alexi such a thing! "He would think me one of his love-struck hussies—exactly like that Louisa Cochrane. Worse, he would laugh at me!"

"Why not ask *him* if he wishes to drive in the country?" she said, smiling. "No one would ever think you a hussy, dear."

"I would never do such a thing! Mother! A lady does not throw herself at a gentleman!"

"Louisa Cochrane doesn't seem to mind making her interest known, dear, and she is not a hussy—she is our neighbor and a lady."

Elysse's eyes widened as her mother walked away, a smug look on her pretty face. She didn't know why she had ever liked Louisa. Last night, Jack had gone on and on about how attractive she was, and that if he was a marrying man—which he was not—he might take her on, himself.

Virginia had noticed that Louisa was pursuing Alexi and had thought enough of it to mention it to Elysse. What did she expect her to do about it? Alexi's sordid affairs were not her concern. Alexi was a dyed-in-the-wool bachelor who tired of his affairs very, very quickly. Their affair should hardly cause her stomach to hurt.

Her heart thudded, far too hard for comfort. When had

her relationship with Alexi become so complicated and confusing? He was an old and dear friend, that was all. But last night it had taken her hours to fall asleep. She'd kept thinking about Alexi and his tea, Alexi and Louisa, and the way he had looked at her, as if he meant to kiss her.

She had probably imagined that.

She heard the hacks outside before she saw them, their hoofbeats distinct upon the graveled drive. Elysse ran to the window and saw Alexi and his pilot astride two of his father's magnificent Thoroughbreds. Montgomery was early—and she was a bit disappointed.

The men were dismounting. Alexi carried a large parcel, wrapped in brown paper. Almost certain it was her gift, Elysse turned and hurried into the library, seating herself on the sofa and carefully arranging her skirts. Her color felt high. She touched her hair, which was curled and coiffed. Every strand felt as if it was in place.

Alexi sauntered into the library alone, clearly at home and not needing a servant to usher him in. He set the parcel on a chair. "Hello, Elysse," he said softly. "What's wrong? Couldn't you sleep last night?"

She stood, flushing. He couldn't know what thoughts had kept her up last night. She eyed the parcel but restrained herself. "Hello, Alexi. Did you sleep well?" she asked sweetly.

"I slept very well," he drawled, as if amused.

She tore her gaze from the package. "Where is Mr. Montgomery?"

"He is chatting with your father, Elysse." He came closer. "Let me guess." His tone was a murmur now. "You were up all night, dreaming about your outing with Montgomery."

She trembled. Why was he using that seductive tone on her? "And if I was?" she challenged, wetting her lips. "It is hardly your concern. Besides, you look ragged today, too. You did not sleep well, either."

"Oh, I didn't say you looked ragged. You are lovely as always, and you know it. So let me guess again. You couldn't sleep because you were thinking...of me?" He laughed out loud.

If she'd held a purse, she would have thrown it at his broad chest. "My mother thinks you have turned into a fine, upstanding man of character. I beg to differ. You are rude and unbearable, more so than ever."

If anything, his expression grew more pleased. "You are so easy to bait, sweetheart," he said. Then he turned and picked up the parcel, very casually. "Don't you want to know what's inside, Elysse?"

She tried to keep her eagerness from her face. "Is it for me?"

He smiled slowly at her. "Yes, it is." He handed her the paper-wrapped gift.

Her heart leaped and she felt like a child, wanting to tear the wrapper apart. Somehow, she restrained herself, slowly untying the ribbon. Her fingers suddenly felt clumsy as she tried to open it.

He came up from behind her, reaching past her, enveloping her with his body's heat. "Here." His breath feathered her nape and she went still. "Let me help you."

She didn't move—she couldn't. Didn't he know that he was crowding her? That she was practically in his arms? Then he stepped past her, filling her with relief and disappointment. He began to slowly unwrap the paper. He glanced up at her, sidelong, and smiled.

"You are being a tease."

"Yes, I am."

He finally tore open the paper, and Elysse glimpsed the

gleaming dark brown fur. She gasped as a sable coat fell into his hands.

"Alexi! You remembered—and you even made it into a coat!"

"Let's see if it fits." He settled it on her shoulders, and she slid her arms into the sleeves.

Elysse wrapped herself in it. "It fits perfectly." She met his gaze. "You didn't forget."

"I said I'd bring you a Russian sable," he said roughly. "I never say what I don't mean. I never forget a promise when I make one."

Tears came to her eyes as she was cocooned in the fur coat and she became aware of his hands on her shoulders. "How can I accept this?" she asked unsteadily, her eyes searching his. She didn't know why the coat meant so much to her. It was the most precious gift she had ever received.

"How can you refuse?" he returned. "I won't take it back."

He finally dropped his gaze and paced away from her. She watched him, still stunned, feeling mesmerized. She was so happy he was home, she thought nervously. Why did he have to ever leave?

Alexi faced her. "I don't like you toying with my pilot, Elysse."

She stiffened. His eyes were serious. She didn't want to argue. "I am not toying with him. I enjoy his company." She was aware that she dissembled, that the pilot meant nothing to her.

"You flirted shamelessly with him and you know it."

She inhaled, hurt by his words. "That is unfair. Every woman flirts. Why are you doing this now?"

"I am protecting you. Flirt as you will—and I know you will flirt insatiably—but just not with my pilot."

"*You* were flirting even more shamelessly with Louisa."

He smiled slowly, without mirth. "I'm a man and a de Warenne at that. She is a woman—and a widow."

He had just made his intentions clear. He would pursue Louisa, but not for marriage, oh, no. Why did his affair hurt her even more than his criticism? She took off the coat, breathing hard. "I hope you enjoy yourself."

"You sound peeved. No, you sound jealous. Are you jealous, Elysse?"

Was moisture gathering in her eyes? "I'm a *lady*. I would hardly be jealous of one of your paramours." But in that moment, she did not understand her own feelings.

His gaze changed and became searching. "William is my friend. I owe him my life. I am asking you to cease your flirtation and leave him alone. I see no good coming of a relationship between you both."

Because she trusted him, she was almost ready to agree. But would he leave Louisa alone if she asked? She knew the answer to that question. "We are going for a carriage drive, Alexi. He is hardly a suitor! Who is jealous now?"

He flushed. "Playing with his affections is a mistake, Elysse. Trust me. I know."

"I'm just being friendly. He's your guest—last night he was our guest. I don't understand why you are being so difficult."

Alexi approached her. His face was set with determination but his long strides were unhurried. She tensed impossibly. He paused before her, and she started when his fingertips grazed her cheek. "And what will you do if he courts you seriously?"

It was almost impossible to think. "If he wants to court me?" He was tucking a tendril of hair behind her ear.

Elysse felt her pulse explode. "I don't know... It is my choice to make!"

He dropped his hand to his side and said flatly, "I don't trust him."

She wanted him to lay his hand on her face again—or her shoulder—or her arm or anywhere else that he chose. Her entire body felt inflamed. Confused, she backed away. *She had known Alexi forever—no matter how dashing and handsome he was, he was her friend!* "That is absurd. What could he possibly do? He may be a pilot but he is a gentleman—at heart, anyway."

"He isn't a gentleman, Elysse. I know firsthand. I am warning you that his pursuit of a woman can be ruthless."

"Why are you doing this?" she cried, frustrated but uncertain why.

"I am trying to protect you," he said.

She started. For the first time in years, she recalled the promise he had made to her so long ago in Ireland, when they were children. "I am flattered and grateful, but I don't need your protection, Alexi."

They stared at one another and the moment felt interminable. He finally said, "He has been blinded by your beauty and lost all common sense."

"Nonsense," she managed.

"Don't you expect all men to lose their judgment when confronted with the possibility of being with you, even if only for a moment?" he asked, very softly.

"No," she somehow whispered, "I don't."

"Liar," he returned, their gazes locked.

She trembled and reached for his arms. His eyes widened as she clasped his powerful biceps. Elysse felt as if her skin was on fire. It was hard to think. She didn't really know what she was doing, but holding on to Alexi now felt so terribly right, even if her heart seemed to be trying to pound its way out of her chest.

To her disappointment, he pulled away from her. His own cheeks were flushed and his blue eyes glittered. For one moment, he looked at her, his stare shockingly bold.

Elysse backed up as he turned away from her. She hugged herself. Her body was screaming at her. There was no more doubt as to what was happening to her. She desired Alexi, and it was a desire she'd never felt before.

He said roughly, "Could you fall in love with him? A man without a title, a master of the seas? A simple, courageous seaman who is brave and determined?" He cleared his throat, slowly facing her. "We both know Devlin will do anything you want him to do. If you wanted to marry the pilot, he would approve—if it was for love."

What was Alexi talking about? "Are you talking about Mr. Montgomery?"

He nodded. "Who else would I be speaking of? Who else has come here to see you today?"

The room seemed to spin. She had never felt more off balance. "I like him, but I am not in love with him. I doubt I will ever fall in love with him." Why were they discussing the pilot? Why didn't Alexi take her in his arms? Didn't he feel the blinding need, too?

His stare was hard and intense, unwavering. It was a long time before he spoke. "Then maybe you should tell him, very frankly, what you have just told me." He turned to leave, adding, "Instead of leading him on so merrily."

She hurried after him. "We are going for a carriage ride! I am not leading anyone on!"

"I think he is smitten, and you know it! He may even be calculating his chances of a legitimate courtship, Elysse. You are deliberately leading him on."

"I am doing no such thing. Since you have come home, it is as if you think the worst of me!"

"You are always the lady in the room with a dozen admirers."

"I am twenty years old and unwed! Should I turn away from possible suitors?"

"Have you ever turned anyone away?" he demanded.

She shrank. "You make me sound like a harlot!"

"You flirt like one."

She was stricken. "That isn't true."

"Do what you want, Elysse," he finally said grimly. "You always do."

"And you do not?" she demanded furiously.

He strode through the library. She ran after him, then paused on the threshold. What was she doing? She had been watching well-bred ladies chasing him for years. She could hardly behave like that! She clung to the library door, aghast and bewildered.

He glanced back at her. "I'm glad you like the coat," he said. "William is waiting in the other room."

Elysse didn't answer; she couldn't.

CHAPTER THREE

ELYSSE CLUNG TO THE SAFETY STRAP of the black lacquer carriage she shared with her parents and brother as it passed through the heavy wrought-iron gates that guarded the de Warenne property. Those gates were open now, flanked by stone curtain walls that stretched away into the distance. As their coach entered the long shell drive, she could see the house, pale and gray, in the distance. Windhaven was silhouetted against the twilight skies and lights blazed from the windows.

Impossibly dashing in his tuxedo, Jack dug his elbow into her ribs and jeered.

She frowned at him.

"Someone has to bring you down," he said, grinning.

She decided to ignore him. Their mother reproved Jack, murmuring for him to stop teasing his sister.

Elysse stared out of her carriage window, clinging to the strap. Several days had passed since that stunning encounter with Alexi in her father's library. The fact that he had remembered his promise to bring her a Russian fur gave her so much pleasure, yet she hadn't forgotten her disbelief and hurt that he had practically called her a harlot. She was certain he hadn't meant it—he *couldn't* have meant it. Mostly, though, she couldn't stop recalling the explosion of desire she had experienced when he had so casually touched her. And she kept remembering the smoldering look in his eyes, before he'd turned away from her. But maybe she had imagined her desire and his response to it. She wasn't sure what to expect when they came face-to-face again that night.

He hadn't been back to Askeaton since he'd brought her the fur, and she knew why he hadn't called. She'd heard plenty of gossip about his comings and goings. Apparently he was squiring Louisa Cochrane about the countryside on a nearly constant basis.

She shouldn't care who he was carrying on with, but every time she thought of him with the other woman, pain knifed through her heart.

She had tried to remind herself that their dalliance was nothing unusual, not really, for Alexi was always having an affair. He remained her steadfast friend. But for the first time in her life, she didn't feel reassured. Confusion and doubt reigned. She had even debated going to Windhaven on the pretext of calling on Ariella. Somehow she had restrained herself. He would see through such a sham instantly, and mock her desire to see him.

It almost felt as if he were deliberately avoiding her. But why would he do that?

The carriage had slowed, entering the end of the queue of coaches and carriages in front of the house. Cliff had built Windhaven the same year he had brought his son home from Jamaica, in honor of his bride, Amanda. The three-story house was Georgian in design, with four corner towers and a high, sloping slate roof. The gardens surrounding it were magnificent, filled mostly with roses—everyone in the county knew how fond Amanda was of English roses. His stables were of pale beige stone, as were the servants' living quarters. It was a palatial home, and testimony to the success of his worldwide shipping empire.

Two dozen conveyances were lined up ahead of them, Elysse saw. She recognized the gilded coach belonging to the Earl of Adare. Tyrell de Warenne was Cliff's oldest brother and Alexi's uncle. He could have gone to the head of the queue, of course, but he had chosen to await his turn, like anyone else. Clearly, no one had declined Amanda's invitation, but then, there was nothing like an Irish country ball, and these days, with corn so dear, the workhouses full and the National Debt a dinnertime topic of conversation, they were few and far between.

Jack patted her knee. "Don't worry. I'm sure Montgomery will ask you for a waltz or two."

She glared at him. Montgomery was not the man keeping her wide awake at nights, although he had turned out to be a very gallant suitor. Elysse had enjoyed his stories of the sea. By now, she knew almost every detail of what had transpired from the moment Alexi had first met the pilot on the St. Lawrence in Lower Canada. Of course, Montgomery had not told her about the day he had saved Alexi's life. She knew that Montgomery agreed that she was too delicate to withstand those details, just as she also knew he thought her enthralled with his stories. She *was* enthralled, but not for the reason he believed. Through Montgomery's tales, she had pieced together so many details of the past two years of Alexi's life.

Their drive in the country had been a very pleasant one. He was handsome, charming and intelligent, and he often made her laugh. He was very attentive, and she wondered if Alexi was right in insisting that Montgomery was thoroughly taken with her. She did feel a bit guilty that she did not return those feelings.

In fact, their last outing had been somewhat awkward. They had decided to wait out an intense rain shower in a farmer's stable, but when he had helped her out of the carriage she had somehow wound up in his arms. She was experienced enough to realize he had maneuvered her into the position. As they waited for the rain to stop, Elysse had caught him looking at her with open male interest, and she'd been certain that Montgomery wanted to kiss her. That had made her anxious and uncomfortable, as she had no wish to be kissed by him or any of her suitors. Kisses were, of course, highly improper and she'd never received more than a peck on the check or a lingering kiss on the hand. She had wondered briefly if she was leading him on, as Alexi had accused her of doing. But every debutante she knew enjoyed the company of numerous suitors, including those they did not take seriously.

She had kept up a stream of lively conversation and he had never made the advance, much to her relief. Instead, the rain had abated and they had returned to Askeaton.

He'd asked if he could call on her again. It had crossed her mind that she should do as Alexi had asked—she should tell Montgomery, very frankly, that he was just a friend. She did not want to lead him on or give him false hope, not really. But then she thought of how Alexi was ignoring her—and how preoccupied he was with Louisa. Surely she was entitled to a casual flirtation, when he was wildly involved with his paramour!

So instead of telling Montgomery the truth, she had invited him to Adare. The earl had not been at home, but she had introduced him to the countess. Lizzie had insisted on giving them refreshments and her daughter Margery had joined them. It had been a very pleasant afternoon. Afterward she had given him a tour of the ancestral mansion, regaling him with the family's long and convoluted history, which went back to Norman times. Montgomery had seemed at ease with everyone and everything, but when they were driving home he had confessed he had never met a countess before, much less been in a palace like Adare.

"I would have never known." Elysse had smiled. She decided not to tell him that Adare was hardly a palace.

"I have never met a princess like you, either," he had said, his gaze searing.

His look was too bold for her comfort now. "I am hardly a princess! You are teasing me, sir."

"For a man like me, you are a dream come true," he had said, obviously meaning every word. "When I am with you, sometimes I wonder if I am dreaming and I will wake up to find out that these moments have never happened. You are a princess in every possible way, to me, at least."

She had been flattered. Where Alexi thought she flirted like a harlot, William Montgomery thought her a princess. When he had smiled warmly at her, she had smiled back, and then they had driven the rest of the way to Askeaton, chatting, their friendship somehow stronger.

She had received her invitation to Amanda's "celebratory spring ball" a few days ago. A personal note had been enclosed. Amanda had written that the ball was being held in her stepson's honor, to welcome Alexi home from China properly and to celebrate his stunningly successful run.

Her heart skipped a beat or two. She knew Alexi's plans—Montgomery had revealed them. He would not run for China till early summer, as the first pick of tea was in July and it took a good month or more to send it down to the Cantonese warehouses from the interior; it could take another month or more to negotiate for the cargo and its price. And that was if he got the first pick again, which the pilot said was by no means a certainty. The trade was so highly competitive! November was the most dangerous month in which to beat down the China Sea—while the monsoon which came from the northeast was a terrific boon, it was accompanied by terrible typhoons, and few captains would disembark that month. Even Alexi preferred to depart in December. Elysse realized that once he left in June, he would not be home until March—a full year from now.

And he had no intention of carousing in Dublin or London until June. Next week he would return to Liverpool to pick up a cargo for a short Mediterranean run. When he returned from Cyprus, Elysse would be certain to be in London to see him. Maybe by then this strange impasse would be forgotten and they would be friends again.

But did she really want to return to their old friendship? She thought about being in his arms and her skin tingled. Except Louisa Cochrane was the woman in his arms. She had, somehow, been completely forgotten.

But tonight she intended to change that.

It was their turn to alight from the coach. She was terribly nervous about seeing Alexi again. Jack dutifully helped her down, her voluminous satin skirts being somewhat treacherous. She was wearing her most stunning dress tonight. The gown was at once sophisticated and daring— even her brother's eyes had widened when he had first seen her in it. Of lavender silk, the low-cut bodice revealed a great deal of her chest and shoulders. The dress boasted expansive demigigot sleeves while the equally full skirts were intricately beaded and the narrow waistline was banded with darker velvet and a bow. She wore amethyst and diamond jewelry to complete the ensemble. Surely Alexi would notice her now.

As he guided her to the front door, Jack whispered, "I wonder, Elysse, just whom are you wearing that dress for?"

She flushed and glared at him. Elysse kept her voice low. "I have no idea what you mean."

He grinned at her. "After you, sister."

Standing at the front door with Cliff and Amanda was the guest of honor.

Alexi looked directly at her. Elysse paused behind her parents, trying not to make a sharp sound. She hadn't seen Alexi in formal evening wear in years. He was so devastatingly handsome, so impossibly male. Now she knew she hadn't imagined the desire she had felt earlier in the week. Her heart leaped. If she wasn't careful, he would guess that she had somehow become terribly attracted to him. Suddenly, when she was usually the queen of every ball and the center of so much attention, she did not know what to do. How on earth could she get him to realize that she was a beautiful woman?

She dared to glance at him again. Although he moved to greet her parents, his gaze was unwavering upon her.

She wondered if he knew about her second outing with Montgomery. It was now her turn to greet their hosts. She kissed Amanda's cheek, murmuring a greeting, and smiled at Cliff. Even as she gave Cliff her hand, she felt Alexi staring at her. Heat crested in her cheeks. Slowly, she looked up.

"Hello, Elysse." He spoke softly—intimately—taking her entirely by surprise. "You are stunning tonight. Clearly, you will be the belle of this ball."

She knew he meant it and she smiled at him, thrilled. "And you are so very handsome in your tuxedo, Alexi. Surely you are the most dashing gentleman here."

She thought she saw some amusement in his blue eyes, but she couldn't be certain. His dark brows lifted. "Is Jack your escort?"

She felt her tension escalate and she wet her lips. "I don't have an escort," she managed. "So we are no longer arguing?"

His gaze held her own regard. "We are not arguing. I don't want to fight with you."

She smiled happily, but she was aware of remaining incredibly nervous. "Do you really like my dress?"

His long, thick, black lashes lowered. It was a moment before she realized that his gaze had moved down her bodice before jerking back up to her face. A slight flush marked his high cheekbones. "Of course I like the dress. Every man here will like the dress. It is indecent on an unwed woman, Elysse." His tone seemed rough.

Before she could protest that his claim was absurd, he said, "But when you chose it, you knew that you would attract even more attention than you usually do."

She trembled. She had chosen the dress to attract *his* attention, but she could hardly admit that. "Every woman dresses up for a ball, especially when there are so few these days."

He did not respond and she realized they were holding up the line. She lowered her voice and said, "I heard that you are leaving for Cyprus soon."

His gaze sharpened. Without turning, he said to Cliff, "Excuse us for a moment."

"What are you doing?" she asked, as he pulled her from the front of the queue. They moved toward the long ebony console set against the pale stone wall. A tall, gilded baroque mirror was above it. In it, she saw their reflections—his serious, hers almost frightened. From the corner of her eye, she glimpsed Montgomery watching them, but she couldn't care about that now.

"Yes, I will embark for Cyprus within days. How did you hear that?" he demanded.

She hesitated, not wanting to admit that Montgomery had told her.

He laughed. "As if I don't know."

"Are we going to argue again?" she cried, dismayed. "You have been so terribly preoccupied since your return, we have hardly had a word. I was hoping I might even have a dance with you," she said. She felt her cheeks flame at the idea of having to ask him for a dance—and all because she wanted to be in his arms. She did not want to discuss Montgomery now. "You haven't called."

He avoided her eyes. "I have been busy."

She *hated* Louisa Cochrane. How had that fat old hen caught his attention? "Were you planning to call and say goodbye, or did you mean to simply sail away for another two years?"

His gaze shot to hers, filled with surprise. "You sound accusing. Did you miss me, Elysse? Surely you were too busy with your five marriage proposals to ever think of me!"

She fumbled with her beaded purse. She *had* missed him, and she would miss him even more when he left this time. "I never expected you to stay away for so long," she said, at a loss. His brows rose and she whispered, "Two and a half years is a very long time."

After a long moment, he said, "Yes, it is."

It was on the tip of her tongue to ask him to forgo the short run to Cyprus and back. "Why didn't you come home?"

"I meant to do so after I returned from Canada, but I was offered a bonus for a timely run to Jamaica, and I could not refuse the agent."

It had been business, she thought, but that did not make it any easier. "Are you ever homesick, when you are away?" What she wanted to know was if he had missed *her*.

His gaze widened. "Of course I am. I am homesick all of the time. It is lonely on the high seas, Elysse, especially on the night watch."

She imagined him at the helm on his clipper ship in the Indian Ocean, the night black but bright and starry, the ship's mainsails full, canvas moaning in the breeze. "I know how much you love the sea, how you love adventure."

"Loneliness is a small price to pay," he agreed. "The sea will always be my mistress."

A naval captain's daughter, she understood. "Don't stay away again for so long," she heard herself say. She flushed.

"Why would it matter, when you are so preoccupied with your parties and balls, and with your endless parade of suitors?"

"Of course it matters," she said, his stare making her uncomfortable. "We are friends."

"I wonder how many new suits there will be, by the time I next return?"

His tone was mild and she did not know what to say. "I am unwed. Of course there will be new suitors."

"But every suitor does not rate a tour of Adare and a rest in our neighbor's stables."

He knew about her two outings with Montgomery. "It was raining," she managed. "We had to escape the rain."

His eyes flickered. "Of course, he behaved properly."

She almost told him that Montgomery had looked at her as if he wanted to kiss her. "He was a perfect gentleman."

Alexis glanced away. "Then you are very fortunate." His gaze lifted to hers. "I asked you not to play him, Elysse."

She was filled with guilt then. Was she "playing" William? "I do not *play* gentlemen. I am merely enjoying his suit. We have become friends."

"Yes, you *do* play gentlemen, all the time, and you are excellent at it. I have watched you toy with male affections since you were a child." He ignored her gasp of protest.

"Now you are *friends?*" His tone was incredulous. "As we are friends?"

She felt as if she were being backed into a corner. "William is a friend. Of course, I hardly know him as well as I know you."

"You do not know *William* at all." He stared, his face hard.

She knew this was dangerous territory, but she couldn't help herself. Their gazes locked, she said, "And I suppose you think that you know Louisa Cochrane well? And I am certain it is Louisa, not Mrs. Cochrane!"

"Do not bring *Mrs.* Cochrane into this."

"Why not? She is obviously a fortune hunter," Elysse cried, her gaze unwavering on his. "She is desperate to marry above herself, and soon! Why can't you see that? Why do you even bother with her?"

He glanced aside. "I have made it very clear that I am *not* marrying anyone anytime soon."

She felt her cheeks flame. She did not need him to remind her that they were lovers. She turned aside. Why did his affair bother her so much? When had she become so jealous? But all she could think of was Alexi and Louisa in a passionate embrace. It hurt so much. "She is undoubtedly planning on trapping you into marriage, even if it is a year from now."

He caught her arm. "I am not discussing Louisa with you."

"I knew it!" His familiar way of speaking of his mistress added to her hurt.

He didn't release her. "Montgomery is besotted with you. But there is more. He is calculating his chances for a legitimate courtship. He is the one who is the fortune hunter here."

She was taken aback. "That is absurd!"

"Is it? Have you told him that you could never fall in love with him? He knows that your father wants a love match for you. And men like Montgomery marry up all of the time!" His blue eyes sparked with anger now. "You are lucky he did not seduce you in the stables—then you would have been forced to marry him."

She gasped. "What is wrong with you? William would never seduce me! He is a gentleman, Alexi. He is kind and sincere and, in fact, he thinks very highly of me!"

"Why won't you listen to a single word I have said?"

"Because you aren't making any sense!" Why did she feel like crying? "Why are you doing this? You have done nothing but ignore me since you have come home, while chasing after that hussy, and you would deny me a serious suitor."

"Aha! So now you admit that he is seriously pursuing you?" he demanded.

She crossed her arms tightly and he looked at her cleavage. She flushed and managed, "Have you finished nagging at me? My dance card is full tonight."

He dragged his gaze upward. "I thought you wanted a dance with me."

"That was before you decided to be a boor." She turned to rush away.

He took her arm, restraining her, and turned her back to face him. "I am not finished, Elysse." His gaze hardened. "I want you to end this tonight, before you find yourself in jeopardy—the kind you cannot smile and laugh and flirt your way out of."

She tried to jerk her arm free and failed. "You cannot order me about, as if I am one of your crew—or your sister."

"You are making a mistake. Sometimes, Elysse, I feel like taking you over my lap and giving you the kind of spanking reserved for small children. You are truly the most stubborn woman I have ever met. You are playing my pilot and it is selfish and dangerous."

She shot back, "You are playing Louisa, are you not? I wonder why you are so set against William but not my other suitors like James Ogilvy? Could it be that you are jealous?"

His eyes widened. "I am not jealous of you. I think of you as *family*. Not as anything else. We have known one another for thirteen years!"

She stepped back, stricken. "We aren't family. We aren't related at all!"

"Oh, ho! Wait a moment—are *you* jealous? Do you want my attentions?" He was incredulous.

"No, I do not!" she cried with panic.

His stare was skeptical, piercing. "I know you as well—no, better—than I know my own sisters! I know how you think and what you want—I know who you are. Sometimes I think I know you too well! When I walk into a room and I see you, I think, why, there is Elysse, the pretty, spoiled little princess I have known for most of my life!"

She was trembling. Tears were arising, and she didn't want him to see. "Are you saying that you think of me as a sister? That you don't even notice that I am an attractive and entirely grown-up woman?"

His mouth hardened. "Obviously you are good-looking, but I don't think about it."

She stared, terribly hurt.

His gaze slammed down to her lavender ball gown. "I hate that dress," he said tersely. He strode away.

She did not move, in shock. *When Alexi saw her in a room, he saw a spoiled little princess. He didn't see a beautiful woman, he saw the girl he'd known his entire life, someone similar to a sister.*

"I like the gown," Montgomery said softly. "I think you are lovelier than ever. Elysse, don't cry."

She turned and found his concerned gray gaze upon her. Vaguely, she realized he had been eavesdropping. She couldn't care. It was her heart that was broken.

Somehow, she smiled at him.

He reached for and held her hand.

SHE DIDN'T KNOW WHY she had ever yearned to be in Alexi de Warenne's arms. She didn't even know why she had ever considered him a friend. He was hateful. He thought to control her life, treat her as a sister, and all while he ran after hussies like the widow Cochrane. Who cared? She had never suffered a rejection before. She did not know of another debutante in Ireland who had had five marriage proposals in two years. His rejection did not matter—not at all!

And if William decided to press a suit, she might even encourage him. He was kind and sincere, and he did not judge her or accuse her of being a harlot. He did not think her spoiled and selfish. When he called her a princess, he meant it as the highest compliment. When Alexi did so, he meant it as a slur—as an indictment of her character!

Elysse danced her eighth dance of the evening, a smile pasted on her face. The handsome squire, Sir Robert Haywood, was a widower of thirty-five, and considered an excellent catch. He had called on her a few times, but she hadn't ever had any real interest in him until that night. As they danced, she kept smiling at him, refusing to look about the ballroom. She did not want to set eyes upon Alexi, not ever again.

Their friendship was now over. She no longer found him fascinating, much less attractive—oh no. The dashing boy she had once loved as a child had turned into an awful, mean-spirited man. She hoped he stayed away *five* years this time! And she hoped Louisa trapped him into marriage. It would serve him right.

Tears burned behind her eyelids. She could not understand why she felt so hurt. To be hurt, one had to care, and she most definitely did not care about Alexi de Warenne. She batted her lashes rapidly and beamed at her dance partner as they finished the country waltz.

"You have never been as lovely, Miss O'Neill," Haywood said, bowing. "I had no idea you were such a superb dancer."

She took a flute of champagne from a passing waiter, trying to banish Alexi de Warenne from her mind and her life, all the while hoping he had noticed how many admirers she had. Not that she meant to make him jealous, as she did not. She couldn't care less if he was jealous or not, but other men found her beautiful—other men did not think her character defective!

The champagne was delicious. "Thank you, Sir Robert. And thank you for such a wonderful dance. I do hope you won't neglect me as you have done these past few months, sir." She sipped from the champagne, aware that she had drunk more than her usual two glasses. She didn't care. Without the champagne, she might not be able to hold back her ludicrous, inexplicable tears.

"I hadn't realized you wanted me to call again," Haywood said, flushing. "But I will gladly do so."

Elysse encouraged him to call another time. When he had left her side, she quickly finished the champagne before rushing off to the dance floor with Jonathon Sinclair, one of the men who had offered for her. He was very tense and flushed, and she instantly knew he still desired her. He said, whirling her about in a German waltz, "I didn't think you'd give me a single dance, Miss O'Neill."

"Of course I would give you a dance." She smiled at him. "I have been looking forward to it all evening long!"

He started. "Why are you being so kind?"

"Do you think me unkind, sir?" She feigned hurt, slipping her hand across his shoulder.

"Of course not," he said harshly, missing a step. "I think you are as kind as you are beautiful!"

"When you next call on me, I will explain myself to you completely," Elysse said. Even as she spoke, a little voice inside her head told her she was going too far, and she would regret it when he called.

"I will call on you tomorrow," he said instantly. "With your permission, of course."

"And I will be waiting with bated breath," she responded gaily.

After two more dances, she had to beg off, in order to catch her breath. As she stood by a table filled with dessert trays, she caught Montgomery's eye from across the room. He smiled at her and she smiled back. They'd already danced two times and he had been wonderful, light and quick on his feet. More importantly, his regard had been warm and intent. Perhaps Alexi was right—perhaps he was seriously interested in her.

Why *shouldn't* she encourage him? He was a seafaring man and she was the daughter of a naval captain. Her father seemed to like him—everyone seemed to like him—and she did not need to marry a fortune, as she had one of her own.

Pain still throbbed in her breast—in her heart—and threatened to erupt if she were not very, very careful.

She walked over to the tray of champagne, wondering if she dare take another flute, wishing desperately to genuinely be happy and gay. Then she could truly enjoy the ball and her suitors. But she felt unsteady in her heels.

Surely the champagne would chase the need to cry away. In the past, a glass or two had always made her feel merry. Why couldn't she feel merry now?

As she reached for a glass, a hand closed on her wrist. "You have had enough," Alexi warned.

He had come up behind her. She slipped around in such a manner that, for a moment, she was in his arms, her breasts crushed against his chest. His eyes widened. She stared, challenging him silently to deny her attributes. He stepped backward, away from her.

Somehow she knew she had made him uncomfortable. She smiled, pleased. She would never let him see how hurt she was. She was the reigning belle of the ball—the debutante every bachelor wanted—a woman with too many admirers to count and no other cares at all. Surely, he could see that! "I must disagree, Alexi," she said sweetly. "You may instruct Ariella and Dianna on how much they may or may not drink, but not me." She smiled archly at him.

His stare narrowed. "Are you crying?"

Was there moisture on her lashes? "Of course not," she said gaily. Ignoring the pain bubbling in her chest, she smiled as coyly as possible. "Have you suddenly realized that I am a grown woman? Have you noticed how many admirers I have? Have you come to queue up for a dance with me?" And unthinkingly—instinctively—she touched his cheek with her nails and skidded them lightly across his skin there.

He jerked his face back. "I do not want a dance!" He seized her hand, stilling it. "You are inebriated. You need to go home."

"I've only had a glass or two and I am enjoying myself immensely. Aren't you? Have you even danced a single time?" The pain had miraculously dulled. Alexi was angry with her—and she was pleased.

"No, Elysse, I haven't danced and I don't intend to. Cease this absurd pretense! You are going home." He was final.

"I am not inebriated and I am not going home." Then she slowly smiled. "Not unless you are offering to take me? Could you so desperately desire my company, the way every other man does?" She lifted her other hand and stroked his cheek. "Oh, wait, I forgot—you are shackled to Louise."

His eyes were even wider now, his cheeks even redder. "It is Louisa, and I am not shackled to anyone. Are you *flirting* with me? Would you dare?"

"I flirt with everyone, remember?" she murmured, stepping closer to him. Her chest brushed his satin lapels and she heard his breath catch. She knew a woman's sense of triumph. He was hardly indifferent to her now! She ignored her own racing pulse. "I am a reckless flirt—no, wait, I am a harlot. You said so, remember? I suppose that makes me just like your paramour!"

"I said you flirt like a harlot," he said grimly, seizing her shoulders and putting a good distance between them. "Jack can take you home."

"Like hell he can," she said softly, swaying against him again.

This time, he did not move away. Elysse thought a fire burned between them. He finally said, "You are making a fool of yourself."

"Why? Because every eligible man here wants me? Except, of course, for you." She laughed at him again. "You are immune to my charms…aren't you? That is why you are breathing so oddly!"

He inhaled. A terrible pause ensued. He finally said roughly, shifting to put a distance between them, "What is wrong with you?"

"Nothing is wrong with me. I am simply enjoying this

ball, as one hardly knows when we will have another one. But what is wrong with *you,* Alexi? Why do your eyes burn like that? Surely—*surely*—you aren't filled with desire for me? I am a spoiled and selfish princess, after all. Or does that make you my *prince?* Are you my Prince Charming, Alexi? If so, I imagine you will sweep me into your arms! Oh, wait. That's impossible—I forgot—you are a boor, not a prince!"

"You are truly drunk," he said. "Like a sailor, Elysse. You are going home."

"No, I am not." She saw Montgomery approaching, his expression concerned. Montgomery clearly did not like Alexi manhandling her. *He* was her hero and protector now! "I can't go home, because I promised William a walk in the gardens. Have you noticed how lovely the moon is tonight? They call it a lover's moon, Alexi. In case you didn't know." She had never made such a promise, but a walk with him outside was exactly what she intended now.

His stare was disbelieving. "Are you acting this way to thwart me? Or just because you gain so much pleasure from playing the coquette?"

She laughed at him, stepping past him and holding out her hand to Montgomery. "I am enjoying a wonderful country ball, and now, I am about to enjoy a walk in the moonlight with my very favorite suitor."

"Are you all right?" Montgomery asked, looking back and forth between them.

"We are having a *family* argument." Elysse beamed at him, taking his arm. "Alexi is practically a brother to me, after all. Surely he has told you that?"

Montgomery glanced at Alexi again. When he looked back at Elysse, his gaze softened. "Do you need some fresh air, Elysse?"

"I should love some fresh air," she responded, looping her arm tightly in his. As she did, she stole a look at Alexi.

He was angry, of that there was no doubt. "She should go home," Alexi said to Montgomery, his tone hard.

"I'll see her home when she is ready to go," the American returned flatly.

Alexi made a harsh sound. Elysse looked back and forth between both men and knew they were fighting over her. She wished she was thrilled. Alexi deserved everything he got tonight. But instead, she felt the hurt all over again. "Let's go," she whispered to William.

Alexi gave her a dark, warning look. Then he turned and stalked away.

"Are you sure you are all right?"

"I am having a lovely time," she told him, forcing a smile. "Aren't you?"

He smiled at her, guiding her across the ballroom and out of it. "I am having a good time now. I must say, I wasn't enjoying myself very much while you were dancing with all those other gentlemen."

His gaze was serious and searching. He truly liked her—perhaps he even loved her. She had been so wrapped up in Alexi's return that she had failed to realize just how handsome and charming William was. "You don't have to be jealous," she said.

He pushed open a door to the terrace. Because it was late March, it remained chilly at night and no one else was outside, even if the moon was mostly full and very bright. "Not even of Alexi?"

She faltered. "Of course not!"

"Good. Elysse, when I am with you, it is the best time of my life."

She knew he meant it. She hesitated, recalling Alexi's

last, warning look before holding out her hand to him. He instantly took it and pressed it warmly to his mouth. She suddenly tensed. It was a moment before he released her hand.

She glanced at the terrace doors. Of course, Alexi would not follow them outside, not after that last look he'd given her.

"Are you cold?" he asked.

When she nodded, he took off his tailcoat and slipped it over her shoulders. His hands lingered. "I don't want to take advantage of you, Elysse. But I am very fond of you."

"You can't take advantage of me," she whispered, wondering if he was going to declare himself. She so needed a declaration of love now. She gazed into his eyes. Alexi was so wrong about him.

"I am glad to hear that. When you smile like that, a man might think it an invitation."

Her glance strayed past him again. No one was watching them. She did not want to think of Alexi, not now or ever again. Should she encourage Montgomery to kiss her? Why not? He was the perfect suitor—it had just taken her a very long week to realize it! "Perhaps it *is* an invitation," she managed.

He studied her and said softly, "I would like to court you, Elysse. My intentions are truly honorable ones."

She trembled. "You may court me, William."

He touched her chin, tilting up her face slightly, forcing their gazes to meet. "Good. I will speak with your father tomorrow about a proper suit."

She didn't know why she tensed. Her mind raced incoherently. Alexi's image swam there. But this was what she wanted! "My father has always wanted a love match for me," she finally said.

His eyes widened and he grasped her shoulders. "Are you saying that you love me?"

She hesitated, well aware that she did not love William—not yet. But she wanted his suit—desperately. Yet she must not lead him on. "I am becoming very fond of you," she finally said.

He murmured, "Let's walk out of the house lights."

She wasn't certain they should walk into the shadows at the edge of the terrace. But he smiled, taking her hand. "I want to kiss you, Elysse, and I don't want to be interrupted," he said softly. "Can you blame me? You are the most beautiful woman in Ireland—and you have just agreed to allow my suit."

Should she allow him a kiss? Elysse paused, knowing Alexi would be furious if he learned of such behavior. Would a real kiss hurt? Hadn't she enjoyed being in his arms on the dance floor? And Montgomery loved her—it was so obvious.

Realizing she had acquiesced, he led her across the terrace to the far side, where it was cast in shadow. He had a firm grasp on her arm, and she realized he meant to walk down the three steps onto the lawns. Suddenly she was confused. Did she really want to step so far away from the house?

"You are so beautiful," he said. And then he caught her face in his hands and kissed her slowly and gently on the lips.

Elysse felt her tension soar. She had never been genuinely kissed. His mouth was very firm but gentle. It was pleasant, but not stunning. When Alexi had touched her in the library last week, her heart had exploded with desire. There was no such explosion now.

Tears butted up against her closed lids. Was this really happening? What *was* she doing?

"I love you," he said thickly. "You are a dream come true."

Elysse met his smoldering gaze and her heart raced. He loved her. He was a good man. Surely she could come to love him in return?

He suddenly put his arm around her. She thought he meant to kiss her again, but she found herself stepping down onto the lawns with him. He took her in his arms and kissed her again.

This time, his mouth was insistent, moving over hers again and again, and somehow she knew he wished for her to open her lips. She held firm, aware that she wasn't ready, but she reached up for his shoulders. He grunted, the sound very male and shockingly sexual.

Some alarm began. They should stop—he had had his kiss.

But his grasp on her tightened. His mouth moved more roughly, more determinedly, on hers. His kisses were becoming frightening. She wanted to tell him that they should stop, but he loved her. She hesitated. Instead, before she could speak, his tongue thrust deep.

Alarm began as his heavy tongue filled her mouth. What was she doing? She choked. She did not want to be kissed like this! He was a stranger! She pushed at his shoulders, becoming very frightened now, but he didn't notice.

Fear turned into panic. She told herself that the kiss would soon end—wouldn't it? And he did love her. But one hand clasped her buttock and pulled her close, and she felt his stiff manhood against her hip. She had never felt that part of a man's anatomy before, and she wanted to protest, her fear escalating. Instead, she froze.

Still holding her intimately, he broke the fierce kiss. "I love you," he said, panting.

Before Elysse could protest and tell him that they must

go back inside, he swept her back into his embrace, this time taking her down to the wet grass with him.

As his huge body covered hers, Elysse seized his shoulders to press him away—to push him off. Instead, his mouth tore at hers, his breathing heavy and harsh. She felt his hand move beneath her dress and underclothes to clasp her bare breast.

"William!" she somehow cried, but his kiss covered the sound of panic and protest. His arms were like a vise, his body like a clamp. She didn't know how his huge thighs had gotten between hers. Her skirts seemed to be tangled up around her knees. What was he doing? She couldn't do this!

And then she felt his hand high up on her thighs, beneath her skirts, only a thin soft layer of cotton between her and him. She bucked and twisted wildly now, desperate.

And suddenly Montgomery wasn't on top of her anymore.

Elysse saw a blur of movement—and then Alexi was throwing Montgomery aside, his face a mask of rage.

She cried out. He had come to rescue her! She scrambled to stand up as Montgomery turned. Alexi tackled him viciously, head-on. Both men went down to the ground, struggling. Alexi was now on top, pummeling him furiously. She knew he meant to kill him. But Montgomery seized his throat.

Elysse screamed. "Stop! Both of you—stop!"

Alexi glanced at her, the American still choking him. Montgomery used the moment to jerk his knee up at his groin. Alexi twisted quickly away from the blow, and as he did, Montgomery thrust him off, and scrambled aside. Both men leaped to their feet simultaneously, crouching, facing one another.

"I am going to kill you," Alexi said.

Montgomery said, "I am going to marry her."

Elysse choked. *What had she done?*

Alexi suddenly looked at Elysse, his eyes hard and furious. "Are you all right?" he demanded. But his gaze widened as it held hers. She knew her hair was a mess. She thought her lip was bleeding. His gaze slammed down her body and she cringed. She was fairly certain that her dress was askew, possibly torn, and covered with grass stains.

She backed up, panting. *She would never be all right, ever again. How had she allowed Montgomery such liberties? What had she been thinking? Why had he turned into such a beast?*

"Elysse!" Alexi cried.

Elysse met his gaze, and felt the tears begin in a flood. She wanted to rush into his arms. He had been right. Montgomery wasn't a gentleman. He had touched her, kissed her, grossly violating her body. She choked and staggered to the wall, to cling to it or fall down.

"I would never hurt her," Montgomery said harshly. "I would never hurt the woman I love."

Alexi said softly, dangerously, "Did you think to seduce her to assure that marriage? Don't you know I would kill you first?"

Montgomery looked at Elysse. "If I hurt you, I am sorry."

She shook her head, hating him. More tears fell. She trembled, the urge to vomit sudden and intense. "That wasn't a kiss," she heard herself whisper. "You touched me."

"You fucking bastard," Alexi growled.

Montgomery smiled coldly. "Get lost, de Warenne. I will take care of Elysse now. She is merely a frightened virgin."

"No!" Elysse cried, horrified at the idea of being left

alone with him again. But Alexi was oddly silent—and she saw the knife in Montgomery's right hand. She froze.

It gleamed.

"Leave us," Montgomery said. "I need to speak to Elysse alone. She needs to understand how a man can become so aroused that he loses all control."

She felt even sicker now. She had been fooled by Montgomery's charm, his declarations of love. A true gentleman—a man like Alexi—would never force himself on any woman.

"Leave the two of you? *Like hell*." Alexi smiled dangerously. He began circling the American. Montgomery turned, so that the two men continued to face one another.

And Elysse knew her presence was forgotten by them both. This had to stop, she thought frantically, before someone was seriously hurt—or worse! Elysse cried, "Alexi, I am fine. No one is marrying anyone! Let's go home! You can take me home now!" She heard how terrible she sounded, sobs choking her tone.

Alexi launched himself at Montgomery, reaching for his right wrist. Elysse screamed, afraid that the American would stab him with the knife. But the blow glanced off of Alexi's shoulder, and Alexi seized his wrist. Both men now strained at one another, their expressions murderous, Montgomery wanting to get free so he could wield the knife and Alexi not daring to release him.

Suddenly Montgomery grunted and dropped the knife. Alexi dived for it. Montgomery dived for Alexi, tackling him from behind. Elysse screamed as both men became entangled, wrestling on the ground, making it impossible to see what was happening. She thought Alexi had the knife. She wasn't certain. She prayed it would get kicked away from them both!

And suddenly the knife was skidding across the terrace

and both men were diving for it. Alexi landed on top of the pilot, grunting, as he seized it. A loud, sickening crack sounded. And Montgomery went still beneath Alexi, cheek pressed against the stone terrace.

Suddenly neither man was moving.

Elysse froze. Alexi got onto his hands and knees, staring down at the American—and she saw that Montgomery's eyes were wide-open, eerily so.

Elysse gasped in shock. *Montgomery was dead?*

Alexi slid off him slowly. As slowly, he looked up at her, the answer in his eyes.

Her own horror began.

Alexi looked back down at the pilot. "He's dead."

She cried out. "He can't be!"

Alexi inhaled harshly. "He's dead. He hit his head on the stone."

William Montgomery had hit his head—William Montgomery was dead?

"Damn it," Alexi gasped, trembling. He was fighting his emotions now.

And it hit her. This was her fault—wasn't it?

Alexi looked up at her again. "Elysse," he said thickly.

She began shaking her head, backing away. Then she seized her skirts and fled.

CHAPTER FOUR

STILL IN SHOCK, Elysse ran into the house, choking on a raw sob. She could not believe what had happened. *William Montgomery was dead!*

She stumbled, leaning against the wall. They had been fighting because of her. They had been fighting over her. Oh, God—this was all her fault.

Elysse collapsed against the wall. She couldn't stop shaking. She was so sick. How had this happened? She hugged herself, crying. Montgomery had wanted to court her! Yet he had turned into a beast! He had said he loved her, but if he had, he would have never treated her with such disrespect! Alexi had been right about him! And now he was dead!

Gasps sounded.

Elysse started, wiping her wet face with her fingers, looking up. A pair of women stood at the other end of the hall. They were frozen, staring at her in shock.

Suddenly Elysse realized how she must look and what they must be assuming. She knew that her hair was coming down, her face was tearstained, and her skirts probably dirty. Any rational person would just think that she had been accosted—and she had.

She recalled William Montgomery's hands and mouth and she felt even more violently ill. Why hadn't she listened to Alexi, who was her oldest and dearest friend? What would have happened if Alexi hadn't come outside and intervened?

"Miss O'Neill," one of the ladies began.

No one could know about the horrid events of that evening! No one could know that she had allowed a kiss and that it had turned into something more, and that William Montgomery was now dead! Crying out again, she whirled to flee back down the corridor. Alexi was rushing up it.

She had never needed anyone more! She shouldn't have left him alone outside with Montgomery's body! She rushed to him. Alexi seized her arm, their gazes locking. Then he jerked his head and turned, dragging her back down the hall with him. Behind him, she heard both women in a frenzy of whispering.

Oh, God.

She was ruined now.

Alexi pushed open a door and they fled inside the room there; he closed and locked it behind them.

Trembling, her heart pounding with sickening force, she managed, "They know."

"They know nothing," he said, pulling her into his arms.

Elysse cried out, collapsing against his chest, her cheek against his lapel. He held her, hard, in a bearlike embrace.

When he spoke, his mouth moved in her hair. "Tell me you're all right, Elysse. That he didn't hurt you." His tone was raw.

She was crying now, incapable of speech. She reached for his shoulders and clung as never before. He rocked her. Why had she allowed William Montgomery to kiss her? Why had she ever even considered his suit? The events of that evening began to replay in her mind—her terrible, endless flirtations; her argument with Alexi; the awful, aggressive kiss; and the fatal confrontation she had just witnessed between the two men.

"I am so sorry," she wept. "I never meant for this to happen. Oh, my God! Alexi!" She looked up at him. His face was spinning. She felt faint. The horror was consuming.

He clasped her face in his hands. Tears shimmered in his eyes, too. "I know you didn't. Damn it, Elysse. Why did you go outside with him?"

She buried her face against his chest. She didn't want Alexi to ever know that she had allowed Montgomery to kiss her.

"I would never let anyone hurt you."

It was so hard to think—all she could remember was that William Montgomery had turned into a beast and he was now dead and it was because of her. "This is my fault, isn't it? Because I played him—because I went outside with him. Because I didn't listen to you."

Alexi's face hardened. "Stop!" He pulled her tightly against him. His taut body was shaking as wildly as hers. "He had no damned right to kiss you—he knew you were trying to fight him off!"

His embrace felt so safe. She had never been so scared. All she could think of now was that she was safe, finally. But Montgomery was dead—because he had been fighting with Alexi over her. Surely Alexi would not be blamed? Elysse didn't speak, breathing hard, fighting the tears, her cheek pressed against his chest. She wrapped her arms around him. "It was awful. Don't let me go," she managed. She wished they could stay that way, in one another's arms, forever.

Images whirled wildly in her mind. She would never forget the sound of his skull hitting that stone staircase!

Worse, those two ladies had seen her in the hallway. She started to cry, soundlessly.

Alexi was in trouble and she was ruined....

His grasp tightened. She didn't know how long they stood there that way, each grappling with their own demons. She finally became aware of his harsh breathing, which sounded suspiciously like choked sobs, and her own heavy, anguished breaths. The sound of a shutter banging against the house filled the night. A clock was ticking loudly in the corner of the room. The trembling of Alexi's body had slowed. Her own wild shaking had not.

Slowly, she looked up.

He slid his hand up her jaw, then into her hair. His cheeks were damp. "We need to get you home."

"I'll be fine," she whispered. "It was an accident, Alexi, wasn't it? Everything was an accident!"

He inhaled loudly. His gaze blazed through his tears. "I warned him not to take liberties." Agony flickered in his eyes and she knew he was thinking of what she had suffered. "I wanted to kill him, Elysse."

"What are we going to do?" More tears fell, slowly but steadily, an outpouring of torment and guilt.

He caught her face in his hands. "I'm going to take care of *everything*," he said.

Their gazes locked. Suddenly the nausea roiled, too much to bear. She ran across the room and retched in a small wastebasket. *A man was dead because of her foolish flirtation. This was her fault, not Alexi's!*

"Can you stand?"

She nodded and he helped her to her feet. She didn't realize she was still crying until he brushed his thumb across her cheek, as if to stop the flood. "I want you out of here," he said roughly.

She wanted nothing more than to run away and

hide—forever, if possible. "How can I leave you now? After what happened? I can't stop thinking about…him."

"In time you'll forget—we both will," he said, not meeting her gaze.

She knew Alexi well enough to know neither one of them would ever forget—he was lying to her, to make her feel better. "Yes. Because it was an accident."

He met her gaze abruptly, and she thought about the fact that the men had been shipmates and friends—and that the pilot had saved Alexi's life. Stricken with guilt, she looked away.

"I need to think, Elysse." Alexi's tone was rough and raw. "Montgomery is dead—and the body is outside."

And suddenly her mind came to life. Could Alexi be accused of murder? Could he wind up in prison? The future flashed vividly in her mind—a sensational murder trial, her reputation in ruins, Alexi behind bars.

"Stay here. Don't move. I mean it!" He whirled for the door.

Elysse followed him nervously. "Where are you going?"

"I'm going to get my father—and yours."

She seized his arm. "My father can't know!"

He faced her and said, "Devlin has to know."

Elysse gasped as Alexi strode from the library. Then she shut the door behind him, leaning on it, breathing hard. What were they going to do? Alexi couldn't be charged with murder! It had been an accident!

But she was the only witness to the fight. Everyone knew how close Alexi and Elysse were and how close their families were. She might not be believed. How had this happened? She had *liked* William Montgomery. She thought of his forceful kiss, his disgusting touch. Hadn't he known she wanted him to stop? More tears welled. She should have never walked outside, alone, with him!

"Elysse," her father cried, stepping into the room. "Alexi said there is a problem!" As his glance moved over her, he paled impossibly.

Her mother, Cliff and Alexi were with him. Alexi shut the door and locked it.

She somehow straightened, clutching her churning abdomen, more tears falling. Speech was now impossible.

Her mother ran to her, embracing her, and Elysse sagged in her arms. Devlin choked, his eyes wide with shock as he stared at her hair, her face, her dress. "Who did this? Who? Wait." His handsome face enraged, he turned to look at Alexi. "Where's Montgomery?" he snarled.

"He's outside," Alexi said harshly. "And he's dead."

Virginia gasped. Cliff strode forward, seizing Alexi by the shoulder. "What the hell happened?"

"It was an accident!" Elysse cried, before Alexi could respond. "It was my fault. I encouraged him. I have encouraged his attentions all week. Alexi found us...kissing." She thought she flushed. "They fought." She looked at her father, begging him now. "It was an accident, Father. They fought and he fell and hit his head. Please, you have to protect Alexi!"

"What did he do to you?" Devlin demanded.

"I'm not really hurt," Elysse cried.

"Not now," Virginia warned her disbelieving husband. To Elysse, she said, "Darling, we are going home. We'll go out the back. And you needn't worry about Alexi." She smiled reassuringly at her.

"I am not going home, not until this is all sorted out! He is dead, Mother, and—" She stopped. "And it was my fault, not Alexi's."

"If Alexi fought Montgomery, then he was hurting you," Devlin roared. "I want to know what happened!"

"It was just a kiss, a terrible, disgusting kiss!" she shouted back.

A silence fell. Virginia pulled her closer to her side. Elysse wiped the incessant tears, wishing she hadn't spoken so openly. Finally Alexi said, his tone firm, "The pilot was making improper advances. Elysse was rudely accosted, but nothing more. *Nothing* else happened."

Devlin jerked to stare at him, clearly uncertain of whether to believe him or not.

Elysse flushed as Cliff demanded sharply, "Where is Montgomery's body?"

Alexi's gaze was unwavering on her. Elysse trembled in her mother's arms. He said flatly, "The body is outside on the terrace." Alexi added in a grim, matter-of-fact tone, "We fought hand to hand and he hit his head on the stone steps."

Devlin said, "So they were on the lawns, not the terrace?"

Alexi looked coolly at him.

Devlin was red. "Where was he taking you?" he asked Elysse.

"I don't know—I didn't want to leave the terrace!"

"When I saw them, I wanted to kill him."

Cliff paled. "Did anyone else see anything?"

Elysse bit her lip. She didn't want to bring up the two women in the corridor now.

Alexi apparently agreed, as he sent her a cautioning look. "We can't go to the authorities." Alexi spoke rapidly and firmly. "If we do, the events of this evening will be made public, sooner or later, during an investigation and maybe even a trial. Elysse will never recover from that."

She knew he would do anything to protect her now.

Cliff turned to Devlin. "We need to get rid of the body."

Devlin nodded, his face ruthlessly set. "Agreed."

Virginia whispered, "They will fix this, darling. Alexi will be fine and so will you."

Elysse prayed that her mother was right.

Devlin and Cliff locked gazes. Devlin said, "We'll bury Montgomery at sea. No one will ever know."

HE HAD JUST KILLED A MAN.

It was half past four in the morning and Windhaven was silent now, its women soundly asleep on the second floor. Alexi followed his father, Devlin and Jack into the kitchens, the four men having surreptitiously entered the house from the back. He had shed his tailcoat long ago and his white ruffled shirt was black with dirt and oil, his sleeves rolled up to the elbows. It remained difficult to think clearly. What he was aware of was the pounding pain in his chest, the hammer in his temples. Even his ribs hurt, as if they were bruised or broken, so much so he'd had difficulty breathing the entire night.

William Montgomery was dead.

But Elysse was all right.

He trembled in exhaustion. Elysse had been accosted—assaulted. She had been struggling to get free of Montgomery, her skirts tangled around her thighs. The moment he'd seen them, he had felt her alarm, her fear and her panic.

He had instantly wanted to destroy the other man. And he'd gotten his wish.

He was no stranger to death. But killing savage American Indians or bloodthirsty Africans or equally barbaric pirates in self-defense was one thing. What had happened that night was an entirely different matter—one he was having a hell of a time comprehending.

Montgomery had been his shipmate, his pilot and his friend. He'd saved Alexi's life. And he had just killed him....

It remained utterly incomprehensible.

The other men were in a similar state of disarray and filth. No one had spoken a word since leaving Limerick Harbor. In silence, they now followed Cliff through the vast kitchen, which was in darkness except for a small fire, down an equally dully lit hall to the library. Cliff did not bother to close the teakwood doors. He lit several gas lamps, instead.

Devlin walked over to the gilded bar cart and poured brandy from a decanter into four glasses, his face grim. He, too, was lost in thought. Alexi simply stared, watching him without really seeing him, his head aching as never before.

He had misjudged Montgomery entirely. If he had known what he was capable of, he would have never brought him home, much less to Askeaton Hall. It made him sick to think of the fact that he had introduced the American to Elysse.

He knew he would never forget the sight of Montgomery on top of her, in the throes of lust, with Elysse, so tiny and fragile in his arms, trying to push him away. He would never forget the sound of that kiss, either—the American's heavy breathing, punctuated with short, rough grunts. Elysse had whimpered in fear, and maybe pain.

He forced the horrific memory aside. Instantly that memory was replaced by an equally unpleasant one—Elysse's tearstained face filled his mind. He saw her in his arms, weeping, hurt and frightened. Dear God, she had never been as beautiful or as vulnerable, and he had never known such an intense urge to protect her.

His gut churned. He knew her so damned well. He had known her since they were children.

I am not inebriated and I am not going home. Not unless you are offering to take me there....

Are you flirting with me?

I flirt with everyone, remember?

His tension had reached unbearable proportions. She was a reckless, impossible, insatiable coquette. She had flirted with every eligible male that night. She had flirted with Montgomery. And she had flirted with him. But no matter what she had done, no woman deserved the treatment she had received.

It was his fault, for bringing Montgomery to Ireland....

His mind reeled with sickening intensity. Images danced—Elysse and Montgomery in a torrid embrace; Montgomery diving for the knife just as he reached for it, too; his pilot's body, being heaved overboard into the night-black sea.

Devlin handed him a snifter. He accepted it, but he saw only Elysse now, smiling seductively at him.

You are truly drunk, like a sailor. You are going home.

No, I am not. I promised William another dance—and a walk in the gardens. Have you noticed how lovely the moon is tonight? They call it a lover's moon, Alexi....

His blood boiled, and he felt as if he must smash something, anything, soon. Of course she hadn't listened to him. She never listened to him! Instead, she had gone outside with Montgomery, flirting impossibly, heedlessly, dangerously. And now, the American pilot was dead.

He had killed him because of her. He would do it all over again, if he had to, even though the damned American had saved his life.

"Well, it's done," Devlin said, breaking into his thoughts. "The bastard is at the bottom of the Irish Sea."

Alexi downed the brandy. His hand was shaking still. The drink didn't ease his tension, not at all.

"This will pass," his father said firmly, clearly willing it to be.

Alexi didn't believe him. He would never forget this evening—he would never forget what had happened to Elysse. He would never forget his part in it.

Cliff clasped his shoulder. "It's done, Alexi, and dwelling on this night won't help matters. You need to put this behind you. We won't ever refer to this night—or the pilot—again."

Alexi realized he had nothing to say. He was in that odd state of exhaustion where he was so tired he would never be able to rest or sleep.

A fresh wave of anger took him by surprise.

So many memories returned that he was briefly paralyzed—he and Montgomery, side by side in the snow, behind a barricade of logs, fighting for their lives against a band of Hurons in a blinding blizzard; he and Montgomery, hunkered down in the cabin afterward, drinking whiskey, shocked to be still alive and suddenly laughing about it; he and Montgomery, in Gibraltar, in the small bedroom of a public inn, sharing the favors of a very lush whore; and on his ship, about to run through the Sundra Strait, a stiff nor'easter behind them now, watching the last mizzen and topsails unfurling, Montgomery at his side, grinning. Later, as the ship had raced past Java Head and into the Indian Ocean, they'd shared a mug of rum to celebrate their homeward-bound run through the China Sea...

"Alexi," his father said.

With a jolt he returned to Cliff de Warenne's library. He

felt how wet his face was. Because in the end, Montgomery hadn't been his friend, not at all.

In that moment, Alexi knew he was going to be sick.

"You have had a shock, and killing a man is no easy matter," Cliff said. "Son, it was an accident. You were protecting Elysse."

Alexi crossed the room in a rush and went outside. On the same terrace where he had found Montgomery with Elysse, he heaved up the brandy. Afterward he just stood there, clinging to the rail, willing his stomach to calm.

He had murdered his *friend*. But Montgomery wasn't genuinely his friend, was he? He had been a calculating fortune hunter and a cad, and he had been forcing himself on her….

He was sick with guilt and sicker still with fury. Cursing, he smashed his fist into the rail. None of the events of that evening need to have happened! More tears filled his eyes. Damn Montgomery! Damn Elysse O'Neill!

Cliff said, "Do you want to talk about it?"

"No." His anger roared. It was better—safer—than the guilt. Anger he could withstand. Slowly he turned to face his father.

Cliff's gaze was searching. "You had every right to defend Elysse, son," he said. "But I know how close you and Montgomery were. You were friends—you were shipmates."

Alexi trembled, fighting the shocking need to cry again. He had trusted Montgomery with the lives of his crew. The safety of his ship. Damn it! "It doesn't matter. He's dead."

Cliff slid his hand over his shoulder. "No one blames you, and certainly not for what Montgomery tried to do. Of course you would protect Elysse. You have cared for her since you were children. I remember the day we arrived at

Harmon House and the look on your face when we walked inside and you saw her for the first time."

He pulled away. He did not want to hear about that! "There was no *look* on my face, damn it! And if there was, she was probably flirting with me!"

Cliff stared, not speaking now.

Alexi cried in frustration, "Montgomery is dead—she was assaulted tonight—and she will be flirting madly tomorrow as if nothing has happened. You wait and see!" He could barely believe how angry he was with her.

"That isn't fair and you know it," Cliff said quietly. "She has been through hell tonight. She will hardly be in good spirits any time soon."

He was so angry now that it was hard to think straight. "I warned her not to lead him on. Will she ever learn?"

"Everyone learns from life, son," Cliff said softly.

Alexi folded his arms stiffly across his chest. "She will never learn from this," he said savagely. "She will never grow up."

"You have every right to be angry."

"I am furious," he shouted. Just then, he wanted to take Elysse by her shoulders and shake her until she became an ordinary woman with common sense. "I told her to stay away from Montgomery! I did not trust him with her! I knew she would go too far! As always, she did exactly the opposite of what I wished for her to do. Knowing her, she probably encouraged that damned kiss. Damn it!"

"Maybe it is time for the both of you to admit to an attraction that has been simmering for years," Cliff said, his gaze searching.

Alexi started. Then he growled, terribly uncomfortable, "I don't have any idea of what you mean." He turned and paced, feeling ruthless and savage now. Devlin needed to set her down. He needed to discipline her. He needed to end her damned flirtations! He needed to marry her off immediately! Elysse had proven she had no common sense; she needed a husband to look out for her.

He froze in midstride. Then he looked at his father, who was sipping from his brandy far too calmly, his gaze watchful.

Alexi rushed back inside, Cliff following more slowly.

Devlin was seated, and staring into his empty glass, obviously brooding upon the events of that evening. Jack was pacing.

"I wish *I* had killed him," Jack spat, trembling with rage. "Those two bitches have probably told half the world that my sister has been ruined. And she *has* been ruined, God damn it. No one will want her now!"

Alexi felt his tension increase. Jack was right. He had thought it his responsibility to warn Devlin about Mrs. Carrie and Lady O'Dell. The fact that the women loved to gossip had been in the back of his mind all night. It was obvious that Elysse had been seriously compromised.

Jack said tersely, "I know Elysse is a flirt. But she is stunningly beautiful. She can't help the fact that when she enters a room, every man looks twice. The pilot was no exception."

Alexi did not want to get into a debate over her reckless affair with Montgomery, not with Jack. Her brother would defend her behavior, of course.

"She was the catch of all Ireland," Jack said. He glanced at Devlin. "No one will want her now. No matter how we deny the gossip, it will be on the tip of every lady's tongue." He scowled.

Devlin looked up. "There is one way to end the gossip,

Jack, other than to refute it. Remember, she is an heiress. I can buy her a very suitable, very prominent, husband."

Alexi's tension was undeniable now. Hadn't he known this tangent was coming? He had just reached the same conclusion—that she needed to be married off immediately—even if he had used slightly different reasoning. And the moment he'd realized that, he'd known that a husband would offer her all the protection she needed from the gossips. Devlin was no fool. He knew as well as Alexi that he could quell the gossip generated by those two biddies if he found her a good match.

"You have always wanted a love match for her," Cliff said mildly.

Alexi stood very still. This was a new battlefield, one filled with hidden mines. He knew he must tread carefully.

"Yes, I have. But that won't be possible now, will it?" Devlin glanced at him.

The ocean seemed to roar in his ears. He recalled that foolish young boy of nine or ten, the one who held the secret assumption that one day he'd grow up and make Elysse O'Neill his wife.

"When she is married, this tragic episode will truly be laid to rest," Devlin said. "I know my daughter. She won't withstand scorn and ostracism well. I am going to find her an exceptional groom—the sooner, the better."

"You could send her abroad for a year or two," Cliff said, glancing at Alexi.

"That won't end this gossip. If she is a wealthy, powerful matron, no one will think twice about this evening." Devlin stood. Clearly, his mind was made up.

Alexi breathed hard. "Stop," he said. "That won't be necessary."

Devlin stared at him. "What do you have in mind?" But his gaze was hooded, as if he knew.

He inhaled. "I came to her rescue once this night and I will do so again."

Devlin raised a brow and slowly began to smile.

Alexi said, "If you intend to marry her off, I will be the one to marry her."

CHAPTER FIVE

MONTGOMERY LOWERED HIS FACE to hers and her heart lurched with dread—somehow, she knew what would happen next. She felt his lips move on hers, fiercely demanding. His tongue thrusting deep, and panic became fear. She began to struggle, aware that she was now on the ground, and he was on top of her. Suddenly Alexi was glaring furiously, accusingly at her. She looked behind him and saw William lying on the ground, his eyes wide and sightless.

"You did this!" Alexi cried.

She wanted to deny it. Instead, no words came and she screamed....

Elysse sat up, her heart thundering, her entire body drenched in sweat. For one moment, shock immobilized her. In that moment, she thought she was on the terrace at Windhaven. She looked down, expecting to see the American pilot lying dead on the ground. Instead, she stared down at her pink floral bedcovers and ivory nightgown.

She exhaled, shaking. She was in her own bed, the bedroom cast entirely in dark shadow. She tried to breathe, her heart continuing to pound wildly. William Montgomery was dead, and it was entirely her fault!

Guilt engulfed her.

Hadn't Alexi told her, time and again, not to lead Montgomery on? Hadn't she ignored his warnings, just to annoy him? Hadn't she even, secretly, hoped to make him jealous?

Yet she had liked Montgomery! She had wanted his suit, hadn't she? She had enjoyed his attentions, up until that terrible kiss….

The events of that night flooded her with stunning clarity now. The men had left Windhaven to bury William's body at sea—to cover up the fact of his death. Her mother had taken her home, leaving through the kitchen entrance to avoid attracting any more attention. Virginia hadn't tried to speak with her during the ride home, but she had kept her arm around her in a futile attempt to offer comfort. No longer crying, but terribly dazed, Elysse had simply stared out of the coach window, icy cold inside her body, inside of her heart.

William Montgomery was dead—because of her.

How could this have happened?

Elysse hadn't wanted to go to bed—she hadn't wanted to be alone with her horror and her guilt. So she had sat up with her mother, sipping hot chocolate in silence, a fire blazing in the hearth. The chill had remained, deep in her bones; she didn't think it would ever go away. Virginia hadn't tried to chat and Elysse had been grateful. But the events of the evening had kept replaying in her mind, relentlessly—cruelly. At half past three, she had sent her mother to bed. Elysse hadn't been able to fall asleep. Pulling the covers to her chin, she had stared at the ceiling, seeing Alexi and Montgomery struggling, watching as Montgomery fell, hearing his skull crack, hopelessly wishing the night hadn't happened….

It had been worse when she closed her eyes. Then, almost every moment of the past week had replayed ruthlessly in her mind, as her unyielding flirtation led inexorably up to Montgomery's death. She kept telling herself that it had been an accident, but she knew better—it was her fault and her fault alone….

I would never let anyone hurt you.... I wanted to kill him....

Elysse clutched the bedcovers and screwed her eyes shut. Was Alexi finally at Windhaven, in his own bed, having buried Montgomery at sea? Had he realized that this was entirely her fault? Would he protect her all over again, if he had to do so another time?

Elysse threw the covers off, leaping to her feet, shivering. She would regret what had happened for the rest of her life; she would never act so recklessly and selfishly again. Not that she would be given the chance. For she was ruined now.

Elysse walked to the closest window and pulled aside the heavy mauve draperies. The sun was shining brightly outside, amidst many fluffy white clouds. It was at least midmorning, if not close to noon. She wondered if she should hide in her room all day.

She almost laughed, desperately. By now, the entire southwest of Ireland knew she had been compromised last night. Every lady in the county who saw her would approach, pretending to say hello but really wanting sordid details. But she would not entirely avoid the gossipmongers by staying home—there would be so many callers today! Even her girlfriends would want to know who she had been with last night and what had happened.

If anyone ever found out that she had been in Montgomery's arms, that Alexi had assaulted him to protect her and caused his death, she would be ostracized and shunned.

Her life as she had known it was forever over.

She was no longer the most desirable debutante in Ireland. No one would ever want her now.

Elysse seized her pounding temples as a knock sounded on her door. Her reputation was in shreds. She could not imagine how it would ever be salvaged. It was just sinking in—her prospects for marriage were over. And if the events of that night were ever discovered, Alexi might very well go to prison....

"Elysse?" Virginia slipped into her bedroom. She held a breakfast tray in her hands. "Are you feeling any better this morning? Did you manage to sleep at all?"

"I had nightmares." She caught a glimpse of her pale reflection in the mirror behind her mother. There were dark, unbecoming circles under her eyes. "How is Alexi? Is he all right?" She wet her lips. "Are they back?"

"Your father returned at sunrise, while Alexi went home. Everything has been taken care of," her mother said, unsmiling. She set the tray down on a small round table next to a window that showed a view of the lawns below. "You should eat, darling. It will help settle your stomach."

"I can't eat. My head hurts and my stomach is churning. William Montgomery is dead, Mother. *Dead.*"

Virginia uncovered the plates. "It is not your fault!"

"I wanted to make Alexi jealous," she cried. In that moment, she knew it was the truth. "What is wrong with me?"

"You hardly foresaw what would happen," Virginia responded firmly. "You are not the first young woman to try to make a man jealous! Montgomery pressed unwanted attentions on you. Had he behaved as a gentleman, he would still be alive. You make certain to remember that fact!"

"So it is his fault that he is dead?" she cried, not believing that for a moment. She felt moisture well in her eyes. "He told me he wanted to press a proper suit. He wanted to marry me, Mother."

"He wanted to marry your fortune," Virginia said sharply. "I was going to speak to you about it, but I delayed, believing he would be leaving Ireland shortly."

Elysse stared, realizing her mother meant what she said.

Still, she wasn't comforted. Slowly, she said, "If I hadn't gone outside with him, intending to encourage him, wanting a declaration from him, he would also be alive."

"This is not your fault," Virginia repeated. "It is over, Elysse. We must all recognize that and let this go."

Somehow, Elysse didn't think she could simply forget about William Montgomery or her atrocious behavior. She didn't believe the nightmare would ever end. "I need to speak to Father," she said. She wanted to know if Alexi blamed her for Montgomery's death. Then, hesitantly, she added, "I need to see Alexi, too." She was afraid he might refuse to see her in the light of a new, horrific day.

"Your father wants to speak to you, as well. There is some news." Virginia smiled. "It might even be considered good news. Why don't you put on a wrapper and I will call him up?"

Elysse couldn't imagine what good news Devlin might have. She felt as if she had aged a lifetime in a few hours.

A few moments later, Virginia returned to her room with her father. Devlin looked drawn and tired, but resolute. Elysse couldn't speak, suddenly imagining what he had been through that night, as well. She knew she had a special place in her father's heart, as most daughters did. Of course he would be devastated by what had happened. "I'm so sorry," she managed. "I regret my behavior, Father, and I will never behave as such a reckless and silly fool again."

He went straight to her, embracing her. "You do not need to apologize. Montgomery was not a gentleman, and I should have chased him away from the start. I will always take care of you, Elysse," Devlin said. "You will always be my little girl, and you are not reckless or silly."

She trembled. "You cannot blame yourself."

"I am your father. It is my duty to look after you."

"This is my fault, Father, and I am intelligent enough to realize it. You must be so terribly disappointed in me."

"I could never be disappointed in you."

Feeling even more guilt, she finally asked, "Is Alexi all right?"

He studied her. "He is upset. Very much so. I think you know as well as we all do that he would never tolerate any ill will toward you. I think he remains in some shock. But he will get through this. He is a strong young man, and a de Warenne."

"Is he at home?"

"I assume so. That is where Jack and I left him this morning at dawn."

She hesitated. "Does he blame me for what happened?"

"I believe he blames himself," Devlin answered.

"Father, it was my fault."

"It was not your fault," Devlin said calmly. "And at this point, what is done is done. It is useless to lay blame. The two of you need to move on."

Elysse was silent, certain she would blame herself until the day she died. But she couldn't bear Alexi blaming himself.

"We have one last obstacle to overcome," Devlin said carefully. "And that is the matter of your marriage."

She started. "What are you talking about?"

"I know Mrs. Carrie and Lady O'Dell saw you in your disheveled state last night. I wish to quell the gossip immediately. Marriage is the perfect way to do so."

Alarm began. "I can't discuss marriage—today of all days!" Did her father mean to buy her a husband?

"Alexi will marry you, Elysse, if you will have him."

She went still. Had she just heard Devlin correctly? "Alexi will *marry* me?"

"Mrs. Carrie and Lady O'Dell saw you in the hallway with Alexi, did they not?" Her eyes widened, as she began to realize the tangent her father was on. Her heart raced. "They probably assumed he is your lover. If you will marry him, no one will ever care that you were in his arms last night, or that the moment got out of hand."

She sank into the closest chair. "Alexi said he will marry me? But...are you certain? He doesn't want to marry at all."

"That isn't true. He wants to end any gossip as much as I do. He has said he will marry you," Devlin stated firmly.

The room seemed to be whirling about her. She clung to the pale, bone-colored arms of the chair. Alexi had protected her from William Montgomery earlier, and now he had stepped forward to do so again.

But hadn't he promised her when they were children, so long ago, that he would always protect her?

He was the most heroic man she had ever met. "He *wants* to marry me?" she heard herself ask, her tone high and uncertain.

"Since when does Alexi de Warenne do anything he does not wish to do?" Virginia murmured.

"I cannot say I am surprised," Devlin said. "Although I did not expect this match for another five years or so. You are certainly ready for marriage, but twenty-one-year-old males are terribly immature—and he is a seafaring man, as well."

She barely heard. She had to pinch her thighs to make certain she wasn't dreaming. A slow thrill unfurled, like a topsail in a gentle breeze.

Alexi wanted to marry her.

The nightmare began to recede.

Together, they would manage to forget. Together, they would heal. She was certain.

"Elysse?" Virginia cut into her shock. "Your father and I have always wanted a love match for you. We have wondered if that match might not be Alexi—the two of you have flirted for years. He is a good man. He is your friend. He is fond of you and you are fond of him. And now, in a crisis, he has stepped forward. If you will accept him—happily—we both approve."

"And if you have doubts, I will do my best to eradicate the gossip," Devlin added.

On the heels of horror, there was the beginning of joy. It was delicate and fragile, like a spring bloom in winter. Elysse somehow stood up, the room still tilting, but slowly, like a carousel. And finally, a smile began. "Of course I will marry Alexi."

"ARE YOU ALL RIGHT?" Devlin asked, tucking her arm even more firmly in his.

Elysse barely heard him. She could scarcely breathe. The bones of her white lace corset were digging into her ribs. She looked up at her father, who was handsome and elegant in his tailcoat. She clutched her bridal bouquet even more tightly.

"Every bride has nerves," he told her, patting her white-gloved hand.

She inhaled, somehow nodding. This was her wedding day. She felt as if she had been waiting for this moment her entire life. Finally, the tragedy that had brought her to this moment no longer mattered—finally, for the first time in two weeks, it was forgotten. Instead, she stared into the church, past the pews filled with her family and Alexi's. Her heart beat wildly.

Alexi stood at the end of the nave with his best man,

Stephen Mowbray, the Duke of Clarewood. The Earl of Adare's minister was beside them, as was her brother, Jack, and Ned de Warenne, the earl's heir and oldest son. Facing the men were her mother and Ariella. Virginia was beaming and Ariella was gazing expectantly up the aisle. The music began, and every head in the church turned toward the doorway where she stood with her father.

Alexi stared at her.

He was devastatingly gorgeous in his tailcoat. But something was very, very wrong. His face was hard and set, as if with distaste and determination.

This was their wedding. But he didn't seem happy.

She hadn't seen him since the night of the ball. When she'd sent him a note, asking him if they'd have a chance to speak before the nuptials, his reply had been brief—he would not be back in Ireland until the night before the wedding. He had left for London two days after the ball to take care of his business affairs. Elysse imagined that there were many loose ends to be tied up, as they would surely take a honeymoon on the Continent. Yet no plans had thus far been made. She had expected a note from him, or even a letter, but there hadn't been a word.

The bridal march was being played by the organist. Devlin murmured, "Shall we?"

Elysse couldn't speak. Her gaze locked with Alexi's as she let her father guide her down the aisle. As she approached, her heart lurched with dismay. She knew Alexi too well; there was no mistaking his anger.

She panicked. This wasn't right—it wasn't how it was supposed to be! He was only marrying her to protect her! Was that why he was angry—because he was marrying when he really didn't want to?

Had he changed his mind, but was too much of a gentleman to jilt her?

Weren't they marrying on the heels of an innocent man's death?

Suddenly she balked, refusing to go forward, so terribly frightened.

Her father looked down at her, concerned.

What if he did not want to marry her? He was only doing so to protect her, after all....

"This is a mistake," she whispered. Her gaze riveted on her bridegroom, she opened her mouth to tell her father that she could not marry under these circumstances. But no words came out.

"Elysse," Alexi said, and while his tone was low, it was unmistakably a command.

Somehow she moved forward, somehow, she stood with Alexi, staring into his cold blue eyes. The minister began speaking. Her knees buckled. Alexi reached out to hold her elbow, keeping her upright.

She felt dazed, almost disembodied, as if an unwilling participant in a dream. But his eyes were locked with hers, telling her not to move. The reverend kept speaking, but it was hard to hear what he was saying. There was only Alex's unyielding gaze. And then she heard Alexi say, "I do."

She tensed, unable to look at the reverend as he said, "And do you, Elysse O'Neill, take this man in sickness and in health, for better or for worse, until death do you part, as your everlasting husband?"

She stared at Alexi. Her heart lurched. He was angry—but she loved him. Dear God, she knew that now. She had always loved him, hadn't she? Ever since they had first met as children.

Would he ever forgive her for what she had done?

"Elysse," Alexi prompted, his grasp on her elbow tightening.

She heard herself murmur, "I do."

She felt so oddly detached now. She looked down and watched Alexi slide a heavy gold band on her finger. Her vision blurred. *Please don't be angry with me.*

He grasped her arm again. Her gaze shot up to his. For one moment he met her eyes before looking grimly away.

"Then, with the power invested in me by the Church of England and the State, I do hereby pronounce you man and wife. You may kiss the bride."

Elysse was desperately afraid. For one moment, she thought he was going to refuse to kiss her.

He leaned forward, brushing his heavy, closed mouth over hers.

Her heart leaped at the contact. The odd feeling of being disembodied vanished. He hesitated, their mouths brushing, his grip firmer now on her arm, refusing to let her fall. She heard his breath escape and felt his mouth open; even more dazed, she opened her own lips and nudged his mouth with hers. And for one long, interminable moment, she thought he would actually kiss her back.

Instead, his grasp tightened painfully and he stepped away from her.

"I am sorry." He released her abruptly.

She gasped, their gazes still riveted. It was done. For better or for worse, they were man and wife.

But as their families descended upon them, he turned his back on her. His cousins and uncles began pummeling him. His father hugged him. Elysse felt the tears rising up swiftly. He was so distant and so angry. She told herself she would not cry, not now and not ever.

"I am so happy for you!" Ariella exclaimed, behind her.

Elysse plastered a smile on her face and turned to her

aunts, uncles and cousins. Beaming, she somehow nodded at everyone who held her, kissed her and congratulated her. But every minute or two, she glanced around to see where Alexi was and what he was doing. He remained with the men, smiling and at ease, a flute of champagne in his hand. He did not look at her a single time, his back kept partly toward her. No gesture could mean more.

He wasn't angry, he was furious.

LATER THAT NIGHT, Elysse would not be able to recall a single conversation from the entire evening other than the final one she had with Alexi.

It was some time after the wedding ceremony—it was impossible to say how much time had passed. She was in his arms at last, on the dance floor in the ballroom at Askeaton, but she was still filled with dread and hurt.

Alexi had always been an indifferent but naturally graceful dancer. He held her lightly, loosely. It was the first time he had looked at her since they had exchanged their vows.

"Alexi," Elysse said hoarsely.

"Everyone is watching us." He forced a smile. It was cool. "Now is not the time."

She ignored him, moisture rising in her eyes. "I am so sorry about…everything."

"I do not want to discuss anything!" he said tersely.

She inhaled, trembling. "So you have come to blame me for William Montgomery's death."

He stopped in his tracks and stared down at her. "I have realized that you wanted me to come outside and discover the two of you together. You wanted me in a jealous rage, Elysse. And you got what you wanted—you always do."

"Yes, I wanted to make you jealous, I acknowledge that—and I regret it!"

"He was my friend—until you came along. He saved my life. And I killed him." Abruptly he tightened his hold on her. "I don't know if I can ever forgive you, Elysse, for what you did. But what I do know is that I will never forget that night and what *I* did." His eyes were blazing with pent-up anger as he swept her back into the waltz.

"It was an accident," she cried.

"Yes, it was. But none of this would have happened if you hadn't led him on."

He was right. Tears filled her eyes. "We can't fight now, like this," she managed. "Everyone will know that you hate me." It was a question.

But he didn't answer. And that was answer enough. She fought the tears of hurt and disappointment, of grief and heartbreak. Had she been a fool to think they were starting a life together? To think that they could get past this sordid, tragic, painful beginning?

"You changed your mind, didn't you?" she cried, balking. She wasn't going to dance with him now, even if this was their first dance as a married couple. "You offered to marry me to protect me, but you have only done so because you were too much of a gentleman to jilt me."

His mouth was hard and tight. It was a moment before he answered her. "No, Elysse, I don't want to be married to you."

She cried out. Now what should she do? "But we *are* married," she managed. "I want to be a good wife to you, Alexi!"

He shrugged indifferently. "Do whatever you wish. You can be a good wife or a rotten one—I don't care, Elysse. It just doesn't matter."

She gasped. "What are you saying?"

"I'm saying, do as you will. You always do. Just leave me out of your future flirtations."

"You're my husband! There won't be flirtations!"

"Really? I doubt that!" he mocked. "I mean it, Elysse. You can do whatever you want. I've given you my name. I will support you, put a roof over your head, clothe you in pretty gowns and prettier jewels. But that's as far as this marriage goes." He gestured at the table. "Why don't we sit and try to pretend we can get on until this farce of an evening is over?"

He couldn't really mean what he had just said, could he? He was speaking in anger! He wanted to hurt her. But did he know just how much pain he was causing? She opened her mouth to confess the extent of her feelings for him—to tell him that she loved him, and she wanted to make their marriage a good, loving one. Before she could utter a word, he said, "You may as well know, my ship leaves tonight. As soon as our guests leave, I am casting off."

She was stunned.

"I don't know how long I'll be gone," he added with some satisfaction. He watched her closely now.

Reeling, she managed, "But you aren't leaving for China till June."

"I didn't say I was going to China," he said brusquely.

She began shaking her head. Hope started to die. "What about our wedding night?"

He gave her an incredulous look.

He wasn't going to stay. He wasn't going to consummate their marriage. She trembled. It was so hard to speak. "Where are you going, Alexi?"

"Singapore," he said.

Her marriage, she realized in that moment, was entirely a sham.

PART TWO
"Love Waged"

CHAPTER SIX

London, England

Spring 1839

ELYSSE LOOKED DOWN HER LONG, elegantly set dining table at her twenty-three dinner guests, smiling slightly. Candles flickered in silver candelabra, crystal tinkled, gilded flatware clinked and laughter interspersed the hum of voices. Several animated conversations were taking place at once. The dining room had dark red and gold wallpaper, with two large crystal chandeliers overhead. A fire burned in one fireplace, beneath an ebony marble mantel brightened with a stunning bouquet. Smaller floral arrangements graced the table. The room was lovely; her guests were well fed and amused. It was, of course, just one more success of many.

After all, she was one of London's most renowned socialites and her invitations were coveted and fought over.

As the hostess of this supper party, she sat at the very end of the table, clad in a magnificent sapphire evening gown with sapphire jewels to match. Her escort of the evening, Mr. Thomas Blair, one of the nation's leading bankers, had been given the host's seat at the opposite end of the table. He was a very handsome gentleman of ambition—which one must never openly talk about—and means. He was also a bachelor. She had sprinkled the evening with two debutantes and a young widow, as was proper for a catch of his stature. He now raised his wineglass and smiled at her, his regard steady and unwavering. She knew he approved of far more than the dinner party.

She smiled back at him as Lord Worth said, "Who cares if the Chinese buy opium? Other than their own leaders?" He laughed, his tone patronizing. "I say, let them have their opiates!"

"It is wrong," one of the debutantes, Felicia Carew, declared. She was very young, rather pretty and not particularly bright. Blair had not glanced at her even once. "Everyone knows how horrid opium is—and I am sure it is the same for the poor Chinese! We should not encourage them!"

"My dear," Lord Worth intoned condescendingly, "the opium is worth a fortune—to our merchants, of course. It's damned good trade—free trade, I'd say."

A chorus of agreement sounded. The debate over free trade and open markets was all the rage, perhaps even more popular than the discussion over the National Debt and the country's possible impending bankruptcy. Of course, the latter all rather depended on whose point of view one listened to.

"But to go to war over opium?" an elderly gentleman inserted. "I hear our gunboats are all over the China coast."

Blair was looking at her again. Catching his eye, Elysse replied, "Silver pays for our tea, Mr. Harrison. And the country's firms get paid for opium in silver. But if there were more ports open to our trade, there'd be more markets for our manufactures—to pay for the tea."

"Are you a free trader?" the elderly Mr. Harrison asked. "I am afraid of free trade, I confess."

Before she could respond, Blair said, "How could she not be an advocate of free trade?"

"Of course she prefers free trade," Lord Worth declared. "As her husband is up to his ears in trade all over the world. How is the dashing captain, anyway, my dear Elysse? I certainly hope he is avoiding any unpleasant encounters with the Chinese!"

How would she know? She was aware of Blair staring at her now, but her smile never faltered. She hadn't seen Alexi in six long years. If he was caught up in the gunboat war, she hadn't heard about it. Nor would she care. "He is very well, thank you," she murmured, smiling. "And you are correct. I am a free trader."

She did not want to think about him now. It would spoil her evening. There had only been one note, within months of their marriage, when he had insultingly asked if she could be with child. She had been so angered by the question that she had crumpled up the letter without bothering to reply to it.

Of course, he sent her funds, loving husband that he was. In fact, every month her accounts in both London and Ireland received deposits made by his agents. At first, she had refused to touch his damned money. Now, it paid for *everything*—the beautiful apartment she had leased on Grosvenor Square, the furnishings within it, her wardrobe, her jewels, her coach and horses, her staff.

"There will be war," Blair said lazily, from across the room. "China must open her ports to us."

Elysse looked at him, silently agreeing with him. Society assumed he was her latest lover. He was not, much as he would dearly like to be.

If only she could take him as her lover. She was tired of so much pretense.

"The captain, my dear? Your husband?" Lord Worth insisted. "Will he be returning soon?"

Elysse smiled at the heavyset baron. "I imagine he will

be in London any day now, as he left Canton December 8." A naval packet had relayed the information. Her father had casually conveyed it. As always, she had thanked him for the news, insisting that she was eager for Alexi to get home.

Devlin had looked at her sadly. She could pretend all was well, but she wasn't fooling her family. From the moment Alexi had left her after their wedding, they had known that she was deeply hurt, and no amount of carefree living would change that. Thank God they were too polite to ask her directly about the state of her marriage. Only Ariella and her mother meddled these days. Rather incessantly. Every time she saw either of them, one of the first things they would ask was if she had heard from Alexi. She would always smile and pretend that it didn't matter that she had not.

There hadn't been another letter, not in six years.

"It's only the tenth of March," Blair said. "If he made another one-hundred-and-three-day run—and the odds are unlikely—he'd be back tomorrow."

Elysse glanced at him, never changing her expression. But there was a new tension now. He would be in London soon. For the first time since their wedding, she would also be in town when he arrived. For the first time in six years, their paths would have to cross.

Unfortunately, he was something of national hero now. The country seemed to think him the most dashing China trader. The East India Company had lost her monopoly on the trade in '34, and Alexi had swooped into the tea trade with a stark determination to best every possible rival. The year of their wedding he'd had a clipper built just for the trade, one with less tonnage and a trimmer design made for speed. In '37, the *Coquette* had set a new record for the homeward run—one hundred and three days. It had yet to be broken. For the past two years in a row, the *Coquette* had been the first of the season to make port with her precious cargo.

The first ship to reach port would get the best prices for the tea. Everyone knew it.

Alexi could return any day.

Her tension had escalated. She was Devlin O'Neill's daughter and, for better or for worse, Alexi de Warenne's wife. She did not think him dashing, not at all, but their interests were now one and the same, so of course she wanted him to be the first captain to make port with the best, blackest tea, commanding the highest prices.

She tried to ignore the rumors and gossip about him but it wasn't easy. She was often approached by gentlemen at various functions who eagerly asked her if this or that was true: Had her husband dueled a rival British captain in Batavia? Had he rescued a shipwrecked crew off the Cape Verde Islands? Had he won a sugar plantation on the Goree Islands in a poker game held in Gibraltar?

As if she knew about any of those things!

If she chose, she could walk into the London offices of Windsong Shipping and find out details of his current business affairs, locate where he had recently been and what he had been doing. But she refused to do so. If she were in a real marriage, he would be writing her letters, telling her of his affairs and his comings and goings. She never went to the London offices; instead, she would pretend to know what he was up to. Occasionally she would make up stories about him. She tried to stay as close to the truth as possible, based on details his stepmother and Ariella mentioned when they called.

But she was so very tired of pretending that nothing was wrong, that she was proud of her seafaring husband, that she expected him to be at sea three hundred and fifty days out of the year.

But there was no other choice. No one must ever know that her own husband despised her—that her own husband didn't want her—that he refused to consummate their marriage. No one must ever know that she had been abandoned.

She hadn't stepped out in society that first year. She had been devastated by his betrayal in leaving her on their wedding night, in refusing to even consummate their marriage. Her father had been furious with him. Jack had even threatened to hunt him down and drag him back to her! Elysse had found herself in the absurd position of defending him to just about her entire family. But she had believed he would return to her. She had been so very wrong.

He hadn't come home. In the autumn following their wedding, he'd put into Liverpool with a cargo of tea. Elysse had heard the news from Ariella. She'd had her hair trimmed and waved, her best gowns prepared, and had bought new shoes, all in anticipation of their reunion. She was still hurt and angry, but she was also determined to patch things up. After all, they were married—for better or for worse. But he hadn't come to Askeaton or Windhaven—he'd gone to London for a week, only to immediately set sail for Jamaica with a cargo of textiles and pistons. It had been an obvious and deliberate slap in the face. No message could have been as clear—he did not care that she was his wife.

Devlin had exploded in rage, demanding to know if she wished for an annulment.

Elysse fingered her wineglass. She had been so naive and foolish to think that they could have a genuine marriage after what had happened. If she had known then what she knew now—that six entire years would go by with his ignoring her, as if she did not exist, as if she were not his wife—she would have accepted her father's offer of an annulment. It was too late now. She had survived the gossip for all of these years and she had no intention of doing anything to set the gossips off now.

From the moment she had first moved to London in the winter of '35, there had been whispers about her being an abandoned bride. Some of the gossip had been dangerously close to the truth. How many times had she heard jealous young ladies who would have been her rivals if she were still single discuss the fact that he'd left her right at the altar, without even a wedding night? She had heard whispers, too, that Alexi had found her with a lover, just before he had married her! She had instantly put forth the story concocted by her parents, that he had kissed her at the ball, causing them to realize their love for one another, and that they had spent a honeymoon in a small, picturesque lodge in Scotland. That had diluted the rumors, but it hadn't completely dispersed them. Every now and then, she still overheard whispers about her.

An annulment now, after six years of a supposedly happy marriage, would enflame the gossips.

Blair was staring at her. He'd been pursuing her for a few months now, and while she truly enjoyed his company, she knew she could never leap into his bed. Elysse knew that society thought she had a string of lovers, and she encouraged the illusion. When she was alone in the middle of the night, stricken with insomnia, refusing to think of her errant husband, she wished she had a lover. But she couldn't take a lover. She didn't dare. If the fact that she was a virgin ever got out, her humiliation would finally be complete.

He was a very astute man. One did not rise up from the middle class of society into the upper echelons of both finance and government otherwise. He'd asked her about Alexi. Elysse had held firm to her course—she respected, admired and liked her husband, and his long absence was the nature of maritime transport. Yet she knew he suspected that they were estranged.

"Well. I have news," Felicia's father, Mr. Carew, said. "A pair of ships was spotted by watchers in Plymouth, earlier today. Our offices got the news late this afternoon with the mail. And yes, they were clippers."

Everyone at the table sat up.

Elysse felt her heart lurch. One of those ships had to be Alexi's.

"Mrs. de Warenne, do you believe that one of the clippers is the *Coquette?*"

A dozen of her guests shouted at once, demanding to know if one of the ships was Alexi's—and if he might be beaten to the docks. She realized her hands were trembling and moved them to her lap, beneath the table. "Captain de Warenne is very ambitious. Barring a natural disaster—of which there are many in the course of a long sea voyage—I do think he will be among the first few ships to arrive." She had always known that this day would come, but it had been years since she worried about it. Suddenly, she felt unnerved.

"I wonder who captains the other ship?" one of her guests cried.

"Oh, Mama, I have always wanted to watch the tea ships come into town," Felicia said excitedly. She looked at Blair, blushing. "Could we go to the docks and await them?"

"We should all go to the docks, for it sounded like a very good race is at hand. According to my reports," Carew said, "only a few leagues separated both vessels."

Elysse managed, "Was a third or fourth ship espied anywhere upon the horizon?"

"No, madam, I am afraid not," Carew said.

She wet her lips, certain of only one thing—Alexi was on one of those two ships. The *Coquette* had last been seen off Cape Coast in West Africa, where the British had their naval headquarters. It was unlikely a disaster had overtaken him since then. Every nerve in her body told her that he was racing for home against one of his rivals.

After all of these years, there would finally be a reunion.

Everyone at her table was discussing who the second captain could possibly be.

The anger, so carefully contained, simmered. The hurt, long buried, stabbed through her. She kept a perfect smile on her face. *How could he have done this to her?*

"My packet said the ship was not identifiable," Carew announced.

"It might be one of Jardine's—the house is always in the running," Blair remarked drolly.

Elysse dared to look at him, hoping he hadn't remarked her state of nervousness. She said, "Their shouting was the loudest, I believe. Because of Jardine, Matheson and Co., our gunboats now cruise up the Pei-Kang River, threatening the Chinese authorities."

Blair eyed her. "Are you changing the subject?" he mused, as if to himself.

She knew she flushed. Suddenly, she couldn't wait for the evening to end—she needed at least one excessive brandy. *Alexi would be home by the morrow.*

"Jardine's got a very young, very shrewd captain in that John Littleton," Carew remarked. "And they have built several ships just for the trade."

Elysse stood up. "Are the gentlemen ready for their cigars and brandies? I know we ladies are eager for the best port in this house."

"I'll wager on de Warenne," Lord Worth said, standing. "I know the man, and he is almost invincible."

"I'll take the wager," Carew said. "Odds and all, Captain de Warenne cannot be first into town three years in a row!"

"Fred," his wife interjected, "if you are going to await the ships, then Felicia and I are going with you."

"Personally, I like a long shot," Blair said, standing, as well. "I'll join you in that wager—a gentleman's wager, of course. I'll bet on Alexi de Warenne. And who will you gamble on, Mrs. de Warenne?"

She somehow smiled. "I never gamble, sir, but if I did, I would be loyal to my husband."

"Of course. You must be thrilled that he will be home tomorrow."

She kept smiling. "Of course I am."

"Are we going to the docks to watch the ships come in?" Lady Worth asked her husband. She was as thin as he was portly, as pale as he was flushed.

He smiled and took her hand, fondly patting it. "I wouldn't miss it for the world!" He turned to Elysse. "You will join us in the morning, will you not?"

Elysse was so surprised she almost gaped.

Blair ambled around the table to her side. "I will gladly escort you to St. Katherine's myself."

Her heart was racing so swiftly now that she felt lightheaded. Of course she had no intention of going. A public reunion was far too dangerous—the pretense she had lived with since their marriage could be exposed.

Blair touched her elbow, a soft caress. "You seem a bit... distraught," he said.

"I am hardly distraught." She was amazed at how competent she sounded. She was now adept at maintaining a perfect facade, and she was determined to continue doing so. "I am eager for my husband to win this race and command the best prices for *our* tea."

"Well, depending on the winds, they should arrive in town around midday tomorrow. I'll pick you up at half past ten."

And Elysse realized that there was no possible way she could refuse to go to the docks to watch her errant husband return from China.

EIGHTEEN OF HER TWENTY-THREE guests congregated at the docks that morning, amongst a much larger crowd of Londoners numbering perhaps four or five hundred. Word of the clippers' arrival had spread the day before, as it always did. Watching the arrival of the first great ships of the season was both business and pleasure. Foremost amongst the crowd were the various brokers who would inspect the tea the moment it arrived, before the ships were even unloaded, sending samples on to their consigners before brokering their deals. Elysse had heard that both common men and women, as well as ladies and gentlemen, turned out to await the great tea ships, but she hadn't realized how excited the spectators would be, or how festive the occasion. Even children had come to await the great ships, most of them street urchins. They were shrieking and running about madly.

Alexi was coming home.

It felt unbelievable. She hadn't slept a wink all night, despite two and a half very large brandies taken after all of her guests had left.

She knew better than to consider pleading a migraine. Blair would instantly see through such a sham.

She had dressed with great care in pale blue and aquamarines. She held an ivory striped parasol to shield her complexion from the sun. She intended to look her very best. Blair had picked her up exactly at the specified time, and it had taken forty-five minutes to drive to the docks. They had chatted about the previous evening and the weather during the carriage ride. It had been terribly difficult to maintain her mask of composure.

No matter what had happened in the past—no matter the circumstances in which they had married—Alexi should have returned to her years ago to take up his duties as her husband. She did not think of William Montgomery often, but she would never truly forget the events of that week and that evening. Once in a while, there were still nightmares. Afterward, she would remind herself that she had never intended to cause harm to Montgomery, and that all three of them had had a hand in his accidental death. She had matured enough to rue how spoiled, selfish and foolishly young she had been, but she was wise enough now to have forgiven herself for her part in his death. On the anniversary of his death she lit candles for him, wondering if Alexi were doing the same thing, in some faraway, exotic port. Alexi had had every right to be angry with her for all that had happened. Montgomery had been his pilot, his shipmate and his friend, and Elysse had deliberately led him on. But Alexi had no right to have abandoned her as he had. He had chosen to marry her, under tragic circumstances, and he owed her more than a few pounds here and there. She certainly needed more than his name and his wealth. She needed a husband.

If she had loved him once, she no longer did. But they remained married, and that meant that this deliberate separation had to end.

She had spent all night tossing and turning, thinking about his return. She did not expect a new beginning; he would undoubtedly leave town the moment he realized she was in London. But they had to find another, more satisfactory, arrangement than the current one. It was time for Alexi to acknowledge her as his wife. He could not continue to avoid her as he had been doing. They did not have to share very much, but once in a while he was going to have to appear at her side in public. Surely he could manage that!

Just before they had arrived at the docks, Blair had bluntly asked, "Will we be forced to sever our acquaintance while your husband is home?"

She had had no trouble answering Blair. She was an expert at encouraging her suitors while setting limits, and then never giving an inch. She had no intention of going out at night without a handsome, attentive, elegant escort. Blair was, by far, the most interesting of all of her escorts and she was quite fond of him.

"My husband is at sea most of the time. We have a very convenient arrangement." She would hardly jettison the relationship she had built up with Blair for a brief encounter with Alexi.

"I had hoped so," he said. "But you seem…distressed, today."

She turned away, trepidation consuming her. She could not imagine what would happen when she and Alexi came face-to-face, but she was determined to cling to her dignity and pride. She hoped he had matured, as well, and would be as composed in return. She had no wish to dredge up the past. There was no point in casting blame. "I am excited to win this race," she murmured, although she could not care less. "A fortune is in the *Coquette*'s hold."

"And did he name the ship after you?"

Elysse had smiled without answering. He had probably named the ship after one of his mistresses. He would never name a ship after her.

Now, they stood at the edge of the wharf, where they

could properly see the incoming ships. Most of her guests from last evening were with them. Many vessels were at anchor, up and down the docks, but none were China clipper ships. Cliff de Warenne stood on an adjacent wharf with a group of gentlemen. She tensed, wanting to hide.

Blair turned and followed her gaze. "Ah, your father-in-law."

Elysse wet her lips. Her relations were strained with the de Warenne family. She was certain that Ariella knew that she had remained faithful to her husband, but Alexi's sister refused to take sides in this war. From time to time she had run into Alexi's father and his wife at one affair or another. Amanda was always welcoming and kind. But Cliff was never very pleased to see her, especially when she had one of her "lovers" with her.

Still, he was a gentleman. Cliff had seen her. He raised his hand, nodding. Elysse managed to smile and waved back.

"It seems like a good day for sailing," Blair remarked. He took a small pair of binoculars from his pocket and gazed out to sea.

She glanced at the sky, the briskly moving clouds, the frothing waves, which boasted many small white "horses." "I'd guess it's a good fresh breeze of seventeen or eighteen knots."

He handed her the glasses. "There are two ships on the horizon."

Trembling, Elysse took the glasses and lifted them. She had never seen the *Coquette* in person, but she had seen the sketches and drawings when it was being designed. The moment she saw the first clipper racing the breeze, she inhaled loudly.

"I take it that is your husband?"

She stared through the glasses at the *Coquette*'s fine,

sleek lines and swollen sails. "Yes," she said, lowering the binoculars. "I imagine he will be here in less than a half an hour. The appearance of distance is very deceiving and he is not holding back."

"And the second ship?"

Elysse lifted the glasses. The other ship was just a speck on the horizon. "It's impossible to see." She handed the glasses to Blair. "But she is in hot pursuit. If you look closely at ten o'clock, you will see her as a dot on the ocean."

Blair lifted the glasses. "By God, you are right." He lowered them and looked at her with sudden, open admiration. "You are an extraordinary woman, Mrs. de Warenne. I have heard your rivals call you cold and calculating, but I sense so much fire beneath that perfect demeanor."

"I am accused of being cold and calculating?" She was actually hurt. She tried so hard to be proper and polite, all of the time!

"They are jealous of your success, your beauty and your power. I, on the other hand, find it terribly attractive."

Blair was no more than thirty, very good-looking and very male. She'd heard he was a magnificent lover. She did not doubt it, but she would never know. She was suddenly afraid that Blair somehow knew the truth: she was married to one of London's most acclaimed China traders, but it was a marriage in name only. She had had a half a dozen suitors in the past four years, yet not one of those men had warmed her bed—or her heart.

She stared at Blair. He couldn't have guessed the truth. No one could be that astute.

"I am really rather ordinary," she said.

He slowly smiled. "I beg to differ."

As the *Coquette* glided up the river, the crowd cheered ecstatically. Balloons were released into the air; confetti rained down upon everyone. The children screamed and shrieked more loudly. Elysse knew she clung to Blair, but she could only stare at Alexi.

He stood on the deck of his ship, not far from the helm, one hand on his hip, shouting out orders to his crew. Sail after sail was furled, slumping. Anchors were dropped. Small launches filled with merchants were already racing toward the ship. Elysse forgot the man at her side, the crowd, the other ships, everything, even her intentions. There was only Alexi de Warenne.

The anger seemed to have vanished. As she watched him shout out the last orders in the final moments of this voyage, the pain from all those years ago tried so hard to rise up. She choked on it, paralyzed as she watched him. He had hurt her so much. How could he have walked away from her as he had?

Didn't he love her just a little?

God, could she still love him, after so many years of hurt and betrayal?

He was so magnificent!

"Are you all right, Elysse?"

She jerked, abruptly releasing Blair's arm, blinking back the sudden moisture in her eyes. She was impossibly dazed, and she didn't know how she would manage the next few moments. "I am overcome."

"I can see that." He lifted his glasses. "The other ship isn't a China clipper. It's Danish, I believe."

She didn't hear him. The launches had reached the clipper and a rope ladder was being thrown down. A dozen dealers were asking permission to board. Alexi was waving them up. From his gestures and movements, she saw how high his energy was. As the dealers charged across the decks, he greeted them with slaps on the shoulder and laughter. The gentlemen mobbed him, giving him a true hero's welcome. Someone handed him a bottle of champagne. She thought she heard the cork pop, the sound traveling across the water. He threw back his head and laughed and the sound was rich and vibrant, filled with triumph.

Alexi had come home.

She realized she was slowly walking up the wharf toward him. His hair was terribly long, she thought. He needed a trim desperately. He wore a simple white shirt open at the neck, exposing his hard, bronzed chest. Did he go shirtless at sea? He'd done so as a boy. The shirt was tucked indifferently into tight, fitted breeches, revealing hard, muscular thighs, and he wore worn, knee-high leather boots. She watched him take a long swig of champagne directly from the bottle. Behind her, the crowd cheered.

Several beautifully carved tea chests had been brought up from the holds below and various dealers were kneeling on the port side of the deck, inspecting the tea. Alexi watched, arrogantly, almost like a king with his subjects. She had reached the end of the dock. He was so bronzed from the sun, she thought. His dark hair had reddish glints in it.

Then his eyes went wide; in disbelief, he froze. He had spotted her on the wharf.

Was she even breathing? She was immobilized, except for her heart, which hammered hurtfully in her chest.

The docks were oddly silent now, despite the dealers exclaiming over the tea samples, as some of his sailors shouted to one another in the background. His gaze was hard and unwelcoming. He no longer smiled. Suddenly she realized that she stood alone on the end of the wharf, facing his ship—facing him. Perhaps two dozen yards separated them. Some sanity returned. She had to speak! From the corner of her eye, she realized that the crowd was watching them expectantly. She heard the whispers—"It's his wife!"

What was she doing? Panic began. He would humiliate her all over again. Clearly, he wasn't expecting her, and as clearly, he wasn't pleased to see her. The panic escalated. Somehow, she smiled and twirled her open parasol casually, as if indifferent. Somehow, she would pretend that nothing was amiss with her marriage! She had every right to be there.

She had to find her composure—she had to greet him as a loving wife would.

She inhaled. "Welcome home…Alexi." She heard how tense her tone was. She doubted that he heard her, so she lifted her hand.

He moved. Shoving the bottle at a sailor, he stepped down from the deck. Like a panther, with grace and strength, his stride long and lazy, he walked to the closest railing. Their gazes locked.

A cutter remained at the end of the dock where she stood, and she knew she could get a man or two to row her to the ship if she asked. But he should be the one to come to her, not the other way around.

Alexi smiled slowly and suggestively. He climbed gracefully over the ship's railing, using the rope ladder, and landed in the launch. He said something to the oarsmen. Elysse felt her heart thunder as the launch closed the slight distance between them.

The bow of the boat hit the edge of the dock. Alexi's gaze slid from her eyes to her mouth and down her low-cut blue bodice. It shot up to the very expensive aquamarine necklace she wore. "Hello, Elysse."

She wet her lips. All she had to do was welcome him home, yet words failed her.

Before she could summon up the proper words, he had

leaped across the prow of the launch onto the dock, the jump somehow masterful and impressive, at once. Another single stride brought him onto the wharf—and face-to-face with her.

He remained the most attractive man she had ever laid her eyes on, she realized, her mouth now cotton dry. Had he grown even taller in these past few years, or was that an illusion fostered by the mantle of power he wore so casually, so carelessly…so indifferently? He appeared to be exactly what he was rumored to be—a heroic and daring China trader accustomed to challenge and crisis, to triumph and success, a man of vast worldly experience. He stood there as if nothing and no one could move or shake him, as if the world were *his* oyster, and he damn well knew it.

He was so male and so beautiful, she thought helplessly. How could he get better with age?

His gaze simmered as it moved back to her necklace and décolletage. "So my lovely wife has chosen to greet me." He reached for the aquamarine pendant that was hanging from the tier of gemstones. "A pretty and expensive bauble. Did I buy it?"

She could hardly think at all, with his fingertips on her collarbone—on her skin. Her cheeks were on fire. Surely everyone would notice. She stared into his eyes as his gaze lifted. "Of course you bought it," she managed, realizing too late what he had meant.

He made a disparaging sound. "To what do I owe this honor?" he asked. His gaze briefly moved behind her and she knew he had noticed Blair.

She shouldn't have come to the docks with the financier, she managed to think, although she had every right to a proper escort. "You are first again," she somehow said. "You are victorious. Congratulations."

He looked past her. "The *Coquette* is undefeatable—if I am at her helm."

Elysse half turned as Blair walked up to them. Fortunately, he was with Cliff, who went right up to Alexi, embracing him. "Welcome home, son," he said, smiling. He clasped his shoulder, then looked grimly at Elysse.

She felt guilty, when she had done nothing wrong. "May I introduce Mr. Thomas Blair, Alexi?"

Alexi smiled coldly—dangerously. "You may. Another honor. I am overcome."

Blair put forth his hand, clearly unperturbed. "I have enjoyed making the acquaintance of both your wife and your father, and I have looked forward to meeting you, Captain." Elysse hadn't realized that Blair knew Cliff—but then, why wouldn't he? Blair seemed to be involved in so many aspects of the nation's economy.

But Alexi's gaze was narrowed now. "Your name is familiar. Have we met? I rarely forget a face…or a rival."

"Are we rivals?" Blair murmured, his brows arching innocently.

Cliff interrupted. "Blair is Executive Director of Northern Financial and one of the bank's major stockholders."

Blair turned to Alexi. "I have enjoyed underwriting your operations, Captain. In fact, I was eager to finance this voyage."

Elysse stared at Blair, stunned. He had financed Alexi's voyages?

Alexi smiled indolently. "Then you will be very pleased with our profits. And our run."

"I am pleased—and impressed. You managed to tie the record you previously set of one hundred and three days from Canton."

"Actually, I have set a new record of one hundred and one days. I left Canton on December 10. Feel free to make the calculation." He grinned triumphantly and looked directly at Elysse.

She inhaled, too overwhelmed by his presence, his proximity and his masculinity to smile back. Now, she realized he wasn't sunburned, he was flushed with elation from this latest success. "You didn't leave on the eighth?"

"You may check the ship's log if you doubt me, madam." He turned, pointing to the southern horizon. "There is no one even close behind us. That's the *Astrid,* out of Denmark, and she's carrying cane sugar from the West Indies. Our nearest competitor was becalmed off the slave coast. I suspect you'll greet her in about a week or so, although she left Canton three days before we did—but not with the best tea!" He laughed again.

She couldn't blame him for openly gloating over what he had achieved. Elysse was shocked to realize that she was proud of him. He turned his gaze on her and the flush on his face increased.

He reached for the aquamarine pendant again. His lashes lifted. "I will be able to buy you more baubles, madam, after this day," he said softly. His chipped nails scraped the flesh below the hollow of her collarbone.

She couldn't move.

"So." He leaned toward her. "You never answered me. To what do I owe this honor? Surely…you did not miss me?"

His face was so close that she felt his breath. It was clean and bright, like lemon and mint. His scent was as strong—the tang of sea brine, the sweetness of freshly cut teakwood, the musk of man.

She had missed him. Dear God, she didn't want to admit it, not even to herself, but she had! Elysse stared into his smoky eyes, afraid to answer.

"Kiss her," someone in the crowd shouted. "Kiss her! Kiss the wife!" More shouts sounded.

And Alexi slowly smiled.

CHAPTER SEVEN

HIS GAZE SHIMMERED as brightly as her aquamarines. There was no mistaking what that glitter meant. Elysse was breathless. He was going to kiss her and she had never wanted to be kissed more.

Instead, Cliff seized his shoulder. "Alexi," he said. "I want you to meet Georges Lafayette and James Tilden."

Slowly, Alexi straightened, his gaze still on her. Elysse exhaled, trembling.

Alexi turned. The two gentlemen who had approached them had invested heavily in this voyage and the two previous ones, and she had met them on several occasions. Handshakes and congratulations were exchanged. "One hundred and one days!" the Frenchman exclaimed, beaming. "I never expected you to break your own record, *monsieur!*"

Alexi accepted the flask they handed him, laughing. "I was a bit surprised, myself." He grinned, but he glanced at Elysse. His eyes upon her, he raised the flask to his mouth. She watched the thick cords in his throat move as he swallowed. She lowered her gaze to the deep, open *V* of his shirt. Her skin still felt inflamed. She almost wished that he had kissed her, right there on the docks, in public. What was wrong with her? He had abandoned her! It had been six years!

"I've had three tea chests removed to the office," Cliff said. "I am sure you gentlemen would like to see your investment for yourselves. Thomas? Will you join us at the office? I think a bit of a celebration is in order."

"Only if Mrs. de Warenne is not in a rush to return home," Blair drawled.

Alexi jerked his head to stare at him, his brows slashing upward. Then he turned his brilliant blue gaze on her, his eyes narrowing.

Before she could speak, Blair said, "Quite a few of us were at Mrs. de Warenne's last night for supper, when we heard news that two clippers were sighted off Plymouth. Obviously the Danish vessel was mistaken for a clipper. Most of us wagered on your being first to port, Captain. I offered to escort Mrs. de Warenne here today, and it is my duty to see her home—unless, of course, you wish to do so."

Elysse froze. Had Blair just flung a gauntlet at Alexi?

She was afraid of Alexi's answer—of his rejection. With a determined smile, she said breathlessly, "I intend to see the tea, Mr. Blair. After that, I am sure both you and my husband have quite a few responsibilities to attend to this afternoon. I am certain I can manage to get home on my own." She was amazed at how calm she sounded.

Alexi's gaze skidded between her and Blair.

"Alexi is going to detail every moment of his homeward run to me," Cliff said flatly. "Only then will he escape my company."

Elysse glanced at her husband. How could he make her feel all of twenty again—or eighteen—or even sixteen? She had to find her composure.

She genuinely hoped that she did not harbor a small, secret hope of making him jealous. She had learned her lesson. And clearly, he was not jealous of Blair or anyone else. Jealous husbands did not stay away from their wives for six years.

Fortunately, no reply was needed, as both Lafayette and Tilden were anxious to leave the docks and sample the tea. Windsong Shipping's offices were just a few blocks away, along with many other merchants and brokers. "I have a case of the best French champagne awaiting you, *Capitaine*." The Frenchman grinned, slapping his back. "Ah, we have made a fortune, have we not?"

"This is the best tea I have ever had," Alexi boasted. "And we have most definitely made a handsome profit on this voyage."

His arm around his son, Cliff led the way from the docks with both gentlemen beside them. Elysse trailed behind. She felt deliberately left out and she hoped it was her imagination. To distract Blair, who was watching her closely, she called out to Mr. and Mrs. Carew and their daughter, and to Lord and Lady Worth. "Come celebrate with us at the Windsong offices. There's champagne for everyone!"

Blair took her arm. As they followed Alexi, Cliff and the two gentlemen to a queue of their waiting carriages, his gaze slanted over her. "If I were Captain de Warenne, I would not be going to the offices now."

She scrambled to think of a suitable reply. "I am always in the mood for champagne, and I am eager to sample the tea."

"Really? You mean you wouldn't rather spend time alone with the captain?" They passed several warehouses, the Carews and Worths behind them. "You seemed rather smitten with your dashing husband, a moment ago."

She looked at him, afraid that he had struck upon the truth. "I have known Alexi since I was seven years old. That is a very long time."

"So you are bored?"

If she lived to be a hundred, Alexi would never bore her. "We know each other a bit too well." She desperately wanted to change the subject. "Aren't you eager to sample the tea?"

He laughed. "I can't tell black tea from green, my dear. My interest lies in his balance sheets. You know, I heard a rumor the other night—I heard that you and Captain de Warenne were estranged."

She stumbled.

Angered by the truth, Elysse withdrew her arm from his. "One should not heed rumors, sir. And in any case, I will reiterate my previous point. We have known one another for almost twenty years."

"I see," Blair said. "Even after twenty years, I would not choose to go the offices right now."

"That is very kind of you," Elysse said, but she was too distracted to be flattered. They had reached the line of coaches and curricles. Alexi clearly meant to ride with his father. Was he snubbing her deliberately? She had accompanied Blair. She hesitated, uncertain.

Alexi's mouth curled with disdain. She tensed as he followed the other men into the coach. He pulled the door closed, not even looking at her.

The exclusion was obviously deliberate. It hurt. Blair touched her arm, startling her. His gaze was steady and searching.

She smiled brightly at him without saying a word, and climbed up into his smaller vehicle.

Windsong Shipping took up an entire two-story brownstone building. The celebration was already in full swing when they arrived. Champagne had been handed to Cliff, Alexi, their investors and even the two clerks behind the long reception counter. Everyone remained in the lobby. The front door kept opening and closing as more and more guests arrived.

It was a spacious reception room with richly waxed, dark

wood floors and ebony pillars supporting a high molded ceiling. Two vast crystal chandeliers hung there. Costly Persian and Oriental rugs covered the dark floors. Magnificent oil paintings adorned every possible wall—all of ships at sea. A gilded console table was against the lobby's farthest wall. On it were ship replicas, including the very first vessel ever to be launched by Windsong Shipping, which Cliff had sailed to the Far East several decades ago. A replica of the *Coquette* stood on the table, too.

Elysse sipped her champagne, the lobby now crowded to overflowing—one could not move without bumping elbows. Apparently everyone involved in the China trade had heard of Alexi's return, and had come to the office to congratulate him. Some of their guests were even simply passersby. No one seemed to care.

Alexi stood by the fireplace, holding court. He was surrounded by ladies and gentlemen, sailors, dockworkers and a woman who appeared to be a barmaid, as well as his father and the investors. As he sipped champagne, he regaled the crowd with stories of China, the trade and his run home. Blair moved around the room—he seemed to know almost everyone present. She did not mind. She never had the opportunity to stand alone at a soiree and simply observe the crowd as she was doing now.

Except she was staring only at Alexi. Taking her regard from him, even if for a second, felt impossible.

He was home. She almost felt like that debutante again, the one who had been so eager to see him when he had come home after two and a half years. Every now and then, his gaze heavy and indolent, he looked across the crowd at her. *Déjà vu.*

She refused to remember that day at Askeaton, when he had arrived with William Montgomery after his first

China run. Instead, she stared back at him, aware that her color was high, until he looked away.

He didn't seem angry with her, but he didn't seem warmly inclined, either. Yet she was certain he would have kissed her earlier, if those investors had not appeared.

She felt as if she knew him intimately; she felt as if she hardly knew him at all. He had changed. He was even more worldly than he had been the last time she had seen him—as if he had experienced all life could offer, as if he knew he could withstand any crisis, any challenge. His confidence was obvious. So was his power. He was a successful, dashing sea captain, basking in the glory and the triumph of his record-breaking run home.

The one thing he was not was a husband, eager to return to his wife after a long separation.

Elysse wondered if he'd escort her home when the celebration was over. There was so much to discuss….

A woman leaped into his arms, interrupting her thoughts. Elysse tensed, but only for a moment, for she quickly realized it was Ariella he was embracing. Brother and sister parted and laughed.

"Is that his wife?" a man asked, his foreign accent thick.

She glanced up at a tall, striking man. His shoulders were broad, his pale hair tinged red and gold. His skin, which would have been fair, was bronzed from the sun. She knew instantly that he was a seafarer. He smelled of well-oiled decks, wet canvas and the ocean.

He smiled at her. "Baard Janssen, at your service, madame."

She couldn't decide if his accent was Swedish, Norwegian or Danish. "Are you in the habit of speaking to strangers without a proper introduction?" she asked coolly.

"I know better," he said, his gray gaze a bit too direct,

"but I rarely follow the rules of society. I speak to strangers when I choose—especially beautiful female ones."

She asked carefully, "Are you a friend of Captain de Warenne's?"

He glanced at Alexi, unsmiling. "We have had a drink or two on Jamaica Island, while sitting out a storm."

Her brows rose. So he knew Alexi. "That is Captain de Warenne's sister, sir."

"And you, my lady, are the most beautiful woman in this room."

"You surely exaggerate, but thank you. So may I assume you trade in sugarcane?"

"Yes, I do. In fact, I have just returned from the islands, with my holds full. My ship is the *Astrid,* madame. You will not find a finer vessel in the North Atlantic trade," he said proudly.

She finally smiled. Every captain she had ever met had boasted to her about his ship.

Janssen turned to look in Alexi's direction. "I've heard his wife is quite lovely. Does half of London turn out every time he has a good run home?"

Elysse regarded Janssen. Were they rivals? Alexi no longer transported sugar from the Caribbean plantations— the price was too low—but other Windsong ships did. Alexi was scowling slightly at them. She faced Janssen. "It was a very good run. He deserves the flattery, the praise—and the highest tea prices."

Janssen glanced at her sharply. "I'm sure he enjoys the worshipful crowd. But it *was* an exceptional run—if the rumors I heard are true." He added, "You know quite a bit about shipping, it seems. I would love to take you for a sail some time, Mrs.….?"

Her wedding band and engagement ring were obvious. "It is Mrs. de Warenne."

He started. "*You* are his wife?"

"Yes, Captain Janssen, I am."

He began to smile. Before she could decide why he was entertained, someone seized her from behind. Elysse whirled. Ariella stared in surprise at her. "You're here!"

Elysse glanced at Janssen. "Enjoy your stay in London," she said politely. She took Ariella's hand and pulled her away from the Dane and into a corner of the lobby. "I wanted to sample the tea," she lied.

Ariella took her by the shoulders and shook her. "Have you said hello to my brother? Has he said hello to you? Does he know you're here? Have you made up?"

In a way, Alexi had come between Elysse and Ariella. They'd never had secrets—until Montgomery's death. Elysse had never confided in Ariella, although she had frequently wanted to. She had kept up her pretense that she had a lovely life and did not mind having an errant husband, not at all. She smiled now. "Of course we greeted one another, Ariella."

Ariella cried, "And what happened?"

"Nothing happened." But she thought, *He almost kissed me.* To her surprise, she caught Alexi watching them. He turned away, lifting a glass of champagne to his lips. He drained it, then laughed at something one of the ladies standing in his group said. Alexi was obviously flirting with an attractive brunette. A twinge of dismay went through her.

She reminded herself that he had had many affairs over the years—she had heard all kinds of gossip about a mistress in Singapore and his lover on Jamaica—and that she did not care. She was about to return her gaze to Ariella when she caught his glance slanting back to her again. Her heart slammed. Their gazes locked, he took a flute of champagne from a passing clerk with a tray of champagne. This time, as he sipped, he stared openly at her. His gaze was even bolder than Janssen's had been.

"He beat his own record," Elysse managed, hoarsely.

"I know. He told me. He is telling everyone. Actually, he is becoming rather foxed." Ariella searched her eyes. "Did the two of you speak at all?"

"Of course we spoke," Elysse said, incapable of keeping her gaze on Ariella. Alexi was smiling at a different woman, a very beautiful redhead. Her dismay intensified. She wondered if she should go over and introduce herself—and throw cold water on that redhead's plans. But then Alexi's gaze shot to hers. Suddenly he lifted his flute and saluted her with it.

"Is he flirting with you?" Ariella seized Elysse's hands. "Please make up with him. I don't know why the two of you have refused to speak for six years, but please go speak to him! He is in such a good mood. You can get whatever you want when he is like this, Elysse, I am certain!"

Ariella knew Alexi better than anyone. Was it possible that Alexi was in an amenable and forgiving mood? And in that moment, Elysse knew what she wanted—forgiveness, reconciliation and a real marriage.

After all he had done—after all the hurt and humiliation—she wanted him back as a friend and husband.

Ariella tugged on her hand. "That redhead was his lover years ago. Her name is Jane Beverly Goodman. Go over there before she takes him into a back office and rekindles their affair!"

Elysse hesitated. If Ariella was right that they might finally sit down and discuss their differences, the living hell of her existence might be finally over. If Ariella was right, she could rid herself of all deception and finally be alive again.

She so wanted to talk to Alexi without anger, without rancor. But the redhead was whispering in his ear. If she went over, what would happen? Could they both forget the betrayal of these past six years? Could they forget the circumstances under which they'd wed? Could she forget the hurt and pain?

She wet her lips. What did she have to lose? She had his name, his wealth, but nothing else. There was nothing left to lose except the pretense that had become her entire life.

Elysse smiled nervously at Ariella and moved away. She bumped directly into Blair, who caught her by both her shoulders. "Can I take you home?" he asked. "I can't stay any longer. I have some meetings I must attend before supper."

Afraid that Alexi might have noticed them, she stepped backward, forcing him to release her. "I'm going to stay a bit longer."

"I see." His gaze moved slowly over her. "I am disappointed. But I am a patient man."

Her heart thundered. She didn't know what the outcome of her discussion with Alexi would be. It would be foolish to jettison Blair, yet that was exactly what she wanted to do. "We have plans for the opera," she said softly.

"Yes, we do, on Saturday." He took her hand and kissed it, his mouth lingering. His eyes were gleaming when he straightened, and he was obviously disappointed to leave her.

She turned to watch him go. She should not be flirting with Blair, not now. When she turned back around to find Alexi, he was standing in front of her.

She started nervously. "You surprised me!"

His gaze was watchful and wary. "You did not go with him."

She tried to breathe. "I was hoping to talk to you."

His eyes glittered. His hand closed around her arm and she barely contained a gasp.

He said slowly, "You never sampled the tea."

She trembled. "I haven't had the chance."

She felt his mind racing, as if he were debating her reply.

"Good," he finally said. He slid his arm around her waist, pulling her against his muscular body.

She gasped. "What are you doing?"

"The tea," he murmured.

"Of course," she managed. As he moved her through the crowd, she surrendered to the urge to lean against him. His body was overpoweringly male and being in his arm felt so perfectly right. It was so hard to think straight.

"Are you drunk?" he asked with some amusement.

"No." However, it was obvious that Alexi had had a bit too much to drink.

"You act as if you've never been in a man's arms, which we know isn't true." He led her down the hall, into a dark room. She didn't dare dispute him. He didn't bother to close the door. Releasing her and walking over to the desk, he lit a lamp. Still breathless, Elysse saw three beautifully wrought black-and-orange tea chests on the credenza behind the desk. He straightened, looking at her, his gaze blue smoke.

Her heart thrummed heavily now. "I am very happy for you." She meant every word.

"Really?" He was staring at her décolletage, at her waist. His gaze lifted. "Are you happy for Thomas Blair, too? His interest rates are high."

She tensed. "I don't want to discuss him. Surely we are not going to fight."

"Of course you don't." He laughed, without mirth. "I

have no intention of fighting with you tonight," he said, very softly.

Her heart leaped. He almost sounded as if he had a seduction on his mind.

"You look well, Elysse, in spite of that 'doe being trapped by the hound' look in your eye. Do you feel trapped? Do I make you feel trapped?" He seemed to relish the idea.

She had never been as nervous. She was aware that nothing stood between her and the door, which was open behind her. She could rush out at any time, but she had no intention of doing so. "You are acting differently than you used to."

He slowly smiled. "I wonder how many men tried to gain your attention this afternoon. I see that you met Janssen."

"It's been six years, Alexi. In case you have forgotten."

"I haven't forgotten a thing." He settled his narrow hip against the desk.

It felt as if he was toying with her, the way a mighty lion might with a poor, frightened mouse. He wasn't welcoming or husbandly, but he wasn't rude or dismissive, either. She couldn't decide if he remained angry with her or not. "Six years is a very long time," she tried.

He made a harsh sound.

She hesitated. "I haven't forgotten, either."

He launched himself off the desk. "I don't want to discuss the past." In a stride, he closed the distance between them. "I want something…else."

"But I do!" she cried, as his hands closed on her shoulders. Her heart slammed.

"Too bad," he said roughly, and before she could blink, she was drawn up against his shockingly hard body, every inch of which was muscle.

"What are you doing?" she gasped. "Are you inebriated?"

"Like a sailor," he said, with a harsh laugh. "You know exactly what I'm doing." Roughly, he tilted up her chin with his thumb. "God damn it," he said slowly. "I had truly forgotten how beautiful you are."

His words might have exhilarated her, for hadn't she wanted him to notice how attractive she was, all those years ago? She had never seen so much raw lust, ever. But she saw that he was very angry—and that was frightening.

She didn't know if he intended to passionately kiss her, or far more. She didn't know if she wanted more, not just then, without even a discussion of the past six years. Alarmed, she started to back away. His response was to pull her into an uncompromising embrace.

"Alexi!" It crossed her suddenly frantic mind that he *was* going to seduce her. But before she could protest, his mouth covered hers.

Elysse went still. His mouth was possessive and fierce, hot and hard. His arms tightened, making it clear that there would be no escape.

She could no longer breathe. She clenched her fists against his chest. He kept kissing her, and in spite of the alarm, his strong arms felt so terribly right. It was Alexi's chest she was pressed against; Alexi, whom she had always loved…. She felt her mouth soften and yield to his.

"Kiss me back," he demanded harshly. "You know you want to." Breathing hard, he began kissing her again, but now his lips were softer and coaxing against hers. "Kiss me, Elysse," he whispered.

He was right—she wanted to kiss him back. She was a woman now. *It had been six years.* Her body quivered uncontrollably, melting against his. He was angry—and so was she—but she didn't want to resist him. Instead, she grasped his shoulders, moaning.

Her knees buckled and her body throbbed more acutely. His erection pulsed against her hip. She shifted instinctively against him.

"Elysse," he rasped.

The hurt had dulled. The anger seemed gone. There was only the powerful man in whose arms she stood, his body hard and restless against hers. She needed him desperately now. Elysse caught his broad shoulders more tightly, clinging to them, and did as he had ordered.

As she tasted his lips, he went still. She tasted salt and champagne and man. She swept her tongue into his mouth and he grunted. As he pulled her more tightly against his hard frame, slowly reclaiming their kiss, emotion burst in her chest. *She still loved him so much.*

For one more moment, he kissed her gently, slowly, as if savoring a great delicacy. Then he came to life. His mouth tore at hers. Their tongues entwined madly, and it didn't matter to her if they made love now, without any discussion of the past. She kissed him back even more frenziedly. "Hurry!" she cried.

His head lifted and his blue eyes were wide and stunned. Suddenly he turned her and pushed her down on the desk. She went willingly, eagerly, and the lamp crashed to the floor loudly, glass shattering. And then Alexi's weight settled on her. Their gazes met—his flaming hot.

"I want you," he groaned, sliding his hand into her hair. He came down fully on her, accidentally pushing her partly off the desk. Realizing what was about to happen, she tried to warn him. But instead, they both crashed hard to the floor.

Even inebriated, Alexi had the reflexes of a cat. He caught her, jamming his body beneath hers and breaking her fall. Instantly he was on his knees, crouched over her, his arm beneath her. His expression was dismayed.

Elysse was as dazed.

"Is everything all right in here?"

Still on the floor, Elysse looked past Alexi at one of the company's young clerks. The clerk turned red.

"I…I beg your pardon, Captain, Mrs. de Warenne!"

Alexi quickly got up, reaching for her, as the clerk ran out. She took his hand and let him help her up as shock set in. *They had been about to make love on the desk!*

He flushed. "Are you all right?"

She touched her wrist, which she had twisted in the fall, aware that she remained in the throes of the kind of desire she had never before felt. What had just happened?

She was confused. She was afraid. It had been six terrible years. She wanted to rush back into his arms, touch his beautiful face and tell him that she loved him. She didn't move.

"Elysse! Are you all right?" His tone was sharp now.

It took her a moment to exhale, to find words. "I think… so." What would he do if she told him how she truly felt? That she loved *him?* Did he care for her—did he love her, too? Did that kiss mean that everything was all right? She slowly looked at him, wide-eyed.

He dropped her arm and stepped backward, away from her. "If I hurt you, say so."

"It's just a bruise," she managed. "You prevented me from hitting my head."

He looked away from her. "I'm sorry."

"Alexi!" She reached for him.

He shook her off. "Stop. I'm drunk. Very, very drunk. I've been at sea for seventy-seven days—but that is really no excuse for my behavior."

"I don't understand," she said.

"It was a helluva long voyage, Elysse."

"What are you saying?" she asked.

"I'm a rake, remember? And you, my dear, are a very desirable woman."

If he meant to hurt her, he had succeeded. Surely he didn't mean that he had kissed her only because he hadn't been with a woman in months?

He inhaled sharply, shoved hair from his brow. His blue eyes simmered, but with anger now. His hand was trembling. Raw frustration roughened his tone. "I mean every word, damn it. Nothing has changed. Where's Blair?"

"Blair," she echoed. Her entire body continued to throb. Why was he bringing up Blair? Why didn't he take her into his arms? How could he be so cruel, to treat her like a whore? "Alexi?"

Alexi gave her a cold look. "Let's go. If he won't take you home, I'll get one of the clerks to do it."

CALLING BEFORE NOON WAS considered the height of bad manners. At half past ten in the morning, Elysse alighted from her hansom black carriage, indifferent to the early hour. She was too hurt and angry to care what time it was!

Besides, Ariella and her husband were early risers. Ariella had met and married the dashing, enigmatic Romany Viscount St. Xavier a year ago—shocking all of proper society. But it had been a love match, and Ariella was still deeply infatuated with her husband. If anyone knew where Alexi was, it was Ariella. In fact, there was a good chance that he was staying with her and St. Xavier.

She could barely breathe as she fought not to rush up the walkway. Last night Alexi had kissed her as if she were the only woman in the world that he wanted. But then he'd said she was but another pretty face and body. He had treated her as if she was a dockyard whore! He had left her to suffer all kinds of humiliation and abuse for six years, but clearly that wasn't enough punishment for the past that they shared.

She refused to entertain the desire she had felt last night. She didn't know why she had been undone by his kiss, or worse, her incredibly foolish and romantic expectations. It would never happen again. Maybe all twenty-six-year-old virgins would have responded to a rake like him that way, but she had come to her senses. She did not desire him, and she didn't love him—she had stopped loving him six years ago.

She couldn't believe that she had briefly lost her mind as she had.

He had no right to remain angry with her, but she had every reason to be furious with him.

She could not bear their marriage a moment longer, not as it was. But an annulment remained out of the question—her pride came first. Therefore, he must leave town immediately. London was not big enough for them both.

Dressed in turquoise silk and diamonds, Elysse reached the house's front door. If Alexi was inside, he had better prepare himself for their battle. This time, she would win. Her life—and sanity—were at stake. But before she even took the door knocker, the front door opened, revealing the viscount. Emilian's eyes widened when he saw her.

"Hello, Emilian," Elysse managed. She was incapable of summoning a smile. "I believe Ariella will not be surprised that I have called at such an ungodly hour."

In his frock coat and trousers, Emilian St. Xavier was terribly handsome and rakish, all tawny golden good looks. He was somewhat of a recluse, although less so since his marriage to her friend. His mother had been a Gypsy, and to this day, society did not know whether to revere or malign him. "She is expecting you, Elysse. I pray the two of you do not cook up some fantastic scheme involving poor Alexi."

"I'm his wife. I hardly have to scheme in regards to my *poor* husband."

"Really? You might be interested to know I saw him last night."

She tensed impossibly. "I didn't see you at the shipping offices."

"I wasn't there. But Clarewood stopped by to save him from himself. Then they both came here to retrieve me. Alexi was entirely foxed. Have no fear, we took him to supper, not to a club. Not that that stopped him from drowning his sorrows in whiskey and brandy."

She was very still. "He was celebrating last night."

"Not by the time I arrived," St. Xavier said.

She didn't have a clue as to what could have upset Alexi. "He's a grown man. If he wants to drink himself into a stupor, I hardly care. He seemed deliriously happy last night at the shipping offices."

St. Xavier smiled. "There are two sides to every coin." He tipped his hat at her and continued down the brick path to his waiting coach, a grandiose six-in-hand.

Elysse stepped into the house, ripping off her gloves angrily. She was miserable and hoped Alexi was, as well. Unfortunately, he was probably still patting himself on the back for his successful China run. About to fling her gloves aside, she stopped when she saw Ariella hurrying into the elegant entryway. Elysse cried, "Where is he?"

Ariella frowned. "He isn't here. You look terrible, Elysse. Have you suffered from more insomnia?"

"I am suffering from this marriage." She had never meant her words more.

Ariella paled. "I know you are. I am so angry at him!

Don't worry—after you left I gave him a good piece of my mind."

She held her head high. Alexi had practically dragged her out of the shipping offices, a clerk in tow to drive her home. She had felt as if she were a football, being kicked outside. Everyone had noticed, of course. Her coiffure had been ruined, her color had been high and she had been so upset, she doubted she had appeared composed. Alexi had obviously been enraged. The crowd had become silent as they left and she'd glimpsed Janssen watching them. When he had handed her up into the carriage, he had had the gall to tell her to enjoy her evening. To make matters even worse, Elysse had seen Jane Beverly Goodman standing in the window, watching them.

The gossips were having a field day, Elysse was certain.

She didn't know what to do—pull out her own hair, throw something at the wall or go after him and wring his neck. She felt tears rise up. How could he continue to hurt her so? She took a breath and said rather calmly, "Did he go off with that trollop, Jane Goodman?"

Ariella took her arm and led her into the breakfast room, where a breakfast buffet remained in covered dishes on the sideboard. "I don't know. Have you eaten?"

"I am not hungry. Please, do not think to spare my feelings. I do not care what he does—or with whom he does it."

"Mowbray appeared," Ariella said. The Duke of Clarewood had stood up for Alexi at their wedding and was Alexi's best friend. "I doubt he had time to have an assignation."

"He probably met up with her after dining with Clarewood and Emilian." She'd heard the rumors about his lovers for years. Besides the mistress in Singapore and the lover on Jamaica Island, last summer she'd heard gossip that he was carrying on with a beautiful Romany girl.

"Elysse, what are you going to do?" Ariella asked kindly.

Elysse did not hesitate. "I intend to make certain that he is not staying in town. If he leaves right away, I think I can manage—as long as we do not set eyes on one another again."

Ariella looked very worried.

Elysse stiffened. "What aren't you telling me?"

She bit her lip. "I believe he intends to stay in London for a bit."

She cried out. "I won't have it!"

"Elysse…" Ariella began.

"No!" Elysse began to pace, forgetting all about pretending to be calm. "Hasn't he embarrassed me enough? Why would he stay in town? So he can whore and humiliate me even further?" She refused to be hurt again. She whirled. "I think I finally hate your brother!"

Ariella grimaced. "Please don't say that—don't even think it! I wish the two of you would sit down and calmly discuss whatever it was that happened between you to make you so angry with one another."

She breathed hard, thinking about how he had kissed her—and then sent her home. She would never let him touch her again, of that she was certain. "I will not allow him to remain in town." She fought for composure. "One of us has to go—and I am *not* leaving."

Ariella hesitated, and Elysse knew she was hiding something. "Oh, God. He is with her, isn't he? Is that where he is staying? With that tramp, Goodman?"

"No. He isn't with Lady Goodman. Elysse, he purchased a house in Oxford."

She went still. Had she misheard? "What do you mean, he purchased a house in Oxford?"

"It's a very beautiful house, with vast gardens, a hot-house, a fine stable and a racket hall." She bit her lip again. "That is where he is—in his new home."

Her mind spun crazily. This was impossible! Absurd! "Alexi bought a house *here?* In London?"

Ariella nodded.

"And the sale is final?"

She nodded again.

"When did this happen?" she cried, still shocked. "Why would he do such a thing?"

"His agents bought the house about two months ago. Alexi had seen it and admired it years ago, and when he learned it was up for sale he made an offer. Clarewood dropped him there last night." She wrung her hands.

Elysse looked for the closest chair, stumbled to it and sat down. Alexi was staying in London.

"What are you going to do?" Ariella whispered worriedly. "We both know you will never convince him to leave unless he wants to."

Elysse looked at her, still astounded. In that moment, she knew exactly what she was going to do. She stood up. "I am going home to pack my things and move in with my husband," she said.

CHAPTER EIGHT

"YOU ARE MOVING IN WITH HIM?" Ariella gasped.

"I would prefer to have him leave town—and the country. In fact, I would prefer that he never return. But I'm his wife. I deserve more than his name and wealth."

"Oh, Elysse. He has hurt you again—I can see it. My dear, I am entirely on your side!"

"Do you know how much humiliation I have managed to withstand, these past six years?" Elysse cried. "I pretend I am ignorant of the gossip, but I have heard every ugly rumor there is, including the ugly truth—that he left me at the altar, right after our vows."

"He is so angry with you," Ariella whispered.

"And I am equally enraged! Can you imagine the gossip if he is living in Oxford—in a *palace*—while I live in rented apartments on Grosvenor Square?" Elysse asked, shaking. She felt ill, imagining her friends and acquaintances whispering behind her back. "They're already laughing about the row we had last night—I am sure of that!"

Ariella took her hand and held it tightly. Elysse felt tears of self-pity well up. She brushed them away. She was not going to feel sorry for herself. She was finally going to deal with Alexi, as she should have done years ago.

Ariella was wide-eyed. "So you are going to share his home with him? As if the two of you have a *real* marriage?"

Her stomach twisted. She was incapable of answering.

She and Alexi couldn't get along for five minutes. How would they manage to cohabit? "I know he is your brother, but he is the rudest, cruelest man I have ever known," Elysse said harshly.

Ariella did not defend him.

"Many couples reside together in a marriage of convenience," Elysse finally said, but she was beginning to have some doubt. Images flashed of his attempt to seduce her. She could barely breathe. "I can't live in my apartments while he resides in Oxford. But I agree—I can't force him to leave town."

"I understand." After a moment, Ariella said, "Maybe this will be for the best. The two of you might finally come to terms with your relationship—and your feelings for one another."

"I am not interested in his feelings for me." But that was not entirely true. She wondered, did Alexi hate her? "Why didn't you tell me about the house, Ariella? We are friends!"

"He asked me not to tell anyone. I knew he meant that I shouldn't tell you. I am sorry!" Ariella cried.

Elysse hesitated. The enormity of what she meant to do became crystal clear. She could not continue to live apart from Alexi if he stayed in town—it would give the gossips far too much ammunition against her. But to live with him as his wife seemed equally impossible.

Instantly, she recalled his kiss.

She had no intention of ever letting him touch her again. She despised his whores but it was far better that he showered them with his attentions, instead of her. Let him keep all of his lovers—she no longer cared. And if he hated her, so be it.

"How will you approach him?" Ariella asked uncertainly. "I mean, you can't just pack up your things and simply appear on his doorstep with your baggage."

Alexi would be furious. He was not going to welcome her into his new home with open arms, not under any circumstance. She was very certain of that.

Her mind raced. She had rights as his wife, and she was going to demand those rights be fulfilled.

"I don't think he will be very amenable to your moving in," Ariella continued.

"I need leverage."

"I am even more worried now! What kind of leverage could you possibly have?"

"I have to think about it." She breathed hard. "I will not lose this battle, Ariella. My pride is at stake."

"I know."

"I need the address," Elysse said. "I am going over there right now. We will discuss this situation and settle it." Dread arose. She had no choice but to confront him but she was hardly a fool. The encounter would not be pleasant.

Ariella took her arm. "They were out all night. Emilian got home at three in the morning. I don't think today is a good day to approach him."

She pulled away. "By tonight, Ariella, half of this town will be gloating over the fact that he is in Oxford, in bed with that Jane Goodman, while I am alone in a damned rental apartment—especially after what they saw at Windsong Shipping yesterday! I will not be this town's fool!"

"It is a lovely apartment! And anyway, everyone thinks you are with Thomas Blair!" Ariella added, "Alexi probably thinks so, too."

Elysse had never admitted to Ariella that she had never taken a lover, and she said nothing now. "He can think whatever he wants. I have no control over his thoughts."

"Elysse," Ariella objected.

"I am wasting time. May I have his address, please?"

Ariella groaned. "Will you please consider waiting till tomorrow, Elysse? When he is not suffering from the effects of last night's binge?"

Elysse smiled grimly. "Absolutely not."

SUDDEN BRIGHT LIGHT POURED into the room. Alexi growled in annoyance, pain exploding in his temples. He sat up, dizzy and very, very groggy. "What the hell?" He squinted into the brilliant sunshine.

For one moment, he didn't have a clue as to where he was. He was on a very handsome gold-and-green, pin-striped sofa in someone's equally handsome library. He struggled to recall whose home he was in. A woman in a black maid's dress with a white apron was dusting the heavy emerald-green draperies she'd just opened. There was a park outside and he glimpsed a maze and flower gardens. "God damn it." His head hurt so badly he felt as if someone had drilled holes into his skull while he was sleeping.

The blonde maid whirled with a cry of fright.

"Who the devil are you?" he demanded, his stomach churning. Somehow he lurched to his feet. He realized he still smelled of the sea—and of brandy and whiskey. And did he smell cheap perfume, as well? His mouth tasted horrible, too. He began to realize he had overimbibed last night. "And more importantly, where the hell am I?"

The maid was no more than twenty, and actually very pretty, although pale with fright. "My lord, sir! I am so sorry! I didn't know you were sleeping on the sofa. You are in the library, sir—my lord!"

He blinked at her, noticing her lush figure. Reflexively

he turned on all of his charm. "And who are you, my pretty lass?"

She blushed. "I am Jane, sir—er, my lord."

His mind began to function and he recalled the night before—an old lover, Jane Goodman, pressing her card into his hand at the Windsong offices. His father beaming at him amidst the reveling crowd, the hugs and slaps from friends and strangers. Stephen and Emilian, toasting him with brandy at a fine restaurant. His ship, securely berthed, all sails furled, his men celebrating with mugs of rum. My God, he had done it. Together with his fine crew, his superior ship, he'd run home from China in one hundred and one days!

Triumph surging in his chest, he looked around. He realized that the library belonged to *him*. He was in his new London home. Mowbray had dropped him there late last night—or rather, early that morning.

He looked at the maid, trying to remember if he'd ever met up with Jane Goodman last night. Hadn't he been randy as all hell? He always took a woman, or several, to his bed the moment he reached land. But Jane would never wear the cheap perfume he had caught a whiff of on his shirt collar. "It is Captain. Or you may call me Mr. de Warenne."

She curtsied, blushing madly now, her gaze on his chest. His shirt hung open, not tucked into his breeches. He often went shirtless when at sea, and he was as dark as a native from India. "I will summon your valet, sir," she breathed.

He was about to flirt with her. Then he froze. Suddenly he recalled Elysse standing in a dark back room at Windsong Shipping, dressed in pale blue silk and aquamarines, her hair coming down and her face richly flushed—after he had kissed her and thrown her down on the top of someone's desk.

He groaned, clasping his temples. *What had he done last night?*

He staggered to the wall of bookshelves, where a gilded tray with decanters and glasses had been left. The pitcher there was empty. He ignored the decanters of brandy and Scotch.

Elysse had dared to meet him at St. Katherine's docks yesterday. He inhaled. He would never forget looking past the dealers as they charged onto his decks, only to see her standing there, at the edge of the wharf, the most beautiful woman in the world.

Just recalling the moment, his heart slammed to a stop and then raced wildly again.

On the one hand, a part of him was almost savagely pleased that she had been there to witness the greatest triumph in his life. On the other hand, he was furious that she had dared show her face.

Because of her, he had killed a man.

He cursed. He was a man of extreme passion. Everything he did, he did with utmost intensity and gut-wrenching feeling. After the shock of Montgomery's death had worn off, the horror and guilt had set in.

They had been friends until Elysse O'Neill had come between them.

He had not been thinking clearly in the weeks following the accident. By the time she had walked down that aisle, he had been in a quiet rage, as furious with her as he was with himself.

In the years since their marriage and Montgomery's death, he had learned how to avoid his guilt and bury all of his memories of that week. Remembering was too difficult and too painful.

But once in a great while, usually at night when he was alone at the *Coquette*'s helm under a canopy of glittering stars, the memories suddenly returned. He would remember the first moment he had seen her, upon arriving at Askeaton Hall, and the joy leaping in his chest. Then he would recall the night of the ball—Elysse's flirtation—and the death struggle would flash again in his mind. He would never forget the sight of Elysse's tear-streaked face. It would take a vast effort to turn the tide of remembrance back....

But when she had met him at the docks, she had released the flood tide that was the past. Damn it, he had hoped never to set eyes on her again. He had gone out of his way to make certain their paths did not cross. He had been determined to avoid her.

But she was his wife.

He had married her to protect her reputation. When it came to protecting Elysse, there was no choice. He might not have been trapped into the wedding, but he had been trapped into marriage—a marriage he wasn't ready for, a marriage he hadn't wanted, a marriage he *still* did not want!

His wife's reputation was as notorious as his. She was London's most infamous seductress....

He almost laughed, but it was no laughing matter. He would never have dreamed that Elysse O'Neill would become London's most outrageous courtesan. He cursed, then moaned at the pain in his temples. But hadn't she always been an outrageous flirt?

Elysse de Warenne, the reigning socialite of London, never stepped out without one of her paramours....

He paced. He'd heard about all of her lovers. He'd made it his business to know whom she kept company with. And when he was in town, his friends and enemies alike were only too eager to name names. Only his cousins seemed reluctant to meddle.

She was sleeping with his banker. He could barely

believe it. She must have intended to undermine him in some way, as she had once done with Montgomery. Why else would she flaunt the affair by bringing Thomas Blair to the docks with her?

He knew Elysse better than anyone. She was vain and selfish, a spoiled and insatiable flirt, so accustomed to male attention that she was incomplete without it. Nothing had changed. She was stringing Thomas Blair along, enjoying his bed. Soon, she'd be playing Baard Janssen and sharing his bed, too. He thought to warn her that the Dane was untrustworthy and dishonorable. But she wouldn't listen…

What had been wrong with him last night?

He recalled the episode in the back office of Windsong Shipping in shocking bits and pieces, disbelieving. He *despised* his wife. He wanted to forget the past—all of it. They were no longer friends—they would never be friends again. He would ignore the tiny stabbing pain that thought brought him. He didn't want to be married, not now and not ever. That boyhood dream had been just that, the foolish dream of a young, naive child.

Yet, last night, desire had raged. Worse, he had acted on it. He had held her, touched her and kissed her. If he wasn't mistaken, he had wanted her very, very badly, more so than ever before….

He hoped that he was wrong.

He didn't want to remember the feeling of her soft body in his arms, her breasts crushed against his chest, or the way her mouth had felt, at first oddly tentative, beneath his. He had been entirely aroused. In the end, she had kissed him as if she were as desperate to be with him…

"Damn it," he cried. He was always out of control after a particularly good run home. There were always women and wine—and too much of both. He'd set a record yesterday that wouldn't be broken for years! There was no way to describe the triumph, the passion, the adrenaline that coursed through a man's body after such a successful voyage. It was inflammatory.

He decided that he would have kissed just about any attractive woman last night. Elysse just happened to be the victim of circumstance—the most convenient outlet for his lust and euphoria.

"Captain, what can I bring you?"

Alexi looked at the dapper blond man now standing in his doorway. He vaguely recalled meeting the staff his agents had hired for him last night. He sighed. "I'm sorry, I don't remember your name. I was deeply in my cups last night."

"My name is Reginald, Captain, and no one minds." Reginald smiled widely. Although no more than thirty, he was already balding. "Congratulations, sir, on the record you set. The staff is thrilled to be in the employ of such a famous man. No apology is necessary—not from you!"

He smiled wryly. "I wouldn't mind a light breakfast, Reginald. Something to settle my stomach, please."

"A bit under the weather, are we?" Stephen Mowbray, the Duke of Clarewood, stood in the doorway.

"Your Grace!" Reginald blanched. "No one showed you in?"

"I let myself in. The captain hardly minds," the duke said. He was tall, dark and impeccably attired.

Alexi waved dismissively at everyone and sank down into a chair. "He may come and go as he pleases—insufferably arrogant as he is, he is also my best friend." Reginald remained aghast. Mowbray was the wealthiest, most powerful peer in the realm and everyone knew it.

"I will not be sharing breakfast," Clarewood instructed, "as I can't stay for very long."

"I beg your pardon, Your Grace." Reginald nodded and rushed off.

Alexi began buttoning his shirt. "I suppose I should thank you for seeing me safely home last night?"

"Do you remember anything?" Clarewood asked, amused. "You wanted St. Xavier and me to leave you at a bordello with not one, but two rather high-priced courtesans."

"And that was a problem because…?" He glowered.

Clarewood almost smiled, a rare moment for him. His mood was naturally dark and dour, which he claimed was the result of having so many responsibilities. "Alexi, you passed out in the carriage. We chose to protect your notorious reputation as an unsurpassable lover."

Oddly, he thought of Elysse and the brief eruption of passion which had consumed him at the Windsong offices. *Had he really pushed her down on that desk, intending to make love to her as if she were a passing trollop?* He scowled and more pain exploded in his head. He was afraid he might not have stopped if that clerk hadn't come in and interrupted them. "Do you like my house?"

"I've already seen it. When Ariella mentioned you meant to buy it, I came over to inspect it to make certain you would not be taken."

Alexi hadn't realized that Stephen had involved himself in the acquisition of his home. But then, he'd known Stephen since they were children. And with good cause—Stephen happened to have been fathered by his uncle, Sir Rex de Warenne, making them cousins. It was a well-kept family secret.

Clarewood's gaze was narrow. "I realize you are hungover from last night, but why aren't you gloating over your record-setting voyage and all the profits you have made for your investors?"

"I am in an excellent mood," he lied.

"Really? So I take it you enjoyed your reunion with Elysse?"

Alexi stared coldly. Mowbray alone knew the truth about the night of the Windhaven ball.

Clarewood moved a chair and sat down in it, crossing his long legs. "I have known Elysse as long as I have known you. She is terribly vain, impossibly flirtatious and rather imperious, but she is your wife, for better or for worse. Isn't it time to forgive and forget?"

He began to regret ever having confided in Clarewood. "I am *not* going to discuss my marriage with a man who has spent more than a decade supposedly looking for a bride."

"Why not? It was all you could speak of last night. I might be able to offer you some advice, even if I am a bachelor."

Alexi vaguely recalled complaining loudly and repeatedly about Elysse daring to be at the docks and the offices. Had he even complained about her lover, Blair? He began to flush dully. "She has nerve," he managed. "Do you know Thomas Blair?"

"Yes, I do, and I happen to respect him vastly. I have actually borrowed some tidy sums from him for some of the Foundation's projects." Clarewood was one of the country's leading philanthropists. He was always funding asylums, hospitals and schools for the poor—in between fending off the daughters of society's leading matriarchs.

"His interest rates are highway robbery."

Clarewood raised a brow. "Can you really condemn him for pursuing your wife? And can you really blame her for seeking comfort elsewhere—as you do?"

He stood. "I don't care what she does or with whom."

"I am glad you think so." Clarewood also rose. "Now

that you have decided to stay on land for a while, I think this season might be entertaining."

"You are annoying me," Alexi warned. "I might even throw you out of my house."

Clarewood finally smiled. "Good. Because you annoy me all the time. We are finally even."

Suddenly the unmistakable click of a woman's high heels sounded. Both men turned. Alexi felt his heart leap uncontrollably as Elysse paused in the doorway, a shockingly beautiful sight in turquoise and diamonds. He felt his cheeks heat, his heart explode.

He saw that her color was also very high. She was angry. Savagely, that pleased him.

Reginald looked bewildered. "Captain, you have a caller. I asked her to wait but—"

"I refused to wait in the hall until you decided whether to see me or not," Elysse said, her tone strained.

He was glad she was upset. "I suppose you are allowed to barge in. Good morning, Elysse. Say hello to Clarewood. Reginald, Mrs. de Warenne happens to be my wife."

The butler paled.

Elysse glanced at Clarewood very briefly. "Hello, Stephen. Are you talking him into selling this monstrosity and returning to the sea, where he belongs?"

Clarewood bowed, seeming rather merry in spite of a straight face. "Actually, I find this house very pleasing. I am encouraging him to remain in town for a while."

"Thank you very much," she said darkly.

"I am taking my leave—immediately—so you two may go at it, although I do wish I could be a fly on the wall," he said, his mouth curling. With another slight bow, he turned and strode rapidly out.

Her eyes like daggers, Elysse said to Reginald without turning, "Please leave us."

Reginald started to leave. Alexi said, "Stay."

Reginald faltered, looking back and forth between them in utter dismay. Elysse spoke, her gaze distinctly challenging. "We have private matters to discuss."

"Not that I recall," he taunted, crossing his arms. What the hell did she want?

She finally looked at Reginald, her stare cool but not imperious. Her manner was dignified. "I am the lady of this house. Would you please bring some tea and refreshments? And would you bring some proper attire for Mr. de Warenne? There is an odor in this room."

Reginald nodded, his color even higher now, and fled.

Alexi clapped his hands slowly, somewhat impressed by her bravery. He watched as she went to the door and closed it, then realized his gaze had drifted across her petite, lush figure. He frowned, jerking his eyes upward as she turned to face him. "Well done. But you are *not* the lady of this house."

Her purple gaze was icy. "I am your wife."

"I prefer that you do not remind me."

She slowly shook her head. "Why did you buy this house?"

He was surprised. He looked carefully at her and decided he did not blame himself for nearly ravishing her last night. He hadn't imagined how beautiful she was—or how seductive. She was the sexiest woman he'd ever laid eyes upon—and that said a tremendous amount. "I like it. Why are you here? Are you stalking me?" He started forward, his blood racing.

She tensed, folding her arms. "Don't be absurd. As your wife, I have every right to be here."

"You are my wife in name only," he said, pausing within inches of her. He knew he had purposefully boxed her in.

But if she couldn't play his game his way, she shouldn't have come.

"You almost sound disappointed."

He laughed. "Come, Elysse, you know me better than that. What do you want? Are you here for more of what I gave you last night?"

She gasped.

"Ah, well, I didn't think so." He couldn't help looking down her dress. Her diamonds weren't as expensive as the aquamarines. He studied the thin, simple chain. "Did I buy that, as well?"

"Damn you," she hissed. "Of course you did!"

He slowly looked up, into her blazing eyes. He was thrilled that she was so angry. "Then you are keeping the wrong company," he stated. "When a man truly enjoys a woman's favors, he rewards her with some pretty token of his affection. I am shocked that Blair is so tight."

She struck him, hard, across the face.

Pain erupted in his already throbbing head. He seized her hand, harder than he would have if he had not been provoked, and she cried out. He lessened his grip but did not release her. "I cannot imagine why you are here," he said coldly.

"Get your hands off me," she hissed again.

He hesitated. The gentleman within him—and he was a gentleman with every lady except his wife—knew his behavior was appalling. He released her.

"This situation is unacceptable, Alexi," she said.

Her tone was hard, but there was a tremor in it. He looked very closely at her now. Behind the anger, she was hurt. He tensed, refusing to feel sorry for her. "I happen to agree. This marriage is out of hand. Are you here to ask for an annulment?" He intended to tell her he would gladly give her one. Instead he stopped and waited, watching her as closely as if she were his mortal enemy.

She drew herself up even straighter. "I have suffered vast humiliation for six years. I would never give my enemies such fodder for their gossip by asking you for an annulment."

He almost felt relieved. He searched her eyes and thought tears lurked behind them. "Then why are you here?"

"If you truly intend to stay in town, we must discuss our living arrangements."

It took him a moment to comprehend her meaning. Then he stepped back from her. "There is nothing to discuss," he said warily. "You have apartments—which I pay for, handsomely—and I have this house."

"I will not be further humiliated by living apart!" she cried. "I have spent six years pretending to be happily married!"

It took him another moment. "Are you telling me you want to move in here? With me?" He was incredulous.

"Of course I don't want to live with you!" she snapped. "But there is no other choice. I won't fuel the gossips now, with your living here and my living in my flat!"

He folded his arms and stared at her. "No."

She trembled. "We are married. I have rights."

Images flashed, of her beneath him on that desk. He recalled the feel of her writhing body, her eager mouth, her greedy tongue. "I have rights, too, Elysse."

She went still, blanching.

He was glad she understood. "I married you long ago to protect you from the gossips, period. I have no interest in attempting a marriage of convenience by sharing this house with you. If you do not wish for an annulment, then my only intention is for us to continue living as we have—apart."

She said hoarsely, "I don't want to share this house, either, but we do not have a choice. Our marriage will remain a pretense. There will be separate rooms. But I am moving in, Alexi, with or without your consent."

That was a challenge, if he ever heard one. He didn't move, ready for another thrust, another blow. He began to smile. "You are very brave. Do you really want to battle me?"

"I am moving in. Tonight." Her gaze held his.

She was frightened and uncertain; he saw it in her purple eyes. While he wanted to relish her turmoil, a part of him had the oddest urge to retreat. "You do not want to fight me, Elysse. I always win."

"We have been fighting for our entire lives." She blinked rapidly. "I am not afraid of you!"

She was foolish, he decided, and brave. Suddenly, he recalled a little girl trembling in the ruins of an Irish castle. He shoved the regret aside. He refused to respect her courage. He tried to imagine them residing in the same house, and it infuriated him. He had meant it when he had said he did not want to be married. "There is a simple solution. Return to Ireland until I go back to sea in the summer."

"No. I will not be run out of town by you!"

He kept recalling her beneath him, on that desk. He slowly said, "If you move in, it is at your own risk."

"What does that mean? Are you threatening me?"

He pictured them together, in a big four-poster bed, surrounded by fine furnishings and every possible luxury. "It means," he said, "that there will not be separate rooms."

She cried out.

"It means, this marriage of convenience is over—and I will demand my rights. All of them." His smile vanished and he stared, aware of the heavy weight in his body.

It *was* a bluff. He was almost certain he didn't truly

mean his words. He wouldn't go near her under any circumstance. But she would never move in now, not after such a threat.

Her eyes blazed. "You would never touch me against my will. I am moving in tonight!"

She turned, blindly reaching for the door. In surprise, he realized she was about to cry—he had distressed her that greatly. He almost reached out to help her open the door, but he caught himself. He refused to feel guilty, much less ashamed. He refused to consider her pride and dignity—or that she might have changed. She finally pushed the door open and stumbled out.

She turned, wiping the tears from her cheeks. "My door will be locked," she warned, trembling.

He didn't answer, as in that moment, he had nothing to say. She had seen through his bluff. Or had she?

CHAPTER NINE

BY THE TIME ELYSSE RETURNED to Alexi's Oxford home, it was almost five in the evening. She had brought her housekeeper and her personal maid with her, to help her settle in more quickly, along with three large bags containing the most essential items of her wardrobe; her Grosvenor Square staff was packing up the rest of her belongings. She still had eighteen months left on her lease of the apartment, so she hoped to sublet it out as soon as possible, and had sent a note to her solicitor to that effect. Only the most basic items would remain in the flat for the new tenants, such as rugs, bedding, linens and some of her paintings. Otherwise, her bric-a-brac, collectibles and finest paintings, her best rugs, her kitchenware and fine china would be packed up and moved to Alexi's new house. She would find a place for everything; the Oxford mansion was huge. Undoubtedly it would take a good four or five days to move all of those belongings. The task seemed monumental.

She had been in a rush to make good her intentions, before she realized she was truly provoking the beast in its lair.

Now Elysse stood by the door, incredibly exhausted and uncertain. What was she doing? Alexi was home and staying in town—and she was moving in with him. He was hardly welcoming. The only thing she was certain of was that her pride was at stake.

Matilda, the middle-aged housekeeper who had been

with her for the past four years, and Lorraine, a French maid, were unpacking and hanging up her gowns; she had brought half a dozen each for morning, day and evening. Her undergarments were being folded and placed in a beautiful Louis IV armoire. Toiletries went directly into the bureau in an adjoining dressing room.

She had spent an hour touring both wings of the house, having been apprised that Alexi was not at home, before choosing the bedroom that would be hers. The master suite was in the west wing, on the second floor, and Alexi had taken it over. It was a very large, dark blue and gold affair, with a huge black marble fireplace, opening onto an equally vast sitting room, in the same bold, masculine colors. The suite suited him perfectly.

Common sense had dictated she take the largest guest suite in the east wing, as far from Alexi as possible. However, she had hated it on sight—it was too masculine, too formal, too cold. After much hand-wringing, she had chosen a smaller guest room in the west wing, never mind its proximity to the master suite. She had fallen in love with the bedroom instantly, for it was done up in pale robin's-egg blue, with dark gold and cream accents. The mantel over the fireplace was ivory, streaked with veins of apricot, and the bed's skirt was ruffled and pin-striped with the same apricot hue. The blue shams were pin-striped with gold, while the pillows boasted blue and gold tassels and fringe. The draped canopy was blue on top, and an iridescent cream color streaked with coral beneath. One plush floral chair was in front of the fireplace, an ottoman at the foot of the bed. A very small table with a blue toile tablecloth was in front of the bedroom window, out of which she could gaze on the house's magnificent park and its grazing deer. As it was late March, the gardens were beginning to bloom, and everything was lush and green.

The room seemed as if it looked out on the countryside, rather than London.

Matilda had already put fresh flowers on the table—hothouse lilies, and Reginald had said more would be forthcoming for the gilded console table. It was a lovely, feminine and inviting room—except she knew that she wasn't welcome at all.

Alexi had certainly made his feelings clear earlier that morning.

It had been a relief that he hadn't been in residence when she had arrived. It was as reassuring that he had given Reginald no instructions for supper, either. In fact, he hadn't told anyone when he would return—a behavior that would have to be corrected.

Elysse trembled. He was out for the evening, of course. He had undoubtedly been deluged with invitations. Friends, family, acquaintances and even business associates would all be clamoring for his company—as would the likes of Jane Beverly Goodman.

Would he be surprised when he came home to realize that she had meant her every word and that she had already moved in?

She stared past the lovely bed, the tufted ottoman at its foot, the plush chair and fireplace. There was another drawback to this particular bedroom. The door adjacent to her fireplace opened onto the master sitting room, which they could obviously share.

Alexi had known her very well, once upon a time. He didn't know her at all now. He might not realize that she had become a woman of resolve. A lump of dread formed in her chest. She hadn't forgotten his last words to her—that he would claim all of his rights if she dared to disregard his wishes.

She had been strong enough to put on a merry face and

survive the past six years. She was certainly strong enough to survive whatever he decided to do when he came home later that night. She was angry with him, but she didn't want to fight—not when they must reside together in the same house.

He would never hurt her, she thought uneasily. But he was still angry with her. Was that because he did not want to be married or because of what had happened to William Montgomery? He had made it clear that he had not forgotten the past; neither had she.

The door to the sitting room they shared was wide-open. Elysse stared into the huge room with its higher ceiling, gold upholstered walls and dark blue and gold rugs. It contained a large fireplace, a blue damask sofa in front of it. A small desk resided behind the sofa with a gilded Regency chair. Beneath a wall of windows, on the room's other side, was a pedestal table that seated four. The views from this room were even better than the ones from her bedroom.

There was a huge armoire at the room's far end and an equally impressive bookcase. In between the two items of furniture were a pair of massive mahogany doors, and they were open.

Front and center was Alexi's king-size four-poster bed, with its navy blue and gold velvet furnishings.

This marriage of convenience is over—and I will demand my rights, all of them.

Elysse walked over to her sitting-room door and shut it firmly, unwanted images of their embrace in that dark office dancing in her mind. Even as she thought about it, her cheeks felt too warm for comfort. He might attempt to knock on her bedroom door, but he would never force his way in—or force himself on her. So why was she so unnerved?

Everything had happened so quickly—his triumphant

return, his purchase of the house, her decision to move in with him! She reminded herself that this was a marriage in name only—she was simply protecting what was left of her reputation. She despised him for his behavior, and he despised her. He had even said so. And she would not allow herself to be hurt by that! She must never be hurt by him again.

It would be so much easier for everyone if he simply left town.

"We will keep this door locked," she said, snapping the lock closed and inhaling harshly.

Matilda and Lorraine straightened to look at her in surprise.

Elysse realized how that had sounded. She unlocked the drawing-room door. "I am overwrought. Moving so suddenly like this is daunting!" She went to the chair before the fireplace and sank into it. What was truly daunting was the fact that Alexi was going to be sleeping in that bed, just a short distance away.

"Would you like to rest for a bit?" Matilda asked kindly. "This has been very sudden, and you seem quite tired."

Elysse tried to smile at her. Matilda was her rock and her anchor. She never asked questions, but always knew when to send up a cup of chocolate or a glass of brandy. The moment they had arrived, Matilda had asked her if she would be keeping her appointments for the evening. Elysse knew she would never be able to attire herself for the evening and be at Mr. and Mrs. Gaffney's for supper at seven that night. The first thing she had done was to pen a proper excuse with her regrets: due to the sudden return of her husband from his latest voyage, she would not be able to attend supper that night, but she looked forward to their next engagement.

Her headache intensified. She hadn't meant to make it

sound as if she would be with Alexi that evening. But by the morrow, most of the town would know that she had spent this night moving into his house, and her pride would be salvaged—although not entirely. Anyone who saw him out alone tonight might think the worst—that he didn't give a damn about her. That they were irrevocably estranged. And the worst part was, that was the truth.

She knew he would be furious with her for moving in, uninvited and unwanted. But she was just as furious for these past six years. She didn't dare think about the passion she had experienced in his arms yesterday.

She couldn't help recalling his insulting declaration that he had only wanted her because of the state of celibacy he'd endured during this past sea voyage.

She wondered if he enjoyed hurting her.

"Are you all right, madam?" Matilda asked.

"I am tired, that is all," she managed, with a smile that felt wan.

"Let's leave Mrs. de Warenne to rest," Matilda said. Reminding her that iced tea and ham sandwiches were on the tray on the table, she and the French maid left.

Elysse got up and paced the room. She should eat—she was always losing weight—but she had no appetite. She was too worried about what would happen when Alexi came home. She wondered where he was—and whom he was with.

She covered her face with her hands. What if Alexi were squiring Jane Goodman about? She had refused several callers that afternoon, instructing Matilda to explain that she was in the midst of a move to her husband's new home. She hoped that would quell any unpleasant gossip about how Alexi had forced her to leave Windsong Shipping yesterday. But if he was out with another woman there would be more fodder for the gossip mills.

It was never-ending, this battle to save her pride. And it was all his fault.

She was so tired of fighting the gossips! If he was going to be with another woman, he had to be discreet, she decided. He had to stop flaunting his affairs for all the world to see!

She got up abruptly, went to the sitting-room door, opened it and strode through. On the threshold of his bedroom she paused, staring at his bed.

He was going to have to play the role of a proper husband, she thought, shivering. She had just spent six years telling everyone how wonderful he was—how wonderful their marriage was. He was going to have to pretend that they had a good marriage. That he enjoyed her company somewhat. He was going to have to squire her about for a few weeks. After that, no one would care if they went their separate ways.

Behind closed doors, he could do whatever he chose—without her.

Elysse backed away from the threshold to his room, certain of her course. But how on earth would she convince Alexi to play the part of a devoted husband, even if it was only in public? She'd had to fight tooth and nail to get him to allow her to move in! As she had told Ariella, she needed leverage.

In her own bedroom, she shut both doors and poured herself a glass of iced tea. Then she sat down and tried to decide how best to convince him to behave in a suitable manner.

And then she thought of Blair.

She smiled, realizing she had all the leverage she needed to bring Alexi de Warenne to heel.

SHE HADN'T BEEN ABLE TO SLEEP. As was her habit, she had turned on a small lamp, gotten comfortable in the plush chair and, with the fire dancing in the hearth, finished reading that day's newspapers. Alexi's record-breaking return from China had made the front page of the *London Times*. But the article hadn't made her sleepy, so a treatise on an obscure point of law had followed. That was so terribly boring that the words blurred on each page, but she was still wide-awake, thinking about his notoriety and fame.

It was only midnight. Elysse finally picked up a weighty biography about Queen Elizabeth and became so engrossed that she forgot her desire to sleep. She hadn't realized that it was in the reign of Queen Elizabeth that the intent to open up routes to the Far East had first materialized, in the midst of England's rivalry with Portugal and Spain. History usually didn't really interest her, outside of the history of Ireland—she was half Irish, after all—and the seafaring stories her father told about the Napoleonic wars and the war of 1812. But now she read how men like Alexi had dared to blaze routes across the ocean to India and China, seeking fame and fortune and the queen's favor.

She was about to turn the page when she thought she heard a sound in the hallway outside of her locked door. Elysse went still, straining to hear.

At first, she could only hear her pounding heart. Then she heard the unmistakable sound of footsteps coming up the stairs. She almost forgot to breathe. *Alexi was finally home.*

She glanced at the clock on the mantel—it was half past two.

Alexi's gait sounded unhurried and even. Her mouth dry, she stared at her door as he approached.

She thought she heard his steps falter. She waited for him to seize the doorknob and attempt to open the door. Instead, he passed her room.

She slumped in her chair, her heartbeat deafening. He hadn't tried to come to her room. She was relieved, wasn't she?

Elysse leaped from her chair and raced to the door that opened onto the sitting room they shared. She pinned her ear to it and heard Alexi moving about within.

More footsteps sounded, but they were rushed. Reginald cried, "Captain, sir! You must ring for me when you return home!"

"You needn't wait on me hand and foot, Reginald," Alexi drawled.

He sounded sober, she thought.

"Of course I must—it is my duty, sir. Here, let me help you disrobe!"

"Reginald! I can manage very well, thank you."

There was a sudden silence. Elysse had the oddest notion that he was staring at the door she was pressed against. Suddenly he said, his tone wry, "Might I assume that my wife has moved into the adjacent room?"

"Yes, sir, Mrs. de Warenne moved in this afternoon."

There was another brief silence.

"May I assume you were helpful? That all her needs were met?"

"Of course, sir."

"What time did she return? She did go out this evening, I presume?"

"She did not go out, sir. If I might say so, she seemed a bit fatigued. She did not eat at all, and Chef prepared a delightful meal."

There was another pause, as if Alexi considered his butler's words. "Thank you, Reginald. You may go. I not only can, but I intend to undress myself. And in the future, do not wait up for me. That is an order, my man."

Elysse heard the two men exchange good-nights, and

Reginald leaving. She bit her lip, afraid Alexi might catch her eavesdropping if he heard any movement coming from her side of the door. And then she heard him approaching.

She tensed impossibly as he paused on the other side of the door. The doorknob rattled. "Elysse." He knocked once, a short, sharp rap. "I know you are awake. I can see the light."

Very slowly, she straightened.

"I can also see the shadow of your feet."

He was amused, damn him. She inhaled, a bit too loudly.

"And I can hear you breathing. I am not about to accost you," he added. "Not yet, anyway."

His mockery was unmistakable. She wet her lips nervously, then unlocked and opened the door.

His gaze was narrow with speculation and amusement. "What did you expect to find behind my doors?" he asked. "A lover?"

She said harshly, "I never know what to expect from you."

He glanced at her French silk wrapper, which was securely belted over a silk chemise. Both items were costly, flimsy and gorgeous. She had the distinct impression he had somehow looked right through her clothes. "You chose an adjoining room," he purred. "Is this a game?"

"My door was locked," she said. "And contrary to what you seem to believe, I do not play games. Have you had an enjoyable evening?" She wondered, if she stepped closer, whether she would remark the traces of a woman's perfume on his shirt collar.

"I do not feel like arguing with you tonight," he said flatly. "If you truly think to reside here, you are doing so at your own risk."

"You don't even like me," she snapped, trembling. "I know a false threat when I receive one."

He reached out, took a long, loose tendril of her hair and rubbed it between his fingers. "I haven't seen you with your hair down in a decade, at least."

Inhaling, she pushed his hand away. "Are you drunk?"

"A wise man never imbibes two nights running. I do like you, very much, Elysse," he said softly.

She knew exactly what he meant. He desired her. Elysse reached for the door to slam it in his face. He caught it. "What do you expect, when you are dressed like that? I am wondering if you want to provoke me. That garment reveals *everything*."

She released the door. "Actually, I want to discuss some other matters with you—in the morning, before either of us goes out."

His gaze narrowed again. "You look well in blue, but that pale pink suits you even more perfectly."

The flush in her cheeks felt as if it were spreading throughout her entire body. "Now I understand. You won't beat down my door—you will politely knock and then try to seduce me."

"You're my wife." He laughed. "I can do whatever I choose, actually."

She reached for the door again. He braced it open. Frustrated, she cried, "At what time can we speak in the morning?"

"Speak now." He shrugged. "I am standing right here. Frankly, I can't wait to discover what is so important."

She exhaled harshly, already furious with him. "Moving in was not enough."

He seemed genuinely surprised. "I am confused."

"I am trying to quell the gossips, Alexi. But if you are running about town without me, they will gloat about the state of our marriage behind our backs. You don't care, but I do."

He folded his arms.

"Were you with Goodman tonight?"

His eyes widened. "Is that really your affair? And do you really want to know?"

"You can do whatever you want," she cried, but she was absurdly hurt. "But you must be discreet! More importantly, for the next few weeks you must squire me about and pretend to be a doting husband."

Slowly, he began to smile. "Like hell, Elysse," he said, with laughter.

She felt like slapping his smug face. "I mean it. I have spent six years pretending that I am happily married. The least you can do is pretend that we get along. And that requires us being seen together."

"No." He wasn't smiling now.

"I am not telling you to give up your paramours," she barreled on. "When the night is over, you can do whatever you want, with whomever you choose—in private. Keep all of your lovers, Alexi! But we must pretend that we are happily together, now that you are home!"

"Are you insane?" he demanded. "Why would I bother to play this latest game of yours? I have no interest in your company, Elysse—well, not unless it is at this late hour, in such private circumstances." He gave her a lewd glance.

She smacked him, as hard as she could.

He caught her wrist and pulled her up against his body, his eyes gleaming. "You struck me yesterday," he remarked. "This is becoming a very bothersome habit."

"Do you want me humiliated? The boy I loved was a gentleman!" she cried, not even trying to struggle to become free, as she knew it would be useless.

His eyes widened. "No. I do not want you humiliated."

"Good! Then for two or three weeks, we can pretend to be doting spouses in public! Beginning tomorrow, at the opera." She had plans to attend with Blair, but now she was determined that Alexi escort her. He still held her wrist. Her knees grazed his legs and her breasts brushed his torso. Her nipples ached, suddenly erect. It was impossible to ignore the fact that he was a very sensual male.

As if he felt the sudden desire, too, he released her. "I am not taking you to the opera, or anywhere else. I did my duty by marrying you and saving your good name. Many couples are estranged. It's not my fault you have carried on this sham for the past six years!" But his blue eyes were hot, and they drifted to the points piercing her silk wrapper.

A little voice inside of her head warned her to back off and approach him tomorrow. "When is your next voyage?" she asked, a bit hoarsely.

He started. "I'll run for Canton in June or July."

"That's what I thought. They start picking the tea in July. By the time it is packed and sent downriver, ready for negotiations, you will be in Canton."

His gaze was wary. "If I am lucky, I could have my holds filled in October and head home before the November monsoon."

She couldn't control her breathing. "And has Northern Financial underwritten this voyage, as well?"

He went still. "Ah. Elysse. You don't want to go there."

"Go where? Oh, wait. I can ask Thomas if he is financing your next voyage."

Alexi's face turned red. "What do you intend?" he demanded, leaning over her. His breath was warm on her cheek.

"I need a proper husband—just for a few weeks," she said, managing not to cringe.

"Or what? You will whisper in your lover's ear to charge me higher interest rates?" His eyes blazed.

She was breathless. "Thomas is very fond of me."

He cursed, slamming the door closed behind them. She leaped in fright. He caught her arm. "Are you blackmailing me?" he shouted. "Do you know how many bankers want my business?"

"And then there is Captain Littleton," she gasped. "He surely needs financing, too!"

His blue eyes had become black.

"Maybe Thomas will want to finance Jardine's." Her cheeks felt damp. She wondered if she was crying.

He choked, jerking on her arm. "My God! You *are* blackmailing me!"

"All I want is to live without humiliation! All you have to do is pretend to be a proper husband!" But even as she spoke, in the midst of so much anger, there was heartbreak—and she knew she wanted so much more.

"No one blackmails me, Elysse, not even you."

He was so strong that she tripped as he flung her aside, but she caught the poster of the bed and righted herself. Then he started toward her, his face a mask of fury.

"What are you going to do?" she cried.

"You want me to be a proper husband? Do you?" he shouted. When she didn't answer—she couldn't even nod—he said, "Invite me into your bed, Elysse. Then I'll be a proper husband!"

She clung to the poster, terrified. She had gone too far and she knew it.

He was so enraged he was shaking. He seemed unable

to continue, but when he spoke, his voice was raw. "If Blair finances Littleton—or any other of my rivals—you will have made yourself clear. And you do not want to be my enemy, Elysse."

She cried out.

He stared at the bed for a long time, as if thinking about doing what he truly wished to do. Then he gave her an ugly look and slammed from the room.

Elysse ran after him, locked the door and slowly dropped to the floor. Hugging her knees to her chest, she cried for a very long time.

CHAPTER TEN

ELYSSE SMILED BRIGHTLY AT BLAIR, aware that she had been uncharacteristically quiet from the moment he had picked her up for their evening at the opera. They were standing in the large marble lobby of the Piccadilly Opera House, surrounded by other operagoers, the ladies in jewels and evening gowns, the gentlemen in tailcoats. She had chosen to wear red that night, with diamonds. She was hoping the crimson silk would hide the fact that she was shockingly pale.

Blair smiled back, but his gaze was searching.

Her smile felt forced and brittle. She had never felt as distressed. Her temples ached.

Before Blair could ask her any questions, she began a long and enthusiastic monologue about the Italian opera they were about to see. She knew Blair well enough to be concerned that he might realize how low her spirits were. She could not deny it. Alexi had come home, and he had brought nothing but grief into her life.

Her heart had never felt so trampled upon, so raw.

She had barely slept at all last night after Alexi had stormed from her room. Their angry exchange was all she had been able to think about, and it had kept her up well past dawn. She could hardly believe that they had come to such a terrible impasse. She couldn't accept that Alexi had become so cold and indifferent that he would refuse her request. Except he wasn't entirely indifferent, now, was he? She would never forget the sexual nature of their exchange.

Recalling the heat in his eyes and his demand that she invite him into her bed, her body throbbed uncontrollably. If she desired her husband, she was determined to deny it!

She had almost sent Blair a note, begging off from their evening. A tiny voice in her head told her that seeing him just then might not be the wisest course. But the knowledge that Alexi would undoubtedly gloat if she stayed home due to their quarrel had caused her to keep her engagement. So had the fact that he refused to be discreet with his lovers. Besides, she liked the opera and she liked Blair. She wasn't sure she could survive another night alone in that house, with only her dismal thoughts for company, while he was out and about with his various paramours, being worshipped by all of society.

"Are you sure that you are feeling well?" Blair asked quietly, his hand on her elbow. His tone was concerned.

This was the second time that he had asked her if she were unwell. She smiled at him. He was becoming more than an escort and a pretend lover—he was becoming a friend. "I have a bit of a migraine. I'm sorry, Blair. I know I do not look all that spectacular."

"You are always, without question, the most stunning woman in the room," he said firmly. "When will you admit that this sudden move has taken its toll on you?" His dark gaze was searching.

She tensed. "Moving is never easy."

"No, it never is." He spoke flatly. "I am rarely taken by surprise, but you never let on that your husband had a home in Oxford. I might even conclude that you had no clue that he had bought the house and that this decision to move was an impulsive one."

She inhaled. She did not want to lie to Blair. "It must have slipped my mind," she said, turning to study the crowd. She was surprised to see Ariella and her husband, then relieved to have a new subject to digress upon. "Ariella is here, with St. Xavier." She was thrilled to see her friend. She had never needed her more. Ariella had actually called that afternoon, but in her exhaustion Elysse had fallen asleep, and Matilda had sent her away.

"Ah, yes, your sister-in-law." Blair was wry. Then he murmured, "And I do believe that is your husband with them."

Elysse tensed impossibly. Alexi stood with St. Xavier, dashing and handsome in a tailcoat, chatting pleasantly with a dark-haired woman. She was incredulous. What was he doing there? Had he come on purpose, to annoy and unnerve her? She had asked him to accompany her when she went out—not to appear separately at the functions she was attending! She had no wish to see him now. He would erupt when he saw Blair. And he did not look as if he had spent a sleepless night. His smile seemed genuine, his spirits seemed high. Apparently, their quarrel had not bothered him!

The ramifications of his presence struck her hard. She was with Blair, not with her husband. Was Alexi escorting another lady? She prayed not. In any case, everyone at the opera would remark this circumstance.

Blair murmured, "You seem distraught, Elysse."

"Why would I be distraught?" she managed, unable to look at Blair, her gaze on Alexi.

He leaned close. "Because he is with someone else and you are jealous?"

She jerked around to face him. "I am not jealous, Thomas," she said, but her tone was high and those closest to them turned to look at her. She flushed. She had been overheard, and that would add fuel to the fire. "Alexi does as he pleases—he always has. I am quite used to it." She took his arm possessively and smiled brightly at him, recovering her facade of composure. Or so she hoped.

Blair seemed dubious. "He is hardly ever in town, so how can you be accustomed to anything he does? I thought your marriage solid, but your reunion yesterday was one of the most anxious I have ever witnessed."

She did not know what to say. "We have an unusual marriage," she managed at last. "But it is solid, Thomas, very solid," she lied, desperate to convince him.

The look he gave her told her that he did not believe much of what she claimed. "I hope," he finally murmured, "that you have begun to have real affection for me, regardless of any feelings you might harbor for Captain de Warenne."

Her alarm knew no bounds. This was not the time to confess to any feelings at all—not with Alexi standing just out of earshot, not with the passersby noticing her and Blair standing together, apart from her husband. Of course she was fond of Blair. But her gaze shot back to Alexi. He had yet to notice her or Blair. Then the woman he was speaking with turned ever so slightly, so Elysse could glimpse her face. She stiffened. He was conversing with Louisa Cochrane! Of course, she was now Mrs. Weldon, as she had remarried years ago. Mr. Weldon did not appear to be present. Louisa was smiling at Alexi.

Louisa clearly meant to renew their liaison, she thought miserably, if they hadn't done so already. She was dismayed.

The evening could not get worse.

"When will you admit the truth to me? I will keep your secret, Elysse. You and your husband are estranged—and at great odds," he said. "But it is not your choice."

She faced him, trembling. "Thomas, that isn't fair." She wanted to claim that she and Alexi were very fond of one another, but she couldn't get the words out.

He touched her cheek. "I want to help, Elysse. I don't like seeing you this despondent. I know how proud you are. Captain de Warenne's appearance with another woman right now is very painful for you, never mind that everyone present thinks we are paramours."

She bit her lip. How could he be so astute? "We are hardly the only couple in this room to have separate lives, which is hardly the same as being estranged. How could we not live separately? As you have pointed out, he is rarely on land. We have an understanding." She clutched her purse so tightly her knuckles turned white. She thought about how he had walked away from her at their wedding reception, refusing to share their wedding night. No couple could be as estranged.

He studied her. "But you don't want to have a separate life, do you? Or an *understanding?* And your marriage isn't good, as I have heard you claim to anyone who might listen, is it?"

She wanted to deny it. Images from their encounter last night blazed in her mind. Their marriage was unbearable. But she couldn't tell anyone, much less Blair, even if he had guessed so much of the truth.

He suddenly took her arm firmly, giving her a brief and warning look. He glanced past her. "Good evening, Captain de Warenne. I hope you don't mind my escorting your beautiful wife this evening in your stead."

With dread, Elysse slowly turned—and her gaze clashed with Alexi's.

He was angry—his eyes glittered—but he was under control. Alexi smiled tightly at Blair. "Why would I mind? I am usually at sea. My wife is a grown woman with her own life. I would frankly be shocked if she were *without* an escort. How convenient that she has chosen you, my banker, as part of her loyal, steadfast circle of *friends*." His smile hardened.

Elysse tried not to cringe. She could not miss his reference to her foolish attempt to use Blair against him. "Hello, Alexi," she tried. "I forgot that you would be here tonight."

"Really? I don't believe you knew I would be here tonight, my darling, as I didn't know myself until an hour or so ago." His gaze moved back and forth between her and Blair, then down over her low-cut crimson bodice. "And how are you tonight, Blair? Don't tell me you enjoy the opera? Ah, how foolish of me, it is my wife's *company* that you enjoy."

Blair's smile was perfunctory—and just a bit mocking. Clearly, Alexi could not unnerve him. "I am hardly an aficionado—of the opera, anyway. But I am a huge fan of Mrs. de Warenne's. I greatly enjoy her company, and if she wishes to attend the opera or a circus, I will do my best to accommodate her—in every possible way."

"Of course," Alexi said, his tone very harsh now. "What gentleman would not accommodate my beautiful wife's every need and desire?"

Elysse was beyond dismay. She was mortified. How could they argue this way, over her? Alexi obviously remained furious with her. But she was as furious, perhaps more so. His appearance with Louisa was exactly the opposite of what she had asked him to do last night!

"Thomas and I have had plans to attend this opera for at least a month, Alexi," she said, amazed at her neutral tone. She touched his arm, as a true wife might. He jerked. "If we had known you wanted to see this performance, we could have all come together. In fact, I haven't seen Louisa

Weldon in at least a year, and I look forward to renewing her acquaintance."

"I am sure you made your plans while I was still at sea," he said. "Just as I am sure you hardly needed to exercise your powers of persuasion to convince Blair to attend the opera, no matter how he might dislike it. Crimson suits you, by the way…darling." He leaned close and brushed his mouth over her cheek. "You must wear red for me some time."

She leaped away, shocked, her heart pounding. She knew he had kissed her because she had stroked his arm—just as she knew he had been rudely suggestive for the very same reason. Damn him! Elysse tried to signal to him silently that she did not want to fight now. They were being remarked; passersby were eavesdropping. This was exactly what she had meant to avoid! She could not bear more humiliation—why couldn't he see that?

"Mrs. de Warenne need only ask, and I will gladly do her bidding," Blair said dryly. "Just as I am certain you are as eager to please her. And the pleasure of her company far outweighs any ennui I might suffer during the performance. But of course, you are aware of that, aren't you? No man, especially not a husband, could fail to appreciate her vast charm."

They were in a bitter battle, Elysse realized, over her. Blair was being so gallant, taking Alexi to task for his indifference toward her. She couldn't imagine what Blair would do if he ever discovered that she had been abandoned at the altar by him. But she didn't want him to defend her, not now, not in public. She took his arm and silently begged him to cease. In fact, she and Blair should probably leave. They could attend the opera another time.

Alexi's gaze shot to the way she clung to Blair's arm. "Yes, my wife has vast charm—even I can appreciate that."

Alexi stared at her now, his bright blue eyes glittering. "She certainly managed to *charm* me last night. Didn't you... darling?"

Elysse prayed he wouldn't reveal what she had attempted to do last night. She felt Blair looking at her closely and she knew she blushed. Did Blair think she had tried to seduce Alexi? He had certainly made it sound as if they had had relations last evening. "Gentlemen are meant to be gallant, and ladies must be equally charming, a wife all the more so." She turned to Blair and smiled at him. He did not smile back and she rushed on. "It is wonderful that we are all here, isn't it? We can begin to make up for lost time." She was aware that she was babbling. She so wanted to escape!

His gaze locked with hers, Alexi said softly, "Ariella insisted I come." Then he looked at Blair. "I knew Thomas would be here, and I thought I must get to know him better, as he is my financier." His smile was dangerous.

"We should have lunch," Blair stated. "I am sure we will find many topics to address."

Elysse's mind raced. She knew she must never allow the two men to speak alone. She couldn't imagine where a business conversation might end up. As for Ariella insisting that Alexi come to the opera—which he despised—hadn't she mentioned to her friend that she would be attending on Saturday with Blair? And she had asked Alexi last night to go with her—surely he had known she would be present. She stared at Alexi, realizing that Ariella had wanted them to cross paths. He stared back. She could only wonder why he had bothered to appear. After his refusal to escort her last night, she could only conclude that he wanted to hurt her.

Ariella approached with St. Xavier and Louisa. Elysse controlled her rising temper as they hugged; later, she would give her friend a set down. "I didn't know you would be here tonight, Ariella. You never said a word." Her tone was accusing, and rightly so. Why would her best friend do this? Didn't she know that the gossips would love to spread rumors that she and Alexi had been out with their respective lovers? And that their happy marriage was a sham?

"We have the box, and we decided to come at the last moment." She turned to Blair, who kissed her hand. "It's a pleasure to see you, Thomas. Elysse, you remember Louisa, don't you? It is Mrs. Weldon now."

Elysse managed to smile at Louisa, rudely deciding that the woman looked her age. She had to be at least thirty-five. She remained attractive, but surely not enough to regain Alexi's attention.

"Won't you join us in our box?" Ariella asked, glancing at everyone uncertainly. "There is no reason to sit separately, is there? We are all friends! And family," she added firmly.

Elysse could think of nothing worse than suffering through the performance just a few seats away from Alexi, but there was no way they could make an excuse to sit by themselves. Blair took her arm, then turned to Ariella. "We would love to join you, Lady St. Xavier."

Elysse looked at her husband, praying her migraine would vanish—just as she prayed he might walk out of the opera and vanish. If she had to watch him whisper to Louisa all night, with her clinging to his arm, her head would surely explode.

Alexi gazed at *their* linked arms. He smiled coolly at her. "How perfect. Blair and I can have a brandy during the intermission—and clear up some matters."

"An excellent idea," Blair said calmly.

ELYSSE'S MOUTH HURT FROM the effort of forcing smile after smile all night long. Blair's coach had finally halted on the graveled drive in front of the stone steps leading up to the door of the Oxford house. The evening had been interminable. She had barely seen or heard LaScalla's performance; she had spent most of it watching Louisa leaning against Alexi, her hand on his arm as they whispered to one another. She might thoroughly despise him, but he still had the power to hurt her.

As discussed, Blair and Alexi had gone off together during the intermission. Ariella had sent St. Xavier after them, perhaps to act as referee. She had almost bitten her nails, waiting for them to return. But when they had come back to their seats, neither man had seemed terribly put out. According to Blair, he and Alexi had merely discussed the state of the British economy, its current recession and possible remedies to the National Debt.

With Louisa present, Elysse had not been able to demand just what her friend had been thinking to invite Alexi to the opera, much less with his latest paramour. She had done her best to be amiable to the other woman. Unfortunately, Louisa had been quite pleasant—and rather likable. She had even dared to take Elysse's hand and tell her how fortunate she was, to be married to such a dashing hero. Somehow, Elysse had managed to agree, while inwardly seething.

Ariella had seemed quite chagrined by the time the opera ended.

Elysse looked toward the house. At least Alexi was still out. She would lock her doors, drink a brandy, and cover her eyes with an eye patch. She might even use earplugs. She was exhausted and she meant to retire immediately.

Blair leaned past her, shoving open the carriage door.

Elysse got out and he followed. Then he took her gloved hand in his.

She trembled, meeting his gaze. The evening had been a disaster. She had barely survived the knowing looks from her acquaintances, each and every one of whom had managed to bring up Alexi's name when they had greeted her—gloating in her discomfort and, quite possibly, the exposure of six years of pretense and lies. Her attention had been on Alexi the entire time, not Blair—who deserved so much more.

Blair hadn't even tried to make conversation during the hour-long ride to her house. Instead, he had seemed deep in thought.

"I realize you are tired," Blair said as they walked up the stone steps to her front door. "Even though your husband is out, you won't invite me in, will you?"

She looked at him. Why couldn't she love him? He was powerful, strong and, most importantly, kind—unlike her damned husband. She felt like crying. "I *am* tired, Thomas. I'm sorry the evening was so unpleasant. "

"We both know that your tiredness isn't the reason you won't invite me inside."

She couldn't invite him in because her husband had returned to town. But Alexi was with someone else, so her reasoning didn't even make sense, Elysse thought.

When she didn't speak, he added, "It wasn't your fault. I am sorry you are so unhappy."

She so needed a friend and confidant. She couldn't tell Blair everything, but she wasn't going to dissemble again. "Alexi and I no longer get along."

"Thank you for telling me that." He took her other hand. "Yet somehow I don't think I have a chance."

A tear welled. She refused to entertain it. "He won't stay on land for very long—he never does. My life will soon return to normal." She winced, thinking of what *normal* was—a vast pretense at being happy.

"But you love him anyway."

She closed her eyes tightly. Was it possible? Surely her love had died when he had treated her so rudely and callously upon his return home, as if she were a whore—if it hadn't already been destroyed in the past six years.

"I loved him when we were children. We were close friends. But that boy is gone, Thomas."

"People change, Elysse, as the result of life's experiences. Perhaps you should admit that you love the man, in spite of the changes?" His gaze was searching.

Loving him now was impossible, wasn't it? It would only bring more pain. "We fought horribly last night. You may trust me, there is no love between us." She felt an unbearable tension within her. "We lead separate lives and have done so for years. I have no desire to change that, but as we are both in town now, he must pretend to enjoy this marriage somewhat."

"I find his behavior toward you insufferable." He studied her, then touched her cheek. "He is a fool to hurt you this way. Should I hang on, Elysse? I am terribly attracted to you. But I don't care to be where I am not wanted."

"I don't know what to say." She squeezed his hands in return. "I am so fond of you, Thomas. I am afraid to lose you…as a friend." Her traitorous mind recalled that once, Alexi had been her friend. Once, he had been the man she could depend on. Once, he had been her hero.

"I want more than friendship," he said softly.

She hesitated. "I know."

"Do you know what makes this even worse? I actually like your husband quite a bit."

"Oh, God!" she cried, horrified.

He half smiled. "He is daring, determined and clever. I also happen to like his balance sheets."

Elysse couldn't smile back.

Seriously, he said, "I am tempted to press my suit. But I see how upset you are—and I worry that even if I succeeded, no matter how I pleased you in my bed, the outcome would not change. You would remain unhappily in love with your errant husband."

"Alexi and I go our separate ways," she cried. "You have seen that firsthand!" She couldn't lose Blair. She was afraid. "I don't love him—I can't!"

"No, Elysse, the truth is obvious. You don't want to live separately. You are terribly hurt—and terribly in love." He shook his head. Then, suddenly, he leaned close and feathered her mouth with his.

She clasped his shoulders, keeping her face turned up to his. But this time, there was no desire—there was only misery.

He straightened. "I will leave. But, Elysse, if you need me, you know where to find me." He added, "I will always be your friend." He turned and started down the steps to the waiting carriage.

She hesitated, almost calling him back. After all, she deserved kindness and happiness. She deserved the respect of someone like Thomas Blair. She even deserved passion.

She trembled, but did not call him back. She reassured herself that she could contact him anytime—tomorrow, or any day after that. Blair cared. He was solid. He would not be so quick to find someone else.

Then she turned and opened the door. The entry hall was well lit but empty. As she closed and locked the door behind her, she reached for the buttons on her red, fur-lined cape, watching Blair's coach as it left. It was as if things had ended between them somehow.

She felt utterly alone.

Strong fingers stilled her hands on the buttons of her cape. A hard chest pressed against her back and she cried out. Shocked, she realized Alexi was home—and apparently waiting for her.

She turned in the circle of his arms.

He smiled tightly, his fingers rapidly releasing each button. He took the cape and tossed it onto the floor.

She froze. His gaze was very hot. There was lust—and anger. "What are you doing here?"

"I live here, my darling. But you already know that."

He hadn't stepped back, not even an inch. They stood so close that her chest almost touched his and her skirts covered his knees and shoes.

"You didn't invite your handsome lover in," he purred.

Had he seen Blair kiss her? "I didn't believe that inviting him in would be proper." She whirled to rush past him.

Reflexively he caught her wrist, stopping her abruptly in her tracks. He jerked her back to him. "As if you care about propriety. And I don't mind if you invite him in."

She shook him off. She wasn't going to discuss Blair. "Where is Louisa? My God, is she upstairs?"

He laughed at her. "Even I am not such a callous cad, Elysse."

She trembled, her relief instantaneous. Then it vanished, fury growing in its stead. "I asked you to be a proper husband last night! How dare you come to the opera with another woman?"

"But you were there with Blair—clinging to his arm, smiling coyly at him, hanging on his every word for all the world to see."

"As if you care!" she shouted, wanting to throw something at him. "Did you want to humiliate me tonight?"

"You're right, I don't care. Why would I care if you give

that spectacular body to Thomas Blair—or James Harding, or Tony Pierce?" His gaze was hooded now.

Those were the three men society thought were her lovers. How had he heard about Harding and Pierce? Had he put runners on her? What else did he know?

He couldn't know how her pride had suffered these past six years.

"You look frightened, my dear." He laughed again, as if pleased by that. "Don't you know that when I come home, my friends can't wait to tell me what my delectable little wife is up to—and with whom?"

Ariella would never tell him how much he had hurt her. Then his words sank in. How dare he be so rude! He caught her wrist before her hand could slap his smug face. "You will not hit me again," he warned, but he seemed pleased that she had tried.

Panting, she said, "Last night I begged you to pretend that we have a happy marriage. I asked you to the opera! Instead, you appeared there with Louisa. Surely it was not a coincidence! Did you want to humiliate me? Did you seek to inflame the gossips?"

He eased his grip. "I hardly need to humiliate you, when you do so all by yourself."

"Let me go, you bastard," she cried.

He released her. "And you didn't *ask* me to be a proper husband, Elysse. You tried to blackmail me—loyal wife that you are."

Elysse ran into the salon, so angry she was almost blinded by her rage. She stood there, shaking. How could he accuse her of disloyalty?

His chest brushed her from behind. She went still. Reaching past her, he poured two stiff shots of whiskey.

It crossed her mind that he liked crowding her—this was the second time he had done so. Acutely aware of his muscular body pressed against her, she fought for calm before turning, not even trying to move away from him. "You must have known that if you appeared at the opera with another woman, while I was there with another man, the gossips would be delighted at having more grist for their mills."

"I have never given a damn about gossip, Elysse," he said. "Most men are indifferent to shrews."

She flushed. "I have spent six years trying to quell the gossip about me—about us," she said. It was so hard to breathe properly now. "I have made certain that no one really knows the truth about our marriage."

He tossed back the shot, poured another one, his gestures almost casual. "Yes, you have had *such* a difficult time. Being my wife has been a terrific hardship. Can I assume I bought those diamonds, that dress?"

She so wished to strike him. Instead, she stared, refusing to reply but wanting to tell him how horrible the past six years had been—wanting him to understand what she had suffered. Living like this, having to pretend happiness, was unbearable.

He was staring far too closely, as if trying to read her thoughts. She couldn't admit to any of the anguish, she realized. He wouldn't care—he might even gloat. "I have spent six years being the perfect wife," she managed, swallowing. "I have spent six years pretending that this marriage is exactly as I want it—I have praised you and your successes a hundred times, to everyone who would listen!"

"So you equate perfection with infidelity?" He saluted her with the small shot glass, then drained it. "Yes, everyone must think us the perfect couple, with you keeping company with so many gentlemen."

"You keep that whore in Singapore!"

His gaze hardened. "Soo Lin is not a whore, Elysse,

she is my mistress. She is refined, highly educated, the daughter of a great merchant, and I am fond of her."

She flung the whiskey at his face. "Then go back to Singapore."

He caught her wrist and she froze. He instantly released her. Using his sleeve to dry his face, he walked away from her.

She trembled. What was happening to her? Dear God, she had just thrown her drink in Alexi's face.

He cared for that woman. She had never expected such an admission. She covered her heart with her hands. The anguish threatened to erupt.

He turned abruptly, his eyes slamming to hers.

She dropped her hands and rearranged her face, but his gaze was narrow and speculative. "Neither one of us is faithful. But I have been loyal."

"I am sorry. I should have never said what I just did about Soo Lin." He was terse.

She shrugged. "I am very fond of Blair, so we are even."

He darkened. "That is obvious. It is obvious you are more than lovers. You are *friends*—the way we once were."

No, she thought, Blair was not the kind of friend Alexi had once been, so long ago. That boy had always been there to protect her—he had been the anchor in her young life. Yet Blair could become precisely that if she allowed it. But why did the notion hurt so terribly? "You make that sound worse than a love affair."

He stalked back to the bar, pouring a third shot. He stared down at the glass, not drinking.

The pause gave Elysse a moment to think. She was devastated by his admission about his mistress. But hadn't his abandoning her at the altar also devastated her, and she had survived. She had survived six years of gossip, of betrayal, and she would survive his feelings of affection for someone else. She had to consider the present, not the past—and not the future. They could not go on this way. She might be able to salvage their marriage's reputation, in spite of this evening and last night, if she were careful and clever now. That must be her single, consuming ambition.

He looked at her, clasping the tiny glass to his chest. "You shouldn't be residing here, Elysse. It's insane. No good can come of it. We might end up truly hurting one another."

She was already hurt. "As long as you own this house, I will live here, Alexi—to save my pride."

He glanced at her sidelong, his expression utterly grim. "In China, it is called saving face."

Pain lanced through her. "And did Soo Lin teach you that?"

He didn't answer. His gaze moved slowly over her face and for one heartbeat, he stared at her mouth—as if recalling their kiss.

He wasn't angry now.

Elysse took the shot and tossed it back the way he had. She'd never consumed an entire ounce of whiskey that way before, but she refrained from choking. She waited for the whiskey to burn its way down her throat to her stomach before she spoke. "Living here is not convenient." She hoped she had mistaken that direct, measured look. "My flat is only twenty minutes from the theatre and shopping. But I am determined to continue claiming our marriage is successful."

His thick dark lashes lowered, hooding his eyes.

Was he finally listening to her? "I agree, living this way and fighting so often is terribly unpleasant—even hurtful. Once, long ago, as children, we were friends." Their gazes collided and she was the one to look away. "That seems like a different life, doesn't it?"

"What is your point?" he asked flatly.

"You could leave town, Alexi. I know you won't run for China till the summer, but you could go to Dublin or Windhaven, or even France."

"No."

She trembled. But the whiskey had had an incredibly calming effect—it was as if she could think clearly and rationally now. "Then we must get on." It would be so simple, she thought, if he would just accept her proposal from the night before. "Why won't you consider pretending to be my doting husband, just for a few weeks? You can keep your lovers. All you have to do is be discreet. We will go out together, hold hands, smile at one another—and then, later, you can return to Louisa Weldon, or whomever you wish to be with."

"While you go off with Thomas Blair?" He spoke very, very softly.

She knew she must ignore that. Yet she flushed. "I am sorry I was so foolish as to try to blackmail you. I apologize."

He sipped the whiskey. When he looked up, he appeared somehow predatory. "Has anyone ever told you that when you cajole it is far more effective than when you throw whiskey in a man's face?"

"I am sorry about that, too," she said, meaning it. Her behavior had been beyond the pale.

"I am more than happy to pretend to be a proper husband, Elysse, and I said as much last night." He slowly smiled at her.

It took her a moment to realize what he meant. *If she took him to bed, he would play his part.* Her pulse exploded.

She was stunned by her response to his words and the

smoldering look in his eyes. Her body flamed and her senses sparked with dismaying urgency.

"After all, if I must be married and live with my wife, why the hell shouldn't I enjoy my matrimonial rights?" His eyes gleamed.

He would be a magnificent lover and she knew it. A part of her desperately wanted to accept his unacceptable proposal! But surely her desire was the result of her age and inexperience—not anything more! "This marriage is a terrible sham," she heard herself whisper. "And you do not want to be married—you said so."

"I might feel differently if I were enjoying your favors. After all, I am not getting *anything* out of this marriage." He finished the whiskey and set the glass down, hard. It seemed an eternity before he spoke. "No man likes being trapped into marriage, Elysse."

She started, taken aback. It took her a moment to comprehend the swift change in subject. She was afraid to begin such a dangerous discussion—even though she knew that, one day, they must discuss the past. "You married me to protect me," she said, very carefully. "I am not sure I ever thanked you."

His gaze was impossible to read.

Elysse tried not to give in to the memories that were returning. Was this why he was so angry with her? "It wasn't a trap, Alexi."

"There was no choice. That makes it a trap."

She inhaled. "Is that why you stayed away? Is that why you are so furious with me?"

"It was my duty to protect you." He made a harsh sound. "I made you a promise, remember?"

She was shocked that he recalled that long-ago day at Errol Castle in Ireland. Before she could speak, he said roughly, "A man died because of us—a man who was my friend."

She hugged herself, and their gazes locked. Images filled her mind—Alexi dragging William Montgomery off her; the dead pilot lying in his arms, Alexi looking up at her in horror; Alexi holding her tightly in the library, demanding to know if she was hurt, if she was all right….

Once, he had cared so much about her.

Now, she was afraid to continue the discussion. She had stopped thinking about Montgomery's assault years ago. It had been Alexi's betrayal which had caused her so much grief and pain. But she was beginning to understand why he had left her at the altar. He had been twenty-one. He'd stepped up to marry her—but only after a fatal struggle with the man who had once been his good friend.

After all these years, she had managed to forgive herself her unwitting role in that terrible tragedy. But she hadn't known Montgomery as well as Alexi had. "It *was* an accident."

"Maybe. But I killed him—not deliberately, but nonetheless, I *killed* Montgomery," Alexi said. His eyes burned.

In that moment, she realized he still blamed himself for the American's accidental death. "Alexi, it was not your fault."

He made a mocking sound. "But *you* led him to his death."

She gasped. "You blame me? I went outside for a stroll in the moonlight. I expected Montgomery to behave as a proper gentleman!"

"I warned you repeatedly and you led him on deliberately, to make me jealous."

She pressed back against the shelf of the wall unit. The air seemed to sizzle between them. Alexi's gaze was as accusing as his tone had been.

"I regret what I did, Alexi. You are right, I led him on. I think I wanted to fall in love with him, if that is any defense to make. But I knew how close you were. At the ball, foolishly, I wanted to make you jealous. I am sorry."

"I will never forget that night, Elysse, or what has come because of it."

He hated their marriage because the foundation was his friend's death. In that moment, she knew there would never be a genuine marriage between them. They would never find common ground; there would never be a truce—it would never be the way it had once been.

Their friendship was really over. He would never take her in his arms again, seeking reassurance that she was all right. He would never smile with warmth and affection at her. There was no hope for them—not as long as Alexi remained haunted by Montgomery. Not as long as he blamed her—and himself—for his death.

The past was a huge gulf between them.

She trembled uncontrollably now, with monumental regret. The pain of heartbreak returned. She knew she must hide it. But his gaze narrowed suspiciously as she spoke. "I have learned how to live with guilt, Alexi. I was young and so foolish. I regret it all. I will never forget, but I prefer not to remember. I know it was a terrible, unfortunate accident. No one is to blame." She hugged herself.

He said harshly, "If you believe that, you are lucky."

Had her heart ever felt so raw? "I have learned from my mistakes. I do believe that there is no more blame to be had."

He stared at her, his intensity unnerving. "If I didn't know better, I'd think you had changed. You almost sound wise."

Of course he meant to be rude and insulting. "I *have*

changed. I am hardly the same foolish and selfish girl I once was."

His brows lifted. "Really? When you are obviously leading Blair on?"

"I am not leading anyone one," she said stiffly. She couldn't explain that she genuinely cared for Blair.

His eyes hardened, as if he knew her very thoughts. A long time ago, he had been able to easily read her. She doubted he could do so now. "He is smitten with you, but you know that. You do not return his feelings—it is déjà vu."

It was a moment before she could respond. "Clearly," she said harshly, "the past is a huge obstacle between us. What do we do now?"

He gave her a rude once-over. "Oh, I can think of a thing or two. Our current impasse has not changed."

She realized that he would take her in his arms another time—but not out of concern, not to reassure her or to heal the past. His blue gaze was brilliant. "We can't change the past—or the fact that we are married," she managed to say. "No, our impasse has not changed."

His smile was mocking. "Your dilemma is foolish and unnecessary." He paused and murmured, "Come closer, Elysse. You know you want to."

Her heart rate escalated wildly. "A long time ago, we were friends. But we're not friends now. You keep taunting me, Alexi, as if you enjoy it. I wonder if you want to hurt me. Using me would accomplish that."

"No. We're not friends. We are man and wife, Elysse, and I am tired of this situation."

She was alarmed—and equally aroused. But if she slept with him, she would regret it in the morning. Of that, she had no doubt. "I can't share your bed. Not like this."

"Why not? I know you're accustomed to passion. There *will* be passion, Elysse, but you already know that."

She recalled being in his arms the other afternoon, in the back offices of Windsong Shipping. For one moment, she locked gazes with him, knowing that their passion would be an inferno, should it ever be released. Because deep in her heart, she still loved him. And that terrified her.

She resumed the disguise she was so accustomed to. She spoke quietly, sensibly, calmly. "I am asking you to consider what I asked yesterday. I will even bend. You don't have to be with me every night, just one or two nights a week. I will plan a supper party. You may provide the guest list. But I will need you to be present—so we can begin this game of keeping up appearances."

His gaze was piercing as daggers. "And why should I do anything that you ask, when I get nothing in return?"

She lifted her chin. "We are married, for better or for worse. I didn't ask you to step forward six years ago. You must take some responsibility for our current situation. I am not moving out. You have admitted that our relationship is intolerable. I am offering a very fair solution, but it requires civility from us both."

"Civility—how boring. I will think about it."

She began to smile.

"Oh, no," he said swiftly. "Because you had better think about what I am demanding in return. Quid pro quo, Elysse."

She went still.

He laughed and walked out.

CHAPTER ELEVEN

"ARE YOU TERRIBLY ANGRY WITH ME?" Ariella asked.

Elysse looked up from the desk where she sat. She had discovered a small, cheerful salon on the ground floor of the house, with floral wallpaper and bright, happy furnishings. The windows looked out on the flower gardens behind the house. She had decided to make the room her own personal parlor. In it, she would take care of her correspondence, make her lists, update her calendar and run the household.

Ariella stood in the doorway uncertainly. Reginald was with her. It was early Monday afternoon; Elysse had spent all of yesterday settling in and unpacking more of her things. She hadn't seen Alexi since their conversation after the opera. He had vanished early Sunday morning and when he had returned later that evening she had already retired for the night. Her doors had been locked, but she had been up, waiting to see when he would actually come in. He hadn't paused as he had walked past her bedroom door.

She hadn't had a clue where he had been all day and evening.

Elysse smiled grimly at Ariella, her thoughts filled with her difficult husband. He was considering a new arrangement in which he would pretend that their marriage was a good one, but he expected her to consider taking him to bed in return for his efforts. He still blamed her in part for William Montgomery's death. He felt that he had been trapped into a marriage he did not want. She could never sleep with him under those circumstances. Allowing him such intimacy when he continued to blame her for the past would be too hurtful for her to bear.

She despaired at all that he had said. He continued to judge her for her every action, both in the past and the present. He refused to consider that she had changed. It was as if he was determined to see her as a foolish, selfish coquette.

She understood why he felt he had been trapped into marriage, although that had not been her intention. Surely, he would eventually realize that. But she now knew the cause of his anger. His friend was dead because of her, and they were married—in his mind, it was as simple as that.

It hurt, thinking about the friendship they had once had, and the place they had come to now.

She yearned to go back in time, to well before Montgomery's death, when he had been the most fascinating boy she had ever met—a boy who admired her and would do anything for her.

Did she still care about him? Was it possible? She prayed not! She was terribly afraid that she did care—that she had missed him for years.

Elysse stood, glad to have company. She did not have time to feel sorry for herself. Reginald left them and Ariella came into the room. "Why on earth did you invite Alexi to the opera? It was a disaster, Ariella." But she would never remain angry with her best friend for very long and they both knew it

Ariella grimaced. "I was hoping some good might come of the two of you being together."

"We are living together, in case you hadn't noticed."

"I noticed that Alexi and Stephen showed up yesterday

afternoon, attempting unsuccessfully to drag my husband off to carouse, as if Emilian were still a bachelor at large." She slipped her arm around Elysse. "I also noticed that he is very jealous of Blair, Elysse. Maybe some good did come of his being at the opera. And maybe you should think twice about continuing your friendship with Thomas."

Elysse started. "I can assure you, Alexi isn't jealous—he doesn't care what I do." Hadn't he said as much, several times?

"You can't really believe that," Ariella replied.

"Does that mean you think he cares?" Elysse was disbelieving. Still, she couldn't help thinking how she had told him to keep his many lovers, as if she couldn't care less, when the truth was that his reckless liaisons remained terribly painful for her.

Ariella sighed, walking away. She paused at the terrace doors, as if admiring the flowers and the manicured grounds. "I don't know how he feels about you now. I do know that once, he was smitten with you. But yes, I think he cares very much about your affairs."

She trembled. "He was never smitten with me, Ariella."

"When you were children, he was besotted. If you did not realize that, then you were the only one."

Was it possible? When she realized that she wished that were true, she shook herself free of such foolish yearning. "It doesn't matter what he felt when he was all of eight."

Ariella turned. "He is very proud—as are you. You certainly didn't care to see him out with another woman—anyone could see that—just as he didn't like seeing you out with Blair. He will only be in town till June or July, Elysse. Can't you end things with Blair, even if it is only temporarily, so you have a chance at patching things up with my brother?"

If she thought that ending her friendship with the banker would help her marriage, she would consider it. But Alexi was an impossible rogue. Would he end his liaisons? Would he escort her about town as a man did his wife? Their impasse had not changed. "Blair is becoming a good friend, Ariella, one I should regret losing," Elysse finally said.

"I know you haven't been unfaithful to my brother, in spite of what everyone else thinks. But Alexi doesn't know that you are faithful to him."

Elysse bit her lip. She could not admit to Ariella the true reason for her loyalty. She was Alexi's sister, and she was more than capable of meddling if she thought that doing so was in their best interest. "I am not going to comment on my personal life, Ariella."

"I know that you want everyone to think that you are a free-spirited and independent socialite who casually takes lovers upon whims!" Ariella walked over to her desk and stared down at the papers there before looking up. "I still can't decide if I did the right thing in encouraging Alexi to go to the opera. I do not think he will pursue Louisa Weldon, by the way. How *are* you and Alexi getting along?"

She hesitated, surprised by Ariella's comment about Louisa. "Not very well. I am trying to convince him to pretend to enjoy being married to me, as a matter of pride, so we can offer up a united front to society. It isn't an easy task."

"Seduce him."

Elysse choked. "I beg your pardon?"

"I think you heard me," Ariella said, smiling knowingly. "Elysse, men are fools when it comes to the beautiful women they desire. Alexi is no exception."

She couldn't breathe. "You must be mad! He has women all over the world! He is indifferent to me." But even as she spoke, she recalled the way he looked at her with obvious lust. He was a seductive and sensual man. She couldn't breathe properly, thinking about how clear he had been about what he wanted.

Could Ariella be right?

Did he really want her? Or was he just trying to hurt her in this ugly contest that they battled in?

"Whenever I am at odds with Emilian and I want to patch things up, I lure him to bed," Ariella said brightly. "The next day, he is eating out of my hand."

Elysse paced the cheerful salon. She would never tell Ariella that she wouldn't even have to seduce Alexi; all she would have to do is tell him she had accepted his terms for their living arrangements. She strode over to the desk, where the guest list she was crafting lay. "I am having a supper party on Friday. Will you and Emilian join us?"

"Of course we will." Ariella touched her arm. "You are sad, Elysse. Don't deny it. And my brother is the reason for your heartache."

She couldn't tell Ariella that the past was the obstacle that loomed between them. "Alexi regrets ever marrying me. He has said so. Our arguments are very unpleasant. I dread our next encounter." That was the truth, at least.

"It's true he had no interest in marriage at the age of twenty-one—which is why I wish I knew why he married you in the first place," Ariella said swiftly. "You have never told me what really happened that night."

"We were caught in a passionate embrace, remember?" Elysse said. Ariella scoffed and Elysse moved quickly on. "We are simply going to have to manage to get along some-how." She had barely finished speaking when she heard his booted footsteps in the hall. Her heart lurched with dread and anticipation.

Alexi appeared in the doorway. Instantly, his gaze founds hers.

Her heart leaped and then raced uncontrollably. He was dressed for an afternoon hack, in a riding coat, tan breeches and high boots—as dashing and devastating as ever. Apparently aware of that, he slowly smiled at her.

She reminded herself that he was not dashing or handsome or, worse, seductive. She must not think along those lines. She was so anxious—she hadn't seen him since their argument Saturday night after the opera. It still felt odd and awkward being in his home.

His gaze moved over her deliberately. She was wearing a simple ivory day dress, with a high neckline and long sleeves, but she felt nearly naked now. Warmth exploded in her cheeks. He sent her a mocking smile, as if he knew that she could not dismiss the attraction between them, and turned to his sister.

Ariella hugged him hard. "Stop being a rude husband, Alexi—I mean it!"

He released her and looked at Elysse, his smile vanishing. "I am never rude. My manners are impeccable."

She folded her arms. Did her racing heart and weak knees indicate a continuing attraction? She did not want to believe that he could enter the room and have such a potent effect on her. "Your manners are impeccable with everyone but me."

"But you seek to provoke me, Elysse, as you are doing now—and I admit I enjoy taunting you."

"Little boys provoke puppy dogs, Alexi, and caged ferrets—and little girls. You aren't eight years old, even if you choose to act that way."

"Where are your manners…darling?"

"Quid pro quo," she said, trying to taunt him. He began to smile, clearly amused. She knew she flushed.

"Do you challenge me now?" he asked.

Challenging him was a terrible idea. She retreated. "I would never do such a thing, as I am a proper wife."

"*Proper* wives do not dispute their husbands—or deny them anything." His blue gaze was bland.

She inhaled, well aware of his inference. "We have been arguing since we were children."

Ariella glanced back and forth between them, her eyes huge. "I am a proper wife and I dispute Emilian all of the time."

"You, my dear sister, are a shrew."

Ariella rolled her eyes. "My husband doesn't think so."

Elysse realized she hadn't taken her gaze from Alexi since he had appeared in the doorway. She reached for the guest list she had been working on, wishing he didn't unsettle her so easily. She fought for composure. "I am scheduling our first supper party for the following Friday, in two weeks. It will be a small affair—two dozen couples. I hope that meets with your approval." She spoke briskly, but she felt even more nervous as she faced him.

"I hadn't realized we were actually having a supper party, Elysse." His gaze narrowed. "Does this mean we have come to terms?"

She knew her face flamed. "It means that we are having twenty-two guests and you will be at the head of the table, in the host's seat."

He folded his arms. "Really. So I am to obey *you?*"

Ariella seized his forearm. "If your wife wants to have a dinner party, you will humor her, Alexi. All husbands attend their wives' parties."

His stare never wavered from Elysse's.

"I thought we agreed that you would make a dutiful husbandly appearance, once or twice a week." She swallowed.

They hadn't agreed to any such thing, and she could barely believe she was pushing him now. But she was determined to salvage the reputation of their marriage. It was not a great deal to ask.

"I agreed to no such thing. Quid pro quo, Elysse," he added softly.

All she had to do, Elysse thought, was unlock her door and allow him into her bed and they would have the perfect sham of a marriage for her dinner party.

Ariella jabbed her elbow hard into his ribs. "Enough bickering! Do as she has asked!"

He scowled at her. "Fine. I will tolerate the evening, but this subject is hardly closed."

How had she won this round? Elysse almost felt faint. She approached him and handed him the list. "Is there anyone else you would like to invite?"

He scanned the list quickly, then raised his eyes.

"I don't see Thomas Blair on that list."

She froze. "That is because he is not invited."

"Invite him."

She began to tremble. "Why are you doing this?"

"Doing what? I am not inviting him because he is your lover. He is my banker."

He was trying to strike at her, she thought, entirely off balance.

"Besides, if anyone can learn his plans, you can."

"I beg your pardon?"

"He does finance other maritime merchants. In fact, he finances some of my competitors. I wish for details... darling."

She choked in disbelief. "You want me to spy on Blair for you?"

"Hmm. *Spy* is a strong word. But yes, that is exactly

what I wish for you to do." He smiled triumphantly, nodded at both women and strode out.

Elysse realized she had crumpled the list accidentally in her hand as she stared after him.

Ariella touched her arm, her face rather pale. "Oh, dear," she said. "Elysse, if it is any consolation, from time to time Emilian wishes to know what his various associates and rivals are up to and I am sent on the mission of discreetly discovering their plans."

"I am not spying on Blair," Elysse managed.

Ariella slid her arm around her. "You can't fool me," she said quietly, her gaze worried. "The two of you are at worse odds than ever. Alexi wants to hurt you. I just wish I knew why."

Elysse desperately wanted to tell her best friend everything. Briefly, she closed her eyes and composed herself. "I am fine," Elysse lied. Then she smiled brightly. "Will you stay for lunch? I have brought my chef over from the Grosvenor Square flat, and as you know, he is an excellent cook."

ELYSSE SMILED AT ANOTHER couple in the entry hall, thanking them for coming. Every one of their guests had arrived—except for Blair.

Her stomach tightened as she told Lady Godfrey how thrilled she was to see her again. As they briefly chatted, she glanced between the open front door and her husband. Alexi stood at the hall's far end, receiving everyone as they moved into the gilded salon where they would have sherry before dinner. He was impossibly handsome in his white dinner coat and midnight-black evening trousers. He was smiling, and she knew he was deliberately charming their guests. He was on his best behavior. She wondered how long it would last.

Her heart lurched as she glanced outside, certain she saw carriage lights far down the drive. She remained at the front door, clad in a sapphire-blue evening gown, trying not to let anyone see just how worried she was.

She had meant to raise the issue of Thomas Blair with Alexi, certain his motives were dangerous, but she had barely seen him in the past two weeks. He was out every day, apparently at the Windsong offices or with possible investors, and every evening, as well. If he was with other women, she hadn't heard about it, but he never came home until two or three in the morning. It was fairly obvious what he was doing. Of course, it hurt. But she worked hard to avoid him, too. Often she did not come out of her rooms until he had driven away.

She had kept up her affairs, attending a gala at the London Museum and several supper parties. For the first time in six years, she had been without an escort. She had been asked a dozen times where her husband was, and had carefully made up excuses for him. In those moments, her smile and her careful mask had never slipped. But at home, in the refuge of her rooms, she despaired.

Whomever he was with, and whatever he was doing, at least he was being very discreet. But it was impossible to feel grateful.

It was almost as if nothing had changed. He had spent six years avoiding her; now, he was certain to never be in residence when she was at home or attend the same evening affair.

In the end, she hadn't had the opportunity to discuss Blair's attendance.

It hadn't mattered. Apparently Alexi had seen him in town, extending the invitation personally. She only knew that because she had received Blair's RSVP.

She was determined that the supper party be a success.

She would keep all drama to a minimum—at least until the last of their guests had left. After all, the entire point of the evening was to convince society that she and Alexi were happily wed. Whatever Alexi thought might transpire by inviting Blair, she was determined to carefully navigate around that.

Blair's carriage pulled below the front steps where she stood. Her smile never wavered. She wished he had decided not to come—yet part of her was glad to see him. He would always be a trusted friend.

A woman got out of his carriage. Blair followed, dashing in his black tails. As they came up the front steps, she saw that the woman was blonde, attractive and her own age. She wondered if he might be genuinely interested in her, and she was somewhat dismayed when she had no right to be. She had known he was bringing a guest.

Blair took both of her hands in his. "You are as beautiful as ever," he said softly, so only she could hear. She was relieved, knowing he missed her.

He kissed one of her hands and introduced Mrs. Debora Weir, explaining that she was newly widowed and had recently moved full-time to town. "Her husband has been a client of mine for many years," he added. "Mrs. Weir has inherited a number of highly lucrative coal mines."

"I found it too tiresome to remain alone in the country, with Philip gone," she said earnestly. "I am thrilled to meet you at last, Mrs. de Warenne. I have heard so much about you and your soirees, and so much about your husband." Her glance moved across the hall. "Is that the captain?"

Elysse turned and found Alexi watching them like a hawk. She glanced at Blair, who held her gaze for another moment. "Come, Mrs. Weir, I will introduce you. Our shipping company often transports coal across the world. I am not sure who your agents are, but they should inquire after our contracts and rates."

Blair touched her elbow, moving her forward. "I believe that Windsong Shipping already transports some of Weir Limited's cargo, but I could be wrong."

She realized Alexi was staring openly. In that moment, she wondered if inviting Blair had been a test of some sort. If so, she was determined to pass it. But she still refused to spy for him.

"I hope we are doing business with you," Mrs. Weir cried eagerly.

Elysse turned to her husband. "Alexi, darling. You know Thomas, of course. And Mrs. Debora Weir. We might transport their coal."

Alexi smiled at the beautiful blonde, gallantly bowing over her hand. Then he and Blair shook hands. Alexi's gaze was cold, but Blair seemed unperturbed.

"I so appreciate the invitation, Captain," Blair said drolly. "Your new home is spectacular."

Alexi suddenly slipped his arm around her. "We think so."

Elysse was disbelieving, but she said calmly, "We are so pleased you could join us, Thomas."

His glance moved to Alexi's hand, splayed on her hip.

Her discomfort intensified. Alexi stood on her right, Blair on her left. They stared at one another, unsmiling. And nothing felt finished, not with either man.

THE EVENING WAS ALMOST OVER and nothing terrible had transpired—yet.

Elysse smiled down the length of her dinner table. A myriad of desserts had been served and almost every plate was finished. Her twenty-two guests seemed comfortably sated and were happily engrossed in one another. They had drunk seven entire bottles of wine—four white and three red. She had learned from experience that the more wine that was consumed, the more successful the party.

Perspiration trickled between her breasts. She simply kept smiling. Thus far, the evening had been a success.

She meant to keep it that way.

Alexi, who was at the opposite end of the table, caught her eye and smiled lazily at her. He had been gazing indolently at her through most of the evening, as if they were in a game of cat and mouse. His glances made her uncomfortable—and wary. He was obviously aware of the effort it took for her to maintain her charade, and that keeping scandal at bay remained her utmost priority. She had spent the entire evening ignoring his attempts to bait her with those heavy-lidded looks, speaking instead with her closest guests.

His stare intensified. She saw it from the corner of her eye.

Her breath quickened. She had the oddest notion that he meant to collect his dues from her that night, for his part in the evening's success. Well, he could think whatever he wanted; there would not be any such repayment.

Everyone seemed delighted with the company thus far, and she was certain no one had noticed any tension between her and her husband—other than Blair. Ever astute, the banker had been watching her and Alexi all evening. He was seated a few chairs away from Alexi, at the other end of the table, across from his guest. Blair had glanced at her far more frequently than he had at Debora Weir. He had seen Alexi watching her, and he seemed worried. She had almost forgotten how kind he was—and how protective he could be. Elysse smiled at him. He was an ally, but she could manage the rest of the evening, no matter what Alexi intended.

Alexi and Blair had actually conversed quite a bit during the evening, which added to her distress. Blair had said he liked Alexi, but her husband clearly considered him a rival. She couldn't help worrying about Blair, yet he seemed too worldly to fall for any tricks that her husband might have up his sleeve. Besides, she knew they were discussing trade and global opportunity.

Nothing untoward was going to come of this evening, she thought. They merely had to retire for another hour, the men to their cigars and brandies, the ladies to sherry and port. Then she could go upstairs and lock both bedroom doors. There would be no late-night dialogue, no shared brandy with her husband. It would be too dangerous.

Alexi was gazing at her again, with that suggestive half smile. Flushing, Elysse stood up. Her guests began to rise, as well, two dozen chairs scraping loudly back.

She finally looked at Alexi, signaling him to lead the men aside. He had his wineglass in hand, and he lifted it. "One moment," he said.

She froze.

"I'd like to toast my beautiful wife, without whom this evening would not be possible," he said softly.

As everyone raised their glasses, turning to look at her, she smiled, but her heart turned over. Alexi slowly looked up at her. His eyes were too bright. She tensed, certain he meant to deliver a terrible blow.

"To a *successful* evening," Alexi said, his tone far too bland. "The hallmark of a *successful* marriage…wouldn't you all agree?"

There was a brief silence. Then Blair said, "Hear, hear."

If he humiliated her now, she would never forgive him, she thought, her mind numb with dread.

"I have married the most beautiful woman in the world.

She is charming, clever, witty and a hostess without parallel," he said, still smiling.

Elysse couldn't move. What would he say next?

His gaze was piercing. There was no warmth in his eyes and his tone was mocking. "To my very loyal, very beautiful, very desirable *wife*." He drained the wine. "A woman every man must want. A woman only *I* can have. How very fortunate I am—I have wed a paragon. Wouldn't you all agree?"

Elysse somehow kept smiling, aware that her guests were confused. His words weren't precisely insulting, but his mocking tone was edged with sarcasm. Her reputation was well-known. Some of their guests must sense his anger toward her.

Damn him. He meant to ruin the evening and make certain everyone knew their marriage was a farce!

"Now it is my turn," she said. She picked up her glass. "To the most courageous and skilled sea captain of the times—may his China record hold for years to come! To my dashing husband—a hero and a gentleman."

There was a moment of silence, as her guests glanced at one another for direction. Alexi said softly, "So we are both terribly fortunate, are we not?"

She kept her smile firmly in place. "There is no woman in London as fortunate as I."

Blair broke the silence, lifting his glass. "I'd like to make a toast. To the greatest hostess I have ever known—the greatest hostess London has ever known—as the captain has said, a woman without parallel."

She looked at him and wanted to cry.

Glasses clinked and their guests cheered. She met Blair's gaze, refusing to let the moisture rise in her eyes. Then she looked at Alexi, trembling. His eyes blazed with anger.

Her guests filed out, conversing amongst one another

again. Blair faltered as he passed her, but she shook her head quickly, not wanting him to approach her now, afraid that she might lose the last of her composure. She reminded herself that Alexi had stopped short of maliciously speaking against her. His words had been high praise; it was his tone that had been so sarcastic.

Alexi was the last to walk past her, from the dining room. "Are you pleased, Elysse?" he mocked. "Surely you liked my toast?"

She was afraid of what she might say or do if she responded. Instead, she refused to speak.

He leaned close. "Blair is on your hook. Reel him in."

She hissed incoherently.

Alexi grinned and sauntered away. She was alone in the hallway. Elysse leaned against the wall, trembling. At least he'd had the decency not to say anything untoward about her. Had he ruined the evening? She wouldn't know until she heard the ensuing gossip tomorrow.

"Elysse."

She turned, pleased to see Blair, even though she knew that being alone with him was highly inappropriate and possibly dangerous.

He strode to her and caught her hands in his. "I am very worried about you."

"I will manage."

"Really? Is that how you intend to live your life? By *managing* this terrible dispute with de Warenne? By allowing him to insult you and pretending he did no such thing?"

She trembled, finding comfort in the clasp of his strong hands. "I have no choice, Thomas."

"There is always a choice," he said swiftly.

She pulled her hands away. "I am married to him. For better or for worse."

"And it is worse than I suspected, isn't it?" he said.

She had the sensation that they were being watched. She looked past Blair.

Alexi stood at the end of the hallway, staring at them. His gaze was cold and hard.

"Yes," she said softly. "It is worse than you thought."

CHAPTER TWELVE

THE LAST OF THEIR GUESTS were finally gone. Elysse was acutely aware of Alexi as he shut and locked the front door, leaving them alone in the entry hall. As he turned to face her, she wondered if he could hear her pounding heart. She was very, very angry at the toast he had made.

His smile was a smirk. "Another successful evening. All hail the queen of London, Elysse de Warenne!"

She tensed.

"You must be so pleased. Your friends will be talking about this party tomorrow—heaping praise after praise upon you, whispering about how perfect the food was, the decor, how lovely your gown, the jewels, and how exceptional the company! Except for those who were not invited—they will be slandering you viciously behind your back."

She folded her arms rigidly. "That is how society is. There is always gossip, and some of it is malicious. But that will please you, will it not?"

Still smiling, he said, "And why would you think that?"

She erupted. "You damn well know why! Everyone realized how mocking you were when you toasted me as your paragon of a wife!"

"*Was* I mocking?" He blinked innocently at her.

"You know you were! Did you want to ruin the evening—and the impression I have been trying to make?"

He reached for her. Impossibly tense, she didn't move as he slid his thumb down the heavy cord in her neck. "I doubt the gossips will bother with my toast, darling…. I imagine they will be busy with the fact that you're jumping back and forth between Blair's bed and mine."

She pulled away from him. "How dare you! Have I asked you even once about the hours you have kept—and with whom you are keeping them? I am exhausted. I am going upstairs. Good night."

"Oh, come, the evening is still young," he said, physically barring her way. "Have a drink with me, Elysse."

"I believe that you have had enough to drink—I certainly have."

His smile grew. "Now that is the Elysse O'Neill I have known for two decades—snooty and patronizing at once. I am not in my cups, darling. Everyone present saw how Blair watched you with such concern, with such consideration. He could not take his eyes off you! Everyone clearly realizes your latest lover is your knight in shining armor. You must be thrilled—another man has helplessly fallen for your indisputable charms."

"If anyone saw anything, it was how *you* watched me all night long. Are you going to allow me to pass?"

He didn't move aside. "And how did I watch you, darling?"

Their gazes locked. "You stared as if I were the latest harlot to catch your interest."

"But you *have* caught my interest." He laughed, as if pleased. Then he seized her arm. "I want to share an after-dinner brandy, Elysse. We have so much to discuss."

She did not want to have a drink with him, and not simply because he had tried to ruin the evening. She did not trust him, especially not at this late hour. She wanted to escape to the privacy of her apartments, so she could sort her jumbled thoughts. Mostly, though, she didn't trust herself, not with her body humming as it was in acute awareness of him, no matter how distraught she was. She wasn't strong enough to pull away from him now, so she didn't even try—instead, she reluctantly kept abreast of him as he moved across the hallway. "We can discuss whatever you wish tomorrow."

"Come, you can hardly object. I have played the perfect, proper husband all evening long—I must have some tidbit tossed my way in return."

"You played the proper husband until you decided to mock me with that toast." She stared into his brilliant blue gaze as he guided her forcibly into the library.

He grinned at her. "But did I really mock you, darling?" His warm gaze slid slowly across her features before moving down to the edge of her low-cut bodice. "Did I mention how much I like that gown?"

He was enjoying her distress, just as he enjoyed being as suggestive as possible. She felt like telling him, in no uncertain terms, that she was not allowing him into her rooms that night, much less into her bed. Her decision would not change. His smile widened as if he'd read her mind and did not believe her; he let her go and went to pour two cognacs.

She inhaled, wishing she weren't so terribly aware of him. She wished her pulse were not pounding; she wished Blair was her lover; she wished she were not an inexperienced virgin. She decided to ignore the topic that was so clearly on his mind. "If there is gossip tomorrow about that toast, I will expect you to somehow set the record straight and quell it before it rages all over town."

He returned to her, handing her a glass. "I thought it was a very loving toast," he said. "Have you considered what I want in return for my theatrics?"

Her heart skidded wildly. "I do not want to go out tomorrow and hear everyone whispering behind my back about the animosity in this marriage."

"You are avoiding my question," he said.

She tore her glance away from his, determined to change the subject. "I didn't realize that you and Blair were so friendly. What did you discuss?"

"We aren't friendly—we are associates." Alexi sipped, no longer smiling. "Very well, let's delay the inevitable, shall we? We were discussing the Foreign Office's gunboat diplomacy. We both wish to see the China trade grow. Then we discussed the price of corn and sugar. That led us into a discussion of what remains of the slave trade. What did you and Blair speak about tonight? He was certainly groveling at your feet, before and after supper."

Of course they had discussed trade and economics. She had been afraid to digress from those topics. "Blair doesn't grovel. Is that all you discussed?"

His gaze flickered. "We hardly talked about his interest in you, darling, if that's what you're wondering. Janssen, it seems, has approached him for financing. Did you ask him about his other clients, darling?"

"I said I would not spy on him, Alexi, and I meant it."

He slowly shook his head. "You know, I was hesitant to use the adjective *loyal* in my toast. Next time, I will surely refrain from using it."

He had been referring to her infidelity in his toast, when she was as faithful as a woman could be. Of course, he didn't know that—and he never would. But clearly her refusal to spy on Blair meant as much to him as her supposed love affairs.

"What, no comeback? You must press him, Elysse. After all, my fortune is your fortune. It won't be hard to do—Blair is already enthralled. When will you see him again?"

She stared, her tension growing. "If you want to know when our next tryst will be, I do not know."

"This is now business. I want to know which of my competitors he has chosen to back. You thought you could use him against me? It has backfired, Elysse. I will use you against him." He drained his drink in a single gulp. "I am sure he will tell you just about anything you want—at the appropriate time."

She set her glass down so hard the sound ricocheted through the room. "You have your lovers, Alexi, and that only makes you a rogue, but I am a whore? Is that your meaning? Now I must prostitute myself for information?"

"I am a man." He was calm. "And I did not call you a whore—that was your choice of words."

"I care about Blair!" she cried.

He flushed.

"He is my friend—my dear friend," she added tersely. "Obviously we can't share even a quiet drink together without arguing. It has been a very long day—and on that note, I am going upstairs."

"Like hell." He sauntered toward her.

She could have made it to the door, but she simply waited for him, her heart speeding, her insides acutely hollow. "I told you, I don't care that you and Blair are carrying on right under my nose. Why would I? We married for the most sordid reasons—to cover up your tryst with Montgomery and protect your good name, which somehow remains intact in spite of your various liaisons."

"I know exactly why you married me," she cried, "so stop reminding me at every turn. And I didn't ask you to play the knight in shining armor! You took on that role yourself!"

"And now Blair is your knight in shining armor?"

She hesitated. "He is very protective of me."

"He'd marry you if he could."

Her tension spiraled. "But he cannot."

"Too bad for you both," he mocked. "You will have to remain star-crossed lovers till the very end."

"You know, Alexi, I have my regrets, too. I am sorry I agreed to this marriage—I was such a fool!"

"Ah—we finally agree on something." He tilted up her chin. She froze, as he said softly, "I want to go to bed with you. I wish I didn't but I do. And obviously, you are not indifferent. Invite me upstairs, Elysse."

His eyes were smoldering. For one moment, she imagined being in his arms as he moved over her, his mouth tearing at hers. She pushed at his chest, but he didn't budge.

"You must despise me," she whispered hoarsely. Desire fisted, making it hard to speak. "To treat me this way."

"I think I do," he agreed harshly. "But if we go upstairs together, I won't hate you, not at all—not this night, anyway."

Did he have so little respect for her? His words hurt so much! She pushed at his chest again; he caught her hands and held them there. Her entire body was pressed against his length. She wished she could be oblivious to his appeal, but it was impossible. Every nerve ending she had throbbed.

"Is this a game, sweetheart?" he asked softly. "Because if you think to inflame me by refusing me, you are succeeding."

She shook her head, aware of tears rising in spite of the

thudding desire. "I don't play games anymore, Alexi," she said. "We will never get along if you truly despise me."

"I don't expect to get along." He forced their gazes to meet. "I don't care about our marriage. I care about going upstairs with you, now. Have you thought about my terms? I played the proper husband tonight—now it is your turn to play the dutiful wife."

"No, I have not considered your terms, damn it!" she cried in panic.

"Oh, you little liar. You have been thinking about being in my bed all night." He laughed.

He was right. Those damned terms had haunted her ever since they had been raised, hadn't they? During the evening, his every glance had agitated and aroused her. "I don't understand why you are insisting on marital relations," she said distractedly. "We don't even like one another. You just said so. You have other lovers."

"God, you remind me of a nervous schoolgirl. Except, of course, when you are flirting with other men—then, you are as accomplished as the highest-ranking courtesan." He caught her chin again and looked at her mouth.

Her heart exploded. "Please let me go. I am not a courtesan."

He didn't release her. "I have said repeatedly I don't care who you sleep with. Even Clarewood has agreed you have every right to seek comfort elsewhere."

She felt her eyes widen as she trembled. "My God, *Clarewood* approves? What else have the two of you said about me?"

"That is all we have said about you." His gaze became languid. He added softly, "You are not on the tip of every man's tongue, darling."

She went still. Her fevered body warmed impossibly. As inexperienced as she was, her friends spoke behind closed doors and she was familiar with the nature of many sexual acts.

"What's wrong?" he murmured, leaning closer, his grasp on her chin tightening. "Do you want to be…on the tip of my tongue?"

His words should have been shocking—no gentleman would ever speak to a lady that way. And they were shocking, but not for that reason. She turned blindly away from him.

He let her go but followed her, reaching past her to close the door before she could escape into the hallway. She halted, paralyzed by a debilitating arousal. *What was wrong with her?*

She closed her eyes tightly. She knew what was wrong. She was twenty-six years old and she had never been more than kissed—and Alexi remained the most attractive man she had ever met.

He settled his hard body against hers from behind and she almost gasped out loud. He must never know that she was insanely attracted to him. She fought for composure, but failed to find it. She did not turn to face him. "I want the appearance of a successful marriage," she said hoarsely. "That is all I want." Damn it, she thought, leaning into the door and pressing her cheek there.

"I don't believe you," he whispered, nuzzling her nape with his mouth.

She shuddered in pleasure.

"I think you are ripe for my seduction," he said roughly, sounding satisfied.

She did not want him guessing her feelings! She did not want him to ever know how humiliated she had been, how hurt—or now, how attracted she was, against her better judgment. She whirled to face him. He said smugly, "I'm better than Blair. Trust me on that."

What would he do if he ever knew the truth—that she hadn't ever had a lover?

There was a terrible temptation to let her masquerade crumble, to turn to him and tell him everything.

The boy she had once known would be understanding. That boy would hold her, comfort her—and make love to her.

But Alexi wasn't that boy anymore and that mask of pride was all she had. She had to cling to it. She had to be strong.

He smiled at her and slid his arm around her. She started to say *no,* but his mouth covered hers, smothering the protest.

Elysse went still as his lips brushed hers, firmly, insistently—with mastery and skill. He pressed against her, deepening the kiss, testing her lips with his tongue. She hesitated—and opened for him. Urgency vibrated in his body, in hers.

He grunted with satisfaction, thrusting deep. The ache within her intensified dangerously. As their tongues sparred, she pushed at his shoulders, aware of one coherent thought. *Her pride was all she had.* "Alexi, stop, I cannot."

He started, breaking the kiss to look at her. Trembling, avoiding his smoldering eyes, she slipped past him, ducking beneath his arm. He slowly turned as she ran to the sidebar. She felt certain his desire had been so intense that he was somewhat shocked.

She hardly knew what she was doing. His heated kiss was all she could think about. She quickly poured another cognac, her hand shaking wildly. Maybe moving in with him had been a terrible mistake. There had already been too much hurt, too much humiliation and far too much pain. Now the desire was unbearable and it seemed to intensify every time they were in contact. If he pushed her, she would succumb, she was certain.

"I think you mean to punish me," he finally said roughly. "Either that, or you intend to play me until the very end. And if that is the case, you are superb, Elysse."

She sipped once, then twice, afraid of how her voice would sound. "Think whatever you want. You will do so anyway." She refused to look at him. She swirled the contents of her glass, still dazed from the desire they had shared.

"You're shaking like a leaf." His own tone remained hoarse and hard.

She took a deep breath but it was hardly calming. "Am I? I have already said I am *exhausted*. I think I will sleep in tomorrow." She finally glanced up. His eyes glittered with arousal. "And, Alexi? Do not think to seduce me again."

He slowly smiled at her. "Why not? Are you afraid your carnal desires will get the best of you?"

"No, I am not," she said curtly, lying yet again. "Unlike you, I am in complete control, always."

He laughed. "Really? Then I must make certain to be the one to shatter that control, Elysse."

She stiffened, knowing exactly what he meant. The intensity of her desire told her there would not be any control. She did not have to be experienced to know that.

"Why even bother to resist me? When we are in bed, it won't matter that we don't like one another."

"It will matter to me."

Suddenly his smile vanished and his gaze widened. "Dear God. Are you in love with Blair?"

She started, surprised.

"Damn it, why didn't I realize?" he said harshly, flushing. "He is so protective of you—you are so tender toward him!"

She debated setting the record straight. But if his thinking she was in love with another man would keep him away from her, maybe it was better to stay silent. She crossed her arms defensively and stared mutely at him.

"Are you in love with him?" he demanded, almost shouting.

It took her a moment to find her voice. "I won't even dignify that question with an answer," she said. "I am going to bed."

She hurried past him, careful to keep her shoulders erect and her head held high. Then she felt him following her into the front hall. She tensed, glancing over her shoulder at him as she reached the stairs.

He was very angry now.

She moved up the stairs but he paused at the bottom of the staircase. "If you are in love with him, you can tell me," he said, his tone suddenly cajoling. "I would never begrudge you true love."

He did not mean it and she knew it. There was no response that she could make to appease him, as he wouldn't believe a denial. "Good night." She didn't look down the stairs at him.

A moment later, she heard glass crashing.

Cringing, Elysse lifted her skirts and ran up the rest of the flight of stairs.

"Captain, can I be of assistance?"

Alexi looked up, a shaving brush in hand, clad only in a pair of riding breeches. Reginald stood in the doorway holding a breakfast tray, which contained toast and jam, coffee and the morning newspaper. He was clearly horrified by the state of Alexi's apartments.

"I have been packing, Reginald," he said briefly, scowling. One large trunk was empty on the bed. A great deal of his wardrobe was otherwise strewn about the room amidst broken glass from the mirror he had shattered the night before.

If he spent another day in the same house with his wife, he would explode. Therefore, he was leaving.

Which meant she had *won*.

"Sir, are you going somewhere?"

Reginald sounded shocked. Alexi sighed, so stiff with tension it hurt. "I am going up to Windhaven for a week or so. I wish to visit my father and my stepmother," he said. That was not quite the truth. He was leaving the Oxford house in order to calm down. He had never been in such a terrible mood. He felt like ripping Elysse's clothes off. If she spent a night with him, she might not be so impassioned for Blair.

Hands on his hips, he stared across the sitting room at her closed door. *She was in love with Blair.*

He was in a state of disbelief.

He had spent most of the night trying to comprehend it and he could still barely grasp the concept. All he had been able to think about was their childhood. They had been best friends from the moment they had met, despite her airs and the fact that she was a girl. The adults around them had been so amused. They are destined, he had once overheard someone say fondly. He hadn't minded; he had been pleased.

Everyone had always known that Elysse O'Neill loved him, even if they were just children. Even he had known!

Her feelings for him—her friendship, admiration and love—had been an inescapable and solid fact of his life.

But she was in love with another man.

Why else would she deny the attraction raging between them? She had almost come out and admitted it. In fact, if she told him one more time how *dear* a friend Blair was, he might put his fist through the closest wall.

But what did he expect? They weren't children anymore. A man had died because of them—because of her. And he had subsequently been trapped into a loveless and faithless marriage.

She was in love with his banker—the man who could and probably would finance several of his closest rivals. And on top of it all, she meant to be *faithful* to Blair!

The pounding in his head increased. He was furious—not jealous. He felt cuckolded. If she should be faithful to anyone, it was her husband. But no, leave it to Elysse O'Neill to be faithful to another man! Hadn't she deliberately set out to attract Montgomery? Hadn't she succeeded? Maybe she had known all along that Blair was the underwriter of his voyages. That would make more sense than anything!

He wanted to break something.

"Pack up my things, Reginald," he said brusquely. He had been trying to pack for himself, but he hadn't been able to focus. He kept seeing Elysse and Blair together in bed, Elysse in the throes of rapture.

"Sir, may I bring a maid in to clean up the broken vase and glass?" Reginald asked.

He nodded, his gaze trained on her bedroom door. He hadn't slept a wink all night, while she had surely slept like an infant. He should have never let her move in; he should have never agreed to host her party; he should have kissed her until she was senseless; he should have taken her to bed, making love to her until she was sobbing uncontrollably with pleasure—until she had forgotten Thomas Blair.

Alexi thought about the moment he had seen her on St. Katherine's docks. The wind had been knocked right out of him, the way it had when he'd first glimpsed her that day he'd arrived at Askeaton after his first China run; the way it had when he'd first laid eyes on her in Harmon House after arriving in London from Jamaica. God, he should have walked away immediately!

But he hadn't. He had stayed—and now, they were sharing the same house, but not the same bed. If she could give her favors to Blair, she could certainly dispense them to her own husband. He deserved something in return for his having given her his good name.

He stared at her door. Women never denied him—but his own wife had. In fact, a rival held her passion. She loved Blair, not him. And he knew that while he might be able to forgive her for an affair, he would never forgive her for falling in love with someone else.

Elysse didn't love him anymore.

"What will you need, sir, for your trip?" Reginald asked, having come up behind him. A maid was silently sweeping up the broken glass in the room, her eyes downturned.

"Riding clothes, evening clothes and perhaps a suit." He turned back to her door. He knew he should walk away; he hardly had to explain his departure or even inform her of it. But he recalled Blair holding her hands and worrying about her in the hallway. He pounded on the door. "Are you awake? Elysse! I want to speak with you."

When there was no answer, he pounded again, aware of Reginald fleeing. He banged again. "I am leaving town, Elysse. You have chased me from my own house. Open up the door and savor your moment of triumph."

The door opened and she stood there, her long blond hair falling in disheveled waves about her shoulders, her purple eyes wide in alarm, a piece of silk with two tiny straps revealing every perfect inch of her body. She was so sensual and so beautiful that his mouth watered, while his loins stiffened impossibly.

"Hello." He smiled, feeling lusty and nasty at once.

She took one look at his bare chest and started to shove the door closed. As if she were as bothersome as a fly, he ignored that gesture and walked into her bedroom. "Don't you wish to give me a proper goodbye?" he mocked.

She was blushing, as if she had never seen a man in such a randy state before. "Why don't you get fully dressed and we will meet downstairs," she said hoarsely.

He looked more closely at her face, no easy task, as he preferred studying every inch of her body. There were circles under her eyes. Maybe she hadn't slept well, either. Slowly, he smiled, hoping that were the case. "What's wrong? Couldn't you sleep? Wait, don't tell me, you were dreaming of Blair—no, you were dreaming of *me*."

"You're not dressed."

"Neither are you. I find it incredibly convenient." Alarm bells went off in his mind as he reached behind him to shove the door closed. He knew what he wanted, but he would never force her against her will. Still, he felt so mean at the moment that he was almost worried about it.

Especially as he fixated on the image of her in Blair's arms and his bed.

He folded his arms and smiled at her. "What are your plans for the rest of this day?"

She blinked at him as if he had spoken Chinese. "Where are you going?"

"Windhaven. You know, I truly liked that dress you wore last night, but I like your nightgowns even more." He cupped her shoulder; he couldn't help himself. Her eyes flew wide-open as he slid his hand down her entire arm in a sensual caress.

She trembled. "If you don't open that door right now, I will scream."

"Why? Am I frightening you? Are you afraid of your

desire, Elysse? Do not deny it. You may love someone else, but it is me that you truly want."

She wet her lips. Fiercely aroused, he caught her hand and began to reel her in. "I want a proper goodbye before I go," he murmured, meaning it. "Damn it, you are my wife."

She caught herself from falling against him by pushing at his chest. Her cheeks furiously flushed, she said, "I can't do this, Alexi."

She truly loved Thomas Blair. She was trembling and breathless and he knew desire when he saw it, but she had made up her mind to deny him—to succour his rival, instead.

He released her.

She jerked back a few steps, panting.

Itching to throw her down and run his hands over every inch of her—even if she fought him—he inhaled, trembling.

"I am going to Windhaven," he said bluntly. He turned and pulled the bedroom door open. He knew his decision to get away from her was the right one—for both of their sakes. "I take it you will hardly miss me. But I have one request."

She trembled, swiftly finding a wrapper, which she put on. He snorted. The wrapper did not cover her bare legs, and he could easily imagine what the rest of her looked like.

"You may see whomever you wish to see while I am gone—but not in this house," he said. "Use the Grosvenor Square flat or a hotel chamber."

She hugged herself, shivering. "I would never disrespect you the way you are suggesting—and I would appreciate it if you spoke to me with a modicum of respect."

He didn't answer. Instead he simply stared—at her

perfect features, her gorgeous hair, her petite, lush body. He couldn't believe what he was doing. He was going off to Ireland and she would be free to run about London with his rival—the man she loved.

For one moment, he saw the little boy he had once been, dashing about the gardens of Harmon House with his cousins, knowing that, in a few moments, they would all troop inside and she would be there, waiting for him. And when she saw him, she would smile and his heart would turn upside down….

It made him furious all over again, because this betrayal felt worse than every other one.

"Alexi?"

He turned and strode for the door, wondering if he hated her now. He hadn't meant it when he'd said it last night. Hating Elysse O'Neill had always been as foreign to him as walking on the moon. Now, though, he wasn't so sure. It felt as if his entire world had been toppled over somehow. The solid ground was splitting open beneath his feet. When he looked outside, he expected to see a sky devoid of a sun.

And it was all because of her.

She loved someone else.

"When will you be back?" she cried to his back.

He never faltered. "When I damn well feel like it."

CHAPTER THIRTEEN

SEATED PRIMLY IN THE backseat of an open carriage with Ariella, Elysse held her gold silk purse with her gloved hands. It was the first week in May and a gorgeous spring day, filled with bright sunshine and big white fluffy clouds. Hyde Park was packed with ladies and gentlemen, both in carriages, on hacks and on foot. Children were also present, some of them street urchins, others with nursemaids, all eager to play outside in the fine weather. An elderly gentleman was walking his King Charles spaniels not far from where they were driving. The elm trees lining the carriage road were lush and green, and daffodils bloomed along the walking path. For her outing, she had chosen to wear a pale blue ensemble with her aquamarines, forgoing any kind of coat or pelisse, and a jaunty blue hat with bright blue feathers.

Elysse smiled and waved in greeting at the two ladies who had just passed by in an adjacent gig.

Both women had been at the dinner party she had attended last night. They were longtime acquaintances and had been to her home on many occasions. Both women had remarked upon her lack of an escort—and then they had asked about her husband.

"Is Thomas Blair avoiding us tonight?" Mrs. Richard Henderson asked, her eyes wide and innocent.

"I wouldn't know," Elysse said stiffly. The innocence was obviously feigned.

"Really? But he is always at your side—or he was at your side, until that handsome husband of yours came home. We so miss his presence at these affairs, my dear, you must insist that he come! He rounds out the table, you know."

Elysse assured them that the next time she saw Mr. Blair, she would let him know that he was sorely missed.

Susan Craycroft chimed in. "I have heard that he escorts Mrs. Weir everywhere."

Elysse kept smiling. "I have found Debora very personable and charming. I am sure that Mr. Blair enjoys her company—anyone would."

The two gossips exchanged glances. "You are so gracious and forgiving," Susan said. "I should be rather jealous. Blair is such a catch!"

Elysse meant to walk away, but Beth Henderson's next question prevented that. "What can Captain de Warenne possibly be doing in Ireland for three entire weeks?"

As if Elysse knew! "I do believe, after so many years at sea, he is enjoying the company of his parents and younger sister." Elysse was acutely aware of Beth's obvious glee.

Beth Henderson drifted off with Susan Craycroft after that, but Elysse heard them whispering anyway.

"Lady Jane Goodman is in Ireland, did you hear? And she does not have a single Irish relation!"

"She must so enjoy the countryside there." Susan giggled. "I mean, don't we all love the rain?"

Ariella reached across the space separating them and took her hand. "You are so despondent."

She forced a bright smile, very glad to have her thoughts interrupted. She felt abandoned all over again, and terribly lonely. The hurt that assailed her on a daily basis was both old and new.

"I am not despondent, Ariella. I am tired. I have been

suffering from insomnia again." Another pair of ladies in cream-colored dresses and matching parasols was on the walkway beside the carriage path. Elysse waved.

"I can imagine why you can't sleep at night," Ariella said grimly.

Elysse did not want to admit to any of her feelings, not even to herself. To avoid that, she had spent three weeks madly redecorating the house—and madly socializing, when she wasn't too tired from decorating to do so. She usually went with a casual acquaintance. Most of the gentlemen were quite elderly—or very young and wet behind the ears. She had also ordered an entire new wardrobe. There had been days and days of fittings. She was planning a trip to the Continent—an expensive tour of the finest hotels in the best cities. And she had had three more supper parties. Each and every one had been a huge success.

Blair hadn't been invited.

He had sent her flowers four times in the three weeks since Alexi had left for Ireland. Thoughtful, caring notes had accompanied the flowers. He continued to worry about her and he wished to see her as soon as possible. He refused to give up, especially not now, when he understood her situation. He might be squiring Debora Weir about town, but Elysse was certain he remained her ardent protector.

She missed their friendship and his quiet strength, but she didn't dare see him. Alexi had been furious over the conclusion he had erroneously reached. Not that she cared if he was angry, but she was struggling to hold on to the pretense of their marriage. It was no easy task, not with the gossips on fire over the subject of their marriage and relations. And allowing Blair back into her life felt as if she were leading him on—and that reminded her of the tragic past, when she had so foolishly set her sights on William Montgomery, hoping to make Alexi jealous.

She was truly suffering from insomnia again. At night, staring at the ceiling, she thought about Alexi and Thomas, almost hating her husband for walking out on her again and yearning for the kind of love she would obviously never have. Alexi despised her but he was her husband; Blair was in love with her but she didn't dare go forward with him. It felt so terribly unfair.

When she did sleep, there were far too many dreams. In her dreams, Alexi taunted her and seduced her in their Oxford home, before making love to her in a frenzy. She awoke fevered and gasping from his imaginary lovemaking, just when he was smiling warmly at her….

She also dreamed of their childhood. He and his cousins would be rushing about Harmon House, the place they had so often met during family gatherings. The boys were always in trouble, and she was always awaiting his return. He would boast and brag about their exploits, and she would pretend to be indifferent, but his every word held her rapt. Their rapport was inescapable and unbreakable….

She almost wished she could forget those days but she never would.

She had even had a dream about William Montgomery. She had been flirting recklessly with him, aware of precisely what she was doing, and she had awoken just as Alexi appeared, furiously reaching for him….

Alexi's return had shaken up her life. It threatened the careful pretense of happiness she maintained, and she simply did not know what to do.

If anyone had told her that her husband could come back into her life after six years and hurt her all over again, as badly as before, she would have never believed it. But he had done just that. The abandoned bride was now the abandoned wife.

She could only thank God that she hadn't succumbed to his seduction.

During the day, she kept herself as busy as possible. But when an unexpected caller arrived and she heard the carriage in the drive, her heart always slammed to a stop—and she wondered if Alexi had come home.

A part of her was waiting for that day. A part of her no longer cared. A part of her simply meant to walk the tightrope that was her life.

"I am in the mood for some shopping. Shall we go on to Bond Street? Asprey has sent me a note, inviting me to view the new spring collection," Elysse said, feigning enthusiasm.

"If you bought every piece, it would serve Alexi right," Ariella cried. "I wrote him a letter. I told him in no uncertain terms that his behavior was inexcusable and he must return to town—and you—immediately."

Only Ariella would dare to speak to Alexi that way. "He hardly needs to return to me. I do not miss him at all."

Her words felt like a lie. She had imagined his coming home. Sometimes she thought about changing the locks on his house, packing up all of his things and leaving them outside, on the street.

And sometimes she imagined him walking into the house, going directly upstairs to her room. He would sweep her off her feet and lay her down on the bed and smile at her the way he had, years ago, and then they would kiss passionately....

"I think you do miss him. I think that bond you had as children remains," Ariella said firmly. "Emilian thinks so, too."

She was mad, Elysse thought nervously. The only thing between them was regret and an unwelcome attraction.

"Mrs. de Warenne?" a familiar male voice said.

She started, her gaze veering to Baard Janssen, who was on a big bay hack. He smiled warmly at her. She hesitated before smiling back. She hadn't seen him since their brief meeting weeks ago at the Windsong Shipping offices. She hadn't thought about him since. Now, though, she recalled a comment Alexi had made—that Janssen had sought financing from Blair.

"I saw you go by and thought it was you." His gray gaze was as bold as it had been the day they had met. "I had to gallop to catch up. Fortunately, I grew up on the back of a horse. But I prefer a rolling deck beneath my feet." He doffed his top hat at Ariella, but his gaze returned to Elysse. "How are you? It's a beautiful day for a beautiful woman to be taking an outing in the park."

His gaze remained uncomfortably direct. She rapped on the back of the driver's seat. "Driver? Please pull up." She smiled at Janssen. "I hadn't realized you remained in town. I am well, thank you. Have you been enjoying the sights of London, Captain?"

"I am enjoying them immensely now."

She turned. "May I introduce my sister-in-law, the Viscountess St. Xavier? Ariella, Captain Baard Janssen of the *Astrid,* from Denmark."

Janssen smiled politely at Ariella. "I am still hoping to give you a tour of my ship," he said, leaning a bit forward as he spoke. "I would enjoy hearing what you think of her."

She glanced at Ariella, who seemed unhappy with his flirtation. "I have been terribly busy, Captain. I would have to look at my calendar and see if there might be an available afternoon in the near future."

"I rarely take 'no' for an answer, not from a beautiful, gracious and captivating woman."

She smiled politely. "You are far too kind, Captain. When will you set sail, sir? You have been in port for quite a while. If I recall correctly, you brought cane sugar to our shores."

"Ah, a woman who wishes to discuss shipping with me!" He grinned. "I am awaiting the conclusion of some business affairs, Mrs. de Warenne, and then I will depart for Africa."

She started, as she knew no African traders. Surely, he did not trade in human cargo. "Will you trade in palm oil, then?"

"Undoubtedly—it is in high demand in the manufacturing countries."

"Yes, it is." Had Blair financed the voyage? she wondered. Was this the type of information Alexi had hoped she would glean from Blair? Yet Alexi hardly cared about the trade in palm oil.

He swept her a bow, nodded at Ariella and whirled his horse around, clearly trying to impress her with his horsemanship. She hid a smile. He was not the best of horsemen; it was obvious by the way he hauled on the poor horse's reins, his body entirely off balance.

Ariella clasped her knee. "What was that about?"

She turned. "Alexi mentioned something about Blair financing Janssen. I am a merchant adventurer's wife, Ariella, and I suppose I can't help myself. When it comes to trade, I am always curious."

"You and Alexi are so perfect for one another," Ariella cried.

"We are hardly that." She was wry. "So you wrote him a letter. Did he reply?" she asked, hoping to sound casual, as a handsome carriage pulled up beside their coach.

"He said he will return when he feels like it, and not a moment before."

She couldn't feign a smile now. "I don't know why I asked."

"He sounded angry in the letter, Elysse. What happened? Why would he leave right after your supper party?" Ariella asked. "Why is he being so rude—so insufferable?"

She shrugged, as if indifferent, when once again she was bitterly hurt. Every day, there were whispers about her—about them. She had thought herself humiliated these past six years, but now her humiliation was complete. The entire world knew her husband didn't care for her, not at all—and that he had no respect for her.

"Mrs. de Warenne, Lady St. Xavier."

Elysse turned, her heart leaping, to find Thomas Blair standing beside their coach, having just climbed out of the adjacent carriage. He rested his hand on her door and smiled at her.

She was genuinely pleased to see him and she found herself returning his smile. "What a delightful surprise."

"I think so, myself." He finally tore his gaze from her to smile at Ariella, who was not trying to hide her displeasure. "Are you ladies enjoying the stunning day?"

"We are trying to." Ariella scowled.

"Do not mind her. Yes, how could we not?" Elysse laid her gloved hand on his.

His gaze shot to hers. "Walk with me. I have missed you."

Ariella choked.

Why had she turned Blair away? She was lonely and he was one of the kindest and most attractive men she had ever met. And Alexi was running around Ireland with Jane Goodman, anyway.

"Ariella, I am going to stroll for a bit."

"You will make things worse!" Arielle whispered.

"I doubt it." As Blair opened her door, she gave him her hand to help her alight. "Do you want to wait for me? I can take a hansom home."

"I will take you home," Blair interjected.

"I will wait," Ariella snapped.

Elysse ignored her, tucking her hand firmly in Blair's arm. She was aware of his warm regard, his powerful proximity and his masculine appeal. He helped her over to the walking path. "I was wondering how long you would hold out on me."

She smiled a little. "It hasn't been easy."

"Then why?" His gaze was direct, but not uncomfortable like Janssen's.

She hesitated as they paused, face-to-face now. He still held her arm. "You guessed correctly, Thomas. My marriage is in a shambles. I am trying, without success, to keep up appearances."

He slowly shook his head. "Your husband is unconscionable. He should make an effort to hold up his end…out of respect for you." His gaze had turned dark with anger.

Blair never lost his temper, and she was surprised. "He isn't happy about our relationship, especially considering you are his banker."

It was a moment before he spoke. "I never mix business with pleasure or do anything to jeopardize profits. But…I am smitten with you, Elysse." He started walking again, his expression grim, and she fell into step with him.

"What does that mean?" she demanded. "Will you try to undermine him? Will you finance his competitors?"

He paused abruptly. "I do not intend to undermine him. I am a banker, Elysse, and I happen to like his balance sheets. As for my other clients, I believe that is privileged and confidential information."

"I am sorry!" she cried, reaching for his cheek. She had almost done as Alexi had asked—she had almost spied on Blair, the kindest gentleman she knew—a man she cared about.

He clasped her hand, holding it against his cheek. "I meant it when I said I have missed you."

For one moment, she let him hold her hand before gently dislodging it. "I am trying to do what I think is best."

He studied her. "I realize that. So does that mean that you will avoid me until your husband sets sail for China in June?"

She nodded. "I think that the wisest course of action, Thomas." She hesitated. "And I do not want to lead you on."

"What does that mean?" he asked sharply.

"I led someone on once, to make Alexi jealous. No good came of it," she said grimly. She thought she blushed a bit.

He took both her hands. "My God, is that what this is about? I have come to believe that you care for me. But your feelings for de Warenne are far more complex than I first suspected."

"No! I am very fond of you and I am not trying to make Alexi jealous. But my husband and I are in a terrible battle. I do not want you caught in the cross fire."

His gaze was searching. He finally said, "Do you still love him?"

"Of course I don't!" she cried, taken aback. As she spoke, all she could think of was how Alexi used to smile at her, years ago, before William Montgomery's death, before he had chosen to protect her by marrying her.

He slid his arm around her. "I will always be here for you. I am very concerned about you, Elysse. I have heard the gossips. They enrage me."

"Ignore them. I do."

"Do you?" He caught her face in his hands.

She tensed. Suddenly she was afraid he would kiss her.

He had done so a dozen times before and she had enjoyed it—but that had been before Alexi had returned home.

He dropped his hands. "I will not ask you out again until de Warenne disembarks." He added wryly, "And perhaps I should refrain from sending more flowers."

She smiled, relieved he hadn't kissed her. "I love the flowers."

As they started back along the walking path, he said, "By the way, was that Captain Janssen I saw, on a bay gelding, leaving your coach?"

"Yes, it was."

He halted. "Why on earth would he approach you? Does he know Lady St. Xavier?"

"We met briefly once, at the Windsong offices."

His eyes widened. "I don't trust him, Elysse. He is a scoundrel. Stay far from him."

She was completely surprised. "Very well. But those are strong words, Thomas. What has he done?"

He hesitated. "I refused to finance his voyage, and not because the price of sugar makes the profit margin a bad one. He trades in Africans, Elysse."

She was shocked. "He offered me a tour of his ship!"

"I hope you turned him down."

"I will now," she said. "How is it that our navy has allowed him into port?"

"He came to London with sugar, dear, and his holds are now empty."

Elysse felt her stomach roil. "Thank you for telling me the truth, Thomas. What a despicable man!"

"The entire trade is despicable, as is the institution of slavery itself. Eventually the world will follow Great Britain, and emancipate all slaves. Or so I dare hope."

They had reached her carriage, where Ariella sat, staring avidly at them. Blair's expression softened. "I hope I haven't upset you."

"I am hardly a fragile flower." But she had never met a slave trader before, and she was genuinely appalled.

"No," he said. "You are, in fact, the strongest woman I know. De Warenne is a damned fool."

Elysse got into her carriage, extravagantly pleased but wishing he hadn't brought Alexi up again. He kissed her gloved hand and turned away. She watched him go, and as she did, she thought about Alexi.

She felt cornered, even trapped. She was Alexi's wife, and she wanted a marriage she could manage and live with. Yet Blair wanted to take her as a lover. She had not a clue about what to do, except, perhaps, wait out her husband.

After all, he would run for China in June.

That meant he would have to come to London for his ship, sooner rather than later. And then he would leave her again.

Unfortunately, it felt as if she were waiting for his return.

HIS ARMS FOLDED ACROSS HIS CHEST, Alexi stared at the grand facade of his Oxford home as his carriage approached. He had spent most of the past three weeks at the Windsong shipyards in Limerick, where two clippers were under construction. He had been actively involved in overseeing several changes to their design. He had also begun designing a yacht, which he intended to use for his own personal pleasure. He had spent days at the drawing board. He had done some shooting, hunting and riding with his neighbors, as well. He had even ridden in a foxhunt— and had a sprained shoulder due to a nasty fall from his mount.

There had also been several nights of debauchery in

Dublin; one tavern wench in particular stood out in his mind, as did the night he had lost three hundred pounds in a poker game, not to mention his best pair of boots. He was usually a superb poker player—hadn't he won a sugar plantation in the Goree Islands last year?

He hadn't played well for the same reason he had spent so much time engrossed in ship designs and drawings. In fact, he hadn't ridden well in that foxhunt for the very same reason—he had been intolerably distracted.

He stared grimly at his rosewood front door. Yesterday, as he had prepared to return to town, the dark, dire anticipation had begun. He had left London because of Elysse—to escape her and his deep lust for her—but she had remained in the back of his mind for the past three weeks, no matter what he did or who he did it with. Now all he could think about was Elysse O'Neill and her lifelong penchant for annoying him by flirting with other men.

But she wasn't just flirting. She was in love with Thomas Blair.

Images of Elysse filled his mind. He no longer fought them. Some were innocuous, others were truly dangerous: she was a gracious hostess in blue silk and sapphires; she was impossibly seductive in a tiny silk peignoir; she was managing his household with dignity and grace; she was fending off his advances, her cheeks flushed, her eyes as hot as his own had to be. In all of them she was terribly beautiful—the most beautiful woman he had ever seen—and in all of them, lurking just behind her, he would see Blair.

These past few weeks, he kept thinking about how she had used Montgomery to make him jealous. Her affair with Blair felt like déjà vu.

He had done his damnedest not to think of her with the other man. Had the two of them laughed about how they were humiliating and cuckolding him after they'd finished having sex? Did they conspire to undermine him in trade, as well? Would she persuade Blair to raise his interest rates? To fund Littleton, from the house of Jardine's? For all he knew, the two of them were planning to run off together! She claimed the gossips had humiliated her. Now they must be talking about him. Not that he cared what they said—he held the record for the homeward run from China! No one would ever take that from him.

Of course, he knew he was being irrational. Elysse was his wife and while she might betray him by taking Blair as her latest lover—and daring to fall in love with him—she would never conspire against his business interests. She would never run away with Blair, either, just as Blair, as one of the realm's leading bankers, would never abscond from his power and responsibilities.

It was early afternoon and he wondered if she was at home. His carriage had stopped and someone was holding his door open. Scowling, he leaped out. He did not want to be returning home like this. She had said long ago that London wasn't big enough for them both. Now he agreed with her. The sooner he made sail, the better. She could have the house and her lover.

Reginald greeted him as he came through the front door, smiling widely, and obviously thrilled that he had returned. "Sir! I do hope your holiday was pleasant. You did not send word, but we have been expecting you. Will you be staying in this evening?"

He stared up the stairs, half hoping that Elysse would appear on the landing above, impossibly ravishing, but she did not. "I doubt it." He turned his attention to Reginald. "Where is Mrs. de Warenne?"

"I believe she went to London, sir, to drive in the park

with Lady St. Xavier. Later, she plans to attend a supper party."

He stared at Reginald so intently the butler flushed. "Surely the ladies had a proper escort."

"I did not hear of any escort," Reginald said.

"Come with me, Reginald," he said. He intended to interrogate his manservant thoroughly. The butler followed him into the library, which had become his favorite room. As he poured a scotch, he asked, "Where is she going tonight—and with whom?"

"She will attend a supper party at Mr. Bentley's, sir. I believe her escort is Mr. Avery Forbes. She has stated that she will retire for a bit at your sister's and change her attire there, instead of returning here."

He cradled his glass in both hands. "You mean to say Thomas Blair isn't escorting her?"

Reginald said, sounding wary, "Mr. Forbes escorted her to the theater earlier in the week, as well."

Alexi tried to decide who Forbes was. "I don't know him. Who is he?" When Reginald hesitated, he urged, "Spit it out."

"He is a very elderly gentleman, sir, and a very kindly one, as well."

"Elderly? What the hell does that mean?" When Reginald looked bewildered, he said, "How old is he, precisely?"

"I cannot be precise, sir, but I believe he must be seventy—at least."

Alexi choked on his sip of scotch. He instantly understood. Elysse was using the old man to cover up her affair with Blair. "Has Blair been to this house?" he demanded, setting the drink down.

Reginald went still.

"Reginald!"

"No, Captain, he has not." He flushed.

"Oh, ho. Do you take her side now? That is not a wise course of action."

The butler blanched. "He has not been to the house, but he sends flowers frequently."

"Of course." He had been right—the old man was just a part of a masquerade. He drained the entire glass of scotch, then poured another one, very aware that anger roiled in him. But he was not jealous—to be jealous, one had to care, and he did not give a damn about his amoral little wife. "What kind of flowers did he send?"

Reginald wet his lips, appearing confused. Alexi repeated the question, impatiently this time. "He sent roses, sir."

"What kind of roses, or should I even ask?"

"I believe the first time they were white, the second time they were yellow, and ever since, they have been red."

"Ever since," he echoed. "And how many times has my banker sent my dear wife roses?"

"Today would be the fifth time," Reginald said, sounding helpless and hapless, at once.

"Where are they?" he snarled.

"In her rooms."

He set the drink down and strode from the room, feeling almost violently pleased—as if he had caught her in bed with the other man. And hadn't he? He took the stairs three steps at a time. Her door was open and he saw the dark red, perfect flowers before he even entered. They were front and center on the pedestal table by the window.

He estimated five dozen roses filled the huge vase there.

An envelope was attached to the stems.

He strode in, so overcome with anger he could barely see, much less think straight. He ripped the envelope from the stems and tore it open, jerking out the folded note inside.

My dearest Elysse, I cannot begin to describe the pleasure I received in seeing you today. I am very pleased with the understanding we have reached. I look forward to seeing you again with great anticipation. With Vast Affection and Greater Respect, Thomas.

His hand was shaking. He wasn't sure he had ever been so angry. What understanding did they have? When was their next tryst? That evening? Clearly, they had spent the afternoon in one another's arms.

An image of her entwined passionately with Blair assailed him. He could barely stand it. Had he been fooling himself these past three weeks, thinking he did not give a damn about what she did or whom she did it with?

He thought of William Montgomery. Was she trying to provoke him yet again? But he believed she had learned her lesson from the tragedy of Montgomery's death. She wasn't using Blair—she loved him. He was her friend *and* her lover. Hell, he was her protector. She had admitted it. He wanted to find Blair and pummel him, but he would never act on his rage. He had learned that lesson long ago.

Instead, he would have to accept the unacceptable affair.

He stared at a chest where more red roses, clearly not as fresh, were in a vase. He did not see a note anywhere.

Alexi strode to the chest and scattered the books that had been piled there. No note fell from the pages.

He glanced at the night table by the bed, but only a lamp, water pitcher and glass were there. Then he moved to the small desk. The leather top was vacant except for a pen and sheath of writing paper. He opened the center drawer—and saw a pile of envelopes, tied with a pink ribbon.

He became oddly breathless, instantly recognizing Blair's handwriting on the top one. Then he sat down, taking the envelopes out of the drawer. There were four—and he slowly and carefully read each and every note.

When he was done, he had reached an inescapable conclusion—Thomas Blair was deeply in love with his wife.

He wished he knew what she had penned in reply. But did it even matter? He already knew that she loved him as deeply in return.

The jealousy burned.

Elysse was his wife; she belonged to him.

With a roar, he overturned her desk, toppling it to the floor.

CHAPTER FOURTEEN

ELYSSE ARRIVED HOME ALONE, at half past midnight. Her escort, Avery Forbes, was far too elderly to spend an extra two hours driving her back to her Oxford residence and then returning to London's Mayfair neighborhood. She had gotten into the routine of dropping him at his London apartments directly after whatever engagement they had attended. Forbes, widowed for almost two decades, was thrilled to have her on his arm for an evening or two, and he had proven to be a delightful gentleman—attentive, witty and respectful. She could hardly ask for more.

As she stepped out of the carriage, clutching a red velvet mantle about her shoulders, she thought about Blair. The banker had been at the Bentleys' with Debora Weir. They had managed to find a moment to step outside and chat under the stars. It had been innocent and entirely pleasurable.

She sighed, her toes hurting from her new, high-heeled shoes. If she allowed herself, she would think about how lovely it would have been to have had Blair as her escort that evening, and if she truly allowed her mind free rein, she would begin to think about Alexi. She did not want to go there. That afternoon, Ariella had given her a rousing set down for allowing Blair to continue to cast his attentions on her. Ariella seemed to think that Alexi would care. Elysse knew better.

As she reached the front door, it was opened by Reginald,

his expression worried. Confused, Elysse stepped inside. Before she could ask him what was wrong, a tall, dark shadow filled the far end of the hall.

Alexi was home.

Reginald took her wrap as Lorraine hurried into the foyer. Elysse stared at Alexi and he stared back at her, a slight, somehow dangerous smile on his face.

His powerful presence filled the doorway and the hall. His hair was uncombed and hanks fell over his brow. He had shed his jacket and waistcoat and his shirt was open at the neck, his sleeves rolled up. His strong, tanned, capable hands dangled loosely at his sides, yet he seemed ready to step forward at any moment.

Her tension spiraled impossibly.

"Can I get you anything, Mrs. de Warenne?" Reginald asked.

She could not tear her gaze from Alexi's. "I am fine," she managed to say. Then, briefly glancing at Lorraine, she added, "I will need help with my dress, Lorraine, before I retire for the evening."

Before Lorraine could respond, Alexi drawled, "She won't need any help."

Elysse went still. The tension between them was so thick that it tainted the air and she could barely breathe. The maid whispered an affirmative and fled, her cheeks red.

Surely he did not mean what he had implied? She had made herself very clear before he had left, hadn't she?

"We are fine, Reginald. Good night," Alexi said flatly.

Suddenly it was too warm in the hall. "Hello, Alexi," she managed. "I was not expecting you."

"Why not? Everyone else was." His gaze skimmed over her fitted bodice, then lifted. "You are wearing red."

She went still. Nothing had changed, she thought. That fatal attraction remained.

He slowly smiled at her. "Will you have a nightcap… darling?"

She felt almost mesmerized. Having a drink with him was a terrible idea. Wasn't it? Without stepping forward, she whispered, "How was Ireland?"

"Cold. Wet. Boring…"

Her mind raced. He was finished, then, with Goodman. She was relieved, but she shouldn't even care.

"How was Bentley's?"

"Fine." He crooked his finger at her. She inhaled. "I don't think we should have a drink, Alexi. Nothing has changed, and it is late."

"But you are so beautiful in crimson."

His soft, seductive tone was somehow odd. He hadn't moved since she had entered the house. Worse, his gaze was as predatory as a hawk's. She swallowed, shaken, deciding to be polite for as long as humanly possible. "Thank you. But it is late. You aren't trying to seduce me, are you?"

That slow, dangerous smile of his returned. "When I try to seduce you, you will know it."

"Are we returning to the arrangement we had previously negotiated?" she asked uncertainly. His behavior was so controlled! She did not understand it.

"You mean the arrangement we *failed* to negotiate? Where I play the loving husband—and you play the lusty wife?"

She heard a chilling note in his tone. Something was wrong. "Have you been drinking?"

"Actually, I began drinking at three this afternoon."

Alarm began. "Here…by yourself?"

He launched himself toward her, but his stride was alarmingly indolent. "Here…by myself. Elysse? I am not interested in pretending to be an adoring, dim-witted husband." He paused before her and she stiffened, incapable of tearing her gaze from his. "I might have agreed to such a pretense before, but *not now*."

She had the strongest feeling that she should flee to her room and lock the door behind her. "What has changed, Alexi?"

His gaze slid over her bodice again. "I meant it when I said you may carry on as you will, and I do not care. But I will be damned if I will pretend to devote myself to you while you spend your afternoons devoting yourself to Blair."

She gasped. "What are you talking about?"

"Deny it," he said harshly, leaning over her. "Deny that you did not spend this afternoon in Blair's arms—in his bed—showering him with your passion."

"What is wrong with you?" she cried, shocked. "I saw Blair in the park. We spent no more than ten minutes together—in public!"

"I saw the fucking flowers!" he shouted at her. "I read the goddamned love letters!"

She cringed. "You had no right!"

"I have every right!" he roared. "You belong to me. But you are in his bed—he has that perfect body and what do I have? Oh, yes, a retreat in the cold, wet country!"

She backed up. He seized her and jerked her forward. "Stop—you are hurting me."

"I don't care!" He shook her. "A dozen *gentlemen* have had you. I am your husband, but I am the one denied your bed!"

"Let go," she cried, frightened, trying to twist free.

But he pulled her closer. "I think you should run off with him. I swear, I won't follow! Ride off into the sunset with him, for all I care."

Tears arose. She had never seen him in such a rage. She fought to control her tone. "You are drunk and you are mad. I am not running off with anyone—we are married. Blair and I are friends, Alexi, just friends!"

He laughed at her.

She managed to leap free of him and started for the stairs. His mood wasn't just angry—it was mean. She had the terrible notion that he meant to hurt her. She glanced back over her shoulder. He was watching her with a savage look, as if he knew she couldn't run far enough or fast enough to elude him.

Fear stabbed through her. She lifted her skirts and started madly up the stairs—and tripped.

She cried out as she fell and he seized her from behind, imprisoning her in his arms. "Tell me the truth," he whispered, his mouth against her cheek. "You have enjoyed making me jealous. You have known all along whom Blair was—it was why you chose him to warm your damned bed!"

She tried to deny it, tears falling. "Alexi, no."

"I hate you, Elysse. If he can have you, so can I." He spoke harshly, but he released her.

She didn't pause. Lifting her skirts, she ran up the stairs, consumed with panic. It crossed her frightened mind that Alexi would never hurt her—but she had never seen him like this.

She raced down the hall, trying to listen to him following her, but her heavy panting was too loud. She raced into her bedroom and slammed the door shut, locking it. Only then did she collapse against it, tears streaming. Would Alexi have actually tried to force himself on her?

She had never seen him so dark, so dangerous, so angry!

And then she heard the door that led to the sitting room they shared opening. She had forgotten to lock it!

Elysse whirled.

Alexi was striding toward her, his face a mask of anger, his eyes blazing with raw lust.

She turned, trying to unlock the door, but her hands were shaking so badly she couldn't turn the key. He grabbed her from behind.

"Stop," she screamed.

He lifted her off her feet, crossed the room and threw her down on the bed. "He is in love with you. I read the fucking letters. And you love him. Damn you! Damn you to hell, Elysse!" he roared, towering over the foot of the bed. "You are supposed to love *me!*"

She twisted and started to slide off the bed. He caught her by one ankle and jerked her back up. And he came down on top of her, pinning her with his hands on her shoulders, his thighs over her legs.

She caught his shoulders, her gaze meeting his, and for the first time in her life she was frightened of him. "Alexi, you are terrifying me," she whispered.

He was breathing hard, but he stared, not moving now. Elysse heard the harsh sound of her heavy, frightened breathing—and the equally harsh sound of his angry gasps. She heard the clock ticking on the mantel. She didn't dare move, afraid of provoking him. But as she lay beneath him, their gazes locked, she watched the light flicker in his eyes. She saw lucidity returning. She inhaled. He would never hurt her. *Hadn't he promised to protect her, always?*

"He has had you…I haven't," he said hoarsely.

"No, he hasn't," she insisted. Her heart was still trying to erupt from her chest. "You are frightening me, Alexi. So much."

He inhaled and shuddered. His gaze finally moved from

her eyes to her mouth, smoldering now with desire, not anger. "How can you be afraid...of me?" he asked unsteadily. "I would never hurt you, Elysse."

Beneath his hands and legs, some of the tension lessened. She watched him uncertainly.

He suddenly looked at the tops of her breasts. As his thick lashes lowered, Elysse felt the change in him instantly. The anger vanished; only desire was left in its stead.

He lowered his face to the top of one breast and moved his mouth over the swell. "Don't be afraid," he murmured.

She gasped as he rubbed his parted lips over her skin. She was no longer afraid—she knew he would never hurt her. Tears blurred her vision.

"Not of me, never of me." His mouth twisted, as if he wanted to smile but couldn't. "I will always protect you," he said. "Don't you remember the promise I made? Elysse... don't cry."

But tears of relief fell. The young boy who had been her dearest friend—whom she had secretly loved—had returned to her. He smiled a bit and lowered his face, still staring into her eyes. When she could no longer hold his gaze, she closed her eyes, welcoming his mouth as it moved to hers.

He feathered her lips with his, suddenly hesitant and tentative. She reached for his shoulders, hesitant, as well, but certain of where they were going. Denying him now never entered her mind; she had been waiting for this moment for her entire life. As her body warmed, her heart turned over, hard. She had missed him. She had been waiting for him to come home. She still loved him. She would never stop loving him. Alexi de Warenne was her fate.

Their mouths danced together and paused. Elysse tightened her grasp on his shoulders, her entire body tensing with anticipation, with need. They had reached a terrible brink and were about to go over the precipice. He knew it, too, for he sat up and looked down at her. Overcome by his serious, intense expression, Elysse slowly nodded.

And suddenly he ripped off his shirt, fabric tearing, and her hands found the bare skin of his shoulders. He came down on her. Against her mouth, he moaned. "Elysse."

Desire exploded. With it came love. She slipped her hands across his back and strained for him, kissing him back fiercely. "Alexi!"

He moved fully on top of her and she started at the feel of his arousal, pounding against her hip. He slid his hand into her hair, anchored her, and deepened the kiss. Instantly, their tongues embraced.

Elysse wasn't sure what happened next. His mouth tore at hers; her gown was ripped from her body. He flung off his clothing and rained hot kisses across her face, her mouth, her neck and chest. When he anchored her hips with his hands and buried his face between her legs, his tongue probing and expert, she wept loudly and uncontrollably, giving over instantly to the torrential rapture.

He moved over her. It crossed her mind, incoherently, that she should tell him she was a virgin, but he stroked her, eyes ablaze, and she couldn't think, much less get the words out. A moment later he was buried inside her and she gasped in surprise.

She hadn't known that being with him this way would be so perfect, so stunning, so intense and so right.

Their gazes collided. Alexi looked as stunned as she felt.

All Elysse could think of was how much she loved him, and how right it was to finally have become one.

He slowly smiled, with satisfaction, in triumph. "Elysse."

"I love you," she whispered, holding his broad shoulders, wrapping her legs around him.

He began moving within her, slowly and surely, and he was smiling. "I know," he said.

She couldn't respond, because the pleasure was too great. She shattered, instead.

THE MOMENT HE BEGAN TO AWAKEN, he was aware of his dry cotton mouth, the ache in his temples, the sickness in his gut and he knew he had drunk too much. Sighing, he opened his eyes and squinted against the very bright, late-morning sunshine pouring into his bedroom.

Except that he wasn't in his bedroom.

His gaze widened at the sight of the robin's-egg blue walls and gold trim. He jerked and saw Elysse, lying asleep beside him in her bed.

At first, there was only disbelief.

She slept on her side, facing him, her long hair tumbling over her bare shoulders in absolute disarray, her expression soft and peaceful. She seemed to be naked beneath the covers, which were pulled only partly up her back. She was as beautiful as an angel.

Images tumbled through his mind, blurred and out of focus. He saw her writhing beneath him in release…he saw her running up the stairs and falling in her haste.

He sat up, shocked. What had happened? What had he done?

He choked as he recalled savagely carrying her across her bedroom and throwing her down on the bed!

What had he done?

Alexi leaped from the bed, and as he did, he noticed bloodstains on the sheets. He froze. Had he assaulted her—hurt her? He tried to remember the events of the night. He recalled her weeping in pleasure as he moved inside her; he recalled her moaning his name. But there was more.

Alexi. You are frightening me.

And he began to remember it all. He had arrived home. He had seen the roses and read all of Blair's love notes. He had begun to drink relentlessly—furiously. And she had come home, wearing red.

He turned almost blindly, found his trousers and stumbled into them. Then he looked back at her, his horror growing.

The memories were still hazy and blurred, but he sought them out and they came, jumbled and merciless now. He had chased her up the stairs—she had been trying to flee him! And he had thrown her down on the bed, brutally, almost ready to force her. She had been afraid.

Elysse O'Neill had been afraid of him. Did he really recall her climaxing for him? Or was that wishful thinking? Had he made love to her—or had he forced her?

"Elysse." He spoke hoarsely.

She did not stir.

Alexi found his shirt and put it on. He walked over to her side of the bed and stared down at her. He prayed that his recollection of last evening was wrong. He might be furious with her, but he couldn't imagine ever wanting to hurt her. "Elysse." He hesitated, afraid to touch her. But he finally grasped her shoulder. "Wake up." More memories flooded him—wildly passionate ones.

She sighed, rolling onto her back, and he stared at her bare breasts. She was even more beautiful nude, and he hated himself for wanting her all over again.

He tugged the sheets up. As he did, her eyes slowly opened. When she saw him, she blinked and then went still.

There was no mistaking her surprise.

He trembled. "Apparently we have spent the night together."

She sat up, clutching the covers to her chin, her eyes riveted to his. It was a moment before she spoke. "Yes.... Good morning." She sounded wary, uncertain.

"Could you get dressed? I would like a word with you," he said.

She nodded, her eyes huge and trained on his.

"I'll be next door," he said carefully. "Do not rush." He avoided looking at her again. As he walked out, one thought kept repeating itself.

If he had hurt her he would never forgive himself.

ELYSSE CLOSED HER EYES TIGHTLY, still in bed, recalling the entire evening. Mostly, she recalled Alexi feverishly making love to her—his passion as frenzied and frantic as hers. She thought of his smile as he took her into his arms to hold her tightly. She had fallen asleep there....

She hugged the covers to her chest, consumed with hope. Last night had been wonderful.... Alexi was wonderful.... She was so deeply in love!

Hadn't he made love to her as if he loved her—fervently, passionately, devotedly? She did not want to think about his history with other women, but she couldn't imagine him touching anyone else as he had touched her! She hadn't ever imagined so much passion was possible. While last night had been so new, he had been the Alexi of old; when he had smiled at her, his eyes had been filled with warmth, affection and love.

Surely this was a new beginning for them.

She trembled, the joy impossible to contain, when a knock sounded. Lorraine asked if she could come in. "Of course," Elysse called, snuggling up under the covers. Her entire body felt exhausted and strained, yet she felt delicious, as well. Now she understood the meaning of the word *sated*. She blushed, thinking of how frequently she had shattered in an explosive climax.

They were meant to be, she thought, smiling.

As Lorraine hurried in, Elysse grew thoughtful. Of course he wished to speak to her after what had happened. He couldn't have regrets—that would be impossible. But their relationship had taken a huge turn. A reconciliation of this nature, after six years apart, could not be ignored. Of course he would want to discuss their marriage, now that it was no longer one of convenience.

She smiled and wriggled her toes. Shockingly, her body ached in a now-familiar way, and she wished he were still in bed with her.

I am a shameless hussy, she thought. Then she blushed. She had told him that she loved him—several times—in moments that were highly inappropriate for conversation.

He hadn't declared his love in return. She hadn't expected him to. She had declared her love because she hadn't been able to help herself. But she hoped he felt the same way. How could he feel otherwise?

She bit her lip as Lorraine came over with a robe. When Alexi declared his love, she would be so deliriously happy she would probably float up to the moon. She felt certain that he would hardly do it in their upcoming discussion, but a part of her couldn't help wishing that he would. But wasn't it only a matter of time? Hadn't they loved one another since they were children?

Elysse got up from the bed, Lorraine pretending that it wasn't unusual for her mistress to sleep naked, with her hair down. As she slipped on the robe, she glanced at the specks of blood on her sheets. Alexi should know the truth, she thought, certain he would be thrilled to learn that she had been faithful to him. The one thing he couldn't stand

was losing to his rivals. But Alexi was a man of experience— he must have realized that last night was her first
time.

She thought of Blair then. He would be hurt when he
learned of her reconciliation. She cared enough for him to
want him to be happy. She might even try to find him a
wonderful, outstanding woman.

She hesitated. Alexi had been so angry to discover the
letters.

"You seem so happy this morning, madam," Lorraine
whispered, smiling.

She couldn't restrain herself and she beamed. Blair no
longer mattered, not for her and Alexi. "My husband is
magnificent."

Lorraine laughed. "That is what we have all heard,
madam."

Elysse started, some of her pleasure vanishing. "That
was in the past, Lorraine. The captain and I have reconciled." She was firm.

A half an hour later, Elysse walked into the sitting room
she shared with Alexi, clad in a rose-and-cream-striped
dress. It was one of her favorite day gowns, and she knew
Alexi would admire her in it. She was on pins and needles,
like a schoolgirl in her excitement to be with him again.
In fact, she had been pinching herself ever since she had
begun to get dressed, afraid that she had dreamed last
night. However, she wanted to impress him with her dignity and composure—she had no intention of acting like
a young, love-struck girl.

Alexi was standing at one of the parlor's windows, his
back to her, lost in thought. She assumed he was thinking
about the night they had shared. She paused on the threshold, although she wanted to rush over to him and tell him

that she was madly in love with him. Somehow she simply smiled. Feeling oddly shy, she said, "Good morning."

He turned. He did not smile back at her but his gaze skimmed her from head to toe. If he admired her in her ensemble, he did not say so. His expression was so poker-faced, it was impossible to read. "Good morning." He walked past her and closed the door behind them.

Why wasn't he smiling? She wanted to blurt out that last night had been wonderful but he actually seemed grim. "Alexi? Is something wrong?" Surely he was as thrilled as she was with this turn of events? But his expression was causing concern and uncertainty.

He moved to stand before her, his gaze searching. "How can you even ask that? I terrified you last night."

He was thinking about how the evening had begun, when she hadn't given his anger over Blair's notes a second thought! "It was a misunderstanding, but it was resolved."

"Was it?" He folded his arms, seeming very unhappy. "Are you hurt?"

Her confusion increased. "I am fine."

His face hardened. "Did I hurt you?"

She started, wondering if he'd drunk too much to recall what had happened. "No, you didn't. Alexi, we did fight, but then we made love." She smiled uncertainly at him.

"Oh, I remember," he said grimly. "No woman deserves such treatment."

She was in disbelief. "Alexi, it was a misunderstanding."

"You fled from me in abject fear—I threw you down on the bed." His gaze burned. *"Did I hurt you?"*

She hesitated, then repeated, "We made love."

His expression was so hard it might have been carved in stone. "There was blood."

He didn't know! She stared, wondering how he couldn't have realized that she had been a virgin. She began to tremble. "Yes, there was."

"Why was there blood, Elysse? Or should I even ask?" He laughed harshly, without mirth. "I chased you up the stairs. I threw you down on the bed. You kept saying 'no.' I forced myself on you."

She gasped. "No! It started out...terribly, but then we made love!"

He made a harsh sound. "You are being rather generous this morning. I certainly do not deserve it."

"You did not force yourself on me," she managed. "In the end, I welcomed you into my bed, Alexi, and it was wonderful. This is a new beginning for us."

"Really?" He became grave. "We gave in to the attraction we have had for one another our entire lives, Elysse. It doesn't change the past. It doesn't change the reasons why we married, or why I abandoned you, or the fact that you have love letters from another man in your desk." He scowled. "It doesn't change the fact that you love someone else, now does it?"

She cried out. Their lovemaking did not mean to him what it meant to her. Nothing had changed—except she wasn't a twenty-six-year-old virgin anymore! "I don't love anyone else," she cried.

It was as if he hadn't heard. "You are being magnanimous. I can't understand why. I have humiliated you for six years, and last night, I hurt you, I seduced you and used you." He spoke calmly, but he flushed even more.

She turned her back to him, refusing to cry. That was what he thought?

He did not love her in return.

"We can't go on like this."

She stiffened. She turned, afraid, and their gazes locked.

"You're not happy. Neither am I."

His words stabbed through her viciously. She tried to reach him. "We could attempt to reconcile."

He gave her a dark, incredulous look. "I believe that attempt has already been made. Obviously we are incapable of residing together as man and wife."

Devastation rocked her. She reached for a chair to steady herself, unable to speak.

"I disembark for Canton in June." He spoke briskly, as if addressing a board of directors or a group of investors. "I had intended to set sail midmonth, but I'll do so on the first. That's only two weeks from now. Until then, we must agree to a truce."

"A truce?" she echoed. He wanted a truce? Last night he had made love to her with more passion than she had ever imagined existed! Today, he insisted they could not live together; today, he wanted a truce.

"I'll even play the proper husband—if you still want me to." He walked past her, opening the door. If he noticed her shock, he gave no sign. "And do not fear. I will control myself. I will not come to your door again."

Her devastation was complete.

CHAPTER FIFTEEN

IN SHOCK, ELYSSE RETURNED to her bedroom and closed the door. She stood there, unmoving, blindly staring at the decor.

What should she do now?

Grief rose up, choking her. Last night hadn't meant anything to Alexi. Nothing had changed; he blamed her for the past, thought her London's most accomplished seductress and he did not love her at all. Yet *everything* had changed, because she loved him. She had never stopped loving him—she knew that now.

She had survived so much—William Montgomery's death, Alexi's abandonment and six years of gossip. How could she survive his indifference now?

He wanted a truce.

Not a real marriage, filled with passion and love, but a *truce*.

But she wanted Alexi as her lover, her husband and her dearest friend. She wanted a life filled with passion and love, not some damned truce.

She heard his footsteps outside of her door. Brushing at her moist face, she ran to the door and opened it. Alexi was already halfway down the hall. He was dressed for town. "Where are you going?" She heard how high and terse her tone was.

He faltered, paused and turned. He remained poker-faced. "I am going out, Elysse. If I am to leave for China earlier than planned, I have a great many affairs to conclude. I will be at Windsong Shipping for most of the day and into the early evening."

Was he making an excuse not to come home?

"I will go out for supper," he added. "If you intend to stay home tonight, you need not wait for me."

She had no idea what was on her calendar for that evening. She simply stared at him, wondering if her expression showed her anguish.

"Enjoy your day," he said politely, turning and heading down the stairs.

She backed up into her bedroom and closed the door. Then Elysse sank down into the closest chair, somehow holding back the tears, trembling. After having come so close to having his love, the pain now was simply unbearable. She felt certain she could no longer pretend to be his loving wife, when that was exactly what she wished to be in truth. Dear God. She did not know what to do.

"YOU HAVE A CALLER, Mrs. de Warenne."

Several days had passed since Alexi had made love to her and then dismissed their lovemaking as inconsequential. Her grief was dangerously close to the surface. She had kept to her rooms for the first day, incapable of going out. Then she had taken up the mantle of pretense all over again, going to luncheons, suppers and a charity event. It had been very hard to converse with her friends and acquaintances, to smile on cue, to make the appropriate responses. Several ladies had asked her if she was ill. Gaily, she had lied. Nothing was wrong; she had a touch of a head cold.

She had seen Alexi several times but only in passing, within the house. They did not speak, but he always nodded at her. He was polite, but his expression remained impossibly bland.

She was not interested in luncheons or teas, in supper parties or charity balls. She wasn't interested in callers, either. Now, she looked up from her small desk, in the cheerful parlor that looked out onto the back gardens. She had been reading a letter from her brother, Jack, who remained in the wilds of America, seeking adventure and perhaps a fortune. "I am not receiving today, Reginald."

"It is Lady St. Xavier," he said.

If she saw Ariella, the dam she had erected around her heart would surely break. "Can you tell her I am not well?" She loved Ariella as her own sister, but she could not manage a pleasant facade around her now. Ariella would take one look at her and demand to know what was wrong!

Elysse was afraid that, after all of this time, she might finally tell her the truth—all of it.

Reginald left and Elysse stared at Jack's letter, fighting a fresh wave of grief. And then she heard a woman's high-heeled footsteps pause on the parlor's threshold. Tensing, she raised her eyes.

Ariella's gaze widened. "What on earth has happened?" She rushed forward in concern. "What has my brother done?"

Elysse told herself she must not cry—and she must not confide in Ariella. She smiled but it felt like a grimace. Ariella pulled her to her feet, hugging her hard. "You look as if someone has died!"

In her arms, Elysse started to cry.

"Dear, what is wrong?" Ariella asked.

Elysse managed to step back from her. She whispered, "It is finally, truly over, Ariella. I have lost the love of my life."

Ariella's eyes grew huge. She cupped her friend's cheek. "I am here, Elysse. I am always here for you. Come, let's sit down."

Ariella guided her to the sofa and Elysse sat, accepting the handkerchief Ariella offered. She used it to wipe the tears away. It was so hard to think lucidly. There was too much pain.

"What happened?" Ariella took her hands and clasped them.

"We made love." She looked up. "I love him. I have always loved him. But nothing has changed for him. He doesn't love me—he never will. He wants a truce, Ariella, a truce! Until he leaves for China."

Ariella hugged her again. "I know you love him. You have loved him since you first met him, when we were all small children!" She released her. "What is wrong with Alexi? He loved you, too, once. It was obvious. You *must* tell me what is really keeping the two of you at such odds."

Just then, Elysse couldn't recall why she hadn't told Ariella the entire, tragic truth. "Do you remember Alexi's pilot, William Montgomery?"

Ariella nodded. "The American. He visited us at Windhaven years ago—and left rather abruptly, as I recall."

"He didn't leave Ireland after the Windhaven ball, Ariella. He died that night."

Ariella cried out, blanching.

Suddenly the past felt so close, and his features were so clear. "I led him on to make Alexi jealous, even if I didn't quite realize it. Alexi kept warning me to cease. I was such a vapid fool. He warned me that Montgomery was no gentleman. That night, Alexi found us, struggling, on the terrace."

"Oh, my God," Ariella whispered, clutching her hand.

"It was an accident. They fought and he hit his head." She wiped at some errant tears. "Two ladies saw me shortly afterward. I was entirely disheveled. Alexi married me to cover it all up—our tryst, Montgomery's death. He married me to save my reputation—not out of love."

Ariella inhaled, clearly trying to absorb what had actually happened that fateful night.

"I have realized over the years that this was an accident. I have stopped blaming myself, though I know how wrong my behavior was. But Alexi won't forget that night. And to make matters worse, he thinks I am in love with Blair."

Ariella put her arm around her. "Now I begin to understand. And I think I understand why Alexi hasn't been able to forgive you. He loves you so much, Elysse. He couldn't stand your flirtation back then with Montgomery. And I know you don't believe it, but he cannot abide your supposed affair with Blair. Maybe he could forgive you if you told him the truth about Blair—and these past six years. I have always suspected that you have been faithful to Alexi, haven't you?"

Elysse flushed. "He has been so cruel...I'm afraid he wouldn't care if he knew the truth. He might even mock me for remaining a virgin for all of these years!" When Ariella was silent, she added, "We have spent six years growing further and further apart—becoming vastly different people. How could I have ever thought we could recover our love, when he was forced to marry me because a man died?"

"You can," Ariella said fiercely, leaping up. "You and Alexi are meant to be. He *chose* to marry you. Have you forgotten about my family? A de Warenne loves once and it is forever. There is no changing course! Alexi fell in love with you when he was a small boy. He is angry and guilty and jealous of Blair—but he still loves you. I am certain of it!"

Elysse stood and faced her. "Ariella, the night we made love was the most wonderful night of my life. I thought we were starting over. I thought we would have a real marriage—one based on love, one filled with passion!"

"What did you mean when you said he wishes for a truce?"

"He has moved up his departure plans. He will sail for China on the first of June—not the fifteenth as planned—to get away from me! Until then, we are to cohabit as polite strangers. But he is not a stranger—he is my husband, the man I love. Once, he was my dearest friend."

"So he is running away from you?"

"Yes, he is."

Her brows rose. "That is very interesting, Elysse. Alexi isn't a coward. He is a fighter. But apparently, he fears remaining here with you." Ariella slowly smiled. "Now why would he be afraid of you?"

"You are not making sense."

"Alexi is as tormented by the past as you are—perhaps more so. And now he is running away. Hmm. So what do you plan to do about it?"

"I beg your pardon?"

"Oh, come, Elysse. You have now experienced passion with the man of your dreams. Surely you do not mean to simply stand back and let him sail away?"

She inhaled. Some excitement began. Why had she allowed Alexi to dictate the terms of their marriage? She knew what she wanted—she wanted her husband.

"If Emilian were acting like such a selfish, self-absorbed jackass, I'd fight. I'd fight him tooth and nail for what I wanted—and I'd start by seducing him."

She gasped. Images of the evening they had shared raced

through her mind. Alexi had been desperate to be with her. She was certain that their desire was unusual. Why was she allowing Alexi to run away from her? Did she dare take matters into her own hands?

"You are right. I want my husband and I want a real marriage. It is time to fight."

ALEXI WAS WARY AS HE ENTERED the grand foyer of his Oxford home. It was half past ten, and he had no wish to encounter Elysse. He had done his best to avoid her since the disastrous night when he had chased her up the stairs—practically forcing himself on her. But she claimed they had made love.

Apparently, he hadn't imagined her rapturous cries.

He had made love to Elysse. That was impossible—he was only capable of raw, lusty sex. Most of that evening remained a terrible blur. But now and then he would have a recollection of how he had touched her, kissed her, held her. Surely he had not been as desperate to be with her as he recalled. Surely he did not love her still, after all these years, as he once had as a small boy.

He was trying very hard to forget about that night. But he could not. He remained intensely ashamed of his behavior. He had frightened her with his lust and anger. The man he had once been had only wanted to protect her! What had happened to them?

Living with her this way was proving impossible. He did not trust himself to be around her. He stole about his own corridors to avoid her. The sooner he set sail for China, the better. The first of June was much too far away!

Which was why he had decided to reorganize the outward-bound cargo as swiftly as possible. Sixty percent of the shipment was already in their warehouses; he was working tirelessly now to acquire enough exports to fill the rest of his holds. If successful, he would be able to set sail at the end of the week.

He closed the front door quietly behind him. If she had gone out for the evening, she would probably not be back until closer to midnight. If she had stayed in, she would have retired to her rooms by now. It was unlikely that their paths would cross.

Reginald met him as he crossed the front hall; he refused to heed Alexi, who told him each and every day he need not wait up for him. "Will you need anything else tonight, Captain?"

"No, thank you." He stared up the staircase. "Is Mrs. de Warenne in?"

"Yes, sir. She retired to her rooms quite some time ago."

Alexi looked at the butler. "Good night, then."

Reginald looked as if he had something to add, but the butler flushed and walked away without speaking. Relieved that he would not come face-to-face with her, he took the stairs quickly, wanting to escape into the sanctuary of his own rooms. He doubted he would be able to sleep, so he would read until his vision blurred.

He refused to entertain his hazy memories of the night they had shared. But even now he felt an intense desire, walking up the stairs. He would feel that same desire as he lay in bed, trying to read, listening for her as she moved about her own rooms.

He walked through the sitting room, where a full fire blazed in the hearth. *That was odd*. Then he saw the table.

He halted and turned, incredulous.

The small pedestal table was set with crystal and china. Candles flickered in gilded candlestick holders. A covered silver platter was on the table, and a bottle of champagne was chilling in an ice bucket. "What the hell?"

The door to Elysse's bedroom opened. She stood in the doorway, clad in an ivory-and-lace peignoir and white lace slippers with dainty heels. He was stunned.

"Hello, Alexi." Smiling, she entered the sitting room, her long hair loose and flowing over her shoulders, silk caressing her hips and thighs as she moved.

He stiffened entirely. "What the hell do you think you are doing?"

She walked up to him and seized his jacket lapels, standing on tiptoe to kiss his cheek. Her breasts brushed his chest and the sweet floral scent she wore wafted into his nostrils. "We are having a nightcap."

Their gazes clashed. "Like hell we are!"

Hips swaying, she walked over to the table, removing the bottle of champagne from the bucket. He stared at her as she poured two flutes of champagne. He could barely breathe. He was not going to be seduced! No good could come of any involvement with her. He was leaving any day now and it would be good riddance.

She returned, handing him a flute.

He took it, only to step past her angrily and set the flute down on the table. "Why are you sashaying?"

"I am not sashaying."

"Is this a seduction?"

"Yes."

She sipped from her flute, her regard unwavering upon him. He trembled violently. "Why must I be added to your string of conquests? Do you want me to be one more besotted jackass groveling at your feet? Why are you doing this, Elysse?"

"I don't want you to grovel, Alexi. And I do not consider you a conquest—although you can certainly be a jackass."

His pulse was pounding so hard he could barely think. "And why are you the only one allowed pursuit and seduction?"

He inhaled. "What is wrong? Is Blair unavailable tonight?"

"I don't want Blair. I have never wanted Blair. I want you." She set the flute down and reached for her silk sash.

He was incredulous. "The door is open!"

She untied the sash and shrugged off the silk wrapper, standing before him in the tiniest scrap of ivory silk he had ever seen. "Then close it," she murmured.

He barely heard. He looked at her beautiful, flushed face, at the hard points of her nipples beneath the silk chemise, and at her long, lovely legs. "Why are you doing this?"

"I told you—I want you."

He tried to breathe and failed as she slowly approached, placing her small hands underneath his jacket, on top of his shirt and chest. "And we both know that you want me, too," she whispered.

Her body moved against his. She was soft and warm. She was female. She was Elysse. His arms encircled her without any intent on his part. He crushed her hard in his embrace, his mouth against her hair, his heart exploding. He wanted her so much! He'd lusted for her day and night since they'd first made love. He needed to be with her again! He had never wanted any woman the way he did Elysse. The past no longer mattered.

Alexi tilted her face upward. Her gaze was bright and hot, but tears sparkled on her lashes.

He couldn't think about that. He found her mouth,

covered her lips. A tremor of raw, excruciating need passed through his entire body. She kissed him back fiercely. He exulted. Their mouths fused, open and wet. He found her tongue, mated with it. As he did, he reached beneath the silk chemise, and clasped her naked buttocks, lifting her up against his manhood, holding her there. She gasped and moaned into his mouth, quivering and ready for him.

Kissing her wildly, he grated, "We will both regret this."

"No," she whimpered.

He lifted her and strode to the bedroom, and over to the bed. But he was careful to lay her down gently, recalling all too well how brutal he had been the first time. She smiled at him, extending her hand, long legs splayed open, an unmistakable invitation he could never refuse.

He ripped off his jacket and came down on her. As they kissed, she fumbled with his trousers, finally opening them. He cried out as hard hot flesh met soft wet flesh, and he cradled her face in his hands. He wanted to tell her that he needed her and he always would, but he did not speak.

"Oh, Alexi," she whispered, and suddenly he recalled her telling him, "I love you." He started. Had she really declared such feelings? But didn't she love Blair?

She murmured, "Hurry."

And because he was too inflamed to wait, he obeyed.

Elysse gasped as he filled her, holding him tightly. It felt so damned right.

ELYSSE SIGHED, AS THE WAVES of ecstasy receded. Alexi moved off her. She lay still, reaching for his hand, smiling as she found it. Her body was still quivering and aroused. "Alexi," she whispered somehow. She opened her eyes to look at him.

He lay on his back beside her, absolutely naked and

magnificent to look at. His eyes opened and he stared up at the ceiling.

Coherence returned. Her initial seduction had succeeded. Elysse turned onto her side, still holding his hand. She debated telling him that she loved him. Instead, said, "I love being with you, Alexi."

He turned and looked at her.

She sat up at his expression. "Don't you dare become angry now! That was wonderful and you know it!"

He sat up, throwing the sheets at her. "Yes, we just had great sex."

His words hurt. "We made love."

He leaped to his feet. "Cover yourself."

"Why?" She flung the sheets at the foot of the bed.

He seized his trousers, holding them over his heavy loins. "You seduced me, Elysse, when I specifically said I was interested in a truce."

"Yes, I did—and you were terrifically easy to seduce!" She finally took a sheet and held it over her body.

"You know how beautiful you are—how sexual! You know the effect you have on men." He glared.

"Why are you so angry? We are two adults—who happen to be married to one another!"

"Because I don't want to be married to anyone, much less you!" he shouted at her. He stepped into his trousers with fury, yanking them up and closing them with abrupt, angry gestures.

She knew she could not give in to the rising hurt. "But we *are* married, and I happen to want to be married to you."

He started, seeming incredulous.

"I intend for this to be a beginning for us. I intend to have a real marriage with you." She was aware her smile lacked confidence.

He reached for his shirt, but he did not put it on. "Intend whatever you want. I am not about to become the proper husband. Sleeping with you again is out of the question."

"Why?"

"Because I don't want a real marriage with you!" he shouted again, his cheeks turning red.

She trembled. "Why can't we try?"

He gave her a dismissive look. "You can try whatever you want—I can hardly stop you. I'm leaving."

She gasped. "Where are you going?"

"Back to the offices," he snapped, shrugging on his shirt.

"It has to be well after midnight!"

He turned his hard gaze on her. "My plans have changed, Elysse. I was going to tell you in another day or two, but I will happily tell you now."

Alarmed, Elysse hugged the sheet to her body. "What are you about to do?"

"I believe I can set sail at the end of the week." He seemed calmer now. "In fact, I am organizing an outward-bound cargo as we speak."

"What?" she cried.

"I plan to embark at the end of the week. Sixty percent of the original cargo is already in our warehouses. I have been soliciting the additional tonnage."

He meant to set sail in six more days!

He was leaving her, as fast as he possibly could.

"I am looking forward to the voyage—I have been on dry land for far too long."

"Don't go." She shot to her feet, holding the sheets in front of her.

His gaze slid to her hip and she realized it was exposed. Lifting his eyes, he said, "What difference does it make if I set sail a few weeks earlier?"

She panicked. "You will be gone for six months. We have to finish this!"

"There is nothing to finish." He started for the door.

She ran after him. "There is everything to finish, Alexi." On impulse, she cried, "Take me with you!"

His eyes widened. "I am not taking you with me, to China of all places!"

"Why not? Your mother sailed everywhere with Cliff!" she countered, aghast at what was happening. "Or do you plan to linger in Singapore?"

"I never promised you fidelity!" he exclaimed.

He would visit his mistress! "Please take me with you. We must resolve the status of our marriage. We cannot go on this way."

He was grim. "On that last point, I am in complete agreement. We cannot go on this way—which is why I am leaving."

She covered her face with her hands, dropping the sheet.

He picked up the sheet, his mouth hard and tight, and wrapped it around her. "As for the status of our marriage, there is nothing to resolve."

THE FOLLOWING DAYS PASSED in a terrific blur. Alexi did not come home and Elysse learned he was staying at the St. James Club, an exclusive hotel catering to London's most distinguished gentlemen and its wealthiest foreign visitors. Ariella's advice was to hound him until he came to his senses but Elysse could not take such advice again. She had seduced him once, and the only thing that had come of it was his hardened resolve against her.

She finally wrote him a letter, choosing her words with great care and utter honesty.

My dear Alexi,

If leaving for China is what you must do, then
I support you entirely. I wish you great success, as
always, and Godspeed, on this latest voyage.

Your setting sail cannot change the fact that we
are married. I will remain in London, keeping up our
home and managing our affairs, until your return. It
is my fondest hope that when you do return, we can
resolve the issues confronting us.

Yours truly, Elysse.

She had her coachman deliver the letter in person, two
days before his scheduled departure. The next two days
went by with excruciating slowness. Elysse was certain
he would reply, even if only formally, but by the evening
before he would set sail there had not been any response.
She was sick in her heart and soul. He hadn't left yet, but
she missed him already.

Ariella had come to visit every day with news of Alexi.
"I have never seen him so determined." She did not believe
that anything other than an act of God would stop him from
leaving.

The night before he was to sail, Elysse tossed and
turned, incapable of sleep, wondering if she dared go to
the St. James and beg him to stay. But her pride was all
that she had left.

At dawn, she was at St. Katherine's docks, seated in her
carriage, bundled up in a wool coat, staring at the clipper
ship. Hugging herself, she watched as his men swarmed
about the deck, preparing to make way. Sails were being
hoisted, lines untied. Alexi stood on the quarterdeck,
watching everyone and everything.

He had to have noticed her carriage, as it was the only one present.

All lines had been cast. Anchors had been set away. Elysse trembled and pushed open her door. Incapable of speaking to the coachman to tell him she would only be a moment, she stepped out unsteadily. Then she started down the wharf.

Alexi remained unmoving by the ship's helm, occasionally shouting out an order. Topsails flew first. Then the mainsails swelled.

Her heart in her throat, Elysse paused at the edge of the wharf.

At least a hundred feet of river separated them, but somehow, her gaze locked with Alexi's.

Please don't go, she thought silently, as the great ship began to inch forward.

He kept staring as the clipper caught the wind and began to pick up knots. Alexi seemed smaller as the ship moved away from the docks.

She choked on the pain of heartbreak. How could she let him leave her like this—again?

The answer was clear—she couldn't.

The *Coquette* was beginning to race for the sea. Alexi was only recognizable now because she knew it was him. She thought he still stared at her. Elysse lifted her hand. She didn't think he would return her wave, but then Alexi lifted his hand in farewell.

She had not mistaken the gesture. Elysse bit her lip hard, a new decision made. She could not let him leave her like this.

If Alexi was going to China, then so was she.

PART THREE

"Love Won"

CHAPTER SIXTEEN

ALTHOUGH IT WAS ONLY EIGHT in the morning, two clerks stood behind the front desk in the lobby of the Windsong Shipping offices. Elysse smiled at them as she entered the building. She'd spent the past hour huddled in her carriage, her mind racing. She would not allow Alexi to run away from her or their marriage. She was following him to China. She had never been as determined. But now she began to consider just what sailing alone to China meant.

No voyage was certain or safe. Pirates continued to plague the high seas. Ships were raided and seized, never to be returned, nor were their goods and cargoes. Crewmen were usually ransomed. Sometimes, crewmen were imprisoned for years at a time or forced into shipboard slavery. Ships were also lost at sea in gales or hurricanes.

Fear vied with hope. My God, she was intent on traveling across the world by herself. She either had courage she never realized she possessed, or she was mad.

"Good morning, Mrs. de Warenne. It was a fine morning, was it not, for the captain to make sail?" The red-haired clerk smiled at her.

"Good morning." She shoved all fear and anxiety aside. She *must* follow Alexi. "There was a strong breeze for sailing," Elysse agreed. "Is my father-in-law in yet?"

But she hadn't even finished her sentence when Cliff de Warenne stepped out from the corridor leading to the ground-floor offices. "Elysse? What are you doing in town at such an hour?" He swiftly approached and kissed her cheek lightly.

"I came to watch Alexi cast off," she said, meeting his gaze. "I need a word with you, please."

His blue eyes—which resembled Alexi's exactly—widened. Taking her arm, he said to the clerks, "We are not to be disturbed."

A moment later they were in his office, which took up an entire corner of the ground floor. Corner windows looked out on both the busy street and the even busier docks. A massive desk was in front of one wall of windows. A bookcase displayed various models of ships, and a sofa and two chairs were in front of a fireplace. Cliff closed the door behind them and offered her tea from the setup on a glass tea cart.

"I am fine," Elysse assured him.

He poured himself tea into a porcelain cup that was far too delicate for his large, weather-beaten hands, and gestured to an upholstered chair. Elysse shook her head. "I need your help," she said bluntly. "I am both desperate and determined."

"I am more than glad to help you in any way that I can," Cliff returned, studying her curiously. "So what can I do for you?"

She bit her lip. "I must go to China, Cliff."

He started, spilling tea over the rim of his cup.

"I need passage. I am praying that another Windsong ship will be embarking shortly." She wrung her hands, her pulse racing. In that moment, she imagined herself standing alone on the deck of a clipper ship—the only lady on board amongst a dozen or more rather scurrilous men.

He set the cup and saucer on his desk. "My God, Elysse,

why on earth would you wish to travel to China? If you wished to go, why didn't you sail with Alexi?"

She inhaled. If ever there was a time to be honest, it was now. "I asked him to let me share the voyage and he refused." When Cliff didn't respond, she added, "I cannot be apart from him for an entire year."

Cliff's gaze narrowed. "What exactly is this about? You have been apart from my son for six years. Your marriage is a pretense, as far as I am concerned, and a shambles. Why would another year make any difference?"

She trembled. "Because I love him. I can't allow him to continue to shun me and our marriage any longer!"

Cliff's blue gaze widened.

She continued. "I have tried to stop loving him, but I can't. I have loved him since the day we first met, when we were children! But you know that. I want my best friend back—I want my husband! You are right that our marriage has been a pretense. But I want a real marriage now. I am determined to fight for him—for us."

Still stunned, Cliff approached. "I can't tell you how pleased I am to hear you say that you will fight for my son and right the terrible wrong that your marriage has become." Abruptly, he embraced her, hard.

Elysse felt tears rise up. She loved his father and stepmother. It was so good to have Cliff's approval again. "I love him so much."

"I know you do. I have wondered for years if we did the right thing, allowing you both to marry to cover up the accident that killed Montgomery." He released her.

"I wanted to marry Alexi," she whispered. "To this very day, I regret my behavior. Maybe, if I hadn't flirted so recklessly, Montgomery would be alive—and Alexi and I would be happily wed."

"It was an accident." Cliff was firm. "A lady is allowed

to flirt. He accosted you, Elysse. If I had been Alexi, I would have killed him with my own hands. A man must always defend and protect the woman he loves."

She wondered if Alexi had been doing that and suddenly, profoundly, she knew that he had. He had loved her when they were children; they had just been too young to realize it. "Alexi was fond of me and, if given half a chance, he could be fond of me again. Yet he is determined to resist me."

Cliff smiled. "Alexi is a very proud, stubborn man. You hurt him when you considered marriage to Montgomery all those years ago. You have continued to hurt him with your various friendships, Elysse. I am not sure he will be easy to persuade. But I *am* sure that he has always loved you."

She felt her heart leap in exultation. God, if only his father was right! She bit her lip, hesitating. "I was a fool to toy with Montgomery to make Alexi jealous. I have realized that ever since that tragic night at Windhaven. I have even told Alexi how sorry I am. But he is so stubborn. He refuses to forgive me and he refuses to forgive himself. As for the gossip about my liaisons…they have been merely friendships. I have played a terrible charade these past few years to save my pride and avoid humiliation—and perhaps, to hurt Alexi in return for his betrayal."

Cliff finally asked, "Have you told my son any of this?"

"He would never believe me."

"He needs to know. I believe your affairs in the past six years have damaged your marriage even more than Montgomery's death ever did."

She hugged herself. Was Cliff right? She knew how proud Alexi was, and she was beginning to believe that he could be terribly jealous. "But he has had his own affairs."

"He is a man and there is a double standard." Cliff was blunt.

Elysse knew he was right. Men could get away with the most scandalous behavior, but no lady ever could. She walked over to a huge window and stared out at the busy street, filled with drays, carts and wagons. Beyond, she saw a ship's holds being unloaded; hundreds of sealed barrels were being stacked for transport to warehouses. Cliff came to stand behind her. "That's palm oil, from Benin. We cannot keep up with the demand from our factories."

She turned to face him, not caring at all about African oil. Only one thing was clear. "I intend to bury the past, for us, once and for all. I intend to repair this marriage, no matter what it takes. And I intend to love Alexi, no matter how he fiercely he resists."

Cliff slowly smiled. "Now that your mind is made up," he said softly, "his resistance might not be as fierce as it once was."

Elysse dearly hoped he was right. "Cliff, I can't sit in London for a year, awaiting his return. I am going to follow him to China. But to do so, I need your help."

Her father-in-law's smile vanished. "Elysse, you cannot possibly travel alone to China!"

"Why not? I could take a berth on the next outward-bound ship. When does the next China clipper depart?"

"The next Windsong ship bound for Canton departs on July 15 but it is not a passenger vessel. Such a voyage is inherently dangerous. You are a lady! You could be accosted by crewmen or, worse, pirates. What about hurricanes and monsoons? What about malaria?"

She paid no attention to his objections. The next Windsong ship wasn't leaving for another six weeks—she could not possibly wait that long! "If I took that ship, Alexi might be homeward bound by the time I arrived in Canton. Let me lease a ship, then!" But even as she spoke, she knew she could not afford to spend such a vast sum of money. It was an absurd notion to send a ship without cargo across the globe for a single woman.

"That would waste half of your fortune," he said tersely. "I am not sending an empty ship to China. Didn't you hear me? It isn't safe, Elysse. There is no way on this earth I would allow you to sail for China unless it was in my company or that of your husband. I must remain here, managing Windsong affairs, and Alexi is already gone. And that means you must wait here in London until he returns."

She was about to rebut him but his stare was hard and suspicious. She glanced aside. If he knew that her intentions had not changed, no matter the danger, he would move heaven and earth to stop her. She closed her eyes. Now, she must lie as never before.

Somehow, she looked directly at her father-in-law. "I don't know what is wrong with me. Of course I can't sail alone to China. Only a madwoman would do such a thing."

"You can write him a letter," Cliff said firmly. "He'll be in Canton for at least a month. If you send it out now, you have every chance of his receiving it."

Elysse managed to smile at him. Yes, Alexi might receive a letter—in a hundred and ten days or so. "Of course," she said demurely. "I will write him a letter, explaining everything."

ALMOST A WEEK LATER, Elysse sat in her closed carriage, the window shades half-drawn, wearing a heavily veiled hat. She stared at the front door of Potter's. As if on cue, Matilda exited the establishment, dressed as a gentlewoman, also wearing a hat and a veil to avoid recognition. Elysse breathed hard and sat back against her seat. Matilda crossed the street, keeping her head low to avoid anyone identifying her.

Thus far, Elysse had not found a passage to China. She had made two very careful inquiries through her housekeeper. Now that she knew that her father-in-law would never allow her to make sail for China, she had to operate in the utmost secrecy. She was well-known in the shipping district and she had immediately realized she would have to use a shill to book her passage. Thus far, the two departing China clippers had refused her. She prayed Matilda had met with success at the house of Potter, Wilson and Co.

Matilda opened the carriage door and climbed in, frowning. Elysse's heart sank. "No luck?" she cried, dismayed, already realizing the housekeeper's answer.

"Maybe you should reconsider, madam," Matilda said. "No shipper wishes to transport a lone woman to China, no matter how much you are offering to pay for the passage."

"I want my husband back," Elysse heard herself whisper. Even as she spoke, she wondered if this was the wrong way to go about finding a passage. She had approached the managers and magnates of these houses; what if she went directly to a ship's captain? She became nervous. Alexi was a wealthy gentleman, but many seafaring men were not. Still, wouldn't that work to her advantage? A more modestly backed sea captain might be amenable to transporting her to Canton for a hefty fee. His employers would never have to know.

"James," she told the coachman. "I'd like to drive about the docks and view the ships at anchor."

Matilda glanced at her as their carriage moved off. Elysse pushed open the window shade, staring blindly outside. Alexi had left six days earlier and she felt as if she were racing the calendar. He would probably make a swifter passage than most to Canton, and he undoubtedly meant to run for home before the November monsoons. With every passing day, she worried about just how long he would be in Canton, purchasing tea and then carefully loading it. She must set sail soon. She could not arrive in Canton, only to find that he'd left for home!

Her temples throbbed. She seemed to have a constant headache these days. She had never felt such stress. She had never worried so much—or missed him as much! Sometimes she dreamed that he had changed his mind and returned to London to claim her as his wife. But it was only that, a fanciful dream. By now, Alexi was off the coast of Portugal.

As her carriage rolled along one wharf, Elysse noted a large, familiar sailing vessel. The brigantine was at anchor, perhaps two hundred feet away. Her heart raced and she put binoculars to her eyes. She was right. "It's the *Astrid*," she said, with some excitement. Wouldn't Baard Janssen know who was sailing where—and when? These men knew one another and their plans well. Where had Janssen said he was staying? Would he help her? She was determined to persuade him.

Elysse was about to lower the binoculars when she saw a small cutter racing away from the Danish brig. She moved the glasses and saw Janssen standing in the bow as the cutter approached the wharf.

She thrust the glasses at Matilda, quickly took off the veil pinned to her hat, and stepped out of the carriage. She reached the wharf's edge as the cutter glided up to the dock. Janssen had already seen her. A moment later, as lines were cast, he stepped onto the dock. "Mrs. de Warenne! What a pleasant surprise. I might almost think you are waiting to see me."

She smiled back. Blair's warnings about the man crossed her mind. However, she had to trust him now. "I *am* waiting for you, Captain. Surely you do not mind?" She reminded herself not to flirt too effusively with him. She had no desire to lead him on.

He approached, grinning, took her hand and kissed it. "You are a sight for sore eyes. My heart is racing like a schoolboy's."

She continued to smile. "Somehow I doubt that."

"One of the most beautiful women in London is at the wharf, awaiting me. How could my heart not race?" He finally released her hand. "Have you decided on a tour of my ship after all?"

"I had some affairs at Windsong Shipping," she lied. "Being the daughter of a captain, as well as the wife of one, I cannot come to this part of town without visiting the docks and viewing the great ships here. I saw the *Astrid* immediately."

"De Warenne is a fortunate man," Janssen said, seeming to mean his words. "I heard he has run for China. I'd be reluctant to leave land, if I were him."

"We are in the China trade," she said primly. "And when will you leave town, sir?"

He seemed mildly surprised by her question. "In two weeks, actually. I have been waiting on some repairs to the *Astrid*." He added, "It is interesting—your husband has made sail, and here you are, seeking me out."

She ceased smiling. "I need your help, sir. Very desperately."

His expression grew concerned. "You seem very serious."

"I am. But first, I need your word that you will not reveal to anyone what I am about to ask you."

His gaze was searching. "Why do I have the feeling that you are not about to ask me for a tour of my ship?"

"Do I have your word?" she asked.

"Yes, Mrs. de Warenne, you do." He was solemn, but his gaze was curious.

"I am desperate to get to China. Can you help me find a passage? No one must know, for my family will try to stop me. I will pay handsomely, Captain."

He folded his arms and stared at her, suddenly thoughtful. A moment passed. "Hmm, a lady in distress. I can't help wonder why you are in such straits, that you must chase your husband to China."

She would not deny the truth. "We have been at odds. But I love him." Elysse stared closely at Janssen now. "I must repair things. I cannot wait a year to do so."

He shook his head. "As I said, de Warenne is a lucky man." Elysse could not read his eyes, or his expression. He finally said softly, "And if I can arrange passage, what is in it for me?"

"My eternal gratitude," she said quickly. "And unless it offends you, compensation."

He was silent. "I had hoped for so much more."

She was dismayed. "I am in love with my husband."

"So it seems. Yet I have also heard that you are in love with someone else—Thomas Blair."

She grimaced. "No. I have never loved anyone except for my husband. Blair and I were—and remain—friends."

Janssen absorbed that. He gestured toward her carriage and they fell into step together. Elysse prayed he would help her. His head was bowed, and she glanced at him repeatedly, unable to decipher his thoughts. He finally paused, taking her arm. "I can find you passage easily enough.

In fact, I believe the *Odyssey* is leaving at the end of the week. I know her captain rather well. If he is compensated generously, I think he'll give you a berth. I will make the arrangements for you."

Elysse cried out, so thrilled she almost hugged the Dane. "If I can get a berth on his ship, I will never be able to repay you—but I will try! I will certainly be in your debt!"

"Are you certain you won't accept a moonlit tour of my ship?"

She cried, "I cannot tryst with you."

"I suppose that is for the best—your husband doesn't particularly like me, and one day, I would love to do business with his company." He smiled. "As soon as I have arranged the passage, I will send you word."

Elysse wanted to hug him. Instead, she shook his hand. "Please hurry. The sooner I depart, the better."

When he had walked her back to her carriage and had left, Elysse ordered the coachman to take her and Matilda home. "It is done," she told the housekeeper huskily. "I am going to China—by the end of the week!"

CHAPTER SEVENTEEN

Off Cape Coast, Africa

THREE WEEKS LATER, Elysse stood peering through her binoculars on the *Odyssey*'s port side, not far from the bow, forgetting to be worried about the strong African sun. She inhaled, overcome by the spectacular West African coastline. Cape Coast Castle sat atop a rocky outcropping, a sprawling and formidable fortress, its nearly white stone walls sparkling like diamonds in the sun—except where dozens of black cannon were mounted. Snow-white beaches stretched out endlessly below the castle, framed by lush, emerald-green jungles, as far as the eye could see. Elysse estimated that they were three or four miles from the castle. A dozen ships were at anchor in the stretch of calm water that sat between them and the shore, and it was obvious why—she could make out the violently frothing white Atlantic surf as it pounded upon the coastline. Clearly, even the smallest merchant ships didn't dare anchor too close to shore and that surf. As she watched, some cutters tried to breach the high white rollers and make it to the beaches. It seemed a dangerous proposition.

The *Odyssey* was a hive of activity as her topsails were lowered. Still staring at the scene, Elysse noted a dozen canoes, Africans at their oars, being paddled about the anchored ships. Some were filled with passengers, others with cargoes. She watched as one of the cutters was overturned in the violent surf, spilling its passengers into the ocean. Breathing in, she watched the men struggling to make it to the shore. When they had succeeded, she handed the binoculars to Lorraine.

She had never imagined that Africa would be so spectacular. They had kept far out to sea, out of sight of all land, ever since Lisbon, intending to catch the northeast trade winds. She didn't know why they had come so close to shore now. She was uneasy. But at least the navy was within sight.

"Where are we?" Lorraine asked, wide-eyed.

"Cape Coast, which is our navy's headquarters."

"Are we stopping here?"

"I don't know. Captain Courier didn't mention any stops to me."

"The mainsails are coming down."

She glanced at the mainsails, which were being rapidly lowered. The crewmen were preparing to drop anchor. Why were they stopping?

She saw the captain approaching. The *Odyssey* was a three-masted barque, owned by a Glasgow company but captained by Courier, a Frenchman. His English was very poor, but her French was excellent, and he had spent the past three weeks regaling Elysse with stories of life at sea. He was charming, as most continental European men were, but she didn't trust him. She was careful to remain polite and proper at all times but she tried to keep their contact to a minimum, so he didn't entertain the idea of a shipboard liaison. He still insisted that she and Lorraine join him in his cabin for supper every evening. There was no possible way to refuse.

He smiled at them now, and spoke in French. "We are dropping anchor, Madame de Warenne." Blond and sunburned, he eyed her admiringly. "Have you noticed how calm the ocean is here? We call this calm *the roads*. The winds cannot disturb us here. But the surf? It is very dangerous, madame. Be happy you do not go ashore."

She turned to gaze at him. "Why have we stopped, Captain?"

"We must take on water," he said pleasantly.

She started. They had only been at sea for three weeks—and already they needed water? That was very odd. "How long will we be at anchor here?"

"Just a day or two. I must go ashore, as I have some matters to take care of there, but rest assured, we will be back under sail very shortly." He bowed.

Elysse managed another smile, instinctively reaching for Lorraine's hand. Her maid was blushing. She obviously found the captain handsome and charming. He saluted them and returned to the helm. She stared, wishing she trusted him and knowing she did not.

"What is wrong?" Lorraine asked, keeping her voice low.

There was no point in alarming the maid. "We will get a bit closer to the other anchored vessels, I think, before the rest of the sails are furled."

"I can't believe we are in Africa," Lorraine whispered, awed.

Elysse agreed with her. She could barely believe she had made it this far—all the way to the coast of West Africa. She was so glad that she wasn't alone.

Matilda had tried to insist that she accompany Elysse. But Elysse had thought it far too suspicious, as the housekeeper never traveled with her. She had told Reginald that she was returning to Ireland for a few months. He hadn't seemed concerned. It was usual for Lorraine to travel with her, but Elysse hadn't expected her to come all the way to China with her. To her surprise, the shy maid had insisted.

She was certainly proving her loyalty! Elysse wasn't certain she would have survived the endless days and nights at sea without the other woman's companionship.

No one knew where she was, except for Ariella.

"You are going after my brother?" Ariella has gasped in shock when Elysse had come to say goodbye. "You are chasing him all the way to China?"

"Yes, Ariella, I am following Alexi to China. I intend to fight tooth and nail for his love."

Ariella had hugged her, hard. "It is a dangerous voyage," she had cried. "You are so brave! But I would do the same thing."

"I'm not brave—actually, I'm very frightened."

Elysse had made her swear to absolute secrecy.

Ariella had done so, fighting tears. "We love you so much. I can't wait till you and Alexi return to Emilian and me." They had embraced a final time, until Emilian walked in on them. He had appeared suspicious to see them both so emotional and near tears.

Afterward, Elysse had made one more stop—one she had been avoiding. It had been time to say goodbye to Blair. She had called on him at his offices, which she had never done before. He had taken one look at her face, ordered everyone out of the office and closed the door. "You are ending things," he had said bluntly, his dark eyes hard and anguished.

"I am so sorry," Elysse had cried. She had taken his handsome face in her hands. "You are one of the best friends I have ever had—and one of the finest men I have ever known!"

He had gripped her wrists. "I don't want to be your best friend, Elysse. I want to be the man you love."

She had slowly shaken her head. "I care so deeply

for you…but I am even more deeply in love with my husband."

His eyes had become shuttered then. Elysse hated hurting him but there had been no other recourse. She could only hope that he found his true love one day.

She had refused to deceive him in the course of their relationship, and she wouldn't do so now. She had been evasive when she had told him she was leaving town, refusing to give specifics, not even insisting she was on her way to Ireland. Still, he had appeared suspicious and skeptical. "If de Warenne doesn't come to his senses and treat you as you deserve, I am going to call him out," Blair had said bluntly. Those had been his parting words to her.

She prayed that Alexi would "come to his senses," as Blair had put it.

"Are you thinking of Captain de Warenne?" Lorraine asked, breaking into her thoughts.

She thought about Alexi day and night, and it was always obvious to her maid. "I am thinking about home," she said softly. A launch, slightly smaller than a cutter, was being lowered into the ocean.

Her stomach twisted. Was it safe to be on board without Courier? Should she insist that she and Lorraine go ashore with him? As she glanced at her maid, Courier strode up to them. He'd put on a rumpled jacket and a felt tricorn hat. "I will be back on the morrow," he announced politely.

"Captain, perhaps it would be best if my maid and I went ashore with you."

"Madame de Warenne, that is impossible. My most trusted officers will remain on board with you. There is absolutely nothing to fear."

Lorraine looked at her and whispered, "I am afraid to go to shore, madam."

Elysse was already aware that her maid could not

swim—she had said so a hundred times. "I am placing all my trust in you, sir." She gave him her most earnest smile.

His eyes warmed and he bowed. A moment later, she watched him getting into the launch with five of his men. "Good luck," she called impulsively.

He waved at her.

For the next hour, they watched through her shared binoculars, breathing a small sigh of relief when Courier's launch made it safely through the breakers. Elysse turned. "I think we should retire, Lorraine, and stay below until the captain returns."

Lorraine agreed, and they hurried below to the small cabin they shared. It contained two double beds, one on each wall, and a small dresser and table. Everything was bolted to the floor. Immediately, they locked the door.

That night, as the moon rose, Elysse lay on her bed and stared out the open porthole, unable to sleep. The night was blue-black, sprinkled with stars, while a three-quarter moon smiled at her. The barque rocked pleasantly on the waves, her masts creaking, canvas whispering. She thought of Alexi, who had confessed to the many sleepless nights he had spent at sea, and her heart ached for him. By now he was surely at the Cape of Good Hope. Was he thinking of her? Was he, too, unable to sleep? Surely he thought of the passion they had shared. She hoped Montgomery's poor ghost was leaving him alone.

The masts seemed to creak more loudly now. She could almost see Alexi alone at the helm of his ship, his face turned up to the moon, and she wished desperately that she were with him. She would give anything to be in his arms just then.

Wood groaned.

Elysse sat upright, careful not to hit her head on the

low ceiling. The small hold behind their locked door was absolutely silent. But she was certain she had just heard a footstep.

She strained to hear. Lorraine was asleep, breathing softly. The canvas continued to whisper, the masts to creak.

Then she heard the latch on her door rattle.

Elysse dived for the satchel she slept with, taking out a loaded pistol. As she did, she heard the latch being wrenched off the door.

Lorraine awoke, crying out.

The door was jerked open.

"Come in and I will shoot," Elysse cried, her heart pounding in fright. In the dark, her gaze met a pair of wide, unblinking eyes.

It took her one moment to comprehend that a huge African man stood there. He rushed toward her, seizing her wrist. As Elysse fired, other men rushed into the cabin. Lorraine's scream was cut off. The pistol was wrenched from Elysse's hands and a sack was thrown over her head.

In panic and terror, Elysse fought the pairs of hands clutching at her. Someone spoke harshly to her in a native tongue. She struck blindly at what she hoped was his face and eyes with her nails. She felt a terrible blow on the back of her head.

Pain consumed her. And then the darkness claimed her.

CHAPTER EIGHTEEN

THE LONDON DOCKS HAD never been such a welcome sight. Alexi stood by his pilot at the clipper's helm, barely able to remain still as four great anchors were lowered into the Thames. He had done the unthinkable. With a full cargo bound for China, he had turned his ship around.

He had left these exact docks four weeks ago, but had only run as far as Gibraltar.

His men had been on the verge of a mutiny. Every man jack on board knew the cost of returning to London with the *Coquette*'s holds filled with wares destined for foreign markets.

Elysse's image flashed in his mind, as he had last seen her, a tiny blue speck on St. Katherine's docks, waving forlornly at him. He had raised binoculars at the very last moment, to take one final look at her.

Such a terrible pain had pierced his chest that he had wondered if he had been shot.

But no gunshot had sounded. It was the pain of heartache.

He glanced around at his ship. "Haul the topsails a-bowline," he said tersely. "We'll hang all sails to dry."

"Aye, sir." One of his officers rushed off to obey him.

He had prevented a mutiny by personally guaranteeing each crewman adequate compensation for the four-week voyage. Those funds would come out of his hard-earned fortune. "Lower the jolly," he said roughly.

Elysse's image seared his mind again, but this time as he had last seen her at Oxford House, her expression stricken when he had told her he was leaving at the end of the week.

We made love…it was wonderful.

Nothing has changed.

This is a new beginning for us…

He inhaled, the small jolly boat rocking in the river below the clipper ship. Elysse had told him that she loved him several times. But she loved Blair, didn't she?

He could not stand the idea of her with Blair. Elysse belonged to him—she always had.

She was his wife.

He recalled the day they exchanged vows at Askeaton Hall. He hadn't wanted to marry her. He had been young and very angry, but he had been determined to protect her, at any cost.

He had spent the past two weeks making a choice: walk away from their marriage, allowing her to return to Blair, or take up his duties as her husband and fulfill the vows he had made six long years ago. He didn't want to be married—did he? He was a bachelor with an eye for the ladies, and a sailor—the sea was his mistress! But he simply couldn't tolerate the notion of her with Blair or anyone else. Yet there was more.

He had to face his deepest feelings. He had loved Elysse since they had first met as children; he had never forgotten the promise he had made to her, that long-ago day at Errol Castle. Although spoiled and vain, an impossible flirt, he had loved her then and he still did.

As he had recalled the past few months since his return to London, over and over again, he began to consider how much she had changed. He had been so angry that he hadn't wanted to see the changes. Had she flirted with anyone, a single time? Not that he had witnessed. Had she been self-involved? Self-centered? Vain? The more he replayed their every encounter, the more he began to see how she had matured into a gracious gentlewoman. Even her relationship with Blair seemed more of a mature friendship than a reckless affair of passion.

In fact, if he forgot the child or young woman she'd been, he might not even recognize her now!

None of that even mattered. If she remained a reckless, spoiled flirt, he would love her just as much. That was his deepest, darkest secret.

And that meant he had to turn the *Coquette* around and claim her as his wife.

He felt as if he were on a cliff now, about to step over the precipice. He loved her and he wanted her, but the thought of taking up the responsibilities of a married man was terrifying. The moment he reconciled with her, his life would change forever.

Shoving all reflection aside, Alexi swiftly stepped down the rope ladder into the small, single-masted boat riding against the clipper. He moved easily, not missing a step. He had been climbing down rope ladders and up rigging and masts since he was a small boy, and he'd climbed into similar launches in far more treacherous waters. He nodded at his two oarsmen. As the jolly boat moved toward the docks, his heart pounded. Oxford House was an hour away; she was an hour away….

He didn't know what he would say to her, or how they would manage a real marriage, considering all the hurt and pain caused by their past actions. He wished he could change the past. He also wished that her lovers didn't stand between them, but he was prepared to forgive her. After all, he had taken his share of lovers, and unlike most men, he did not believe that women had to adhere to higher standards. Still, her past bothered him. Foolishly, he wished that she had loved him enough to wait for him to come to his senses and return to her as her husband.

He only knew that they would have to start this reconciliation somehow, because he wasn't ever allowing her to stray from him again.

"Alexi."

The small boat was butting the pier when he heard his father's voice. He looked up, expecting a tirade. Cliff was clearly shocked to see him. Before his father could ask what had happened, Alexi leaped out of the boat. "I will pay for the cost of the voyage, and make sail for Canton within the week."

Color flooded his father's cheeks. "When I heard that the *Coquette* was returning, I thought there had been a disaster! Is the crew intact? You have not been stricken with the plague or malaria? The ship is intact? You were not bombarded by cannon and attacked by pirates?"

"The crew is whole, the *Coquette* is intact," he said, uncomfortable. Alexi did not blame his father for being furious. "I have affairs I must settle—personal ones."

Cliff blinked, incredulous.

Then, to Alexi's shock, his father began to smile. "Really? You have *personal* affairs to manage?"

Why wasn't his father shouting at him for the tremendous waste of time, finances and resources his actions had cost them? For the damage he was causing to Windsong's reputation? For the ire that their backers and clients would surely have? "I left in a temper," he said gruffly. "I must speak to my wife and patch things up before I am gone for most of the next year."

Cliff clasped his shoulder. "I am so pleased to hear you say that! And I think she will be very happy to see you. But she isn't in town, Alexi. She has gone to Ireland."

He started. Why would Elysse go to Ireland? She had nothing to do in the country. Suspicion and doubt began. "Are you certain?"

"Of course I am," Cliff said easily. "She did not speak with me or Amanda, but she was very explicit with your staff. And she told Ariella that she wishes for a period of seclusion."

"Is Thomas Blair in town?" He could not stop himself from asking. Had they gone off together? Was he comforting her even now?

Cliff darkened. "I don't know. Alexi, you must give Elysse the benefit of the doubt. After speaking with her, I certainly do."

"Really?" He felt the tidal wave of anger rushing over him. He fought it. "I may have abandoned her for the past six years, but enough is enough. I am determined to reconcile. That means her friendship with Blair is over. I will not have it otherwise." He saw Cliff's small carriage at the end of the wharf. "May I use your vehicle? I won't be long."

"Yes, you may take it. But where are you going? To Blair's banking offices?" Cliff seized his shoulder. "Take a moment to think clearly. Do not make this impasse with your wife worse. Alexi, you should discuss everything calmly and sensibly with her before you do anything else."

Alexi ignored him, already striding up the wharf toward the curricle. Was she with Blair? He was amazed, because he recognized how hurt he was at the notion, and how jealous. *I love you.* Had she meant those words? She *had* changed; he saw that now. Perhaps she had truly gone to Askeaton to seclude herself there. As he drove away from the docks, he recalled more of their conversations and the letter she had written to him.

*I don't love anyone else...we made love...it was
wonderful.*

I don't want Blair. I want you....

*I want to be married to you.... I intend for this to be a
beginning for us...*

*Your setting sail cannot change the fact that we are
married.... I will remain in London, managing our affairs,
until your return....*

The woman who had spoken so sincerely was mature,
considerate and thoughtful—a woman of experience and
substance, a woman with an iron will. Was it possible that
she loved him? She could not have so blithely gone back
to Blair, not if he was right about her.

She was waiting for him—and all he had to do was find
her.

Of course, Blair might know her whereabouts. And that
insane part of him wanted to be certain that Blair was in
town.

Blair's offices were just off Bond Street. Alexi was
summoned into the banker's office and he was relieved
to discover Blair there. The moment they locked gazes,
he knew that Thomas Blair was no longer his rival. Every
instinct he had told him that the affair had ended.

Blair gestured at a chair, settling his hip on the edge of
his desk. "So, you have returned to town. Where is your
ship—and cargo?"

Alexi did not sit down. "At anchor in the Thames. I'll
embark within the week. I came back to speak with my
wife. Where is she?"

Blair stood. "I don't know. But I am damned glad you
have come to your senses. She is a magnificent woman,
and she deserves your trust, your consideration and your
affection."

Alexi started. "What do you mean you do not know where she is?"

"She came here to say goodbye, but she was in an unusual mood—dispirited and anxious. Most of all, she was evasive. I could not get her to elaborate on her plans—she merely said she must leave town for a while."

"Elysse has told everyone that she has gone to Ireland." But why not tell Blair?

Blair raised his brows. "She did not tell me. She has never lied to me, and I, for one, do not believe that she has gone to the country. I am worried, de Warenne."

Dread began. Elysse was not the kind of woman to isolate herself in the country. But where would she go? She *had* to be in Ireland!

I will remain in London, managing our affairs, until your return....

"Could she still be in town—in seclusion?"

"That would be a difficult feat. Perhaps her housekeeper would know. I did try to speak with Matilda, but to no avail," he said. "Surely she confided in someone."

Alexi looked at him. *Ariella would know where she had gone.* "You're right. My sister is her best friend and confidante," he said swiftly, already heading for the door.

Blair followed, seizing his arm. "There's one more thing."

Because they were no longer rivals, Alexi did not shake him off.

Blair dropped his hand. "This is for her sake, not yours. We were never more than friends."

Alexi inhaled, aware of the relief flooding him. "But you are in love with her."

"Yes, I am. But I can see I am not the only one."

He though he felt himself flush. "I appreciate your candour," he said, meaning it. He held out his hand. "I have known Elysse for a lifetime. Some bonds cannot be broken, no matter the damage done. I cannot be sorry for your loss, Blair, but I wish you well."

Blair took his hand. "I am glad to hear you say that. Good luck, de Warenne," he said.

The next hour was the longest carriage ride of his life, as his mind twisted and turned, considering every possibility. He wondered if Elysse had gone to Paris. Almost every woman he knew sought refuge from their heartache in the distraction of shopping.

He didn't wait to be announced at Ariella's house. He barged into the library where he knew he would find her with a book. She dropped the text, sitting up on the sofa where she had been reclining. "Alexi! You're not at sea!" She turned starkly white.

All of his suspicions were aroused. "I am right. You know where Elysse is!" he accused, striding to her as she leaped to her feet.

"Why aren't you bound for China?" she gasped.

"Because I need to speak to Elysse. If you must know, I have finally come to my senses—I wish to reconcile with her."

Before he had even finished the sentence, Ariella threw herself into his arms, hugging him wildly. "She loves you so much and I know how much you love her! I am so happy for you both! You misjudge her terribly, you know."

He set her apart, sternly. "You know where she is, don't you?" He had lost all patience now. "I am getting damned worried, Ariella! Did Elysse go to Ireland? And if not, where the hell is she? Has she gone to France?"

Ariella blanched and her expression filled him with dread. "Oh, dear. Alexi, try to be calm!"

He knew that he was going to be very upset when he learned of her whereabouts. He shook her once. "I will be calm when you tell me where she is, so I can find her and patch our marriage back together."

She blurted, "She has sailed to China!"

His horror knew no bounds.

PAIN BEGAN, throbbing dully in the back of her head.

Elysse began to awaken, feeling weighted down, as if her hands and legs were tied. The pain sharpened. Somehow she knew she must awaken, but she was in a thick dark fog. She had to swim through it, toward the gray light. She felt something sharp beneath her back and buttocks and grew aware of the rocking motion of the ocean. The ocean? A blurred and hazy memory tried to form. Finally conscious, she opened her eyes, blinking.

Brilliant golden sunshine blinded her.

It took Elysse a moment to realize she lay on her back, staring up at a cloudless blue sky and the blazing sun. Lorraine sat with her back against the side of a narrow canoe, peering anxiously at her, her face sunburned. Three very dark men—Africans—clad only in loincloths, paddled the canoe.

And Elysse recalled the door to her cabin being broken down, and the African man she had tried to shoot. She cried out.

"Are you all right?" Lorraine cried. "Oh, madam, I feared you might be dead!"

Elysse realized her hands and ankles were loosely tied. She somehow squirmed to sit up. Pain exploded in her head—fear exploded in her heart. The African who was not rowing looked at her and spoke. "Sit still."

She had been abducted.

Breathing hard, finally sitting up, Elysse realized the canoe was being paddled toward the beach. Ahead, she saw the violent, frothing surf, as the breakers beat upon the sandy shore. The beach was deserted except for a handful of men, clustered together, as if waiting for them. The canoe remained in the "roads," but the dozens of merchant ships and few British naval vessels that had been at anchor were nowhere to be seen. In fact, their small canoe was the only vessel in sight.

She jerked her frightened gaze back to the coast. A stone fortress sat at the top of a hill on the closest beach, but it was very distant—and it wasn't Cape Coast Castle! "Where are we? Where are you taking us?"

The African said, "Quiet," and turned his back on her.

In abject horror, Elysse realized the extent of her dilemma. She had been abducted—and she was being taken away from the British naval headquarters and the *Odyssey*. The African interior lay ahead! "We were abducted at midnight. Lorraine, it must be midmorning!"

"It feels as if we have been in this boat forever," Lorraine said, tears appearing. She blinked them back furiously. "We are going to shore. I can't swim!"

"Untie me," Elysse demanded furiously, fighting her fear. Courier must have been complicit in their abduction. Thoughts of Alexi and her family filled her mind. Dear God, how would she ever be rescued? What if she never saw Alexi again?

Didn't I say that I would always protect you?

She trembled, fighting tears as she recalled the silly childhood promise he had made to her so long ago in the ruins of that Irish castle. She had been lost and terrified. But Alexi had come back for her.

He would never leave her in the wilds of Africa!

She breathed hard. He had made her a promise and Alexi was a man of honor. Alexi would find her.

"Sir!" she shouted. "Untie me, so I can help my friend get to shore! She cannot swim!" Anger mingled with the fear. Lorraine was not going to drown in the breakers that lay ahead!

The African looked contemptuously at her.

"She can't swim! Do you speak English? I will have to help her if we are overturned by those breakers!" She held up her bound wrists. "Untie me, damn it!"

His knife appeared. Her heart stopped, but then he grinned and sliced through the bonds on her wrists and her ankles swiftly. Elysse exhaled, trembling. He then sliced through the cords on Lorraine's wrists. Her ankles hadn't been tied.

Elysse rubbed her wrists, breathing hard. "Was it Courier?" she demanded. "Did he set this up?"

"Quiet," the African said.

Lorraine whispered, "I don't think he speaks more than a few words. Oh, madam, how will we ever be found?"

"Don't worry. Captain de Warenne will come for us, sooner or later."

Lorraine looked at her as if she wondered if she were mad.

Elysse briefly closed her eyes. It was so hard to think. She desperately wanted to consider their escape, but they had something more dire and imminent to worry about—getting through the breakers without either one of them drowning.

Lorraine choked. Elysse glanced ahead and said, "Hold on to the sides of the canoe, dear. Tightly."

"I'm afraid."

"I won't let you drown." She had never meant anything more. But as good a swimmer as she was, no woman could possibly swim in the many layers of clothing she wore.

The canoe hit the first series of rolling waves. Lorraine screamed as the tiny boat was launched high into the air. The two oarsmen rested their paddles for a moment. Then, as the boat hit the trough below, they delved into the water with their oars. She breathed in hard as the canoe surged forward and was launched upward once more. She realized instantly that these Africans were very skilled oarsmen. They had undoubtedly breached the surf to get to the shore a hundred times. Still, as the little canoe fought the waves, Lorraine was turning green. Elysse, who was never seasick, felt ill, too. Both women held on to the sides of the tiny boat for their very lives.

But a few moments later, the canoe bottomed out in the final trough. Suddenly they were drifting quietly in a lagoon, the thundering breakers behind them. And Elysse saw two men in European dress standing on the beach— an incongruous sight in their dark suits and top hats, the jungle a thick, impenetrable wall behind them. So she had been right—they were waiting for them. But before she could consider what their presence meant, the oarsmen were leaping out of the canoe, as was their leader. The boat was dragged through the water till its prow hit the sand. Elysse was seized by one of the men, as was Lorraine.

The maid screamed. But both women were only carried onto the beach as if they were weightless, and then set abruptly down in the sand.

Lorraine looked at her, wide-eyed, brushing sand from her skirts. "I am barely wet."

Elysse inhaled, her gaze moving to the two Europeans striding toward them. She reached for the maid's hand and held it tightly. She noticed a dirt road beyond the beach, fronting the jungle, and a cart drawn by a mule. "They are skilled, but we are very lucky not to have drowned."

Lorraine turned, having seen the men. "What are they going to do to us? What do they want?"

"They won't hurt us," Elysse said, squeezing her hand and pretending absolute confidence. There was only one possible motive for their abduction. Surely these men wanted a ransom.

The Africans gestured and both women started up the beach, the sand pristine and white but hard to walk in. Elysse realized she was desperately thirsty. As she came face-to-face with the Europeans, her heart sank. The men were unshaven, dirty, and they stank; they weren't gentlemen. They seemed scurrilous in character as well as appearance. "Do you speak English, French or Spanish?" she asked.

She was ignored. Instead, the Europeans handed a large parcel wrapped in oilskins to the African leader. He grinned, flashing very white teeth, one gold tooth sparkling. He pulled back an edge of the oilskin and Elysse saw a musket there.

She shared a glance with Lorraine. The Africans had clearly been paid—with guns—to abduct her. But who was behind the abduction?

The three Africans started back to the canoe. The European grabbed her arm, pushing her forward. "Where are we?" Elysse demanded, and when he didn't answer, she asked him again in French and then in Spanish—to no avail.

The next five or six hours passed with excruciating slowness. They were shoved into the back of the wagon, bound again and given some tasteless gruel and water. The taller European sat in front of the cart, driving the mule, while the stouter one sat in the back with them, holding a rifle loosely and staring unrelentingly at them. When Elysse made the mistake of meeting his gaze, he smiled lewdly at her.

She had never been more frightened or more uncomfortable. The sun was furiously hot, beating down upon them, and Elysse felt her cheeks and nose burning. Lorraine was terribly sunburned now. Their captor continued to stare and she knew exactly what he was thinking. She began to worry about being raped. How would she and Lorraine survive in the wilds of West Africa until they could be ransomed or rescued?

Her dream that Alexi would find her was insane. Alexi was at the Cape of Good Hope by now! It was far more likely that her father or brother would come to her rescue. But she kept recalling that night at Errol Castle as if it were yesterday.

You're not lost. I'd never leave you....

Suddenly Elysse heard noises other than the rhythmic clip-clopping of the mule and the droning of the cart's wheels. She strained to hear and recognized what sounded like childish shrieks and shouts. She sat up, turning to face ahead, and saw thatch-roofed huts ahead, on either side of the road.

"Civilization," she whispered, wondering if they had arrived at their destination. As she spoke, more of the African village appeared, consisting mostly of open huts suspended on wood posts. A few small children played with sticks and a wood ball in the road, and she saw several women, half-clad, their breasts bare. Two women with large urns strapped to their backs stopped to stare at them as they passed.

Lorraine seized her arm. The road had turned and ahead was a huge harbor, filled with ships of all sizes and types. Elysse saw several buildings in the distance, sparkling white in the sun, and apparently made of stone. They exchanged worried glances. Wherever they were, at least they might soon get out of the sun. Elysse glanced at the harbor again, thinking it offered hope.

The distances were deceiving, and the mule plodded on for another hour before she could make out the docks and all the familiar shipping activity. Cargoes were being loaded and unloaded from dinghies, cutters and canoes similar to the one they had arrived onto shore from, and carters were transporting wares about the docks and to warehouses. More Europeans were visible on the wharves. She and Lorraine looked at one another again. Surely someone would help them escape their captors.

Their cart left the harbor, heading into the village. They passed what seemed to be an outdoor café. She could see into an open hut, where black men wearing gold chains sat with very disreputable-looking white men, smoking from pipes. Then she did a double take.

"Is that…a prison?" Lorraine gasped.

They were passing a structure with a thatched roof, built of wood. But unlike the previous huts they had passed, the walls were wood bars. Obviously, it was a kind of a jail cell, as large as a Mayfair salon. Within, Elysse saw dozens of African men and women crowded so closely that no one could possibly move. Shock made her speechless. She realized she was seeing African captives destined for the slave markets.

It was a moment before she could speak. "Those Africans will be transported to Brazil, the West Indies and maybe the American colonies, Lorraine, as slaves."

Lorraine gasped. "But the slave trade is illegal!"

"It is illegal in the British Empire, but not in many other places." She clenched her fists. "Hopefully our navy will raid the slavers leaving this port." Her stomach roiled. It was one thing to read about the slave trade; it was another to witness it in all its cruelty and inhumanity.

She glanced at the harbor, trying to decide which ships were slavers. They would have wider hulls and larger holds. She spotted three.

Two minutes later, the cart stopped in front of one of

the white stone buildings. Up close, Elysse saw that the building was old and weathered, with many stones missing. The shutters on the open windows were warped, the dark paint flaking. They were urged out of the back of the cart, their wrists remaining bound. Elysse was poked with the butt of the rifle in the small of her back. She stiffened, furious and insulted, but did not deign to look at the stout European who had molested her that way. He laughed.

The cooler air inside the hall was a welcome relief. Elysse saw that the single room contained several separate areas: a dining area with a handsome table with six high-backed chairs, a living area with a somewhat worn brocade sofa and two upholstered chairs, and an office area with a large desk. The man sitting there rose, beaming.

She halted, her heart skidding.

He was a slender, well-dressed European with dark hair and fair skin. "Welcome, Mrs. de Warenne, to Whydah." He approached, obviously pleased. His heavy accent was French. He reached for her hand.

"Who are you and what do you want?" Elysse withdrew her hand abruptly.

"I am Laurent Gautier, at your service, madame. I will do my best to make your stay here as comfortable as possible."

"I asked you what you want of us. And I would like my wrists untied."

In French, he snapped, "Cut the bonds."

Elysse lifted her hands as the taller European released her bonds. Lorraine was also freed. She rubbed her red, blistered wrists. "Thank you."

He smiled slowly. "It has been a long time since I have had the pleasure of the company of a real lady."

She cut him with a look of daggers. "And I have never been in such rude company before."

His smile vanished and his stare grew cold. Elysse regretted her words. "You will be my guests until your release," he said. "Your rooms are upstairs."

"And when will we be released?" she demanded.

"When I have received sufficient compensation."

"You are holding us hostage for ransom."

"Ah, you do not mince words. Then neither shall I. Yes."

It was hard to hold back the dread. But at least she now knew the game. "Captain, my family will pay whatever you wish for my release, but you will never be forgiven for this."

He shrugged. "I am aware of the reputation of your father, the infamous Captain Devlin O'Neill. I am also aware of your husband's reputation, madame. I will demand a king's ransom, and when I receive it, I will flee this ungodly place." It was clear he doubted anyone would ever find him once he left.

"Release me now," Elysse said tersely. "Let me go home. I promise you I will pay you whatever you wish."

He gestured, and the women were seized by the European men. "Do I appear a fool?"

The European shoved Elysse toward the stairs. Gautier snapped, "Do not push her, you bastard. She is a lady."

The European released her. Lifting her skirts, Elysse started up the rickety stairs. At the top, she was motioned to a small bedroom. The white walls were flaking and dirty, and a threadbare rug was on the wood floors. A small bed was against one wall, a bureau with a washbasin on the other. A single window was over that. Through it, Elysse saw the sparkling blue harbor, filled with ships of all sizes and shapes.

Gautier appeared, moving in front of the two Europeans

and Lorraine. "I will enjoy your company tonight at seven," he said. He bowed, and the door was closed in her face.

She cried out, rushing to it, as she heard it being locked from outside. "You are locking me in?" she cried. "What about Lorraine?"

"Mrs. de Warenne, don't let them separate us!" Lorraine cried, in tears.

"Your maid will be fine. I will see you at seven o clock," Gautier said.

Elysse heard his booted steps as he left and another door being locked. She could hear Lorraine crying.

Shock finally overcame her, as did exhaustion. Dazed, she turned slowly around, looking at the dirty, horrid room. Tears started to fall.

They had separated her and Lorraine. She was afraid of what they might to do her maid, who did not have the protection of a fortune and a title behind her. More tears fell.

She was being held for ransom. It would probably take a month for Gautier's ransom demands to find their way to her family in Britain. It would take another three or four weeks for her to be ransomed. Her heart lurched. *If she was ever ransomed.*

Now she thought about the stories she had heard of ladies abducted on the high seas, never to be heard of or seen again. But that could not be her fate!

If you are lost, I will find you. If you are in danger, I will protect you.

Alexi's words, spoken over a decade ago, rang loud and clear, as if he stood with her in that very room. She believed in him; she did. But she was so afraid!

She walked over to the window and looked outside. The Whydah harbor was beautiful, the waters bright blue and glittering like gemstones, the canvas sails light and bright, the sun shining. But tears began coursing, until they blurred her vision and she could no longer see.

She laid her hand on her chest, over her aching, frightened heart. "Alexi," she whispered. "Oh, God. Please find me. *Please*."

CHAPTER NINETEEN

"LOWER THE TOPSAILS," Alexi shouted tersely, staring past the ships riding at anchor in the bright blue ocean. He was within two miles of Cape Coast Castle.

"Aye, Captain," an officer shouted in return, his men scurrying to obey.

His heart pounding, he stared at the sparkling fortress through a telescope. He had never been as afraid of anything as he was now afraid for Elysse. He had learned from his sister that Elysse had taken passage on the *Odyssey,* intent on following him to China. He could not imagine her alone at sea, with only a personal maid as companion. His nights had been restless and tortured before he had learned that she had decided to follow him to China. Now they were entirely sleepless, filled with nightmares and vast regret. Any doubt over the extent of his love—or his decision to take up his responsibilities as her husband—had vanished.

He had been off the coast of Portugal, the *Coquette* racing at fourteen knots under full sail with her holds empty, when he had learned that the *Odyssey* had been spotted anchored off Cape Coast. He had gleaned that information from a passing Portuguese ship, using the intricate language of all sea captains—signal flags. After a full week at sea, he had encountered fifteen vessels, but none had seen or heard of the *Odyssey* until then. The information had shocked him.

The *Odyssey* was bound for China. There was no earthly reason for her to drop anchor off the West African coast. The northeasterly trade winds would keep her far from the coast, in fact.

He had already spent three days in London making inquiries into the *Odyssey,* her owners and her captain. His first instinct had been to race for China under full sail, immediately. But the *Coquette* had to have her cargoes unloaded, and he had taken advantage of that time. The *Odyssey* was owned by a reputable Glasgow shipping company, McKendrick and Sons, Ltd. Neither partner knew that its captain had taken his wife on board and was transporting her to Canton. In fact, the agents and owners had been shocked to learn what had transpired. To make matters worse, they did not speak glowingly of Captain Courier. They had used him only once before and his résumé was thin; they could not even speak on behalf of the man's character.

He had sensed trouble then, and his senses never failed him. The dread he had been living with ever since learning of Elysse's flight to China had consumed him. Suspicion began. *Something was very wrong.*

Was Elysse at the Castle? He prayed she was. If the ship were still at anchor, it meant he would have found his wife.

He heard the topsails furling behind him. Lowering the topsails was both a courtesy and a defensive measure—it signaled the British navy that his intent was not hostile. After all, no ship could make any speed without her topsails. Lowering the sails protected his vessel from being fired upon. It was tradition for any vessel passing by the castle or anchoring in her roads to lower their topsails.

"Fire the starboard guns," he ordered, still training the telescope upon the British naval headquarters.

Instantly, nine of the *Coquette*'s guns blasted. The sound of the cannon carried across the water. The castle sparkled white and bright in the sun, except for the black cannons pointing out to sea. A few more moments passed before his nine-gun salute was returned.

His heart thundered as he ordered the jolly boat readied. As he stepped into the jolly, he kept telling himself that Courier might have been forced to stop at Cape Coast for repairs or to change crews. Ships could be badly damaged in a storm; crews could come down with malaria almost overnight. But he did not believe a word he said to himself. None of the passing vessels he had communicated with had relayed such news in the past fortnight.

At least it was believed that Courier could sail. If so, he might make it up the China Sea without running aground, slamming upon a hidden reef or being capsized in a typhoon. But Alexi planned to catch up to the *Odyssey* well before it happened upon the China Sea.

As the jolly was launched, its single sail furled, he stepped forward to stand at the bow. He had to wonder if the *Odyssey* was even on its way to China.

He cursed, wishing Elysse had done what any other woman would have done—wait for him to return home!

What could she have possibly been thinking?

But hadn't she asked him to take her with him? Why hadn't he listened to her when she had said she wanted a real marriage? If anything had happened to her, it was his fault!

Using binoculars now, he scanned the roads, looking again for the *Odyssey*. There hadn't been any drawings of her, but he'd pounded her owners with questions until he could see her in his mind's eye. He'd memorized her tonnage, lines and rigging, and would know her on a moonless night, anywhere. She was nowhere in sight.

Deeply dismayed, he turned his glasses upon Cape Coast. Having been to the Castle several times before, Alexi was familiar with the sight of the fortress, which had its back to the land and was surrounded on three sides by the tropical ocean. Dark, dangerous rocks jutted out of the surf about the battlements and bastions, and Alexi could see a bell tower on the highest part of the Castle. The seaward gate was on the beach, and numerous canoes were depositing passengers and cargoes there.

He put down his glasses. He estimated that he was two weeks behind Elysse—if the Odyssey hadn't lingered at Cape Coast. If it had, he might be a week or even days behind her. With his holds empty, he would soon catch up to the other ship.

A part of him was desperate to go on to the northeasterly trade routes, chasing her under full sail; the saner part of him told him he must stop at the Castle and find out why the *Odyssey* had put into port there.

The frothing white breakers were ahead. Alexi sat down, taking up an oar from one of his men as the jolly boat hit the first set of waves. A few moments later, the jolly glided into the lagoon in front of the beach, Alexi and his men all soaking wet. Some small naked African children came splashing up to greet them, smiling and shouting happily.

Alexi stepped out of the boat into the thigh-deep water, leaving the jolly to his men. As the children came up to him he somehow smiled, realizing he'd forgotten to bring them anything of value. "I'm sorry, I don't have a single thing with me," he said, striding through the water and onto the beach. The children stopped smiling, no longer following him, when they realized he was not going to give them a gift or a treat.

He was greeted at the seaward gate by a young naval

lieutenant before he could go up the stairs. Two armed marines were positioned at the top of the staircase, on each side of the entry gate. "Captain de Warenne, sir, of the *Coquette* and Windsong Shipping," Alexi said, identifying himself and trotting up the stairs.

The lieutenant brightened, holding out his hand. "I have heard all about you, sir. Welcome to the Castle." He grinned, gesturing him inside as he introduced himself. "How can I be of help? My men tell me you have a China tea ship in our roads."

Alexi couldn't smile. They strolled into a small courtyard. "Her holds are empty, Lieutenant. I'm afraid I am in pursuit of my wife."

Lieutenant Hawley gaped, then flushed. They had paused beneath one of the battlements. Alexi let him off the hook. "She wished to join me in my run to China and I refused. Fortunately I had to turn around and return to London for repairs. There I was told my lovely wife decided to travel to China herself, to join me there."

"Good Lord," the lieutenant exclaimed. "But why on earth would you stop at Cape Coast?"

"Have you heard of—or seen—the *Odyssey*? She dropped anchor here two and a half or three weeks ago. My wife was on that ship." Alexi had never been as intense. He was desperate for answers now.

Hawley slowly shook his head. "Name doesn't ring a bell. But we keep a record of every ship that drops anchor here, Captain. If she was here, it will be logged. We'll know exactly when she was here and what she was doing."

"When can I see those logs?" Alexi asked abruptly. "I'm afraid I do not have time on my side if I wish to catch up to her." The lieutenant looked sharply at him and Alexi knew he was wondering if his wife had run off. He added,

"Captain Courier is an enigma. I have a gut feeling he will cause trouble."

"Courier? Courier had supper with the Governor, Captain. I happened to be on duty when he arrived."

Alexi almost choked. "Was a woman with him?"

"No, he came by himself. Wouldn't he have invited your wife to join him and the Governor for supper?" Hawley was staring at him now, his brow furrowed.

"Let's go look at those logs."

Alexi followed the lieutenant into another large bailey. They trotted up a set of stairs, rushed down a long corridor and finally entered an office filled with naval clerks. Alexi sat down with Lieutenant Hawley and began poring over the logs from the past few weeks. Ten minutes later, the young lieutenant found the entry they were both looking for.

"The *Odyssey* dropped anchor on June 23, Captain. She set sail the very next day."

Alexi reached for the log. "That is beyond odd," he said, reading the entry. No ship made port and stayed a mere twenty-four hours. Ships usually spent weeks, if not months, in a port. The log said that Courier had taken on one hundred and seventy-five gallons of water. That was equally odd. Why would he need water within the first few weeks of a voyage? As he read the rest of the entry, he froze.

23 June, 1839. *Odyssey* drops anchor at 3:30 pm. Request for 175 gallons of water made by Captain Courier. The ship is bound for China with a cargo of textiles.

24 June, 1839. 3 or 4 local pirates boarded the ship at 12:30 a.m. Gunshots exchanged with the crew and

locals escaped without incident. No one was injured and no thefts reported. The *Odyssey* raised sail at 6:30 a.m. bound for Canton.

"The ship was attacked by pirates on the morning of the twenty-fourth!" he exclaimed, his gut churning violently with dread.

Hawley said worriedly, "Apparently no one was hurt. But why is there no mention of your wife being on board? Passengers are usually listed, Captain, in the rare event that our merchants transport them."

He turned to look at Hawley, trembling now. "Either he did not want it known that my wife was on board, or she was not on board when he dropped anchor here." He could not breathe properly. Had Elysse been on board when the pirates attacked? Was she still on board? If not, where the hell was she!

"Sir, I couldn't help overhearing," a young officer said, blushing as he turned in his seat, from an adjacent desk.

"Do you know anything about this, Sergeant?"

"I logged that entry, sir. Captain Courier was very boastful about the fortune he was about to acquire from his China run. He was into his cups, and he kept telling me that this was his once-in-a-lifetime opportunity."

Alexi stared, trying to decide if this new bit of information meant anything at all.

"And when he left, he said something about there being nothing as welcome as a beautiful woman—especially a wealthy one."

Alexi inhaled. "He had to be referring to my wife! Are you sure he didn't mention that he had a passenger—two, actually?"

The young sergeant shook his head. Hawley turned to him. "I have a suggestion to make. The pirates were

Africans. We work closely with the canoe men. Word on the coast travels swiftly—we learn of incidents two hundred miles from here in mere hours. The locals use drums, Captain, and old-fashioned word of mouth. The natives know everything. I suggest you begin by interviewing the canoe men, in the hopes of either locating the pirates or learning if anyone espied your wife on board that ship."

Alexi tensed. "That could take days—weeks."

"You might be surprised. It is a small world, here on the West African coast."

GAUTIER SMILED AT HER. "You look lovely tonight, my dear."

Elysse barely smiled back. Two of the longest weeks of her life had passed. She had been kept prisoner in her room ever since arriving in Whydah, except at suppertime, when she was escorted under armed guard downstairs to dine with her captor and Lorraine. She had asked him if she could stroll outside, mentioning that she needed to take air on a daily basis, and he had refused. She had expected him to be a gentleman and accommodate her—she had been astounded. Then she had told him she would gladly suffer an escort, even an armed one, if she would be allowed to take a walk. She would even remain with her hands bound, if he so wished, but his answer didn't change.

"Whydah is a very busy port town." His bland smile remained. "I was told that you are an unusually clever woman, Mrs. de Warenne, with some knowledge of the sea and trade. I have no intention of allowing you to attempt to communicate with the various merchants who come to our small town, or our inhabitants, or any of the missionaries who pass by. Not to mention that the British keep a trading post here, as well. I do not intend to allow you to escape, my dear."

Elysse had stared, dismayed. Communication with someone—anyone—and escape were foremost on her mind. "So I will remain locked up in that tiny, horrid room until my ransom is paid?"

"I am afraid so," he had calmly returned.

She supposed she should be grateful for small favors. Neither she nor Lorraine had been harmed. She had made it very clear that any ill treatment of Lorraine would be taken as a slight upon herself. She had told Gautier directly that her husband was a vengeful man.

Gautier had cheerfully told her that he believed her.

They had been given some clothing and toiletries, paper and pen, and books. She had been allowed to write to her family. Gautier was pleased to post the letters for her, but only after censoring them first.

She wrote Alexi, her parents and Ariella. Of course, by the time they received her letters, she would probably already be back home. Or so she prayed.

Now Elysse walked past her captor to the chair he held out for her. Lorraine was already seated at the table. She did not look well. She had lost weight and there were dark circles under her eyes. Her sunburn had peeled away. She was far paler now than before.

Elysse knew from the small hand mirror she had in her room that she looked just as terrible. As she sat, she smiled at her companion. "How are you, my dear?"

Lorraine looked woefully at her. She did not even bother to speak.

Elysse took her hand. "It could be worse. We could have been accosted. And our ransoms will be paid. Surely you know that?"

"I know," she whispered. "But we have been here for so long."

Elysse had kept track of the days—they had been

imprisoned for twenty-five days thus far. It felt like an eternity. She was determined to be optimistic and keep up a cheerful, hopeful facade, but she felt far more desperate and despondent than she let on. By now, Alexi was probably approaching Madagascar in the Indian Ocean. If he knew the dire straits she was in, he would turn around and come for her—she had not a single doubt.

If you are lost, I will find you. If you are in danger, I will protect you.

He had made that promise to her so long ago, but that no longer mattered. Her faith in him was everything—it was her hope, her salvation. The past six years seemed foolish and inconsequential now. Alexi was with her in her mind, as if at her side, day and night. He was her anchor, her strength. The man she thought about so ceaselessly was the man she had known her entire life. The bridegroom who had betrayed her just after taking wedding vows with her no longer existed. The man who had abandoned her for six long years had somehow vanished. Had he ever really existed? How had she ever doubted his feelings for her? Alexi would move mountains for her. He would rescue her from this hell if only he knew of it. She loved him deeply, as she did no one else, and she always had. Now, in retrospect, she looked at their awkward dance of the past few months and the cause of his anger was clear. He was jealous of Blair, just as he had once been jealous of Montgomery. Alexi loved her in return—she knew it as a fact.

Too late, she wished she hadn't been that young, vain, foolish coquette, and that she hadn't led Montgomery and all her other suitors on. She wished she hadn't misled society with her pretense of domestic complacency and sexual independence. She wished she hadn't fostered the illusion that she was an experienced woman of the world.

When the day came that she was in Alexi's arms again, she intended to tell him *everything*.

As for Montgomery's death, Elysse felt as if she had had an epiphany. There could be no more blame. When they were together again, she would make sure he let go of the past and healed. All that mattered now was survival—and the future they deserved to share.

Supper was always a quiet affair, with Gautier being jovial and doing most of the speaking. Elysse tried to be as polite as possible in return. Remembering her manners was a matter of common sense—she did not want to anger her captor, nor did she want this small freedom of joining him for a decent supper taken away from her and Lorraine.

After supper, Gautier escorted her upstairs, wishing her a pleasant evening as if dropping her at her front door in London. Once he was gone, her door locked from the outside, she turned restlessly around, missing Alexi so much that her chest ached. But she refused to succumb to absolute despair. There was hope, and she clung to it. Eventually, her ransom *would* be paid. She would be freed and they would be together again—and the absurdity of the past six years would be behind them.

She was about to struggle out of her dress and put on the nightclothes she had been given when she heard a visitor downstairs. Gautier never had guests after supper. Elysse went to her door and leaned her ear against it, wondering if there was some kind of news, hopefully about her ransom. But she knew that the ransom demand was probably only just reaching her family.

She heard the rumble of lowered male voices, but could not make out a word. Still, her nape prickled. Was one of the voices familiar?

She wished her heart would stop thundering so loudly.

She took a deep breath and listened acutely again. Then she stiffened, shocked. Was Baard Janssen downstairs?

For one moment, she thought he had come to rescue her.

In the next, she shook her head to clear her mind and wondered if he was in town by chance. She had already learned from Gautier that Whydah was a huge slave trading port. Blair had told her that Janssen was a slave trader.

And then those silly, frivolous thoughts vanished. *Janssen had arranged her passage....*

The men were still talking. Had Janssen arranged for her abduction, as well? Could he be such a cad? Hadn't Alexi warned her about him, hadn't Blair?

Was it possible? Aghast, the anger arose. Elysse tried to tell herself not to jump to conclusions—perhaps, just perhaps, Janssen's arrival in Whydah was coincidence and he was her ally. She began pounding on her door."Let me out!" she cried. "Let me out! Janssen! It is Elysse de Warenne. I am a prisoner here!"

A moment later Gautier unlocked and opened her door, oddly pale. Baard Janssen was with him. The moment their gazes locked, she knew that his presence in Whydah was not a coincidence.

He was neither surprised nor shocked to see her. "Hello, Elysse. For a hostage, you are looking very well."

Shock immobilized her. *He had done this.*

Gautier said grimly, "You should have remained silent, madame."

Janssen slowly shook his head. "But she did not. She's seen me, Laurent."

The meaning of their words escaped her. "You did this!" she cried.

His gaze raked rudely over her. "You wished for passage and I availed myself of a spectacular opportunity, Elysse."

She struck him as hard as she could across the face.

He struck her back, as hard.

Elysse was flung backward by the terrific blow. She crashed into the bed and fell to the floor. Her cheek exploded in pain. She wondered if the bones there were broken. Dazed, she looked up. Stars blinked at her, but Janssen stood there, towering over her.

He had hit her.

He was in her bedroom now.

"Janssen," Gautier protested, sounding shocked. "She is a lady."

"Shut up." His gaze remained unrelenting and there was no mistaking the look in his eyes.

Afraid of being hit again, or worse, she did not move.

"You look frightened."

She exhaled. *He was going to rape her.*

"You are worth a fortune, my dear. So yes, I planned your abduction." He held out his hand. "You made a nearly fatal mistake when you approached me for help leaving London, and you made a very fatal mistake coming out of your room to approach me now."

She refused to take his hand. Her heart surged in fear. "What are you going to do to me?" But she knew. *She could identify him.* He was not the kind of man to vanish into the African continent like Gautier. He would not let her live now.

How many hostages held for ransom were never returned, even after their ransoms were paid?

He slowly smiled. "It would have been a bit tidier if you hadn't heard us speaking or seen me. I have no interest in running from your husband for the rest of my life."

She had been right. He was not going to let her live.

She trembled wildly. "If you hurt me—if you kill me—he will find out—and he will not stop until you are dead."

Janssen chuckled. "But he will never know."

She inhaled, choking on a sob of terror. *What was she going to do?*

Then she heard the click of a trigger being pulled back. She twisted to look past Janssen. Gautier held a pistol, which he pointed at his back. "She is a lady, Baard."

Janssen turned and stared coldly at Gautier. "*Mon ami,* she is a lady who is now doomed, and you had better get used to that. Put the pistol away. I am going to amuse myself tonight."

Gautier said, unsmiling, "Get out."

Her heart exploding, Elysse looked back and forth between both men. Gautier was intent and determined, clearly meaning to protect her, but Janssen was ugly in his fury now. "Fine," the Dane finally said. "But we'll finish this tomorrow. And when the ransom is paid, I will dispose of her. When you are thinking more clearly, you will realize it is best for us both."

Gautier did not speak.

Janssen stormed out. Elysse collapsed, hugging herself, and giving over to tears.

Gautier knelt. "He is a dangerous man, madame. You should have stayed silent when you heard him downstairs."

She managed to look at him. Somehow, he had become her protector. "Thank you," she whispered. But she knew that her time had finally run out.

ELYSSE DIDN'T SLEEP. In her clothes, she stared up at the cracked ceiling where a spider spun its web, blinking back tears, frightened as never before. Gautier did not seem capable of protecting her for very long. She would beg him to hide her somewhere else. But if he hid her from Janssen, would Alexi or her family ever be able to find her?

The sun crept into the sky. That morning it was blood-red. Elysse walked over to the window, watching it rise over the harbor, staining the tropical waters peach and pink. She had never been able to get over the irony of how spectacular the Whydah harbor was. The azure waters, the beautiful ships, the white beaches, the emerald jungles. That morning, her gaze moved to one of the wharves. Perhaps a hundred chained and shackled Africans were being slowly marched down to one of the slave ships. She hugged herself and wept for them, and for herself and Lorraine.

A knock sounded on her door. She was brought breakfast at 8:00 a.m. every morning; she knew it wasn't even six. Trembling, she just stood there as her door opened. Gautier stood there, looking as if he had spent a sleepless night, as well. "I will not allow him to use you and murder you, madame."

She nodded, finding her voice. "Then let me go. Send me home, where I will be safe."

His face tightened. It was a moment before he spoke. "Word travels swiftly in Africa, here on the coast."

She stared, perplexed.

"Your husband, madame, was at Cape Coast three days ago."

Elysse's knees buckled. "Dear God, I pray that is the truth! But Alexi is surely in the Indian Ocean now!"

Gautier was unhappy. "Does he not captain la *Coquette?* She was seen at anchor there."

Alexi had somehow discovered her trail, Elysse thought. The room swam. Gautier caught her and helped her to sit. While her mind felt incoherent, she seized his arms and said, "Send me to Cape Coast Castle! Please!"

"If he followed you there, he will undoubtedly learn what transpired and find you here. I cannot cut all losses. I will try to attain a ransom from him when he arrives in Whydah. In the meantime, I have doubled the guards. Janssen is barred from this post."

When Gautier had left, Elysse lay down, crying in relief. Alexi was coming for her. She trusted him completely. He would never let anything bad happen to her. He had promised....

And then she leaped up and pulled a chair over to the window and sat there, staring into the harbor. The slaver was loaded but the sails were not raised. She wondered if the ship was the *Astrid*. The sun rose higher. Sails appeared on the horizon.

By noon, three ships dotted the horizon. Elysse leaned forward, praying desperately. A three-masted barque became visible. Her heart sank. Then a wide, older brigantine appeared. She cried out, waiting for the third ship to become close enough for her to identify it. Time stood still. The sun blazed. She was standing now. All sails seemed to be unfurled. She stopped breathing, squinting. *It was a clipper.*

She leaned against the window, waiting, her heart pounding with frightening force. It *was* a clipper ship. Her lines were long and lean, trim. She inhaled and tried to make out the flag flying from its mainmast. It was British....

And as the topsails were lowered, the ship tacking now, Elysse could finally make out her lines. She cried out. It was the *Coquette*—she had never been as certain of anything!

She took one more look at the beloved clipper ship, then ran to her door and began banging on it in a frenzy. A moment later, Gautier opened it. "He is here—Alexi is here! Let me go to him! Laurent!" She seized his lapels.

"If you approach him with me as your prisoner, he will see you as the enemy. He will find out where I am and kill you on the spot. Let me go to him now! I will reward you handsomely—I swear upon the Bible!" When he grimaced without speaking, she shook him. "You never expected this! You did not expect Janssen to be such a cad and you did not expect my husband to track me down here. You do not want to come face-to-face with Alexi de Warenne!"

Gautier ran his hand over his face. In that moment, she saw how exhausted he was.

"You have to become my protector. You are a gentleman, sir!" she cried.

He inhaled heavily. "No gentleman would ever condone your abduction, madame, and we both know it. I am a scoundrel, the great disappointment of my family. Dear God, I detest this horrid land!"

Elysse blinked in surprise at him.

"Who would ever wish to make their living in such a place, amidst such human agony and suffering?" he said. "You were my way to freedom, madame."

She bit her lip. "You protected me. And that is what I will tell Alexi. Laurent, I am a woman of my word."

He laughed without mirth. "You need not tell me that. Very well," Gautier said harshly. "I will trust you now, madame, to protect me as I protected you last night. Therefore, we will go down to the docks, together."

Elysse nodded, her heart lurching in excitement. Her ordeal was about to end—surely, nothing and no one would get in her way now. But her gaze locked with Gautier's and she knew he was thinking the same thing—Janssen was out there, and he would stop them if he could.

"We will avoid him, at all costs."

Laurent Gautier nodded. *"Après vous."*

CHAPTER TWENTY

ALEXI'S HEART WAS SLAMMING in his chest as the jolly boat bumped into one of the piers in Whydah's harbor. He leaped out of the boat before a single line had been cast ashore, and almost running, he started up the wharf.

Elysse had been abducted. His wife was being held prisoner in the slave-trading town of Whydah.

That fucking bastard Courier had disembarked from his ship at Cape Coast, setting up the abduction. He did not know who else was involved.

Courier was going to pay with his life. So was everyone else....

He had spent two entire days interviewing African canoe men with a British translator. Then one of the canoe men had told him that his brother had been paid in guns to take two white women from the *Odyssey* to a pair of European men awaiting them on the beach. It had taken mere hours to locate the brother of the canoe man who had given him the information, the African in charge of Elysse's abduction. Alexi had wanted to kill him. Hawley had sensed his rage and had reminded him that the man was making a living the only way that he could—and that he needed information from him. As it turned out, a handful of coins had gained the information he desperately needed. The African had overheard the Europeans talking about taking Elysse and her maid to Whydah.

His strides ate up the sandy wharf. His rage was quiet

now, burning deep inside him, but with it was a quiet terror. *His wife had been abducted, and even now, she was being held hostage, and only God knew where, or under what conditions….*

Elysse was a terribly beautiful woman, in a world filled mostly with savages and brutes, and he was afraid of what they had already done to her. But she was alive. He refused to consider otherwise. Her abductors wanted a ransom— she had to be alive.

I am coming for you, he thought silently, his gut curdling with so much fear and anxiety.

When he found her, he was going to do everything in his power to make up for the past six years. He had done nothing but hurt, betray and humiliate her. God, he could barely believe he had walked away from her at the altar as he had! He *loved* his wife. He had loved her from the first moment he had glimpsed her and he had never stopped loving her, not even when their marriage had been a sham and she had been with her various lovers. He realized he'd been far more furious with her for her affairs than for what had happened that night at Windhaven. He wished he'd realized his genuine feelings years ago and demanded a reconciliation then, instead of turning his back on her and pretending indifference. How could he have thought, even for a moment, that he didn't care? He was a de Warenne. Elysse was the love of his life.

Somehow, he would make the past up to her. Just then, all he could think of was finding her and bringing her safely home.

Surely she knew he was coming for her?

He'd given her so much cause to doubt him, to lose faith. He kept thinking of how frightened she must be. He knew how courageous she was—the past six years had proven that to him—but it had to be terribly hard for her to cling to her courage now. He remembered that long-ago night at Errol Castle, when she had been lost and terrified in the ruins there. Did she recall the promise he had made her? He had meant his every word. *I will always protect you.*

She had to know he was coming for her.

He did not know where in Whydah she might be hidden. But a lady like Elysse would be very hard to conceal. Someone would know where she was, and he would not leave a stone unturned to find out.

He had already received a roughly drawn map of the town from another captain familiar with the area. There were four trading posts within: French, British, Dutch and Portuguese. The British post was there to trade in palm oil, not slaves like the others. His first stop would be the French post in the center of town. After all, Courier was French. It could be a long shot, or it could be the winning shot. He *would* find Elysse. She was not going to be lost in Africa. She was his wife and he intended to share the rest of his life with her....

"Alexi!"

He started, thinking he could not possibly have heard the sound of her voice. Then he whirled—and saw her running toward him, her long hair loose, tears streaming down her face.

His heart stopped. *She was alive.... He had found her!*

He ran. As he reached her, he saw her pallor, how much weight she had lost, the circles under her eyes. But she had never been more beautiful! He swept her into his arms, hard, as she wept uncontrollably against his chest.

"Thank God," he gasped, burying his face in her hair.

"You came."

He caught her face in his hands. "I will always protect you when you are in danger!"

"I know," she said, crying. "Do you remember? When we were children? You said you would always protect me—you said you would always find me if I were lost! Oh, Alexi!" She collapsed in his arms again.

He held her tightly and realized he was crying, too. "I love you, Elysse," he heard himself say hoarsely. "I always have and I always will."

She slowly looked up at him, stunned.

He smiled. "I never say what I don't mean." His tone was rough.

She caught his face in her hands and kissed him, not gently, but hot and hard and with an open mouth. He was shocked, for he was certain she had been hurt and maybe abused. She needed care and comfort. He was thoroughly aroused and desperate to make love to her, but he would wait. He caught her face in his hands, breaking the impassioned moment.

She suddenly pulled back breathlessly. "How did you find me? Why aren't you in the Indian Ocean?"

"I turned around when I was off the port of Lisbon," he said, pushing her wildly disheveled hair behind her ears. "I missed you. I couldn't stand it. I went home to be the husband you deserve."

She began to cry all over again.

He took her more gently into his arms. With dread, he asked, "Did they hurt you?"

She looked up at him, trembling. "I am not hurt, Alexi. But I have never been so afraid. Monsieur Gautier let me go. I owe him." She glanced behind her.

He noticed a European gentleman standing behind them, along with Elysse's maid. Lorraine was as thin and gaunt as Elysse, but she was crying tears of happiness and relief. His gaze veered to the European. Instantly, he knew the man was a scoundrel. Gautier stared cautiously back at him, his expression tense and wary.

Monsieur Gautier let me go. Alexi felt his world still. He felt himself step out of his body, distancing himself from his wife, as the implications began—about who the other man was—and what he had done. "He held you prisoner," he said very softly, but his gaze was on Gautier. It did not waver.

"Yes, he did, but we were not abused and he freed me just now," Elysse said, a plea in her tone.

He only heard the single word *yes*.

The rage simmering within became roaring flames. He carried both pistol and dagger, but he didn't need either weapon. He released Elysse, his gaze on the Frenchman. Gautier blanched. "Monsieur!" he cried. "I saved your wife from a fate worse than death!"

"Really?" Alexi said softly. He had no interest in anything the European had to say.

"Alexi!" Elysse seized him by the shoulders. "He saved my life! He saved me from rape! Baard Janssen did this. He arranged my passage—my abduction. Janssen meant to rape me last night, then kill me. Gautier saved me from him!"

Alexi went still, his gaze locked with Gautier's, as her words began to sink in. "Is that the truth?" He finally looked at Elysse. She was in one piece. Miraculously, she hadn't been hurt.

"He protected me, Alexi. Janssen appeared last night. It was terrifying." She trembled, grasping his arm. "And Janssen is still in town."

"He struck her, Captain, and I drove him off with a gun," Gautier exclaimed.

He touched her jaw. "Is that how you got that bruise?"

She nodded. "It's true that Gautier kept me hostage, but he also kept me safe. I want to reward him, Alexi."

He hated the sight of that purple bruise, and it sickened him to think that she had been violently struck. He also had no desire to reward Gautier, not when he had kept her prisoner. He studied her, and she stared back, determination in her eyes. "Life is full of surprises," she said softly. "It is hardly ever black-and-white."

He softened. His heart swelled with love. Had she grown even wiser than she already had become in the course of their estrangement? "We'll discuss it," he finally said, with the odd feeling that she would win this round. Then he turned to the Frenchman. "Where is Janssen staying?"

"The inn down the street," Gautier said, with evident relief.

Elysse moved to his side, taking his arm again. "Can't you let the authorities go after him? I need you," she whispered urgently.

His heart lurched. Did she intend to seduce him now, to prevent him from doing what a man had to do? "I can't let Janssen get away with this, Elysse, and you know it."

She smiled at him, clasping his cheek. "I wasn't certain we would ever be together again. And murder is against the law, Alexi."

He had a flashback to that long-ago night at Windhaven, when he had fought with Montgomery. "We aren't in Britain. We are in a lawless land."

"Haven't we both suffered long enough?"

He stared, aware that she was thinking about William Montgomery, too. But this was not at all like that night. Janssen had put Elysse in danger. He had meant to kill her.

"We began our marriage because of a man's death," she whispered.

He knew what she was thinking—they were starting their future all over again, and if he had his way, it would be founded on another man's death. But Janssen *deserved* to die.

Elysse stiffened, turning white.

He looked over his shoulder—and saw Baard Janssen farther down the dusty street. The Dane halted in midstride, clearly shocked to see them there. Alexi was equally incredulous. Then his heart exploded in savage delight. *This was too good to be true.*

Janssen turned and began to run.

Alexi slipped his pistol in his hand and took aim. He was going to kill this sonofabitch, never mind that Montgomery still haunted him, never mind that he was not a killer, never mind that Elysse was right and they should not start their future this way.

"You are not a murderer!" Elysse cried. "Don't do this, Alexi. Let the authorities hang him!"

For one more moment, he held his aim. He so wanted to pull the trigger! Then moments from his life in the past six years flashed before his eyes, as did images of Elysse during the past few months in London—a gracious, elegant woman of substance and conviction. *She had fought so hard to maintain her pride and dignity. She had survived heartache and humiliation. There would already be gossip over her abduction—she did not need the gossips inflamed over his murdering Janssen. She did not need to suffer through a court trial, which might arise.* Alexi lowered the gun. "You're right. You deserve more. And I am going to give it to you." He smiled briefly at her and she smiled back, in relief. "But Janssen will be hanged for piracy." Ransoming a hostage was not a hanging crime, but piracy was. Alexi set chase.

Janssen looked over his shoulder and realized Alexi was

in pursuit. He ran harder, turning a corner. Alexi pushed his legs furiously, his heart pumping, running faster than he had thought possible. He rounded the same corner—and saw Janssen coming at him with a knife.

His reflexes were lightning-quick. As Janssen plunged the knife, he jerked aside, dodging the blow, which would have taken him squarely in his back. Instead, the knife was driven into the side of his shoulder. Grunting in pain, Alexi seized the other man, wrestling him down to the ground. On top of Janssen, he got his hands around his throat. "You thought to rape my wife, you fucking bastard?" He was not a killer, but this scum of the earth deserved to die, and he couldn't help himself—in that moment, he wanted to kill him.

"Don't do it!" Elysse screamed, coming up to them at a run. "Please, Alexi, for me—for us!"

He wanted to snap his neck in two. Janssen's eyes were bulging. But they were not going to begin their future this way. He had so much to make up for.

Gautier arrived, holding a gun. Alexi released Janssen, grunting as he moved, aware of the pain burning in his shoulder. Elysse helped him to stand as Gautier held Janssen at gunpoint.

Elysse slid her arm around him. "You're hurt. He stabbed you!"

Lorraine, who had run up, handed her a handkerchief, which Elysse pressed to his shoulder. "It's just a damned flesh wound," he said. He looked at Gautier. "Tie him up. He is going to Cape Coast, to be tried for piracy on the high seas, as well as my wife's abduction. And it will be our word against his—I will protect you from any charges."

Gautier exhaled in relief. "Thank you, monsieur."

Elysse moved into his arms, trembling. "Thank you."

He held her, hard, all over again. And nothing had ever felt as right.

IN ALEXI'S SHIPBOARD CABIN, Elysse watched as he thanked his surgeon and saw the man to the door. She had never been on board the *Coquette,* much less in his cabin, and she was surprised at how sparse and utilitarian the small room was. She was perched on the edge of his bed, a simple bunk with fine coverings, a bookcase built into the wall above it. There was a beautiful Oriental carpet on the floor and a dining table with four chairs, obviously Spanish. His massive, intricately carved desk sat beneath a porthole. Navigational charts covered most of it.

Alexi closed the cabin door and turned to look at her. He was shirtless. His shoulder had been treated with iodine, the wound sewn and bandaged. He had been green during the surgery, and Elysse didn't think the brandy had helped dull the pain of the surgeon's needle. She would have held his hand if he had let her, but he had given her an incredulous look, clearly sensing what she wished to do. She had held her own hands during his surgery, instead.

She was free. The horror of the past month was over and Alexi loved her—and apparently he always had.

Alexi slowly smiled at her. "I can't believe you're here."

She trembled, staring openly at him. As he breathed, the muscles in his chest and torso rippled. Her body was hardly immune to the sight of so much powerful masculinity. She was there, on his ship, with him. She wasn't a prisoner anymore. And they loved one another…. "I never stopped believing that you would find me." Moisture gathered in her eyes. "We are together, at last." She met his regard, thinking not just of her abduction but the separation of the past six years.

His gaze was unwavering. "Yes, we are together." He paused, unmoving, except for the rhythmic rise and fall of his muscular chest. "I was afraid. No, terrified. I was terrified I wouldn't find you—and that you were being hurt."

"I am very fortunate."

"Only you would say that." He launched himself slowly forward. Her heart thrilled. Suddenly all she wanted was to be in his arms, lost in the passion that was their love. But was the terrible enmity of the past six years finally over? Alexi had declared his love and surely all was forgiven now, but he still didn't know the truth.

He sat down beside her, his expression serious, and took her hand. "Are you sure the worst that happened was being struck yesterday by Janssen? You must tell me the truth, Elysse."

She nodded. "I was treated with respect, Alexi, the entire time. It was horrible, being locked up in a tiny, shabby bedroom, but I dined every night with Laurent and I was given books to read. I was also allowed to write letters. In the end, he protected me from Janssen. We have done the right thing, turning Janssen over to the authorities and allowing Laurent to go free, with a reward." Janssen had been turned over to the British navy; a small destroyer had dropped anchor in the harbor that afternoon. Gautier had already left town, richer than he should probably be. They would cast off on the morrow, with Elysse and Lorraine sharing Alexi's cabin. Her maid was spending the night in Whydah's finest hotel, with one of Alexi's young officers serving as her escort.

His grasp on her hand tightened. "I can't believe that you suffered so. I can't believe I allowed you to be in such a predicament." He took her face in his hands. "I can't believe how strong you are—how brave! You are sitting here so calmly, recounting your ordeal. Other women would be in hysterics."

"I am not other women, Alexi," she said softly. She hesitated. She had learned courage long ago. She wanted to make love, but first, they must finally resolve all of their differences. "Once again, you blame yourself when there is blame to go around. I let you believe Blair and I were lovers. On some level, I knew how that would upset you. This was not your fault."

He dropped his hands, staring for a moment. Then, as if he knew her thoughts, he said, "It was terribly hard for you, wasn't it? My abandoning you, having to pretend to be happily wed? The gossips behind your back, every time you went out? But you have never let on."

Now she took his hand and clasped it to her chest. "It was horrible. I lived a lie, a terrible pretense that my life was as I wished for it to be. It was humiliating, Alexi. All I had was my pride and dignity."

He grimaced, staring relentlessly now.

"I had one ambition—to avoid further humiliation at all cost. But there was always gossip. I always heard it eventually, and sometimes, the whispers were the truth." She let his hand go.

"God, I am so sorry!" he cried.

"But that is past now, isn't it?" she asked seriously.

He looked carefully at her. "I hurt you, Elysse."

"Yes, you did. And I know that I hurt you—" she hesitated "—with my supposed affairs."

He said flatly, "Blair told me you never slept with him."

She trembled. "How could I sleep with Blair when I was in love with you?"

"The charade was completely convincing, Elysse." His tone was rough.

"Yes, it was. I deliberately fostered the illusion that I was a carefree, amoral socialite—that was how I wished to be seen." Their gazes locked. "I was afraid that if you knew the truth, you would mock me."

A long, long moment passed. "I was cruel—purposefully so. I am so sorry." He said, low, "If you couldn't sleep with Blair, what about the others?"

"There weren't any others, Alexi," she said softly. "It was all a grand illusion, designed to protect my pride."

He cried out, "You were faithful to me?"

"I could never be unfaithful to you," she said simply.

He stared, his gaze wide, as he absorbed the fact that she had never betrayed him or their love. Then he swept her into his arms, holding her tightly. Elysse felt his strong heart racing in a rhythm she now recognized. Her own pulse was rioting, too.

"I was so afraid I would never see you again," she whispered. "I love you, Alexi. I love you so much."

He nuzzled her cheek, and when he spoke, his tone was rough with desire. "I am so sorry that I left you at the altar six years ago…. I was such a fool! I have never stopped loving you, Elysse, not since I was a small boy. My pride also stood in our way."

She managed to pull back a bit so their gazes could meet. His blue eyes were dark with despair and desire. "We were both terribly young, terribly vain and terribly reckless. I was so jealous of your philandering! I am so sorry I led Montgomery on."

"I know you are. And it doesn't matter—the past doesn't matter—because it is *over*," he managed. He caught her chin and claimed her mouth hungrily. He said roughly, "I am going to show you how much I love you, Elysse." He kissed her again.

Her body ignited as she kissed him back.

He broke the kiss. "You are the woman I have loved since we were children. You are the woman I have never stopped loving. I meant it when I said it earlier."

"I know," she said softly.

He feathered her lips with his and murmured, "You are the woman I will always love. Our future begins today." He kissed her deeply now.

She knew. She had always known that he was the one—that she was the one. She cried, even as they kissed, because where there had been so much pain, now there was only bright promise.

CHAPTER TWENTY-ONE

London, England

Summer 1839

OXFORD HOUSE LOOMED AHEAD, a great, gray stone mansion surrounded by blooming gardens and bright blue skies. Elysse held on tightly to Alexi's hand as their hired carriage bumped and bounced over the graveled drive, thrilled to finally be home. They had dropped anchor mere hours ago after an uneventful return voyage. Alexi's father had been on the wharf to greet them, along with every employee of Windsong Shipping. When she and Alexi were espied standing together on the *Coquette*'s quarterdecks, the waiting crowd had cheered. She had barely put both feet upon that wharf when her father-in-law had swept her into his arms, hugging her so tightly she could not breathe, whispering that he dearly hoped Alexi would seriously set her down for her running off alone to China. Before Elysse could apologize, she had realized that Cliff was crying. But his tears were of joy.

Alexi put his arm around her and pulled her close. "It has been an impossibly long voyage," he said, low.

Lorraine sat on the rear-facing seat, across from them, and she blushed and averted her eyes. Elysse snuggled closer to her husband, knowing exactly what he meant. She and Lorraine had shared his cabin and it had been difficult to steal time alone there to make wild, uninhibited love. Yet they had managed to do just that.

It was as if the past six years had vanished into ancient history; it was as if those terrible years of pain and separation had never existed.

He said against her ear, "I am going to make love to you all day and all night and then for all of tomorrow."

She thrilled. Her skin tingled. She said in his ear, breathlessly, "Is that a warning?"

"Oh, yes, it is," he said, clearly meaning it.

She laughed. She couldn't wait to be alone with him for an entire day—no, an entire week, if she had her way.

The carriage halted in front of the wide stone steps. Alexi got out first, then helped Lorraine down. Elysse smiled at him, extending her hand, but when he took it, he pulled her forward and swept her into his arms.

She laughed in delight. "Are you carrying me over the threshold?"

"Damned right I am," he said. In midstride he halted, kissing her hungrily, as if with weeks of pent-up passion. Elysse felt her insides hollow. Holding on to his shoulders, she kissed him back deeply. They were home, where there would be no interruptions. This would not be a brief stolen moment.

He broke the kiss, his gaze smoldering. Then, without saying a word, he started for the stairs.

Lorraine had gone inside ahead of them, and as they reached the threshold of the entrance hall, Reginald and the rest of the staff began to pour into the room. "Sir!" the butler cried. "Mrs. de Warenne! This is a great day, to have you both home!"

Elysse saw a dozen familiar faces. She was about to tell Alexi to put her down so they could properly greet their staff and at least pretend to decorum, but Alexi's strides increased. Reaching the stairs, he said, "We are *not* to be interrupted, even if this house is burning down."

She felt her cheeks flame and she buried her face in his chest as he bounded up the stairs, taking them two at a time. "Alexi!" she managed. "What will they think?"

"They will think that I am besotted with my wife and that I am making love to her for an inordinately long time."

She met his gaze. It was fiercely determined, but laughter was in his tone. "I love you."

His answer was to kiss her, hot and hard, while striding down the corridor. A moment later they slammed into a wall, but Alexi did not break the kiss and Elysse, in spite of the urgency humming in her body, started to laugh.

He lifted his face, smiling. "Ow," he said.

"Take me to bed, but please, watch where you are going!"

His answer was to kiss her again as he stood with her in his arms, pressed against the corridor wall.

She kissed him back. Her heart thundering, she slipped her hands inside his shirt. It crossed her mind that no one would dare come upstairs and they could make love right there. He read her mind, for he slid her down his hard, hugely aroused body, lifting her skirts. "I cannot wait."

"Good," she said, reaching for his trousers and skimming him with her hand. He grunted, as a door opened and closed downstairs. Vaguely, she heard voices—familiar ones. Alexi had her skirts up about her waist. He began kissing her throat, softly and sensually, while feathering her swollen sex with his fingers. The door closed again. There were more voices downstairs.

Elysse was gripping his waistband now. *Was that Ariella she'd just heard? With Amanda?*

Alexi froze, breathing hard. He finally said roughly, "Did I just hear *Adare?*" He was incredulous.

Elysse straightened. Now, she heard the earl's wife, Lizzie, and her brother, Jack, more loudly than anyone. She half laughed and half sobbed, meeting Alexi's disbelieving, still-smoldering gaze. He began to smile. "Shit," he said. "We have a welcoming committee downstairs."

Elysse touched her hair. It seemed to be pinned up. "They have come to welcome us home. We cannot avoid them, Alexi."

"I could be very, very swift."

She smiled and kissed his cheek. "We have all night and an entire week to be as decadent as we wish."

"Hmm, I do like the sound of that." He tucked some hair behind her ears and tucked his shirt into his breeches and took her hand. They exchanged smiles and walked back down the hall. As they went downstairs, they could see into the marbled entry. Elysse was astonished. It seemed as if every single member of their family had congregated to greet them, when it was late July and no one should be in town! Alexi's father had obviously sent word to everyone that they were home. Cliff stood with his wife, Amanda, both of them beaming up the stairs at her and Alexi as they came down. In fact, all gazes were trained brightly upon them.

She managed to see who was actually present. Ariella was with St. Xavier, of course, and her and Alexi's little sister, Dianna, stood with them. The Earl of Adare was indeed present, with the countess. His heir, Ned, and his daughter Margery had also come. Margery carried flowers. Incredibly, her uncle Sean, who rarely left the north of Ireland, was there, along with his wife, Eleanor, their eldest adopted son, Michael, and his wife, Brianna, whom she hardly knew. Their other son Rogan and his wife, whose name she did not remember because she saw them so infrequently, had even called! Sir Rex, Lady Blanche and their daughters were also there. Clarewood was present, standing beside her parents and Jack, with Sir Rex's son, Randolph, who clerked for him. There were also a half dozen very small children present, whom she did not even know—they were probably Sean and Eleanor's grandchildren. Everyone was beaming at them, but a huge silence had fallen.

Elysse realized that the entire family must have gathered in London, in the middle of the humid, intolerable summer, out of concern for her.

And she and Alexi had been upstairs, acting like adolescents in the spring! Elysse touched her hair. Alexi whispered, "Don't worry about it—everyone knows what we were doing!"

That did not make her feel better. But he was grinning and teasing her as of old. She almost felt like pulling on his ear. "And that pleases you?" she whispered back.

"I don't care if the whole world knows I am hot for my wife."

She blushed, thrilled in spite of herself.

Jack strode forward, grinning. "Welcome home, love-birds!" He was laughing.

They had reached the ground floor, and Elysse blushed anew as she was swept into her brother's arms. He said, "Only you would sail off to China alone to chase a man!"

Ariella reached her and embraced her next. "You did exactly what I would have done, and look at how it has worked out! The two of you are in love!"

Before Elysse could answer, she was in her mother's arms. Alexi's hand was pumped by Devlin, while Amanda hugged him, hard. Tears began. She heard him trying to answer their many questions. Hugging her father, she said to her best friend, "Yes, we are in love—we have always been in love. But then, everyone has always known that, haven't they?"

Ariella grinned.

"Everyone has always known that you and Alexi were destined," Devlin said softly, his gaze moist. "We will talk later about the folly of your actions."

She cupped her father's cheeks. "I have a husband now, Father, and I am not eighteen."

His gaze grew even moister. "Yes, you do, and no, you are not, but you will always be my darling little girl."

She hugged him again. "I am fine," she reassured him. "Absolutely untouched and fine."

"Thank God," Devlin said.

Clarewood had his hand on Alexi's shoulder. "So, you have taken the fall, at last?" He was very amused.

"Not only am I smitten, I am more than happy to admit it." Alexi laughed. "I might even try to convince you of the advantages of being a happily married man."

Clarewood rolled his eyes. Everyone knew his years-old search for a bride was a reluctant one.

Elysse was now embraced by Lizzie, the pretty, plump, countess of Adare, and then by her somewhat intimidating husband, Tyrell. She then moved into her cousin Margery's arms, but almost fell as a small child ran between them. Suddenly she and Margery were in a whirlwind as the troop of children rushed past them, heading for the front door. A small, dark boy was leading the way. Last to follow was a young red-haired girl.

"Where are you off to?" a stern voice asked. Clearly it was one of the children's fathers.

"We are merely going to explore the maze," the dark-haired boy cried, pausing at the front door with the five other children. He seemed obstinate and ready to defend their plan.

"Fine, you may go out, but only to the maze," Rogan O'Neill said. "And I expect you back well before dark."

Elysse's heart turned over, hard, as Alexi stepped forward and warned, "Children get lost in that maze all of the time, my young friend."

The little boy's eyes widened and the redheaded girl seemed frightened. Then the boy said, "You are teasing, sir!"

Alexi grinned. "Yes, I am." He looked across the crowded room at her, his smile fading.

She stared back, knowing they would never forget that day at Errol Castle, especially not after what had happened to her. Then he was waylaid by Jack, Ned and Clarewood, and handed a flute of champagne. Her heart, already swollen with her love, felt like a balloon, as she watched him grinning and laughing with his friends and relations, regaling them with far too colorful descriptions of the great African continent. She heard Jack asking, "Will you leave for Canton on the eighth, as planned?"

Her heart tightened. She was fully aware that he would set sail for Canton as soon as possible. And while she couldn't help being somewhat saddened, because she would miss him terribly, the future was theirs. Alexi was the greatest China trader of the era and she, as his wife, would support him tirelessly, no matter if it meant some small personal sacrifice. Besides, she was already planning to lure new investors into their company while he was away. Her connections in London were vast, she was an accomplished hostess, and she thought she could help him immensely.

They were together—and it was forever. After all, he was a de Warenne.

"We are leaving for China on August 8," Alexi said, his gaze unwavering upon her. "If Elysse wishes to join me."

She cried out. This was the first he'd ever mentioned such a thing!

He slowly smiled and raised his flute at her in a salute. "There is no one I would rather have at my side than the bravest woman I have ever met—a woman of grace, dignity, courage and conviction, not to mention sheer beauty."

Everyone lifted their flutes. "Hear, hear."

"To my wife. I am the luckiest man alive," Alexi said, his gaze fixed upon her. "And to the future—to *our* future."

More cheers sounded.

She walked into his arms, overcome. The future had never been brighter or filled with more promise. "Of course I will sail to China with you."

He handed off his flute, swept her into his arms and kissed her for a very long time.

Later that night, as she lay in his arms, she thought about how they had come full circle from that afternoon when they had first met as children, when she had tried to snub him and he had bragged to her endlessly about his entire life. She smiled to herself and kissed his chest. His promise had been fulfilled. First love had become true love—and Alexi de Warenne remained the most fascinating man she had ever met.

* * * * *

REQUEST YOUR FREE BOOKS!

 HARLEQUIN® HISTORICAL:
Where love is timeless

2 FREE NOVELS PLUS 2 **FREE GIFTS!**

YES! Please send me 2 FREE Harlequin® Historical novels and my 2 FREE gifts (gifts are worth about $10). After receiving them, if I don't wish to receive any more books, I can return the shipping statement marked "cancel." If I don't cancel, I will receive 6 brand-new novels every month and be billed just $4.94 per book in the U.S. or $5.49 per book in Canada. That's a saving of 20% off the cover price! It's quite a bargain! Shipping and handling is just 50¢ per book.* I understand that accepting the 2 free books and gifts places me under no obligation to buy anything. I can always return a shipment and cancel at any time. Even if I never buy another book from Harlequin, the two free books and gifts are mine to keep forever.

246/349 HDN E5L4

Name _____ (PLEASE PRINT)

Address _____ Apt. #

City _____ State/Prov. _____ Zip/Postal Code

Signature (if under 18, a parent or guardian must sign)

Mail to the **Harlequin Reader Service:**
IN U.S.A.: P.O. Box 1867, Buffalo, NY 14240-1867
IN CANADA: P.O. Box 609, Fort Erie, Ontario L2A 5X3
Not valid for current subscribers to Harlequin Historical books.

Want to try two free books from another line?
Call 1-800-873-8635 or visit www.morefreebooks.com.

* Terms and prices subject to change without notice. Prices do not include applicable taxes. N.Y. residents add applicable sales tax. Canadian residents will be charged applicable provincial taxes and GST. Offer not valid in Quebec. This offer is limited to one order per household. All orders subject to approval. Credit or debit balances in a customer's account(s) may be offset by any other outstanding balance owed by or to the customer. Please allow 4 to 6 weeks for delivery. Offer available while quantities last.

Your Privacy: Harlequin Books is committed to protecting your privacy. Our Privacy Policy is available online at www.eHarlequin.com or upon request from the Reader Service. From time to time we make our lists of customers available to reputable third parties who may have a product or service of interest to you. If you would prefer we not share your name and address, please check here. ☐

Help us get it right—We strive for accurate, respectful and relevant communications. To clarify or modify your communication preferences, visit us at www.ReaderService.com/consumerschoice.

HH10R

BRENDA JOYCE

77460	AN IMPOSSIBLE ATTRACTION	___$7.99 U.S.	___$9.99 CAN.
77507	THE MASQUERADE	___$7.99 U.S.	___$9.99 CAN.
77363	THE PRIZE	___$7.99 U.S.	___$7.99 CAN.
77275	A DANGEROUS LOVE	___$7.99 U.S.	___$7.99 CAN.
77244	THE PERFECT BRIDE	___$7.99 U.S.	___$9.50 CAN.
77137	A LADY AT LAST	___$6.99 U.S.	___$8.50 CAN.

(limited quantities available)

TOTAL AMOUNT	$ _____
POSTAGE & HANDLING	$ _____
($1.00 FOR 1 BOOK, 50¢ for each additional)	
APPLICABLE TAXES*	$ _____
TOTAL PAYABLE	$ _____

(check or money order—please do not send cash)

To order, complete this form and send it, along with a check or money order for the total above, payable to HQN Books, to: **In the U.S.:** 3010 Walden Avenue, P.O. Box 9077, Buffalo, NY 14269-9077; **In Canada:** P.O. Box 636, Fort Erie, Ontario, L2A 5X3.

Name: _____
Address: _____ City: _____
State/Prov.: _____ Zip/Postal Code: _____
Account Number (if applicable): _____

075 CSAS

*New York residents remit applicable sales taxes.
*Canadian residents remit applicable GST and provincial taxes.

HQN™

We *are* romance™

www.HQNBooks.com

PHBJI010BL